The Chill From Siberia

a story of Poland in the 19th century

Danuta Gray was born in Poland of Polish parents but brought up and educated in Britain from an early age. She has already had a number of short stories published in, *Brummies All Write*, produced by the Birmingham Museum and Art Gallery, and several others published in Nos. 5, 6 and 7 of the magazine *Salvo*. During her busy and interesting career she has illustrated a book entitled, *Obstetrics,* by Jean Hallum and slides on Iso-immunisation for Professor Denis Fairweather. All her life she had intended to write the story of her immediate forebears and their trials and tribulations in 19th century Poland, and here it is at last in her moving and descriptive novel, *The Chill From Siberia.*

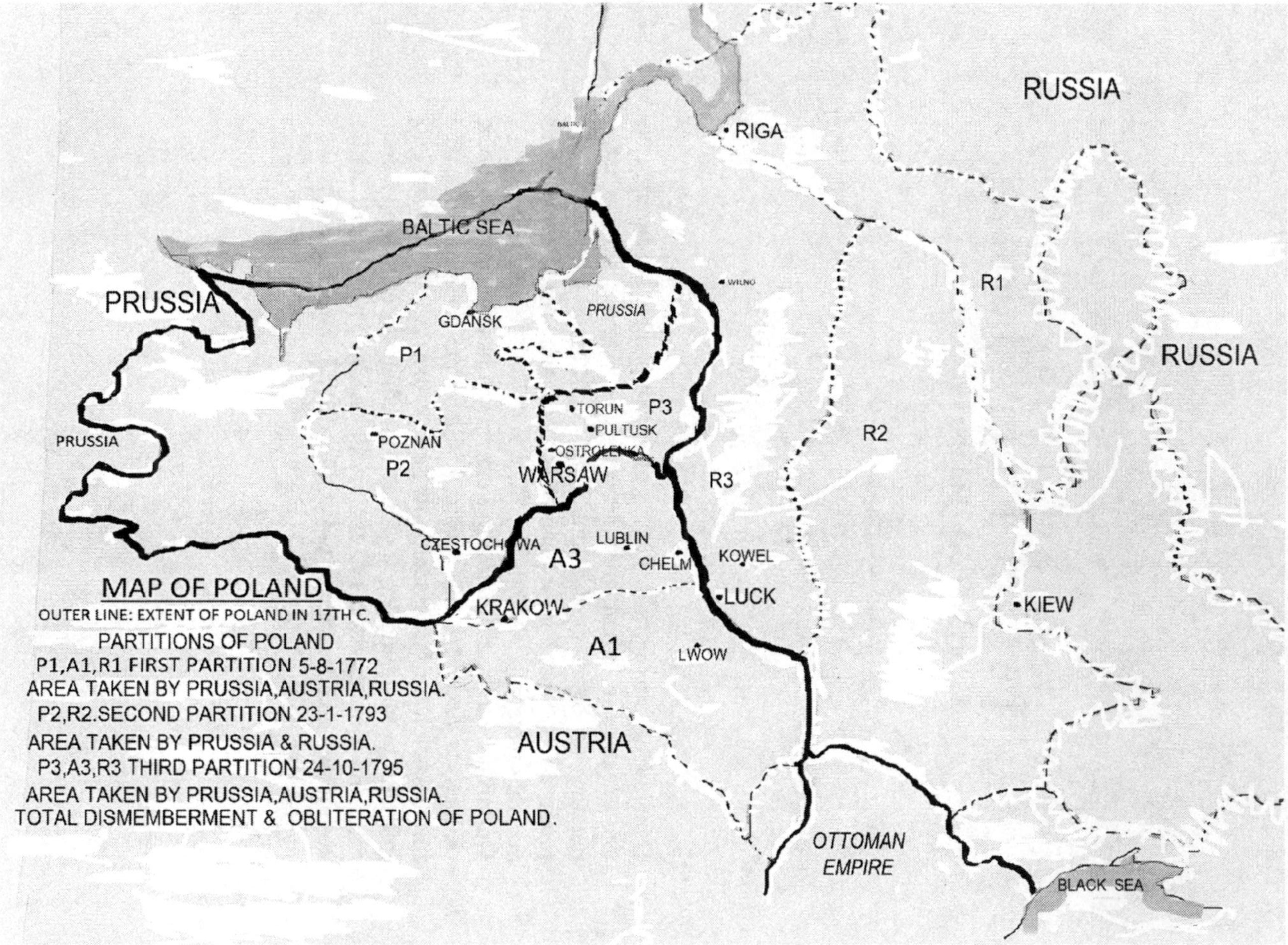

MAP OF POLAND

OUTER LINE: EXTENT OF POLAND IN 17TH C.

PARTITIONS OF POLAND

P1,A1,R1 FIRST PARTITION 5-8-1772
AREA TAKEN BY PRUSSIA,AUSTRIA,RUSSIA.

P2,R2.SECOND PARTITION 23-1-1793
AREA TAKEN BY PRUSSIA & RUSSIA.

P3,A3,R3 THIRD PARTITION 24-10-1795
AREA TAKEN BY PRUSSIA,AUSTRIA,RUSSIA.
TOTAL DISMEMBERMENT & OBLITERATION OF POLAND.

RUSSIA

RUSSIA

R1

R2

R3

KIEW

BLACK SEA

OTTOMAN
EMPIRE

RIGA

WILNO

PRUSSIA

P3

TORUN

PULTUSK

OSTROLENKA

WARSAW

A3

LUBLIN

CHELM

KOWEL

LUCK

LWOW

A1

AUSTRIA

KRAKOW

CZESTOCHOWA

POZNAN

P2

P1

GDANSK

BALTIC SEA

BALTIC

PRUSSIA

PRUSSIA

The Chill From Siberia

a story of Poland in the 19th century

Danuta Gray

Arena Books

First published in 2012 by Arena Books

Arena Books
6 Southgate Green
Bury St. Edmunds
IP33 2BL

www.arenabooks.co.uk

Distributed in America by Ingram International, One Ingram Blvd., PO Box 3006, La Vergne, TN 37086-1985, USA.

Danuta Gray
The Chill From Siberia *a story of Poland in the 19th century*
1. Poland – History – 19th century – Fiction. 2. Poland - Social conditions – 19th century – Fiction. – 3. Historical fiction
I. Title
823.9'2-dc23

ISBN-13 978-1-906791-77-3

BIC classifications:- FV, FRH, FJH.

Printed and bound by Lightning Source UK

Cover design
By Jason Anscomb

Typeset in
Times New Roman

This book is printed on paper adhering to the Forest Stewardship Council™ (FSC®) mixed Credit FSC® C084699.

CHAPTER 1

The horseman slowed down at the outskirts of the city of Luck, but seeing people running towards the centre, he shouted, "What's happening?"

"An execution—a hanging! At the Citadel!" came back a hurried, breathless answer. The rider urged his horse to speed along and quickly covered the distance through the wide cobbled streets. The horse almost reared when he pulled the reins to stop where he could tether the animal, creating a cumulus of dust. A thick crowd had already gathered, and he pushed his way to the front, hearing comments, "…What have they done?…Who are they?,"… cursing the men preparing the scaffold, saying what they would do to *them* if they had a chance.

"Who is it that they've caught?" he asked, looking from one face to another. "Do you know them?" But many shook their head. Then an old bearded man spat on the ground and growled,

"They be from the big estate, northeast of here."

"The name?" the rider asked almost dreading the answer.

"Dunno. There they be!" His informant looked towards the activity. The rider followed his gaze.

"Oh, my God! It's …!" but his voice was drowned as the crowd groaned and shouted. He quickly pushed his way out of the crowd and ran to his horse. He jumped on it with dexterity of an acrobat and galloped out of the city and continued to travel through the forests, past the bog lands that were dispersed in between, and then along the west bank of the river Styr, until they came to a huge mansion.

He jumped off before the horse had even come to a stop, and ran through the front door, just as the butler was coming to him.

"Where are they? The family. Quick, man!"

"The sitting room. Who shall I say…" But the rider was already walking, no, running through the sitting room door.

"Why! Woitek! How lovely to—," said the lady, sitting on the sofa.

"Forgive me for barging in like this, madam, sir. I come in great haste—from Luck. They've caught Adam and Michael and are preparing a scaffold—."

"Oh, my Lord!" The lady jumped up, her hand to her mouth, her eyes enormous with fear.

Her husband was already making large strides and pulled the cord. Edward, the butler entered the room instantly. "Get my horse saddled—no, get two horses—as quickly as possible."

"I'm coming too. Get me a carriage."

"I don't think you should Alexandra. It could be dangerous ," her husband said.

"Jozef! They are my sons too. I'm coming," she said again.

Whilst waiting for the horses, Jozef wanted to know everything that Woitek knew or saw.

"All I know that I had to come and tell you. Maybe you can do something to stop this massacre."

"How many of the police or soldiers were there?"

"Soldiers—I would guess about fifteen, maybe more. We wouldn't be able to overpower them. They were all armed, and looked as if they were prepared to shoot without much provocation."

"Do you know what the boys were charged with?"

"I don't. I didn't stay to ask. We all know that they don't necessarily have to do anything. God what a terrible country this is!"

"No, no! It's not Poland that is terrible! It's the oppressors who are. And we know who they are!"

"I could be equally there, awaiting the same punishment as Adam and Michael. We belong to the same—."

"Shhh!" Jozef placed his fingers over Woitek's lips. "You mustn't say things like that. You never know who could overhear."

The horses were ready and Woitek (now with a fresh horse) and Jozef galloped as quickly as they could, leaving Alexandra to follow with the coach driver.

On arrival at the city square, the crowd was still there, but there was a deathly silence amongst them, with the occasional sobbing of a woman. Many men, especially the old ones wept silently, with tears disappearing somewhere into their beards. Perhaps they too had lost a son or a grandson at the hands of the oppressor, or perhaps they remembered their own rebellious youth.

Jozef was a tall, imposing man and the crowd parted for the two men instinctively. Ahead of them was a vision they would never forget. A young body, hanging from the citadel scaffold, was still swaying. It was Adam. Jozef thought that his heart would break at that moment. He ran towards it but his way was barred by two men with guns.

"No civilians are allowed through at present," said one in a harsh voice.

"Oh, please, please let me through. That is my son. Please, I beg of you let me take him down. My wife is coming any moment now. It'll kill her to see him thus." He rummaged in his pocket and pulled out a handful of money, and offered it to the man. "Please!" His voice was barely a whisper.

"The body mustn't be disturbed for an hour," but all the same he took the money, "but I'll ask," said the man with the gruff voice. He slung his rifle over his shoulder and marched to where there was a group of uniformed men. He waved his hands towards Jozef and the body and carefully showed them the money, and eventually one of them nodded.

They cut the body down. It was still as warm, as his own, when Jozef cradled his son in his arms, and wept, "Oh, Adam, my Adam, my beloved son." The crowd remained silent.

Meanwhile, Woitek went to one of the crowd, "When I was here a little while ago there were two boys. What happened to the other one? Did he escape?"

"Oh, no, he's there as well. He did try to escape. We created a commotion to distract these murderers. But they was wise to it. They shot him," said an old woman. She looked towards the dead boys.

"Where is he? I can't see him."

"He's beyond the group of these bast—murderers. You'll find him there." This time it was a young man who spoke.

Woitek was about to go and find Michael when he heard the wheels of the carriage stop and the crowd silently parted again. The sight could well have been from the bible, when the Red Sea parted for Moses. And through it came Alexandra, pale, drawn and frightened. He took her arm for fear she would faint when she saw Adam cradled in Jozef's arms. She knelt beside her son and put her head on her son's body. After some time she wiped her face, and raised it, looking pleadingly at Woitek, "Where is Michael? Did he escape?" Woitek shook his head, and helped her to her feet and led her to her other son. The soldiers had disappeared. Some of the crowd started to disperse.

When they reached the spot they saw two bodies lying crumpled as they fell, beside each other. Two women were cradling the head of each man. They looked up at Alexandra and Woitek. Alexandra fell to her knees again and held out her arms for her son. As the woman handed her, her son, she said to her softly, "Thank you. Was my son still alive when you first held him?"

"No, ma'am. `E was dead. They made sure of that." She said that with hate in her voice and her eyes. Alexandra looked at the other body, and the woman said, "As this young `un was running and they aimed, `e ran in front of `im to give `im a chance. So they shot `im first. Neither had a chance. There was too many of them. And armed to the teeth, they was."

Alexandra held her younger son as if he was a baby, stroking his face. He now looked even younger than seventeen! How pale! She felt the stickiness of blood on her other hand and between her fingers and saw how much blood there was on the ground, soaked into the soil where he had fallen, the soil which they all loved so much.

"Beg pardon ma'am, shall I bring you a sheet to wrap `im in it? I have one and I only live in the other street. I could bring it in no time at all." The same kind woman touched Alexandra's arm.

"Thank you. You are very kind."

"The other boy—`e be yours too?" Alexandra nodded. "I do have another sheet that's on the bed, but it ain't clean. Shall I bring that one as well?"

"No, the one will suffice, thank you."

When the woman returned, it had seemed only a moment. They wrapped

Michael in the sheet together. Alexandra asked what they accused the boys of, or did they say anything at all.

"Oh, yes, they did that all right, to teach us. They said that these men were accused of treason—against His Imperial Highness the Tsar." She spat on the ground with distaste. "I ask you! When the other one was being led to the scaffold, `e started to sing that patriotic song about Poland, how we love the country and how we should do everything to be free. `E had a fine voice. I can hear `im now. I don't think I shall ever forget it. Every one wept, and some created a commotion so that this lad could run. But `e had no chance." There was such profound sadness and misery in Alexandra's face as she started to tremble, that the other woman at first hesitated and then put her arms around her shoulders, until the trembling stopped.

Alexandra's eyes fell on the other body, of the man who gave his life for another.

"What about this other man? Do you know if he has any family? He looks young too."

"Oh, yes. That's `is wife with him."

"I must go to her. Will you hold my son please?" She didn't want to put him on the ground. She arose and walked quickly to the other man. The woman bending over him, seeing her, stood up, but as Alexandra spread her arms to her, she ran towards her, and they embraced as if they had known one another for years. They stood quietly, united in their grief, one so elegant and the other in much darned clothes.

It was Woitek who organised the transport of the bodies, who found out the names of the women who had helped and where they lived, knowing that Alexandra would never forget what they did for her sons and who would want to show them her gratitude. It was Woitek who led his friends to the carriage and told the coach driver to take them back home. And it was he who rode ahead to warn the staff of what to expect.

"Sir, what are we to say to Miss Kamila? She noticed all the activity and wanted to know what was happening," said Edward, the butler.

"Oh, God! I'd forgotten of her existence!"

"Will you say something to her, sir? She'll come out any moment now—here she is. Please sir—before the rest arrive. Miss Kamila, this is Mr. Woitek."

"I do know this gentleman, Edward. How do you do, sir? You were here a little while ago, weren't you? Do *you* know what's happening? No one will tell me anything!"

Woitek looked at the butler's pleading face, "That's because no one knows anything. Shall we go into the sitting room, Miss Kamila?" He followed her into the room and closed the door. "Shall we sit down?"

Woitek looked at this young girl, barely sixteen, but looked so much younger and he saw grave dark eyes that held his. He had no experience in imparting terrible news to youngsters.

"Your Mother and Father will be here soon. They have received a terrible, dreadful shock, so you must try and help them in any way you can. Do you understand?"

"Well, yes—and, no! What shock? What has happened?"

"Your brothers—they—they were accused—of—of treason—."

"Treason! Never! By Whom?"

"The authorities."

"Oh, them." Kamila said in a withering tone. "So, what happened?"

"What usually happens!" He took a long look at her to see if she was beginning to foresee what he might say. "They—were—executed."

"Executed! Oh, no! No! There must be a mistake! They were only boys! It's not possible! Please say it isn't so!" She looked at him with disbelief.
He put his arms around her and with her head on his shoulder, he stroked her head, "There, there, little one. You must be brave. When your parents arrive they will bring with them the bodies of Adam and Michael. I know it's a terrible shock for you, so cry now but try not to cry when they are here. They have both wept enough. God! How they have!"

Disbelief and anguish hung in and around the house. The servants did their work silently. Alexandra and Joseph tried to keep some form of composure for Kamila's sake. If they discussed the tragedy, they did so when they were alone. Kamila, on the other hand felt that they had become withdrawn and felt desperately alone.

Not being able to stand the silence any longer she burst out, "Papa, why won't you tell me why this has happened? Have you already forgotten it? Why did Adam and Michael have to die? Why ?" Alexandra arose from the sofa and quickly walked to the door. "Mama, please don't go. Please talk to me. Mama, don't you care for me?" Her voice trailed away as Alexandra went out of the room and closed the door.

"Papa—."

"Come here, child." Her father held out his arms as she came to him. "Kamila, my love, my little girl—whatever makes you say such hurtful things? Don't you know that we love you so very much? Can't you see how terribly painful it is for your Mother—and for me—to have lost our sons?"

"But what about me, Papa? What about me? I don't matter—because I'm a girl?"

"Darling, of course you matter—so very much. Of course we love you—just as much. You see the reason we don't talk about this terrible loss, is that your Mother is inconsolable. You can't imagine how she weeps at night. As to why your brothers were executed? You must know how dangerous it is to even talk against the Russian regime now. They have spies everywhere, infiltrating even into families, setting one brother against another, a son against father.

"Ours is not the only family to have suffered thus. Perhaps you are right that we should discuss this? Perhaps it would be easier, but to some extent, it is dangerous, too. Now, go to your Mother. I think you'll find her in her bedroom."

"Thank you, Papa."

Kamila knocked gently on the door and walked in. Her mother was kneeling at the side the bed, her face buried in the bed and encircled by her arms. Kamila ran to her and knelt beside her and put her arms around the weeping lady. She became aware how very thin her mother had become in that short time.

"Mama, I'm sorry, for the things I've said…Please forgive me…."

When the time arrived for her to return to the Academy for Young Ladies in Warsaw for the autumn trimester of 1848, she was glad to go. But before going, her father held her face between his hands and said,

"You know that one doesn't have to actually take part in any uprisings, as there have been this year? You remember what I told you the other day? So, I want you to be very careful and don't discuss politics—present politics—with strangers. In fact it's better not to discuss it with anyone at all."

The classes had finished for the day and the girls poured out into the corridor, laughing, dancing and running until they heard the sharp clapping of strict bony hands.

"Girls! Girls! Stop that noise at once! Have you not learned anything in the years you've been here? If you wish to be called ladies, you must behave as ladies—with decorum. You are not at a barn dance now." It was the headmistress. Her sharp, stringent voice stopped them instantly in their tracks and they stood to attention as if they were soldiers, apology written on each face.

When she let them go, knowing that they were being watched, they walked tall and straight as if a book was being balanced on each young head. But once they went around the corner, one girl mimicked the reprimand they had had to perfection, and as they entered their sitting room they all burst out laughing.

One girl went to the piano. At first she played some popular songs and then some one asked for dance music. At this Amelia started to dance with an imaginary partner.

"She needs a partner. She can't dance with a ghost. Kamila go and dance with her. You like dancing—."

"Katia—we all like dancing. You go. You are taller than I. She wouldn't want a young man who reached only to her chin—."

"It might be a man who had shrunk with age but was fabulously wealthy." At this Amelia stopped and frowned at the girl who had said that, whilst the others laughed.

THE CHILL FROM SIBERIA

"—anyway I don't feel in the mood," said Kamila as she made her way to the window seat, and then changed her mind.

She took a book off the shelf and settled herself on the sofa, whilst some girls danced and some huddled together in groups. Kamila put the book down and went to the chair by the table and started to look through the newspaper. The piano had become silent and the girls were discussing the forthcoming end of term ball. Kamila arose and went to the window seat.

"Kamila! What's the matter with you?" said Amelia.

"Why?"

"I noticed in the class today, you weren't listening and now you've been up and down fifty times. Aren't you well?" She came over to Kamila and put her arm around Kamila's shoulders. "What's the matter?"

"I don't know. I just feel so restless from early morning."

"Come and join us?" But Kamila shook her head.

"Kamila, I wish to have a word with you. Come with me. Please hurry." Kamila heard the voice as if from a great distance. Her mind was hundreds of miles away. On turning her head towards the caller, she found Madame Prust just by her, with her hand on Kamila's shoulder. Kamila jumped off the window seat and straightened her long grey skirt before following Madame Prust. She wondered why Madame had called her by her Christian name. Everything was always so official and polite. *Perhaps it's because I've nearly completed my course here....*

She had spent eight years at this Academy and this year, 1850, was her last. They were taught not only etiquette and how to run a home, but also mathematics and botany and languages, English and French, although they were not compulsory. Polish and Russian, of course, were mandatory. Kamila was eager to learn these other languages and she found them relatively easy, for she considered that once one knew one foreign language, learning other ones was much easier.

They reached Madame Prust's study. It was a comfortable but a dark room and smelled musty. Madame Prust did not believe in opening windows in case all the piles of papers on her desk blew away. Furthermore she was not the outdoor type that liked freezing fresh air.

"Sit down Kamila." Once her command had been obeyed, she continued, "In the kitchen there is a man from your Aunt Elizabeth-."

"Aunt Elizabeth! Why? Wh—?"

"Please let me finish. He was sent here by her to give you this message. I have it here. I do know its content for she sent me a similar one. Here it is. Read it." She took it off the desk and handed it to Kamila.

14th March 1850.

"Dear Kamila,

I can't help that you are alarmed but, my dear, I will explain everything to you when I see you. I want you to pack all your things straight away for you will not be returning to the Academy. It cannot be so. Jordan will drive you back but he must have a rest and so must the horses. You will need to set out as soon as it is light. I will meet you half way and we will complete the journey together.

I will then fill you in.

It's no use badgering Jordan, for he knows NOTHING. Try and get some sleep. It's a long journey. We will meet tomorrow, my dear.

Your loving aunt,

Elizabeth."

Kamila gave the letter to Madame Prust.

"What can it mean? Do you know any more? Does your letter explain this? Can I see it—your letter?"

"Yes, certainly. Now, where have I put it?" She started to rummage through the papers on her desk then looked around the room. "I'm sorry, I seem to have mislaid it. But I mustn't waste any more time. Let me read yours…."

After reading the letter, she returned it to Kamila and said, "No. I know nothing more but we must hurry and pack and you must have something to eat and go to bed early. Go, and start packing. Do you want any help?"

"No. I'll manage, thank you. Perhaps the porter can take the trunks down later?"

"Yes, of course, my dear."

As the door closed behind Kamila, Madame Prust gazed sombrely after her. She pulled out her letter from her pocket and read it again.

"So that's why I felt this restlessness," Kamila said to herself as she walked along the long corridor. When she reached her room she sat on the bed and reread the letter. She didn't see the torrential rain or how the windows were covered with hundreds of crystal drops, or see the thunderous clouds, or hear the wind as it whistled and howled lugubriously around the school.

She started to pack.

She wished that she could fly with the wind to her home, to see her parents. She felt desperately homesick and worried for her parents. She had last seen them at Christmas, and that seemed a thousand years ago. In just three more months she would have been home for good and now she is going tomorrow. The gladness she felt at going home was completely marred by a heavy foreboding, which she could not shake off.

She thought of her Father, always so serious, and her Mother, who had laughter in her voice and how much they still loved each other. She hoped that when she married, her life would be like that of her parents.

But now they only had her.

Her two brothers, Adam and Michael, were dead. Dead, for their beliefs.

For patriotism. Will we ever have peace and harmony in this beautiful country of ours? Not if we continue to be within the Russian Empire. What use is it that we call the country *Kingdom of Poland*, when we are under the Tsarist rule? How often had she heard her Father say that?

It was only thirty-five years since the Kingdom was established and Kamila's parents frequently spoke of it. Because her Father's lands lay in the northeast of the country, they had been subjected to Russian rule, each time the country was partitioned. They fervently believed in the cause of being free of Russia. So did her brothers. And the result? Adam and Michael were dead for openly talking and "inciting revolt" against the Tsarist oppression.

Kamila lay awake most of the night despite having had something to help her sleep. Why had the letter come from her aunt and not her Father or Mother? What has happened that she won't be returning here, to the school? My God! It must be that something has happened to her parents. But what?
With the recent uprisings, there was constant unrest in the country. Perhaps they have been injured? *Oh, God! No! No! Please keep them safe. I mustn't think of such things. They must be safe. Aunt Elizabeth will tell me tomorrow. I must try and sleep.*

But the sleep that came was only light and in patches and all the time she felt a foreboding.

The following morning, all her friends had woken early and together with the mistresses were waiting to say goodbye. It was only when she came to Madame Prust, that Kamila almost burst into tears.

"Please keep in contact with me, Kamila. And write to your friends as well. Don't forget us."

"No, of course, I won't. Goodbye!"

The girls looked on with puzzled, serious expressions, some with sadness for they knew that they would not see Kamila again. As Kamila stepped into the coach, she took one long look at the group of people.

"Goodbye!"

CHAPTER 2

The sky was grey, with dark clouds hanging low, but there was no rain and the wind of the previous day had travelled further on. The roads were slushy, with the horses and the wheels throwing up mud. Inside the coach, Kamila sat as if numbed, unable to believe the events that had taken place and fearful of what was to come. As they left the outskirts of Warsaw, the houses became sparser, with more forests and increasing amount of snow. The March sun had risen and with the increased warmth and the rattling and swaying of the coach, Kamila's eyes began to droop. She fell into a deep sleep.

Having had a brief stop at Lublin, they arrived at last at Chelm, after many hours of travelling. Here they could stop for an hour to change the horses and have something to eat. And it was here that she met her Aunt Elizabeth, who hugged her tightly. Kamila looked at her aunt searchingly.

They were shown into a room with panelled walls and a low ceiling. The large oak table and chairs smelled of wax polish. The landlord pulled out a chair for Elizabeth and then for Kamila.

"The girls will bring you your lunch in a moment," he said. "Meanwhile, shall I bring you some tea?"

"Yes, please," said Elizabeth.

"Auntie, what's happened?"

Elizabeth took Kamila's hands.

"Kamila, once more the chill from Siberia has come upon us." She looked closely at the young girl's face and shook her head. "You don't understand, do you?" Kamila shook her head. "You know your Father's interest in politics and all things patriotic?"

"Y-yes." Her voice was barely audible.

"I always knew that that was a danger—and he knew it too. I think that we all knew, after what happened to your brothers, and indeed so many of our countrymen and my son. This danger has come. They came on Wednesday and arrested him."

"Oh, my God! Why? Aunt Elizabeth, why? Where is he? Where's my Mother? What have they done to them? "

"They are being taken to Siberia—."

"Siberia! Why? For how long? I want to see them. I want to see my Mother. Why is Mother being taken there? She wasn't interested in politics."

"Kamila, your Mother *chose* to go, to be with your Father."

"Chose to go with him? But, what about me? Who's going to look after me? What's to become of me? Oh! What will happen to me? So, after all, she didn't care. She obviously didn't love me—."

"Kamila! Stop it! Stop this hysteria! And listen. You know how your Mother loved your Father—and you and your brothers. Your Father was excellent in politics and his work, but simply hopeless at looking after himself. There is no doubt that if he was to go alone, he'd succumb in no time at all to the harsh conditions in Siberia. Your Mother is very practical and knowledgeable and she'd do her best to keep him alive.

"Whereas you are eighteen, grown-up. Some girls at that age are already married. Most likely you'll be married soon too. So, you see, logically she did what was the best. If I had been in her situation, I would have done the same. I know only too well how useless my brother would be under such conditions."

Kamila was holding her head in her hands. The older lady was looking into the distance as she bit her lower lip. They had experienced this situation in the family before. “Look at me, my dear! As to how long? Have you ever known anyone to return from there? And survive?”

“You mean that I shall never see them again—or are they still in Poland?”

“No. They are no longer here. They did at least allow them to pack a few things.”

“Were you there? When they arrested them?”

“Jordan’s brother, who worked in the fields, at your Father’s, overheard them and took the fastest horse to come and tell me. So at least I was able to say my goodbyes.”

“Are we going home now?” said Kamila.

“Only to collect some of your things, if we are in time. They have confiscated the manor, all the lands, and all the possessions. I bribed one to allow us to collect your things. I don’t know if we will be able to, even so. You’ll have to live with me, my dear.”

“I want to go with my parents,” wailed Kamila. “I want to go to Siberia.”

“You must be the only person on this earth (apart from your Mother) who wants to go there voluntarily!” said Elizabeth wryly. “No darling. You can’t. Your Father asked me to look after you and I will. Besides, your life is just beginning. You must live to uphold your Father’s beliefs. He would want you to live by his standards. Remember the things he and your Mother taught you. He—they were so proud of you—the fact that you are an intelligent girl and not one of those empty headed girls we meet in our society. And I need you, Kamila. I need you badly. I only have Karol, and he—.” She stopped and tightened her lips to check her despair.

“How is he?” Kamila said gently.

“So very ill. I’m afraid he’s dying. Nothing can be done for him.”

This time it was Kamila who held her aunt’s hands and whispered, “Oh, auntie, auntie. What are we to do? How will we live without them?”

“I don’t know. But you see when Karol dies our whole dynasty will die. You are the only one of our family who must survive. There is another matter that I must discuss with you. Your parents and I talked this over a few weeks ago but now there is a greater urgency, because Karol is dying, but we’ll talk of this later. But I’m very tired now. I think we should both have a little sleep. I think we should go back to the coach as we still have a long way to go.”

Elizabeth leaned her head against the upholstery and closed her eyes. Kamila examined her face. Having been so introspective about herself she had not noticed that her aunt looked gaunt and much older than her years. *How pale her face is, apart from those very rosy cheeks. Could it be rouge? But she had never worn rouge before.* She leaned forward and covered her aunt with a fur rug, noticing that the older lady was already asleep. She hadn’t even noticed before, that her aunt was breathless, until now. *What a great effort it must have been for her to come to meet me, and I hadn't even asked her how she was.*

Kamila was filled with remorse. But other emotions kept creeping in. Fear for her parents, a deep sadness over Karol, and now, anxiety over Aunt Elizabeth, and disquiet over her own future. She tried to calm herself by telling herself that her Aunt would advise and guide her.

When Elizabeth woke, she smiled at her niece, "Didn't you sleep, my dear?"

"No. I couldn't. How do you feel now?"

"Oh, much better now, thank you."

"Auntie, what's the matter? You're not well, are you?"

"Nothing to worry about." She patted Kamila's hand. "We have more important things to talk of. You remember what I said before I went to sleep?"

"Yes. You had discussed something with Mother and Father."

"Yes. It's this. And this is the reason why you won't be returning to the Academy. We have decided that you must marry Karol."

"Karol? Is it allowed? But he's my first cousin!"

"Yes, it is allowed. It's not desirable under normal circumstances, but in our case it is necessary. Indeed, I would even say that it is imperative. It will not be a normal marriage because Karol is –very, very weak, and there will be no possibility of having any children. We must ensure that the lands and property don't get confiscated and therefore as his wife you will have that security. After all we wouldn't want those," she searched for a suitable word, "those scoundrels—wastrels—to fritter away our heritage that has been in our family for centuries, do we?"

"But what about you?"

"Kamila, I am an old lady. Have you forgotten, or not noticed that?" She smiled, almost mischievously. "We are nearly home. I've arranged for us to go and collect your things tomorrow. When we get home, I would suggest that you make a list of all the things you'd like to collect from there because it won't be possible to return at a later date."

Kamila thought longingly of her horse and her dog Wolf whom she loved so much.

"All the horses and other animals have been confiscated. As to Wolf–no, he hasn't been shot—he disappeared into the forest once your parents were driven away. Perhaps he's gone into the wild again—to be with his family." Elizabeth explained that unless they were able to retrieve anything from her father's manor, the only possessions she would have would be the ones in her trunks at the moment. In fact, she would be penniless.

They were both tired by the time they arrived at Elizabeth's Birch House. Kamila had always liked coming here. It wasn't as picturesque as Kamila's home but there was a charm about it. The long drive was lined by birches which gave an ethereal quality to the dismal day light. When Kamila was little she always imagined that at the end of the drive there would be a castle with pinnacled towers. There a prince was held captive and they would rescue him.

At the front, which was south facing, there was a wisteria climbing almost to the roof. The house was built in a sheltered valley; so many plants grew in these grounds that wouldn't grow in other parts of the locality. There were already narcissi and primroses in flower in the more sheltered areas along the drive and beside the house.

Kamila asked if she could go and see Karol. She had always loved him for as long as she could remember.

He was eighteen years older than Kamila. She remembered that as a child, she had complained that it took a long time to see his face, because he was so tall. He would then pick her up and sit her on his shoulder as he went about his business, inspecting horses, farm buildings; or held her in front of him as he rode his horse.

"Are you going to continue growing, Karol?"

"Why do you ask, Little One?"

"Because you are already like a beanpole."

He laughed. "Yes, I am. And then my head will be in the clouds and you won't be able to see me because when you are a young lady you won't be able to ride on my shoulders, like this." She had squeezed his neck.

She knocked on the door and entered. Karol was lying in bed. He raised himself to greet her. She quickly ran to him and hugged him, being gentle for he looked so fragile.

"Karol, I missed you so much. How are you? I thought that the news was that you were getting better?"

He smiled wanly. "One must always hope, my dear." He laid his head back on the pillows, breathless with exertion.

"What do the doctors say?"

"They can't do anything now. They don't even advise bleeding." He laughed.

"Pah! My Mother always thought it was a stupid thing to do and I agree. How can that help when the patient is already weak? After all if an animal—or a human—has a bad accident and bleeds a lot, they die from that, don't they? Even if it's a flesh wound." She realised that he was getting tired, so just held his hand. She wanted to ask him so many questions, but instead looked around the room. There were a few bottles of medicines in brown and blue glass bottles with corks on the bedside table. She examined them but they didn't mean anything to her.

Kamila looked at him. How much thinner he looked and so very pale! His eyes were sunken and the cheeks were hollow. Was that the effect of consumption or the result of Siberia? There was such a lot she didn't know. She wished her mother were here with her. *She* would have known what to do. She had seen her treat so many animals that were at death's door with plants and love and tenderness. Kamila's sadness deepened with the knowledge of never being able to see her again.

Karol's other hand had relaxed, and she noticed something red. She peered closely and gently pulled out a blood stained handkerchief. She found another clean one and replaced it in his hand. She must ask Aunt Elizabeth about this. The logs readjusted themselves in the grate with crackling and spitting. She became aware that the room was hot and stuffy. Karol was sleeping so she stroked the hand she had been holding and gently kissed his forehead, and left the room to look for her aunt.

As she walked down the beautiful staircase she decided to go into the library and see if she could find anything about phthisis. She needed to know so much! The library was as large as her father's. It smelled musty and at the same time of polish and leather. She looked for the catalogue and found it.

She searched under the headings; phthisis, consumption, lung diseases but found nothing. Eventually, in a general medical diseases book she found a small piece about it, but didn't find it sufficiently informative. Nothing much was known about this condition. She turned the pages to see when it was printed. In 1830—two years before her birth!

"Ah, there you are, Kamila. I've been looking for you." Her aunt came into the room and sat on the leather bound chair by the table. "What are you looking for? Something to read in bed?"

"I'm sorry Auntie. I did mean to see you after coming from Karol, after he fell asleep, but I thought I might find something about his condition. I feel so helpless, not knowing anything about it."

"I don't think you'll find anything about that here. He and his father read mainly classics. You'll find Homer, Voltaire, Sir Walter Scott and of course ours, such as Mickiewicz, Slowacki. And, of course, Krasinski. He is Karol's, and your father's friend, you know. But he publishes his work anonymously. It's *your mother* who has a good collection of medical books. When we go there tomorrow, we must take everything that you'll need," said Elizabeth.

" Yes, I want to take all those books. She also kept notes. I'd like to get those. You look tired Auntie. All this is too much for you. I hope I won't be a burden to you."

"You, a burden? Don't be silly, child. I can't tell you how glad I am that you are here. For all our sakes." She looked and sighed. "My husband used to love this room….I think I'll go to bed. Don't stay up too late. We have a lot to do tomorrow." Kamila ran to her and put her arms around this dear lady and held her close.

"Good night Auntie. And thank you." She kissed her gently.

She took a book off the shelf and settled herself down in an armchair.

Kamila and her aunt travelled to Kamila's home. The day was bright and sunny with a light westerly breeze. Both of the women kept the conversation light, discussing practical matters and avoiding discussing that which would be painful to either or both. After about an hour, the familiar countryside of her father's came into view. How she loved her home! How beautiful it all looked!

These lands were further to the north from her aunt's place. There was more forestation and the drive to the manor was lined with larches and beech and birch. When their coach approached the front of the building they saw horses and uniformed men. Kamila gripped her aunt's hand as they climbed out of the coach and walked to the front entrance.

A tall moustached man in Russian uniform barred their way.

"Civilians are not allowed here," he said.

"This property belongs to my brother—." Elizabeth said.

"This is a government property now," said the man through tight lips and clenched teeth.

"Would you kindly let me finish? This is my brother's daughter and we've been given permission by—," she searched for the piece of paper in her bag, "here it is—to collect a few of her personal items, like clothes and books."

He looked at the paper and gave it back to her. "Alright, but hurry up." Elizabeth asked her coachman to bring in the trunks.

They entered the large hall. Elizabeth foresaw Kamila's emotions and said briskly,

"No time for sentimentality, my dear. We must hurry. They might change their mind. Let's go to your room first." They started to climb the gently curving staircase. "Run along, child. I know you're eager to start. I'll take it more leisurely."

The building was built in a form of an L. There were windows in between many of the rooms so it was very light upstairs. Kamila stopped at her parent's rooms and opened the door. She thought she saw her mother. She smiled and stretched her arms to run to her and then saw that there was no one here. She fell on the bed and buried her face in her pillow. The fragrance of her mother's perfume of lavender and rose brought vivid memories back. "Come, my dear. It was her choice to go. At least they will have each other. They loved each other so much that it would have been intolerable for either of them to be apart under these circumstances," said her aunt. She was sitting on the bed and cradling Kamila's head. "She knew that you would be strong and wise and in time, understand."

They looked round this room, decorated in blue and gold and white. The ceiling was powder blue with white ornate mouldings and the same colours were used for the bed covers and pillows. Kamila tried to memorise every detail of the room.

They went to Kamila's room. It was a very light, happy room having windows on two sides. The colour scheme was delicate pink and white. She wanted to go to the windows to see if the view was the same, but her aunt grabbed her by the hand, “Let’s get started. Put all the things you want to take on the bed and then we will pack them in the trunks—and hurry.”

Kamila started to pull out her clothes from the wardrobes and chest of drawers. She was surprised that her jewellery was where she had left it and commented about it to her aunt.

“I asked the Colonel who gave me his permission for us to come today, that your room and your mother’s wouldn’t be entered or used until we had been today. And he gave me his word. I must say that I am as surprised as you, that both of the rooms have been left intact. Incidentally your Mother took all her jewellery with her—in case she needed to exchange it for more necessary things.”

“I’d like to take Mother’s little cushion and these miniature portraits of my parents and all her books and notebooks on various medicinal herbs, please Auntie. Do you think they will let me take the big portraits of my parents that are hanging in the sitting room?”

“No, he specifically said we could take things from your room only—only your clothes. So hide these miniatures quickly.”

On the way to her mother’s room, Kamila peered into several bedrooms.

“Ugh! The stench of sweat and feet in these rooms! Thank goodness they didn’t sleep in my room. I don’t think I could have worn any of my clothing, if they smelt like that.”

“Where did your Mother keep her books? In the library?” asked Elizabeth. “ Although I’ve been here many times, I never knew she had her own collection of books.”

“No. She had a small room beside the pantry. Of course! There will be bags of dried herbs that she prepared each year and they will be in that pantry too. We *must* take them.”

The coachman and Elizabeth collected the bags of dried plants that Kamila indicated. Next door was a large kitchen and through the closed door they heard masculine voices, sometimes laughter.

They entered the “kitchen study” as they all affectionately called the room. There were handwritten books with recipes and concoctions and comments as to their effectiveness—of course all to do with animals. She chose the printed books carefully. They were aware of more noise and banging of doors and thought that at any moment some one will come and tell them to leave.

True enough the tall man who met them at the entrance stood in the doorway.

“And what do you think you are you doing? You had permission to take only your clothes.” His voice was like thunder and his eyes burned with anger and hate.

“My niece wants to have some of her Mother’s cooking recipes. That’s all right isn't it? You wouldn't be interested in cooking, would you? You know how we women have to please you men?" Kamila couldn't believe the sweetness in her aunt's voice.

The man grunted his consent.

He waited until they finished and then escorted them to the front door. The coachman had already put up the trunks and now he helped her aunt to climb in. She thanked him. He turned to Kamila. She gave him her hand, and put her foot on the step. She turned her head to take a final look at her home.

"Wait! There's something I've forgotten." She ran round the side and to the back. She wanted to pick a spray of lavender that her mother grew at the back of the manor. But when she came to that bed, she didn't see any lavender. There were just sticks sticking out of the soil. She hadn't realised that the plant wouldn't have any leaves yet. She picked a few sticks. They still had the lavender fragrance. She saw that rosemary had all the foliage and she picked that. She was about to go. Looking up at the window she thought that again she saw her mother.

We have lived here for four hundred years and now all of this, this house and land, and this soil, she bent down and picked a handful of it, *all gone with a wave of the governmental hand, never to be returned.* She took out her handkerchief and put the soil in it, twisting the top and tying a knot in it.

Whilst walking back she met the coachman coming towards her.

Elizabeth looked at the twigs and then at Kamila. "But if you need some of these and other herbs, we have some in the kitchen garden at Birch House."

"I wanted them off that bed, from here. The gardener dug the bed but Mother planted them herself. I know there'll probably be some dried in the bags that we took."

CHAPTER 3

Kamila settled to read her mother's notes. She decided that she must ask the doctor for advice about the things that she read. *I must ask Auntie when the doctor is coming, or perhaps go and see him at his house.* She knew that he would tell her the truth. She had known him all her life. He had delivered her. Her parents liked him and he was almost like an uncle to her.

She left her room and went to see Karol. He was awake and smiled at her as she entered.

"How do you feel today, Karol?"

"Fine. Just fine, my little one." She was overjoyed to hear that. *Perhaps there was a chance that he would get better.*

"Really? Oh, I'm so glad. So very glad." She grabbed his hand and kissed his face.

"Auntie and I went to my home to collect some of my things." She described the soldiers and how they hadn't contaminated her parents and her room…the books that they were able to collect… the herbs. "Oh Karol I want you to get better with all my heart. Perhaps there *is* something that will help you. I want to ask the doctor about this condition. When is he coming?"

"I think he's due to come tomorrow, but you'd better check with Mother."

She realized that she had tired him with her enthusiasm and passion, so she just held his hand to her cheek.

Daisy, the maid came into the room. She curtsied. "Oh, sorry Miss. Kamila. I didn't know you was in here. I just came to see if Mr. Karol wanted anything."

"He's asleep now, but tell me Daisy, does he complain of being cold?"

"No Miss. I make sure that the fire is always stacked up. He hasn't complained."

"Does he eat all the food that's brought to him?"

"No Miss. Not really. Sometimes he eats very little."

"Do you know what he appears to like or dislike?"

"No, Miss."

"Thank you Daisy."

"Thank you Miss." The girl curtsied and left the room.

In the afternoon the priest, Father Dominic came. When Kamila saw him, she looked panic stricken from him to her aunt. *Oh God, he hasn't come to give the last rites to Karol, has he? Karol said he was feeling better, didn't he?*

"Auntie—? Is it Karol? Is he worse?"

"No, my dear, Father Dominic has come to finalise the arrangements of your marriage to Karol. You haven't forgotten that, have you?"

Kamila breathed with relief and smiled. With the recent events, she had pushed this to the further recesses of her brain. Anyway she hadn't thought that it would be so soon. The discussion was mainly between Elizabeth and the priest. Kamila looked from one to the other as an occasional approval was requested from her. They then went to see Karol. He agreed with all the arrangements. Kamila held his hand and every now and then he gave her hand a weak squeeze. The marriage was arranged a fortnight hence, unless Karol's condition deteriorated rapidly.

When Father Dominic left after having tea with them, Kamila asked what she should prepare for the occasion. "Should I get a wedding gown? Should I invite any of my friends, and Karol's friends, Auntie?"

" That's entirely up to you, my dear. You must consider that Karol probably won't be able to get dressed, because even that will take a lot out of him and deteriorate his condition. You can ask the doctor when he comes tomorrow, but I have already asked him that same question. As to friends—I know how you would like to have a romantic wedding with all the festivities.

You are, after all, a young girl and it's natural to want that. If you invite friends, they will want to go and see him, be with him, talk to him….How long are you with him before you see his exhaustion?"

"You are right, Auntie. I was being selfish. I have a white dress that mother had had made for me for this summer—for the debutante's ball. It's never been worn so it will be very appropriate, as I won't be going to the ball. I'll wear that and I'll just write to my friends and explain why they are not being invited. I'll also write to any of Karol's friends if he wants me to. Yes, that will be best."

"Thank you my dear." Elizabeth said. "I'm relieved that you see it this way."

Kamila sat at the desk and the first letter she wrote was to the Academy mistress Madame Prust. Kamila reread the letter and put it down, thinking of the Academy and Warsaw and the friends she had left behind. She must write to those friends that would have been invited to her wedding, had their circumstances been different. But first she must ask Karol if he would like her to write to any of his friends.

She rose from the tall backed chair, smoothed her dress down and went upstairs. She knocked on the door and entered. Mary, the maid, was washing his face. Mary hurriedly wiped his face and hid something in a towel. Kamila noticed that the water in the bowl was reddish.

"I'm sorry Karol. Would you like me to go away?"

"No, no. Come in. You've finished Mary haven't you?"

"Yes, sir. I'll just take the bowl and these bits away, miss," said Mary as she covered the bowl with another towel.

Once Mary had left the room, Kamila kissed him. "Karol, where is that blood coming from?"

"From the lungs. It usually happens when I cough. But don't worry, my love." He took her hand and squeezed it gently. "You had an air of urgency about you when you came into the room just then—as if there was a fire somewhere. Where's the fire?"

She laughed. "I'm about to write to various friends about our wedding and explain why they are not being invited. I thought you might want some of your friends to be told too. I could write to them."

"That's a splendid idea. If you pass me my address book—you'll find it in that bureau—," she held up a book, "yes, that's the one." She was now sitting on the bed, their heads bent together over the book, hers dark brown and curly, his blond. Once the names were chosen she left him and went back to the drawing room where she had left her first letter. She wrote letter after letter, and did not notice that it was getting dark. Lamps were lit. She continued until it was time to change for dinner.

"You're very preoccupied Kamila," said Elizabeth.

"I'm sorry Auntie. I was thinking of all those letters I have to write."

"To your friends?"

"Yes, but also to Karol's friends. It's best if they know why they were not invited to our wedding. That way, there will be no misunderstandings," said Kamila.

"So that's what you were doing all this time! I think it's a very wise thing to do."

"This dipping of the quill into the ink after each word is so tiresome. I wish someone would make a pen that holds more ink." Elizabeth put down the newspaper and frowned.

"There is or was such a pen. I remember your uncle's friend, Count Richard—oh, what was his surname? I must be getting old. Anyway, he was signing some important document, and the whole contents of that ink chamber emptied onto the paper. It was really quite funny, when he was telling us about it."

"Perhaps that had been the problem with all of them and that's why there aren't any available in the shops. How did it look?" said Kamila.

"Count Richard—I wish I could remember his name—said that it was a tube with a cork at the top. Apparently one filled the tube with ink and then squeezed it intermittently to make it flow. Yes, that's how he described it."

"Then it sounds as though it was fraught with possible accidents." She sighed and went back to her writing and Elizabeth picked up her newspaper.

Suddenly, Elizabeth started to chuckle. At first it was a gentle sound, and then a louder rumble—*just like my Father used to do.*

"What's so funny?" Kamila said.

"An English doctor gave a lecture at Krakow University about stays and corsets. He said that they transformed women into cones, with Mount Etna at the top and Mount Blanc at the bottom." She pointed to the newspaper, laughing. "That despite strong opposition, they *are* going out of fashion and the only places they'll still be found to be worn will be the women of the Outer Hebrides and Kamchatka."

Kamila joined in the laughter and came over to her to read the article.

"He is right. They are horrible things to wear. I've seen some of my plumper friends squeezed into them, to achieve the contour they desired and they could barely breathe."

"You are lucky, you are so thin there is nothing to squeeze in or out, Kamila. I don't like them either. Well, I think I'll go to bed now. Good night my dear. Don't forget to look in on Karol before you retire."

"I'd never forget that. Good night Auntie." She kissed her aunt.

In the morning a carriage arrived, which Elizabeth recognised as that of the doctor. Kamila went out to greet him. He was a tall man in his late fifties with white hair, bushy eyebrows and a large white moustache. "Good morning Doctor Roger!" said Kamila, smiling. "I'm so pleased to see you again. It's ages since I've seen you." She felt even closer to him now, because of his associations with her whole family, but especially with her parents.

"Kamila, my child!" His voice was deep and felt as if it was coming out of his rotund belly. He put his case on the ground and spread his arms to her. As he hugged her, she put her arms around him, smelling the tobacco and his woolen coat. He lifted her chin, "My dear! I understand how you feel but you must be strong. Your father would wish it so. Now, Karol will be waiting. Shall we go in? Don't let your aunt see you like this. Put on a cheerful face. She has her own grief."

Kamila drew away. Doctor Roger picked up his bag and gave her his arm. She smiled up into his face and he nodded approval as they walked into Birch House together.

The butler took the doctor's coat and said, "Madame is in the sitting room, sir, Miss Kamila." He went ahead and opened the door for them.

The room was delicately decorated in cream and white colours with heavy brocade curtains with an occasional maroon stripe and small maroon roses and buds. The same pattern and colour scheme was reflected in the upholstery of the furniture. It looked a comfortable room.

"Elizabeth, my dear! How are you—?" He was about to say more but Elizabeth's eyes signalled him not to say it.

He kissed her hand and held onto it, looking into her face, diagnosing, judging and estimating her progress. Kamila noticed all of that and made a mental note to ask the doctor about her aunt too.

"Shall I go and see Karol and then come and see you both here, to tell you of his progress?" he said.

"Yes, please. Thank you Andrew," said Elizabeth.

"I would like to come with you Doctor, if I may," said Kamila.

"Yes, of course you may."

As they were walking up the stairs, thinking that there may not be another opportunity, Kamila said, " Please tell me what's wrong with Auntie. I couldn't bear it if I lost her too. She is not well, is she?"

The doctor sighed. "No, she isn't well. She has a diseased heart. One of the valves isn't working, as it should. There is nothing that I or anyone else can do for that condition."

"How much time has she left? I presume you're telling me that to prepare me," said Kamila, her voice barely a whisper.

"Yes. I do want you to be prepared. She may have a year or two. That's if she took it easy; no worries; no extra exertion." He took her hand and pressed it. "I'm glad that you are here with her. You are young and strong. She can draw on that."

"I understand. Yes, I do. Our family has had so much tragedy. Will it ever end?"

"Kamila, I know that tragedy. I've been part of your family for thirty years, but you know there are many families in this region, nay, in the whole of our *country,* who had suffered so much – no, even more. Unbelievable though it seems."

They arrived at Karol's door. Kamila knocked and entered. Karol was propped up and Mary, the maid was adjusting his pillows.

"Karol, look whom I've brought to see you!" said Kamila. "Thank you Mary. You may go for the moment." The maid curtsied and left.

The doctor and the patient shook hands.

"And how are you today, Karol?"

"Not any worse, Doctor. Better, now that Kamila is here to look after us," Karol said with a smile.

"Yes, I'm glad she is here too. And now I'd like to examine you…"

Doctor Roger and Karol looked expectantly at Kamila.

"I know. You both want me to leave the room. It may be unseemly but I would like to stay. If I am to help in anyway then I must understand and therefore I must stay, unseemly or not," said Kamila firmly.

The two men looked at each other and Karol laughed and nodded. The doctor too assented. Kamila came close to the bed and helped Karol with the removal of his pyjama top. Elizabeth had had these made to make it easier for him to undress on such occasions as these.

"Your mother is a very intelligent lady, Karol. This is the most sensible night attire for men. I don't know why it ever went out of fashion," said the doctor. "Now, Kamila. It's most important that a person with phthisis *at all times* assumes a position which will not restrict the function of his thorax, that is, his breathing. That means, when he is sitting up, he must not slouch forwards. And now, in order that I may examine his chest he will have to lean forwards, so pillows must be placed on his knees up to his neck and his arms must rest on these pillows forwards, like this." He showed her how to position the arms. "Oh, and the knees must be bent and separated, especially if he leans forward—that helps with the breathing."

Whilst he searched for his chest inspector, the stethoscope, in his bag, Kamila observed how Karol's shoulder blades stuck out like a bird's wings, and the spine projected from his body like a shark's teeth. *I must get him better with Doctor Roger's help. I must. There must be something that can be done.*

He put the short wooden stethoscope on the bedside table whilst, firstly he observed the chest. He put his hands on either side of the chest and asked him to breathe deeply. Then he laid his fingers against the chest wall and tapped them. Finally he listened to the chest with the tube, all over Karol's chest, asking Karol to breathe in different ways. The patient was then laid on his back and the examination was repeated at the front.

He then examined his abdomen, hands, fingers and feet. Kamila helped to dress Karol and adjusted his pillows as previously directed.

"You're a quick learner, Kamila!" said the doctor.

"Is there anything else that can be done here? Should the room be this hot? Is that what this disease needs—warmth?" said Kamila.

"No! As a matter of fact patients with consumption should have cool fresh air. But let's go and talk with your aunt, and let Karol rest." He shook hands with Karol and they left the room.

On entering the sitting room, Elizabeth rose from the armchair. "How is my son, Andrew?" she said, searching the doctor's face.

He took her hands in his, "You know how he is. There is no change—to detect."

"If there is no change—at least there is some hope—that he isn't worse. Yesterday he said that he was very well." Kamila was trying to will him to live, to make them believe and hope, just as she did.

"Youth! Such enthusiasm and willpower!" said the doctor. Elizabeth sat down and they followed suit.

"You were going to tell me what I can do to help him," said Kamila.

"Yes. You asked me about the warmth in the room. Consumptive patients should have as much fresh air as possible. So if he could be nursed in the open air would be the best. Ten years ago George Bodington, a general practitioner from Sutton Coldfield, a small village in England, published an essay on treatment of pulmonary consumption. I have great admiration for this man. Not only for what he wrote, but for having had the courage to do so."

"Why what happened to him?" said Elizabeth.

"Poor fellow! Following that publication, the rest of the medical profession closed ranks against him. You see, he wasn't powerful enough."

"Why? What did he say or do?" said Kamila.

"He was scathing over bleeding, leeches, blistering, purgation and starvation and of sending these patients to far away places—virtually to die. He advocated a room that was not closed, to walk, ride and never be deterred by inclement weather. The cooler the air that entered the lungs the better—sharp frosty winter air was most beneficial. The only medicine he used was morphine to sedate the patient at night. His treatment was far superior to the treatments used to date."

"Are you suggesting that my son's bed should be put outside, Andrew?" said Elizabeth with a laugh.

"No, but if you had a veranda it would do very well. I know that you haven't, so have the windows open day and night and place the bed by them."

"He will freeze!" said Elizabeth.

"No he won't!"

"Auntie, let's try these methods that Dr. Roger suggests. It's true that his room is exceedingly hot. Can you tell me if I can use some of these methods my Mother suggests in these notes?" Kamila showed the notes she had made.

“Inhalations aren’t supposed to be used on patients who have haemoptysis—cough up blood— but I see no reason why you couldn’t use these—rosemary and mint—in drinks or rub into the skin in a massage.”

“When should it be done?” said Elizabeth.

“After a bath, which he should have daily. It shouldn’t be too hot or too cold. But who’s going to give him these massages?”

“I think, perhaps, Daisy. She’s a strong sensible girl,” said Elizabeth.

“If I knew how, I’d do it,” said Kamila.

“Kamila! It would not be proper for you to do it!” said Elizabeth.

After showing them how the massage should be done, in a circular movement, the doctor said his goodbyes to Elizabeth and left. Kamila accompanied him to his coach. Before entering it, he turned to face her.

"Kamila, I didn't want to say in front of your aunt, although she does know it. There is no point in rubbing salt into her wounds. Prepare yourself. This disease is a killer. Although it's been called the `The English Disease,` it's present in all the countries of the world. However much you try, Karol will die. Not only has he this direful malady but this was preceded by most severe deprivation and starvation during his years in Siberia."

"But Doctor Roger, only yesterday he said that he was feeling so much better. Isn't that a good sign?”

“No, my dear. Whether it’s beneficial or not, I don’t know, but for some reason consumptive patients have this optimism to the very end. But do your best. After all, miracles do happen.” He kissed her cheek and took his leave. Kamila stood in the drive long after the doctor left and then walked slowly back to the house.

He must get better. He must. She entered the sitting room. Her aunt had her eyes closed but opened them when Kamila was about to leave the room.

“Don’t go, my dear. I’m not asleep.” Kamila settled herself at her aunt’s feet and took her aunt’s pale, smooth hand in her hand.

“Auntie may I have your permission to do these things we discussed?”

“I think we must.” Kamila jumped up with joy, with speed and enthusiasm that only the young can portray, and that made Elizabeth laugh.

Kamila rushed upstairs to tell Karol all the measures that had been discussed. The servants came to put the large bed near the windows. All the windows were opened. Chilly spring air rushed in to greet them all. Pillows were placed under Karol’s arms so that the arms would be away from his chest wall to aid his breathing.

“We must have a bucket of disinfectant here by the bed,” said Kamila.

“What for?” said Karol.

“For two reasons: to refresh the air in the room, and for you to put your dirty and used handkerchiefs into it. So that they don’t contaminate the air as they did before.”

A regime was started whereby Karol had a bath in the morning, followed by a massage with the oil that Kamila prepared according to her mother's instructions and Dr. Roger's guidance, containing rosemary and mint. The sheets and his pyjamas were changed daily as Kamila learned that with this disease there was a lot of sweating. He was then given a breakfast arranged by his mother and allowed to rest for an hour.

Kamila then came to help him out of bed, and having put a cloak on him, took him for a walk in the room. She was little and thin and he was tall and thin. As they struggled across the floor, they made a strange pair and it was not successful. With all the will in the world bursting from her, she didn't have enough strength to hold him. Additionally her wide skirts nearly unbalanced Karol. It was he who suggested that she should allocate this job to one of the menservants. But she insisted that she should be there to supervise.

According to the doctor's instructions, she suggested that Karol walked four times per day. At first it would be for a few minutes each time, later increasing it to a little longer as he grew stronger. In her desire for him to come out of this disease, she had no doubt that he would get stronger. Perhaps it was this very enthusiasm that was so infectious, but her aunt looked happier, and Karol was full of optimism just as Dr. Roger had predicted.

Meanwhile there were a stream of visitors, not to see Karol but Elizabeth and Kamila to commiserate with the family over the tragedy, and enquire about Kamila's future. Many of the ladies—for mainly they were the ones who came—Kamila knew only slightly. And all these visits were exhausting and Kamila tried to spare Elizabeth from the burden of them. But it proved difficult. They all wanted to talk to her, not only about her brother and his wife but about Karol. But Kamila told her aunt that under no circumstance would she allow visits to Karol.

They had made one mistake with the first visitor who had asked to see Karol and allowed her to go to him and seeing what a devastating effect she had had on him, Kamila said to her aunt through gritted teeth, "The next one who insists will have to fight past me for I shall barricade the stairs with my body. If necessary I shall take one of Uncle's swords off the wall and be prepared to use it."

The visitors who were gladly seen by them both were Katarzyna and her husband, Wladyslaw Ludomirski and each one in turn gathered Kamila in their arms, for they had known her since birth, as well as being close friends of her parents and Elizabeth. Although Kamila addressed them as aunt and uncle, they were not related at all.

"Kamila, my dear, my dear," Katrzyna stroked her head as she held her closely, "Thank God you still have your aunt Elizabeth and she's going to take care of you. But please remember that we are here for you too, should you need us. And do keep in contact with us. Come and see us once you've settled down here. You know how my brood long to see you."

"I will. Thank you, Auntie." Kamila detached herself from this warm lady, but Katarzyna still held her by her hands and surveyed the young girl.

"You know, you are so like your Father to look at and in character too, I think. Don't you think so, Elizabeth?"

"Yes. I've always thought so."

"I wouldn't mind being like either of my parents. They were—are—such wonderful people."

"Yes they are. May God look after them both, wherever they are. I can see you want to go to Karol, so go, child. Give our love to him. I'm glad you are here to look after him and Elizabeth."

Kamila thanked them for coming and kissed each one goodbye.

CHAPTER 4

No one had heard a coach arrive until the butler announced that Raphael Karbonski had come to see Karol. He was invited to the drawing room where Elizabeth and Kamila were sitting. The visitor was dressed in the most up to date fashion. He greeted Elizabeth, having met her several times before, by kissing her hand and enquiring after her health.

Elizabeth introduced him to Kamila. Kamila extended her hand and eyed him coolly. He had piercing blue eyes, with what she interpreted as an insolent light in them and these eyes appeared to be laughing at her. His straight blond hair kept falling over his forehead as he spoke. She thought that he was older than Karol, perhaps around forty years of age.

"Ah! The bride-to-be! *You* wrote to me. I thank you for the delightful letter and I bring you my congratulations personally." He put his lips to Kamila's hand. *I can't believe that this—this gigolo—could be Karol's friend.* Kamila withdrew her hand.

After a few enquiries about Karol, Kamila took him upstairs. She walked in silence whilst he talked in a frivolous manner, which she found irritating. Outside Karol's door, she turned to him,

"Please remember that he is very ill. You can stay only a short while—about half an hour. I don't want you exhausting him."

He bowed deeply in an exaggerated manner, apparently unaware of her cool manner . "Your instructions will be obeyed to the last letter, dear lady." She gritted her teeth. She felt sure that he was laughing at her.

As they entered the room, Kamila had no time to say anything to Karol.

"Karol! My dear fellow! It's so good to see you!" Raphael almost flew with long strides, like a stork, to Karol.

Kamila lost some of her frostiness to the visitor. If he could greet Karol with such warmth, perhaps she was mistaken about him.

She adjusted Karol's pillows so that he was well supported and the position was beneficial for his chest. "I don't want Karol to be exhausted," she said again, to the visitor, and left the room. She returned to the drawing room to her aunt.

"I hope that fellow won't exhaust Karol too much," said Kamila.

"Let Karol enjoy him whilst he can. He's his best friend, my love."

"He didn't give a very good first impression—to me, at least. I don't care for him," said Kamila.

"That's just a veil to hide behind. He is a very brave and courageous man. He took part in the insurrection of 1830 you know, and nearly died for Poland. Ask Karol, or better still, Raphael about it."

Kamila tried to suppress the dislike she felt towards the man and certainly had no inclination to ask him. Instead she decided to bury herself in a book. When Elizabeth asked Kamila to ring for some tea and it was brought in, Kamila asked the maid if the visitor had gone and was told that he had not.

"It must be nearly two hours since he came! I must go and see if Karol is alright." She walked briskly out of the room and up the stairs. Outside the room she sniffed the air, not believing her nostrils. She knocked and flung the door open. She didn't quite know what she expected. She certainly didn't expect to see Karol asleep and the visitor to be sitting quietly by the bed, or for him to put up his finger to his moustached upper lip and form his lips into "Shh!"

He jumped to his feet and came to her.

"You've been smoking here," she said accusingly. "Don't you know that that uses up the air—that it's harmful for Karol?"

"Kamila, my dear! Don't blame Raphael. *I asked* him to smoke. It's such a delicious fragrance and it's so long since I've smelt it." Karol was awake and smiling at her concern. "We thought you might be pleased that I've been walking—twice—during the time that Raphael's been here."

"My apologies, sir," was all that Kamila said.

"How many days are you staying?" Karol asked Raphael.

"I can only stay another half hour and then I must go. We have a meeting in Lvov tonight and I must be there."

"I'm only sorry that I can't be with you," said Karol.

And thank God for that, thought Kamila as she left the room.

Months later, Kamila remembered her aunt's words to him as he was departing, "Do be careful."

"Auntie, will you mind if I ask Jordan to take me for a ride?"

"No, not at all. Where do you want to go?"

"Nowhere particular."

"Take Daisy with you, or Mary."

"No, I don't need either of them--."

"I'll ask Mary to go with you." Elizabeth's tone brooked no disobedience. When Kamila went to the carriage, Mary was already standing there.

"Where do you want to go Miss Kamila?" said Jordan.

"Just to the end of the drive and then I'll tell you." When they were out of sight of the house, she asked him to drive on the northbound road and then she'd direct him further.

"Where are we going, Miss Kamila?" said Mary.

"You'll see in a moment. There! That's where I was born. My home. But don't tell Auntie."

"What about Jordan?"

"I've asked him not to tell Auntie, too."

"If she asks us directly, I don't know that we can tell a lie."

A different soldier came out and held his hand up. "Stop! Civilians are not allowed here."

"I know that." Kamila got out of the carriage. "I used to live here and the last time I came, the Colonel was very kind and allowed me to collect my things from the house. I haven't come to collect anything today. But I would be so grateful if you could ask the Colonel if I can see him, please. "The Colonel is not here today."

"Oh."

"He'll be here on Friday. Anyway why do you want to see him—so as I can tell him?"

"My parents were deported—."

"Yes, I know."

"I wondered if the Colonel could give me an address—where they were taken—so that I can write to them. I haven't had any news of them—or a single letter—."

"They are not allowed—."

"I didn't know."

"I'll tell the Colonel when he returns."

"Thank you."

Elizabeth didn't question her as to where she was going, when Friday arrived, but Mary was there to accompany her. The same soldier came out when they arrived.

"I'll get the Colonel," he said and disappeared indoors.

The colonel was a tall man with greying hair at the temples and eyes to match.

"I'm afraid I can be of no help to you, madam. We are not told such information. Indeed, I suspect that this information is deliberately withheld from us. We are just billeted to premises that had been vacated."

"Then can you tell me who is in charge of these deportations?"

"Again, I can be of no help there. It would be the Russian authorities and I would doubt if they would give you such information."

"Is there anyone in Luck who might know?"

He shook his head. "I *am* sorry."

"I'm sorry, too. Goodbye, and thank you."

"Goodbye, madam."

Kamila looked so disheartened that Mary touched her arm. "What are you going to do, Miss Kamila?"

"I don't really know."

Elizabeth had told Kamila that they were going to the second mass on Sunday and to be ready by eight o'clock in the morning. Having seen to the comforts of Karol, they set off, with Jordan driving. The day was dry and warm, and the lakes which were dispersed in the gently undulating landscape, glistened in the sunshine. Farmers, here and there, were preparing the soil for it was mainly an agricultural land, growing different grains. These were transported to Gdansk for export, mainly to Amsterdam. The ships on the river Styr not only collected the grain, but they also brought luxury goods in return.

As they entered the city of Luck, bustle and noise greeted them. Everyone was going to some form of a church, dressed in their best, for there were many churches of many denominations in the city.

The buildings in the city were brick built, covered with plaster and ornate plasterwork surrounded the windows and doors and even under the eaves, and painted cream or white or light yellow ochre colour. The architecture was a mixture of Russian and oriental, with some baroque. Churches had cupolas but these were not of the round onion type as found in Russia but a little more squat and smaller.

The River Styr flowed from the east, westwards, forming a wide semicircle, flowing first northwards and then again to the east. The centre of the city was situated in that loop of the river, almost encircling it, except for the east side. The nearest approach to the cathedral whence they were going, was to go along a road that ran almost parallel to the lower part of the river, but to the north of it. Between this road and the river there was a large expanse of sandy area where the river habitually flooded in the rainy season.

Long before they reached their destination, they could see the cathedral ahead of them, over the sandy expanse and, a little to the left, the Lubarta Castle. The thirteenth century wooden castle was rebuilt in the next century on a triangular ground with bastions on each corner and a surrounding wall and moat, so now it could be seen and admired from afar.

All the roads in the city were cobbled, even the one by the Styr. They were wide and lined by trees on both sides. Although the city had been attacked and ravaged throughout the centuries, from all points of the compass, it still managed to project a gay as well as a careless look.

The cathedral was a tall building with three cupolas and also could be easily seen from afar. It was no longer in the same place that it had originally been at the time of consecration as a cathedral, in 1375. Because it had been burnt down and rebuilt so many times, its site was eventually moved to the Jesuit church site and when the two dioceses were joined, the cathedral was renamed Holy Trinity and St. Peter and St. Paul.

It seemed that whatever political power was raging through the country, be it Knights of the Teutonic Order, Mongols, Turks, Cossacks, Lithuanians, Prussians, they all aimed at destroying this beautiful building with its priceless interior. Other religious buildings were targeted also. And there were many of them in the city. There were Russian Orthodox, Protestant, Evangelical, Unitarian, Catholic churches, and a large Synagogue.

They stopped outside the cathedral. Jordan opened the door and helped each lady down. People greeted them as they made their way inside. Not many of them knew Kamila but they all knew Elizabeth and had heard of the misfortunes that had befallen the family.

The outside of the cathedral was painted in yellow, cream and pink colours so that it looked like an Easter egg. There were three entrances, with three steps to each one. That day, being a Sunday, the congregation filed in through the main one at the front. Situated on either side of the door were two statues, the patrons of the cathedral. On the left stood St. Peter and opposite was St. Paul.

Inside, the cathedral was built in the form of the cross, with numerous Ionic pillars, topped by scrolls and encircling friezes. Each time Kamila was here she marvelled at the beautiful carvings and medallion paintings on the walls and the altar, which was sumptuous in the baroque style. To the east and west of the transept were individual chapels.

During the mass, Kamila felt a desperate sadness, especially when they sang the hymns. Although these were religious, they invariably had something woven into them, echoing the patriotism which each member of the congregation felt. These were even more poignant to Kamila than ever before. During the sermon the Bishop mentioned her forthcoming marriage and the urgency for it. Not that it was necessary to say the bans, because of the special circumstances, but because the family was well known to the parish. They had to pray for Karol's health…

When the mass was over Kamila went to pray at the altar of the Black Madonna. This picture had always had a powerful impression on Kamila. It, like Poland, had had a bloody history. Kamila knelt in front of it. She was so engrossed in her communication, her pleading for the survival of her parents, to be able to be with them again, for the health of Karol and her aunt, that she wasn't aware how long she had been there. She told the Black Madonna how frightened she was of what was to come, of her uncertainty of her future; how she couldn't discuss any of this with anyone, how she felt so alone.

When she arose, she looked around, feeling slightly disorientated, as if she had been in a different world. There was no one about in the cathedral except one or two people lighting candles. Outside, the sunshine was warm and there were still a few groups of people about. Her aunt and the Bishop were talking earnestly. They both turned as she approached and smiled at her. Kamila shook hands with the Bishop who wished her happiness in her forthcoming marriage.

As they made their way to the coach, Kamila asked what they were discussing.

"Your wedding, of course, my dear. The Bishop says that the Civil Registrar has to come to the wedding and we have to have two witnesses. Pity we can't have Raphael here." She felt silent for so long that Kamila looked at her. "Oh! Sorry. I was just thinking. I'll arrange for someone."

The journey home seemed shorter, with both of them being lost in their thoughts. Kamila seemed more at peace. On arrival home they were surprised to see an unknown horse at the front door.

"I wonder whose he is," said Elizabeth.

"Raphael's?"

"No, no. He wouldn't come here by horse."

Benjamin, the butler, informed them that it belonged to a Mr. Thomas Orzel, a local farmer.

"Has he come to sell us something? Why isn't he at the other entrance?" said Elizabeth.

"Mr. Karol asked him to call."

"Karol? Whatever for?"

"I don't know madam. All he said was that Mr Orzel had to come whilst you and Miss Kamila were at church. He said he was not to be disturbed."

"Really? How intriguing! How long has Mr.Orzel been here?"

"About half an hour, madam."

They took off their bonnets and coats and asked for tea to be served in the drawing room.

"Do you know this Mr. Orzel, Auntie?"

"I think I met him once. He's tall and thin, about forty. A widower, I think. Yes that's right. He owns the land south of ours. He breeds horses and livestock. He has two sons. I think they're in Australia—I'm not really sure—some very far away place." said Elizabeth.

When the butler brought them the tea, he said, "Mr. Orzel has just left. I thought you might want to know, madam."

"Thank you, Benjamin."

When Kamila went to see Karol, she asked him what he wanted with Mr. Orzel.

"Why do you want to know, Nosey?" he said.

"Auntie wanted to know as well. Was he selling something? We couldn't work out what you'd be buying from him. I know! You've bought something illegal and that's why you wanted us out of the way. Ah! you bought some diamonds and you've hidden under your pillow?" Her hands dived under the pillow and he caught her and kissed her tenderly.

"No diamonds there, I'm afraid. If I had them I'd have given them to you by now, my love." However she tried he wouldn't tell her why he wanted to see Mr. Orzel.

Letters started to arrive in reply to the ones she had sent out. She read some of them to her aunt but not the ones that considered would be distressing.

"Auntie, if we've had letters like these, is there any chance that my Mother and Father could write to me—to us—from Siberia?"

"I doubt it. I've never heard of anyone having anything from there, unless it was smuggled by some escapee. Certainly we had nothing from Karol. Just silence."

"Or could I write to them?"

"We have no way of knowing where they were sent to. It's an enormous terrain. Anyway, I wrote to the Seym, as soon as your parents were taken away, because the soldiers who were sent to take them, knew nothing."

"And?"

"The reply was that they didn't know and suggested contacting the Russian embassy but they, true to their system of secrecy, could not help either non-stop." They both felt silent. The other letters remained unread on Kamila's knees as she tried to imagine the tundra, the extensive swampland, the taiga and the frozen forest-steppe. Oh! If only she could jump on a horse and ride to them. Then her practical nature took over. *And how far would you ride in that icy and snowy terrain? And side saddle at that? Not very far. But, wait! What if I didn't ride side saddle? Don't be ridiculous!*

That night there was a very heavy frost. The branches of the trees were coated with hoarfrost, which glistened ethereally in the moonlight. The fields looked sugar coated as far as the eye could see. The deep silence was broken by nearby call of the vixens and the distant eerie howling of the wolves. Kamila lay in her bed, unable to sleep. Eventually she jumped out of the bed. Despite the fire glowing and throwing delicate colours of orange and yellow on the walls, it was cold in the room. *And there is Karol lying with the windows wide open. Or has he frozen to death?*

She put on a warm dressing gown and wrapped it tightly around her body, before tying the belt, and looked at the clock. *Two o'clock in the morning*. She put her feet into her slippers and hurried down the corridor to Karol's room. She turned the handle quietly and entered. His fire was also burning but with the windows open made no difference. She shivered as she approached his bed. Gently she touched his face. It was very cold. She lifted the bedclothes at the bottom of the bed to feel his feet.

"What now?" He growled. He sounded really angry. "Oh, it's you Kamila!"

"Did I waken you? I'm sorry. I was worried that you might be frozen stiff. I couldn't go off to sleep for the worry."

"What's the matter with you all? If you all have insomnia, is that the reason to subject someone else to this torture? You're the fourth person to come and waken me." The annoyance hadn't yet left his voice.

"Oh! Who else came?"

"First Daisy, then Benjamin, then Mother and now you. Go to bed and let me sleep."

"Stick your foot out so I can feel it and then I'll go." He obediently obliged and she was gratified that his body was very warm indeed. "I will go, but first, look out of the window Karol. Look how beautiful the land and the world is!" she shivered.

He looked. "Yes it is. If you don't want to go now, then climb into my bed."

"Karol!" Her voice was shocked but she backed away and laughingly bid him pleasant dreams, as she left the room.

At breakfast, she said, "Auntie, would you mind if I went riding this morning? It's so beautiful and sunny. Karol's routine is working well. Would you mind?"

"No, my dear. Go if you want to. Have you looked over the horses? Don't take Karol's horse, Emblem. He can be a bit capricious and needs a firm hand. I think Bessie might be suitable for you, but ask Karol."

When she entered Karol's room, he looked pink, having just had the bath and the massage. "You look very fresh and clean, Karol. I hope you had a lovely restful night."

"No, I didn't. I was the busiest night in my life. A market square couldn't have had more traffic and the damned animals decided to give me a concert. The foxes came right under my window."

"You should be glad that we all love you so." She smiled mischievously and came over to kiss him. "I want to go riding. It's so beautiful outside. I wish you could come too, but I think you're not quite ready yet, are you?"

"No, I don't think so. Take Bessie. She's an intelligent mare, and she won't throw you. Will you be gone long? I can't be left alone for too long. I need someone to disturb me every now and then."

"Do be serious, Karol. There is something else I want to ask you." She lowered her voice, "I couldn't ask, Auntie. I know what the answer would be. Could I use your breeches and jacket and cap?"

"Whatever for?" He craned his neck to look at her.

"I want to ride astride, and not side saddle. If I look like a man, no one will notice. If I ride astride in my enormous skirts, and should meet someone,

my name will be dirtier that mud. They might even deport me!"
He laughed. "My clothes won't fit you. You're tiny compared to me, even as I'm now. I have bigger bones."

"Yes, and they stick out—." She bit her lip, wishing she hadn't said that.

"I *know t*hey stick out," he stretched his hand to her, "don't be upset by that."

"Can I try them—the clothes, at least?"

"Of course you can. Go in to the wardrobe. Try the brown one, the one on your left. Yes, that's the one. That would be the size for me as I am now. You can go behind the screen and try them on there, if you like. I want to see this."

"No, I think I'll go to the next room to yours. I'll come and show you the result."

When she returned, he propped himself on his elbows. The jacket hung loosely on her body. The sleeves were folded over, being far too long. The shirt was too large at the neck, but when Karol's eyes travelled down her legs and saw his trousers in a tight concertina he started to laugh so much that Kamila quickly disappeared into the other room in case some one came in.

On entering his room again, after a longer time, she was impeccably dressed and not one hair was out of place. She put the clothes back into the wardrobe. "You obviously thought I wouldn't get away with that," she said dryly.

"No, not at all. There is something that would fit, though."

"What?"

"The hat," said Karol. "Why don't you ask one of the staff to make you an outfit?"

"Yes, but I'd want it to be like a man's and Auntie would find out and I'm sure she'd not approve. I'll just have to ride side saddle. True, it's an elegant way, but so illogical."

"If Queen Christina of Sweden could wear trousers to ride, why couldn't my Kamila do too?"

"I didn't know that. In fact, I don't know anything about her."

"Didn't they teach you anything at that school of yours? She caused a scandal in Europe when she abdicated her throne. He father, Gustav II Adolphus, ordered that she should be educated as a prince. She was one of the most learned and witty women in the world."

"Ah! That's why I don't know anything about her. She's nothing to do with our history."

"You'd be wrong to think that. When her cousin, Janek Casimir abdicated, she tried to seize his, that is, the Polish crown. She would have made a wise and powerful monarch for us."

"Why did she abdicate?"

"It's thought that she didn't want to get married."

"Was she beautiful?"

"No. Not, at all. But apart from her brain, she must have had tremendous charm."

"Thank you for that. I'll get a jacket and trousers made. Just like yours!"

Kamila put on her riding habit and went to the stables in search of Bessie. Fred, the groom came to greet her. She stopped by a beautiful horse and started to stroke him.

"What about this one? You're a darling, aren't you? And don't I know you?" He nuzzled her face in reply.

"Nay, Miss. `e's got a fierce temper. `E's just foolin' you. Mr. Karol said you was to have Bessie. `Ere she is."

She looked at the stallion she was fondling. True enough, comparing the look in his eyes to the gentle light in Bessie's, she saw the pride and arrogance in his, and thought that he was laughing at her. All the same she couldn't tear herself away from him. She put her arms around his neck and whispered endearments to him.

"Be careful, Miss. `E could turn on you."

"I don't think so. He understands me and I trust him. This must be Emblem, isn't it?"

"Yes, Miss. `E's Mr. Karol's `orse."

The groom saddled Bessie, whilst Kamila talked to her and stroked her. Fred helped her up, she took up the reins and they trotted out of the yard. When eventually they left the immediate grounds of Birch House, Kamila decided to go southwest. The land to the north and east was too generously scattered with bog land and she knew that some would be dangerous. Besides, being engulfed by midges wasn't her idea of heaven. Furthermore they could drive even a placid horse like Bessie, mad .

Quite a lot of the healing plants grew on bog land and she wanted to harvest them. And spring was the best time to pick them, according to her mother. She would go there, but not now, not when she was alone.

The sky was clear, with this characteristic ultramarine-violet hue, which was reflected not only in the rivers, but also on the land. The fields were already ploughed and she could see in the distance, men throwing the seed into the furrows as they walked in between the rows. The earth smelt of spring and hope, having awoken from the deep sleep of winter. Workers' cottages were scattered along the landscape. They were usually built of wood and often brightly painted. Intermittently at road junctions, she came across a metal Christ nailed to a wooden cross, or Mary, Mother of God carved in wood. There would always be some flowers at the foot of them.

Kamila and Bessie came upon the stream that ran into the River Styr, and followed it. There were lots of trees along the banks, and the geese and the ducks leisurely left their resting places on the grass and swam away from these two intruders.

"I think we ought to be going home, Bessie. It must be two hours since we've left. Come on, sweetheart." She patted her neck gently.

At the stables, she jumped off Bessie, hugged her and promised her they would go again. Bessie nuzzled her cheek as if to say that she enjoyed Kamila's company too. She handed the reins to Fred and ran to the house. As she started to climb the stairs, Benjamin came out and coughed.

"Excuse me Miss. Kamila. Madam said she would like to see you when you came back. You'll find her in the drawing room."

"Thank you, Benjamin."

Kamila entered the room, her cheeks glowing and clothes steaming.

"Goodness, my dear! You look as if you've been in a race—and won!" said Elizabeth. "Have you been galloping all over the region?"

"No, not at all. Bessie walked sedately so I wouldn't fall off. It was so lovely. The colour of the sky and the smell of the earth—so beautiful! But I understand you wanted to see me?"

"Yes. Karol is getting crotchety with your being gone so long, so pop along to see him before you change. Let him see you as you are now." Elizabeth smiled and looked her up and down. Kamila laughed as she left.

She knocked on Karol's door and came up to him. "Auntie says you wanted to see me? Oh! What's the matter? You look as if you've swallowed something horrible. Are you still cross?"

"And you look like something the wind has just blown in. I can smell the earth and the fields and trees on you. I missed you. You were gone such a long time."

"Only two hours!"

"No. It was three hours and ten minutes. I'm not letting you go out alone tomorrow. You need a chaperone."

"Don't be silly! I was perfectly safe. And Bessie is gorgeous. She looked after me. Anyway whom had you in mind? Benjamin? *Please*, not Fred."

"No, neither. Me. I'm going to be your chaperone!"

"You! Oh, Karol, does that mean you're feeling better?" She threw her arms around his neck, kissing his face wherever her lips touched it.

"Yes, I do. But also, didn't Dr Roger say it would be good for me to go riding?"

"Yes, he did. Oh, so that's why Auntie was looking so happy. By the way, I'm having the riding suit made, just like yours. But I promise to be dressed like a lady when I'm with you and ride side saddle."

"When will it be ready?"

"In about two days. Did you say anything about it to Auntie?"

"No. I left that for you to do. It's your secret."

"Oh, Karol, I do love you. We will be happy, won't we?" She looked at him earnestly. "And it doesn't matter that we are cousins. We will have lots of children—."

"Hey! Hey! Not so fast! I only promised to go riding with you. And you've got some mud on your sleeve. Shouldn't you change into something more beguiling?"

When Kamila took off her riding habit , there was no mud on the sleeve.

CHAPTER 5

That evening, Kamila and Elizabeth discussed how to get Karol down the stairs. He could walk, but would it be too much? Would he be able to sit on Emblem—and control him? They decided that perhaps he ought to be carried down the long staircase. It wouldn't be a problem as he was feather light.

And that's how he came down. Two of the men made a cradle of their hands and he sat on it, with his arms around the neck of each one.

Karol looked smart in his riding clothes although they were too big for him now. The stables were fairly near to the house, so he felt that he could walk that distance. Kamila watched anxiously his progress. She had arranged that men were around in case he fell. She saw the pride on his face that he had made it, when they arrived at the stables. The horses were already saddled.

He came to Emblem and put his arms around him and buried his face in Emblem's neck for a long time. After a while she put an arm around his waist.

"I hope you're telling that hooligan to behave himself with you. I saw that naughty look in his eyes yesterday and I'm sure he was laughing at me then," said Kamila, patting the horse affectionately. She went over to Bessie and hugged her, "Bessie, tell Emblem what a special day it is and to be very careful." Emblem snorted and Bessie batted the long eyelashes surrounding her gorgeous brown eyes.

Kamila was already sitting on Bessie when she saw that Karol was intending to jump onto Emblem. "Karol!" she said sharply, "Don't even think about that!" She quickly called the men in the yard and Karol was placed onto his horse without difficulty as if he was a lid on a pot.

"What a fussy, bossy woman you are! Just as well I've found this out. When's the wedding?"

"Next week. On Thursday 4th of April. Why?"

"Oh! Good! So I'll still have time to cancel it," said Karol looking cross.

"You wouldn't? Would you, Karol?" Her voice held uncertainty.

"Yes, I would," he said but from his expression she knew he was only teasing.

The horses walked side by side except when they were on the road and had to let carts go by. So frequently, the carts or people who worked on the fields would stop and enquire about Karol's health that Kamila felt that the benefit of his being in the open was being nullified by the constant stoppages. She knew that Karol was popular with the locals for he was friendly, like his father had been, and knew them and their children by name.

"Let's go to the river where we are less likely to meet so many people," she said. They manoeuvred the horses over the slight embankments with ease. Kamila watched anxiously over Karol.

"How do you feel? We've been out about half an hour. Have you had enough?

"Since we both know you're hopeless at keeping time and estimating it, we'll ignore that. I do feel fine but perhaps we should make our way home. After all you wouldn't want the `treatment` to kill me in the process, would you?" Kamila laughed.

She found Elizabeth painting eggs, for the blessing on Easter Saturday. Intricate patterns were painted with warm wax and then the eggs were hard boiled in water containing the outer, yellow layers of onions. When they were ready, the non-painted areas were stained golden yellow and the areas where the wax had been applied remained white, often looking like lace. Those who could afford to buy paints produced daintily painted masterpieces. Elizabeth was still doing the wax painting.

"Oh! Good! You're back. You can start on the painting, unless you'd like some tea?" said Elizabeth. "And over tea you can tell me how the two of you got on. I understand that he is asleep now."

"Yes, he was fast asleep when I looked in, just now."

Elizabeth had prepared two large baskets, lined them with white embroidered linen serviettes. Spare serviettes, for covering up the produce later, were lying folded on the table. Once the eggs were ready, they would add small pieces of bread, cheese, cooked meat, and decorate the whole with sprigs of greenery. But these things wouldn't be done until Saturday morning, just before going to the church for the blessing.

The following day, being Good Friday was a day of fast. Even families who were not the most adherent to the Roman Catholic faith like Kamila's family, they still upheld this fast. It wouldn't, of course apply to people who were ill, like Karol.

In the evening, after the midnight mass it was customary to have a special meal of fish. The whole family would sit at this table if possible, and on this occasion, Elizabeth asked Karol if he could come down to this meal, even for just a little while. They all decided that perhaps that day he would not go riding but do more walking, in the room and the corridors.

They didn't go to the midnight mass, and had the meal set for ten o'clock. Karol was brought down, dressed. Kamila and Elizabeth had dressed in beautiful gowns for the occasion. The fish dish on the table was in stoneware pottery and contained pickled herrings that had been soaked for many hours to remove the salt and then baked with sliced potatoes, placed on the surface like fallen petals in the autumn. All this was cooked in cream with garnishments of onions and herbs. The surface wafers of potatoes were crispy brown and curled upwards invitingly.

"Mm. That smell is so delicious. It's such a long time since I've had this," said Karol. They drank the wine and proceeded with the meal.

"I'm so glad we could have had this day together," said Elizabeth.

On Saturday the final touches to the baskets were done and Elizabeth said, "Kamila, I think that Daisy had better go with you to the church. You won't be able to carry both of those baskets. Jordan is ready and waiting."

When they arrived at the cathedral, there were a lot of people about, all with baskets. They filed into the pews and sat down with the baskets beside them. The blessing of the food went on throughout the day. As the Bishop was passing down the aisle, he picked up the holy water with the brush and flung the droplets in between the pews onto the upheld baskets.

The two baskets brought from the church were identical in content. One was for Elizabeth and her family and the other for the servants. The one basket was placed in the centre of the table in the dining room.

On Easter Sunday, after returning from church, the family gathered together. Karol had not been to church, but was down for the traditional breakfast. Elizabeth took one egg, peeled it and cut it into three parts. She did the same with each of the different foods from the basket. All these were put onto one porcelain plate and shared between them. It didn't matter how tiny the portion was. It was only a token. That it was blessed for this most holy day.

Tradition required that the head of the house should sing the Easter hymn during this time. They stood up and Elizabeth started to sing.

This good day has been left for us because,
It's the day that Jesus Christ arose.....

Elizabeth's voice was low and pleasant to the ear. Kamila suddenly heard how her father used to sing that hymn at this time of the year, in that very deep but still melodious voice.

In the afternoon a carriage drew up and an elegant young lady was helped down. It was Amelia, Kamila's best friend at the Academy in Warsaw. Kamila ran out and flung herself into Amelia's out stretched arms.

"Oh! How lovely to see you, Amelia! Why didn't you let me know you were coming?"

"I wasn't sure to the very end if I was! You know my cousin lives quite near here? Well, they invited my parents and me for the Easter. So I thought I'd come and see you. It's not inconvenient, is it?"

"Of course not. Come and meet my Aunt and Karol. How long are you staying?" She turned to the coachman and told him to go to the kitchen. There, he would be shown where to stable the horses.

"Kamila! Kamila! Hold on awhile! I'm only staying till about six and then we must go. My cousin would be hurt if I stayed here even for one night. The horses aren't tired. The journey was only short. Ruben will get some water for them, though." Ruben followed Kamila's instructions and went in search of food and water—for himself and the horses.

The two girls entwined their arms and walked to the house.

"You look so grown up, Amelia. I think you've grown in height as well since we last saw each other. And what a beautiful gown! Blue does suit you. "

"It's only about a fortnight since we parted! But I suppose it is possible we've both grown. We all miss you so much, you know. Not that you were noisy, but somehow the Academy is so quiet now. It's just not the same anymore. In fact, I'm glad to be leaving at the end of this semester."

"Here we are. Auntie's in here." She opened the door, "Auntie! Look who's come! My dearest friend from the Academy." She introduced the two ladies.

Elizabeth asked Amelia about her family and where they came from and discovering that her origins lay in Lublin, produced a number of families whom she knew who lived near that city. Kamila listened to the questions and answers and smiled. To her, these kinds of conversations always reminded her of looking at a map and trying to get one's bearings. Seeing that her aunt has finally found the place on the map, Kamila asked if the other two would like some tea and went to ring for it to be brought.

Amelia looked around the room admiringly. "What a lovely room. So sunny."

"Yes, it's south facing. It's just right in the autumn and spring and much warmer than the other side of the house. Mind you, during the summer it can be far too hot and we have to have all the windows and doors open. And sometimes even that is not enough."

After tea, Kamila asked if she could take her friend to see Karol.
"I'm sure that he would enjoy meeting such a lovely young lady, my dear." Elizabeth smiled at the two of them. Kamila saw her aunt's eyes rest on her friend. There was no doubt that Amelia was a great beauty, with those large blue eyes, straight nose, full lips, blonde, wavy hair and a trim figure. She was much taller and much better upholstered than Kamila.

When they were outside Karol's room, Kamila said, "I'll just see if he is awake."

She introduced her fiancé and her friend. They shook hands. He didn't kiss her hand. The doctor had advised against that, Karol explained to them both. Once again there was this "map-finding," but only brief. Kamila noticed how easily her friend fitted into the surroundings and thought, *under different circumstances, if Amelia had met Karol, who knows...* But she felt no pangs of jealousy or envy. She loved Karol and liked her friend and was glad that Karol could enjoy her company and feast his eyes on such beauty. She felt sure that this visit would be almost as good as the fresh air for him.

"Karol, I regret I have to take Amelia away. We haven't as yet had time for girl-talk." She kissed him and they left. They walked to Kamila's room.

"I'm glad that we are alone for a little while. I wanted to give you something different for your wedding. After all it's an unusual situation. I had this made for you." Amelia pulled out of her bag, a small black velvet bag.

Kamila took the bag carefully. It was about three inches in length. She undid the drawstring and pulled out what she thought to be a brooch. It was a rectangular piece of silver, smooth on the one side but when she turned it over she drew her breath in sharply. The silver was intricately beaten out, like folds of material around a black face with a scar on the right cheek, and lower down the silver gown, two black hands spread out, palms outward, like a pair of doves. "The Black Madonna!" she whispered in awe. "Oh! How beautiful."

"Hardly the usual wedding present! But you once told me you loved her more than any other portrayal. I've had her blessed at Czestochowa. I thought of having it blessed at the Luck Cathedral as the copy of this version is from there. Wasn't She supposed to have been painted by one of the apostles? St. Mark, wasn't it?"

"No. St. Luke. He painted the Black Madonna on three planks of the cypress wood that came from the table of the Holy Family of Nazareth," said Kamila.

"But how did it come to being in Poland? Do you know how?"

"Yes. It was Ladislaus of Opole, who brought it into Poland in the fourteenth century. He was the palatine for Ruthenia. It hung in the monastery of Jasna Gora, in Czestochowa and attracted pilgrims not only from all over this country but from around the world too. These pilgrims were kings and queens, noblemen, rich and poor, and they donated precious offerings and valuable gifts. In the mid fifteenth century when the Turks—." All this time Kamila was stroking the medallion.

"Ravaged the country, they chopped the Black Madonna into splinters—."

"That's right. The monastery was renowned for its riches and they came to rob."

"Who repaired it in the end? Wasn't it sent to England?"

Kamila looked at the icon in her hand and stroked the black hands. "Yes. There were three attempts to repair it but the glue didn't hold and the paint ran.

It was eventually, restored by West European artists. The wood was glued, a tightly woven canvas was glued on top, painted with thick layers of gesso and only then painted to the original likeness, except that the scar was added to her right cheek."

"I'm amazed that you remember all that—."

"My parents and my brothers have always loved history, so there were always discussions about some aspect of history." Kamila laughed. "You could say that we practically breathed it." She was quiet for a while. Eventually Amelia put out her hand and touched Kamila's hand. Kamila smiled. "So, you see Amelia this made her even more symbolic for Poland. From then on, the Black Madonna, whose origins were from the Byzantium were joined forever with the west, the Gothic. The Black Madonna was like Poland. It was neither east nor west."

"How do you know all this?"

"My Father told it to me when he first took me to Czestochowa. I must have been eleven or twelve. This original restored version showed the Virgin Mary holding the Infant Jesus on her left arm, with her head inclined to the right. There have been many versions of this but as you say, the one in the Luck Cathedral is like this one, without the Infant Jesus. Oh! Amelia! How can I thank you? She is *so* beautiful. I shall treasure this all my life."

"I wonder how they painted her to the original likeness," said Amelia.

"I wondered about that too, for she must have been badly damaged. Perhaps they made copies of the likeness first."

"You mean like a portrait?"

"Mm. I think so."

"Amelia, can I ask you a favour? I know that I wrote to you that no one is being invited to the wedding, but we need to have two witnesses and I was wondering if you could be one? If you're still staying with your cousin, that is."

"When is the wedding?"

"This coming Thursday. At eleven," said Kamila.

"Yes, of course I shall come. Who is the second witness?"

"I don't know. Auntie was arranging that."

After Amelia left she went to tell Elizabeth that Amelia would be a witness.

"That's good my dear, because Dr. Rogers is going to be the second."

"Oh! How wonderful that he is going to be present. I couldn't have wished for anyone else—except my parents. Is he coming to see Karol before the Thursday?"

"Yes, I thought that news would please you. And yes, he's coming to see him on Tuesday afternoon."

"Good. Maybe we'll go riding for a short time in the morning."

"I've never seen the servants work at such frenzied pace, Auntie."

"Neither have I, but then, we've never had a wedding in this house before—not during my time here."

"But we are only having a few people coming, aren't we? Have you heard the clatter coming from the kitchen? You'd imagine that at least five hundred are expected."

"Yes, my dear, but the two most important people in my life are getting married."

Despite that there would be only, perhaps three or four extra people to lunch after the wedding, the cook still wanted this to be a special day. There were cakes to be baked and various pickled and preserved foods to be taken out of the larder. The meats would be done on the day before.

Karol looked no fatter and still coughed. Kamila hadn't seen any blood, but knew from the maid that the water with the disinfectant was bloodstained. His demeanour showed great optimism, but Kamila remembered Dr. Roger's words. *Consumptive patients have this unbelievable enthusiasm and optimism.*

Whenever Karol said that he felt better, Kamila almost skipped with joy, forgetting the warning that Dr Roger had given.

"I feel as if I'm on a see-saw. One day I'm elated and another in despair about him."

"I know…."said Elizabeth.

"Will there ever be a time in my life when the seesaw will remain perfectly horizontal?"

When the doctor examined him on Tuesday, he was pleased with the progress the patient was making but to Kamila he said, "He's not out of the woods yet!"

Thursday arrived. Kamila was dressed by the maids in the white dress that her mother had bought her. She thought that she may have lost some weight but the dress still fitted her well. She added various amulets that signified good luck on these occasions and she pinned the velvet bag containing the Black Madonna on the inside of her bodice. Her aunt had given her, her own veil, which had been so carefully kept over the years, and she had given her an old leather prayer book with gold-leafed edges rather than a flower posy. Kamila surveyed herself in the mirror and then ran to her aunt's room.

"How do I look, Auntie?"

"Lovely. Yes, quite lovely, but that veil doesn't look right somehow. Let me think." She adjusted the veil this way and that and still this did not satisfy her. "Wait a minute! I think that it needs," she rummaged amongst her jewellery, "this!" She pulled out a large but thin gold band with an irregular cluster of fire opals. As she turned it in her hand these fire opals, whose dominant colours in the mainly milky base were reds and yellow, threw out flame-like reflections.

As she was placing this over the veil and Kamila's head, Kamila said, "I won't look like Emperor Nero with that band on my head, will I?"

"Don't be silly, child. It looks lovely. A bit reminiscent of the thirteenth century, but breathtakingly lovely."

"These stones—the opals, are they lucky for a wedding?"

"Well, in ancient India they were a symbol of love. Anyway I didn't think you were superstitious, Kamila! The only bad luck about them is in not having them! I must hurry and finish my dressing. Father Dominic is due any moment for your and Karol's confessions before the ceremony. You stay up here. Don't let Karol see you yet."

"Who's being superstitious now?"

Just before ten o'clock, Father Dominic arrived. A room upstairs had been prepared for the confession of Kamila. She was already waiting there when he came in. They greeted each other. He put his small suitcase on the chair and opened it. Out of it, he took out a carefully folded alb and donned it. Next a white stole was taken out, and having kissed the centre of it he put it around the back of his neck so that the richly embroidered ends hung down to almost the edge of the alb, following the rotund contour of his belly. Then he kissed the ends of the stole.

He looked around for a suitable place to sit, and Kamila pointed to the large oak chair with wide arms. His body filled the chair comfortably and he picked up the left end of the stole and draped it over his hand, holding it lightly between his fingers and thumb, his elbow resting on the arm of the chair. With the right hand he made the sign of the cross and kissed the end of the stole. This was a sign for Kamila to kneel by his left side.

He then went to Karol's room to hear his confession.

The Civil Registrar, to legalise the wedding, had arrived just seconds before Dr. Roger and Amelia. They were all directed to Karol's room. Then Kamila entered solemnly and stood beside Karol who was dressed and seated in a chair. He looked handsome despite that the suit was much too large for him. Kamila and Karol's hands met and held. The Registrar, the two witnesses and Elizabeth sat further back, behind Father Dominic. The room was blessed and the ceremony began.

Afterwards they all went down to the dining room for lunch, which was lovingly prepared by the cook and artistically arranged on the table. There was roast pork and beef and duck, roast potatoes, mushrooms that had been picked in the autumn and dried, in cream sauce. There were pickled cucumbers and pickled cabbage and beetroot. There were cakes with fruit, cakes with poppy seed, nationally so loved, and several sumptuous gateaux. Carafes of wines and vodka stood on the table and crystal glasses and goblets sparkled in the sunbeam thrown across the table from the windows.

Dr.Roger gave them a thick volume, beautifully leather bound, a comprehensive book on herbs, saying, “An unusual present for a wedding, but since you are interested in the subject Kamila, and as it is to benefit Karol…”

“Oh! Thank you so much.” She went to him to kiss him on the cheek. “It’s not the only unusual present I’ve had.” She turned her back to them all and unpinned the Black Madonna from within her bodice, her present from Amelia. It was passed reverently from hand to hand after careful examination.

“And from me, something usual.” Elizabeth produced a thin box. “It was given to me by my Mother on my wedding day. I always intended it to go to the girl who will be Karol’s bride. And I couldn’t have wished for a better one.”

Kamila opened the box. Inside was a delicate, almost lacy, emerald necklace.

“It’s so delicate, so beautiful. Look Karol! Have you seen anything so exquisite?”

“Yes, I have,” he said looking at her face and they all laughed.

“Oh! Auntie, there aren’t words enough to thank you.” She ran to her and hugged her and kissed her.

“I have something else for you—from your parents. But this you must open when you are alone, later. So, I’ve left it on your bed.” She didn’t add that undoubtedly Kamila would prefer the privacy to savour that tenuous contact, albeit so distant with her parents….

“And from me,” said Karol, “the whole of me.”

“That’s a wonderful gift.” She put her arms around his neck and gently touched his face with hers and kissed him. “And I can only give you me.”

Father Dominic gave them his blessing and the Registrar good wishes and both men left. Karol too, was exhausted and was taken to his room. Dr. Roger and Amelia stayed a little longer, but as it was evident that Elizabeth was in need of a rest, and they too left. Kamila and Amelia promised to keep close contact, as they said their goodbyes.

Amelia’s coach was practically out of sight, when Kamila’s arm eventually dropped from waving. She became aware of wood pigeons singing in the trees. It was such a homely, comfortable sound. And then geese flew above her, calling to each other, or were they saying something to her? Surely, this was a good omen? She had always thought that geese in flight signified hope.

In her room she found the small box on top of the envelope, all tied with a blue ribbon. With trembling hands she opened the envelope.

“My dearest, darling Child,

Just a short note because they are hurrying us up. We both wish you happiness in the whole of your life; that you may make the right decisions, that you have the wisdom and strength to deal with the stresses in life. Remember that you can run away from situations and people, but never from yourself. Be honest. Our thoughts will be with you. Don't weep for us. Life is only a short spell on this earth. God bless you, my love.

Your Mother and Father.

She put the letter to her lips and then held it tightly to her chest as if willing for the three of them to be together. She brushed the tears away as she took the box. She recognised it straight away. It was the one that her father had made for her mother when they were on their honeymoon, in the Tatras mountains, in the Austrian Empire, just by the origins of the river Danube. The box was shaped in the form of a travelling chest with a domed top, intricately carved all over, with their initials carved all around the perimeter of the lid. Inside the box was lined with blue satin.

The contents of the box, she also knew. There was her mother's engagement ring, her father's signet ring with the family crest, a ruby necklace that came down the line from her great grandmother and a packet wrapped in tissue paper, containing a pearl necklace, which was a present from her parents for the coming out ball, which she would not be attending. She slid the rings onto her fingers, but they were too big for her. The necklace from her great grandmother she held delicately in her outstretched palms and for the umpteenth time in her life, marvelled at its beauty.

She put them all, but the pearl necklace, back in the box and started to take off her gown. She folded it carefully amongst the tissues back into the box from whence it came. She would not wear it again. Instead, she dressed in a closefitting white bodice with navy trimmings and a navy skirt and put her new pearls on her neck. At that moment she felt that she'd never take them off. They had been chosen carefully by her mother and handled by each of her parents. *This is the closest that I can be to you both, my Mother and Father*.

She looked in on Karol but he was asleep, and looked more tired then she had seen him look for quite a while. Was all that ceremony too much for him? She went to the dining room where the presents had been left. She gathered them up and took them upstairs to Karol's room. She sat in the armchair and opened the book from Dr. Roger. It was *Culpeper's Complete Herbal*. She looked up the treatment of consumption.

The first plant on the list was borage. She read that it was excellent in dispersing melancholy, swoonings and "it helpeth the itch, ringworms and tetters." She started to laugh. At first it was a chuckle and then it spread like a ripple. This woke Karol.

"What's so funny?"

"This book—our wedding present." She told him what she had read. He gave the book a withering glance. Then he looked at the clock.

"The next on the list is cabbage."

"Well you can skip that. We all know what that causes, without needing to refer to a herbal." Karol said.

"I know," she said, her voice still full of laughter, "but listen to this: *with this it's inadvisable to eat bag-pipes or bellows*. He is happy that these are seldom eaten these days."

"He is happy! What about the poor fellow coughing his guts out?" They laughed over the properties of other plants.

"It seems that what you are having—the rosemary and the mint—are really the very best. Saffron is the last herb that he recommends. It has many great virtues but has to be used in tiny quantities. It has been known to lead to convulsive laughter, which endeth in death."

"Enough! Don't you dare give me any of that! I want to live. What with driving me to walk, to ride and planning such an end…"

She snapped the book shut. "You've reminded me—it's time for you to go for a walk!"

Again he looked at the clock as he stuck his thin legs out of the bed. "I'll wait a moment, for one of the lads," he said. He kept looking at the door.

"Shall I ring for help? Is it urgent?"

"No! No! It's not that!" he said. Just then there was a knock on the door and Benjamin entered with a large box.

"I believe this is what you were waiting for, sir." He put the box on the floor carefully and smiled at Karol.

"Yes, thank you, Benjamin." He turned to Kamila, "It's for you. Go on, open it!"

Kamila ran to the box and sat beside it. When she opened it, she let out squeals of delight as she took out a dark brown puppy. "He is so lovely." She kissed and cuddled him and he licked her all over her face and tried his sharp teeth on her nose. "He looks just like my Wolf. Auntie said that he had gone back to the wild. Oh, look how wobbly he is! He's got all his legs mixed up."

"That's why I chose him. Because he's parentage is similar to your Wolf's. His father was a wolf and mother, an Alsatian."

"Where did you get him? You haven't been out anywhere without me. Who brought him here today? He wasn't bred here. I'm sure I'd have known."

"No. He wasn't bred here. One Sunday when you and Mother were at Mass—."

"Oh! I remember. Someone called Mr. Orzel! And you wouldn't tell me what he was doing here."

"That's right."

Kamila came and sat on the bed beside Karol, and they both stroked the delighted little puppy. She learned that the little chap was eight weeks old and his name was Thor but she could change it if she wanted to.

"Did you choose that name?"

"Yes, I suggested it. I wanted him to be powerful, like the God of thunder, and look after you."

"Mm! I like it. Then, I shall call you that too, my darling little Thor." She kissed him again. Then she kissed Karol and thanked him. "I did miss my Wolf *so very* much, but at least he had the sense to run away to his relatives. Otherwise they might have shot him."

"Oh, yes, I'm sure they would have."

CHAPTER 6

Kamila took little Thor to task in house training and he proved to be very intelligent. She recognised his movements when he wanted to go out and wagged his tail ecstatically when he saw that she understood. He seemed to grow in front of her eyes, or at least, his legs did. He followed her everywhere but when Elizabeth was in the room he'd curl himself around her legs, occasionally chewing her petticoats, and when Kamila was with Karol, he slid to be next to his body as closely as he could. At first she hadn't understood this behaviour. She just thought that he was a very affectionate little dog. At night he slept in Kamila's room in a basket with a blanket and a pillow.

Karol went riding with Kamila most days, but never for long. She searched anxiously for dramatic signs of improvement, but saw none. She thought that it was because she was too close in seeing any. When Dr. Roger came, and he came twice per week, he shook his head at her questions.

"It's a vicious disease. As to the improvement, don't expect too much or too quickly."

About five weeks after their wedding, when Karol was saying good night to them both, when he kissed his mother, Kamila thought she heard him say gently, "Thank you." And to her, "Can you stay with me a little longer, my love?"

"Of course, I will. All night if you wish." She pulled a chair near to his bed. "Would you like me to read to you?"

"No, I don't think so at present." Thor jumped on the bed and standing on the pillows, started to lick Karol's face. "All right, Thor, that's enough Boy. Come on! I know you want to get into your favourite place." Karol lifted the eiderdown and Thor snuggled up to his side.

"Karol, do you want to talk?"

"I don't mind. Whatever you like. I just love having you around. I wish, I wish—oh, what's the point of wishing for the unattainable," he said with frustration and some apathy.

She waited for him to explain further but he didn't expand. "*I wish* that you hadn't taken part in the uprisings, then you wouldn't have been sent to Siberia and you would have been fit and well." She quickly put her hand to her mouth, "I'm sorry." Long ago she had made a decision that she wouldn't broach the subject for fear of arousing painful memories. Furthermore she didn't like reproaches. So they had never discussed the subject.

"No! Don't be. I have no regrets. I wouldn't have been able to live with myself if I didn't fight for Poland to be free. Free from oppression. Free to stand by herself, on her own legs. If you were in my shoes, I have no doubt that you would have done exactly the same. Wouldn't you?" He looked at her, but she didn't respond. "As to the consequences, we all knew what we were doing and what would happen to us, if we were caught."

"Yes, but all that suffering!"

"It could have been worse! They could have shot me, or hung me, like they did Adam."

"But you could have turned your head away, and just continued to run your estate! And not take part?"

"No! I couldn't. Can't you understand this overpowering love for our country? You should. For it is in your blood too. Not only that, it's our country's legacy. And believe me, however good God has been to me in that I'm still alive, have you, and Mother, and little Thor beside me," he squeezed the warm body under the bedclothes, "it's still worth while dying for one's country."

"Don't say that word! Spit it out!"

"But you forbade me to spit, do you remember?" He laughed. "Is this some sort of magic?"

"Oh, do be serious, Karol. I don't like that word. It's accompanied our family far too long."

"I'm afraid it's a fact of life and touches everything that lives." She saw that he was getting tired, so she didn't pursue the subject. He closed his eyes. Kamila leaned back in her chair. How and why did she start that subject? After a while she too closed her eyes and fell asleep. When her hand was squeezed, her eyes shot open and she found Karol looking at her tenderly. "Go to bed, my love. I shouldn't have asked you to stay so late."

She kissed him gently and adjusted his pillows, "Sleep well, my love. And be well!" As she walked to the door, Thor jumped out of the bed and followed her.

The house was in darkness apart from a light in the corridor and the stairs. She took Thor down the stairs and outside. He crouched on the grass to make his puddle and then sniffed it with satisfaction. Back in their room, she undressed and put her nightgown on and fell into heavy sleep as soon as her head touched the pillow.

Suddenly she was aware of Thor barking at her face. "Go away Thor. Go to sleep. You've just been out!" But he continued to bark and kept running to the door and then back again to her. She sat up. He definitely wanted to go out. She slid her feet into the slippers and threw a warm shawl over her shoulders. She glanced at the sky through the window and estimated the time to be around five. It was still dark but the birds were already singing their dawn chorus.

When she opened the door she was surprised that Thor didn't run down the stairs, but straight along the corridor to Karol's room. He threw his body against the door but it wouldn't open. Kamila started to run. Fortunately a light was always left in the room at night. Karol was lying on his back, almost as she had left him.

"Karol? Karol, are you alright?"

He didn't answer.

She looked closely. Yes, he was breathing. But this breathing was somehow different. After each breath, there was a long pause, which made her afraid that that was the last. Then another breath came.

"Karol." She touched his hand. It was cooler than hers. He didn't open his eyes. She began to sob. She took his limp body in her arms and listened to the peculiar breathing. "Oh, Karol, don't go! Oh God, don't let him die! Oh, Karol, come back to me!" Even so—it seemed like an eternity to her—she heard him draw the last breath and then there was no more. She continued to hold him with his arms hanging loosely over her shoulders, and quietly wept.

Arms encircled her. Warm arms. Soft feminine arms. "Let him go, my dear. You cannot bring him back." It was Elizabeth. Her eyes were red and her voice laden with sorrow and tears.

"I'll hold him until the doctor comes, Auntie," said the tearful Kamila.

"The doctor can't help him, now. He and Father Dominic will come later. I've sent Jordan to tell them. Daisy, will you lay out my son?"

"Yes, madam. Of course, I will. Come on, Miss. You go with madam and Mary will make you both some tea. Go on, Miss." She peeled Kamila's hands off Karol's back. Her comforting voice and matter of fact attitude calmed Kamila. She let go of Karol, kissed him gently goodbye and went to her aunt.

"Goodbye, my son. May God look after you." Elizabeth cupped his thin face in her hands and kissed him tenderly.

There was no going back to sleep. They sat on the sofa, side by side, with Elizabeth holding her in her arms and stroking her head. "Don't cry my love. We all knew that this was to come. At least be grateful that we have had him for this short while."

"That last evening, we almost quarrelled—about patriotism, I suppose—and I started the subject. How could I have been so thoughtless?"

"No! No! You are quite wrong. He spoke to me about it. That he wanted you to understand. He wanted you to know that there is a purpose in everything."

"Purpose! How can there be a purpose in his dying?"

"Kamila, my love, we all have a purpose on this earth. Some people know what this purpose is—like Karol, your Father and Raphael. Some people never learn why they are here, and just muddle through life, but whether they know it or not, they fulfil this purpose."

"I don't know what my purpose is."

"Perhaps to bring happiness—like you did to Karol and me?"

There was a knock on the door and Mary entered with a tray of tea.

"Thor would like to come in. He's been out on the grass. Shall I let him in, madam?" said Mary.

"Oh yes, Mary, and thank you." Thor run to Elizabeth and licked her hands. "What a good boy you are! Clever boy!" She patted him and then turned to Kamila, "He came banging and barking at my door, you know. That's how he awoke everyone."

"I didn't know. He stood over me and barked into my face and immediately run to Karol's room and threw himself at the door. Otherwise I'd never have known." Her eyes filled with hot tears. "At least I was able to hold him to the end."

"Yes, I know. I was there too."

Dr Roger came to certify the death and Father Dominic to bless Karol and to make the funeral arrangements. Dr. Roger talked to Elizabeth and Kamila at length, once again explaining the hopelessness of the disease and tried to instil peace and acceptance into their minds.

When they had all gone, Kamila went back to Karol and sat in the chair holding his cold hand.

"Oh, Karol, what is to become of us, without you? I do understand that you are in a better place now but *I* can't see it as better. I wish I could. I really thought you were getting better. Oh, Karol, Karol, how can we live without you?"

"There you are, Kamila!" said Elizabeth. "I was looking for you. The undertakers have come, so come away now." She waved a hand to the two men standing just behind her.

"I want to stay to the end."

"I'm sorry Miss. We would rather you were not in the room." He looked imploringly at Elizabeth. "It'll be even more distressing when we put him in the coffin," he said softly.

"No, Kamila. We must leave them to do their job. We will only be in the way. Besides, there is something I must discuss with you. Come, my dear." She held her hand out.

She took Kamila to the study and took out some folders from the shelves. "Since my husband died, Karol took over the running of the estate. Then when he was taken away, I had to hire someone to do that job. His name is Greczko. You haven't met him yet, have you?" Kamila shook her head. "With hired help you always have to keep an eye on them. This is what I want *you* to do. I want *you* to do that job."

"But I don't know anything about running an estate!"

"I know that. But fortunately both my husband and Karol kept a detailed diary of what they did for the estate and the business side of it."

"And I'll have to keep the accounts too?" Kamila was beginning to look apprehensive. "I don't know how to do that."

"Only to some extent. There is an accountant to deal with the final stages, but we have to prepare everything for him. I want you to study these methods and what they did to familiarise yourself with running of the estate."

"Surely it's a man's job, Auntie?"

"Yes, it usually is. But we haven't got a man in the family now. As all of this will be yours, you must learn to do it. You have the intelligence and stamina. I'll help you as much as I can."

"When do you want me to start?"

"How about now?"

They waited until the undertakers took Karol's body away.

They poured over the neatly written diaries and the accounts, discussed what timetable should be made out. Kamila would have to visit the estate cottages where the farm workers lived, check the sowing of grains and the state of livestock. After harvest there would be the selling of the grains at the grain markets. They didn't know how they would manage the latter. These grain markets were male dominated and no woman had ever been allowed into them. But autumn was a long way away.

In the morning, Kamila came down dressed in her riding habit.

"Auntie, I'm sorry that I'm not in black, but I haven't anything suitable to wear—."

"I don't want either of us in black. The colour will only remind us each second of the day of all the recent tragedies we've had. Wear your normal clothes, as indeed I shall. It won't mean that we cared or loved less. I consider this wearing of black is akin to beating one's chest and wailing loudly for every one to see and hear. In my opinion, mourning should be done in private."

Kamila looked at her, "Yes, I think I agree with you Auntie."

The day after, Greczko, the overseer requested to see Elizabeth. He was a sour, thickset man with eyes like coals and black hair that sprouted an inch from his eyebrows. Elizabeth saw him in the study.

"I'm glad you've come Greczko. I had wanted to see you too. What did you want to see me about?"

"I've heard that a girl is taking over my job," he said sullenly.

"I'd be grateful if you could remove your cap whilst in the house." She waited for him to do so. "No one is taking your job. Now that my son has gone, my daughter-in-law is going to run the estate. You will continue your work as before."

"I thought I was running the estate to your satisfaction," he said through clenched teeth.

"Firstly, *you* were not running the estate. *I* was. Your job was to oversee and report to me any problems. As to my satisfaction—I have some doubts about that. I've been over the accounts for the two years that you've worked here and I notice that there has been a downhill trend with almost everything."

"Are you suggesting—?"

"I'm not suggesting anything. You will continue to work under the supervision of my daughter-in-law." Elizabeth looked at him with a coldness that should have sent shivers down his spine.

"I'll not be bossed by a slip of a girl. And that's final."

"Oh? What would you suggest then?"

"I continue to be the boss. And the girl can go back to her needlework."

"How dare you!" She had always disliked him and now she felt like hitting him. There was something cruel about him but she had needed someone and closed her mind to that observation. Elizabeth hesitated a moment and then said coldly, "You'll either accept my conditions or else go."

"I'll not accept your conditions. I'll go, but you'll regret this." Elizabeth noticed the clenched fist., and with the other hand he pointed a thick finger at her and repeated, "You'll regret this."

"Then, please leave me the keys I gave you." He took them out of his pocket, all on a wire loop, and almost threw them on the table. "And you'll vacate your cottage—and leave it in a good condition," she looked sternly at him, showing no signs of fear at his intimidation, "at the end of the week."

"I'll not forget this. You wait and see." he said as he was leaving.

"If there's any trouble from you I'll have the law on you. As it is, I could have you thrown into jail for the obvious discrepancies showing in the accounts. So, bare that in mind!"

When he had gone Elizabeth sat down trembling, but all the same, breathed a sigh of relief. She looked at the clock. It'll be many hours before Kamila was back.

By the time Kamila returned, Elizabeth was in the drawing room having her afternoon tea. Kamila, engulfed by the fresh air from outside, was flushed and smiling as she flopped into the armchair.

"I think that I'll be able to go on my own now. No need for Jordan to accompany me anymore! I didn't lose my way this time. Not once!" she said triumphantly.

"I'm glad to hear it. You sound as if you like the work," said Elizabeth.

"I do. I'm getting used to it. And it's interesting."

"That's good because, from now on you'll have to do more. I've dismissed Greczko."

After a stunned silence, "Why, Auntie? I didn't think you'd ever dismiss him. Surely we need him. And I'm not sufficiently experienced yet. I don't know if I'll ever be."

"Of course you will—in time. To tell you the truth, I've disliked that man from the beginning. The jet black eyes and that narrow forehead made him look cruel, menacing." She poured Kamila a cup of tea. " He wanted to see me about you!"

"Me? But we've not even met!"

"Yes, I know, but he had heard that you were out doing Karol's work and he thought his job was under threat. But when I explained, he said he'd not work under you—as a young girl!"

"I can't help that!"

"I didn't tell you earlier, but there have been substantial losses in the accounts, since he's been here. So I told him to go. He's a dangerous man so please don't go anywhere without Jordan. He must *be with you on all occasions and everywhere you go*. I can't impress this strongly enough, Kamila. I'll tell him that, so that you don't take any risks."

"He does sound dangerous. So I will be careful. With that surname he must be Ukrainian."

"Yes, he is. But we have quite a few Ukranians working for us. I can't quite remember how I came to employ him. It was such a distressing time when Karol was taken to Siberia. I remember everything then as if through haze ."

"Have you anyone else in mind for his position, Auntie?"

"No. I can't think of anyone fit for the job."

"Mm. I wonder.......would you consider one of the workers who lives in one of the cottages?"

"Yes, of course. But they would have to read and write to make notes. And they would need to be completely trustworthy. Whom were you thinking of?"

"I'm not sure of the name. I know which cottage it is. I'll find out more about him tomorrow. I'd better go and change. I feel as if I'm living in this habit. I suppose I couldn't wear the riding breeches for this work? After all it *is* a man's work?" She looked appealingly at Elizabeth.

"Certainly not!"

"Queen Christina of Sweden wore trousers, Karol said." She smiled at her aunt cheekily.

"She was a queen. You're not. You are a lady and must behave and dress like one." Elizabeth pierced her niece with her strict intelligent eyes. "Besides she wasn't the only female Swede who wore trousers. There was Princess Aldwilda of Gotland in Sweden who was a pirate and wore trousers. She probably carried a knife in between her teeth too." This time she had a twinkle in her eyes.

"I don't believe you, Auntie. You've just made this up! When did this Eldwilda live anyway? And how would you know that?"

"Because, my Father told me about her. I was probably your age or slightly younger and because I, too, wanted to wear trousers. And she lived around 500A.D. In fact my Father called her the Barbaric Buccaneer of the

Baltic. She was a terror and with her all-female crew she left a trail of destruction along the Baltic coast."

"Don't worry, Auntie, I have no desire to become a pirate. I'll behave like a lady. You've put me off wearing them now anyway." With a laugh Kamila went upstairs to change her clothes.

On the following day Kamila and Jordan set out earlier than usual. They made their way to the cottage she mentioned to her aunt. The skies were clear. The earth smelt sweet and the trees were bursting with blossoms. The horses trotted side by side contentedly. Kamila tried to explain to her companion which cottage it was that she wanted to visit.

"It's the well-looked after place. He's a tall man and there are lots of children about." She knew that this was an inadequate explanation, since nearly all of them had lots of children. "The house is on a slight hill. We'll come to it in a moment. There! That's the one!"

"That's Lisinski's place, Miss Kamila. Janek Lisinski."

By the time they were at the cottage, Janek Lisinski was outside waiting to take the reins. He greeted Kamila politely.

"You're Lisinski, aren't you?" said Kamila.

"Yes, ma'am."

"Can I come in?"

"Yes, ma'am." He stood aside for her to go through. The cottage was typical of the village dwellings, being single storey, made of wood with a thatched roof.

All the cottages on the estate too, were built in a similar fashion, varying only in size. This one was the larger type with three small bedrooms and one living room. The ceilings were low compared to the tall rooms that she was used to. As she entered the living room she noticed how clean the whole place was. Considering that they couldn't have known that she was coming to see them, Kamila was impressed that the table was covered with a white, spotless tablecloth.

A woman hovered near the doorway, which Kamila presumed led to the kitchen.

"Hello," she said to the woman, and turned to Lisinski, "This is your wife?"

"Yes, ma'am. This is Anna." The woman came forward and curtsied.

"Would you like to sit down, Miss?" She pulled out a chair by the table.

Kamila sat down and indicated that they should sit down too. Two other chairs scraped the floor. "How long have you worked here Lisinski?"

"Why! All my life! And my father before that and his father before him."

He was beginning to look frightened.

"And how long have you been married?"

"Nearly fourteen years, isn't it Anna?" His wife nodded.

"When I was here a few days ago, I think I counted six children. Is that right?"

"No, ma'am. We have eight," he said. Kamila saw his neck pulses throbbing.

"Is there something wrong, Miss?" asked Anna.

"No! No! I just want to know something about you both."

"What is your job? What *exactly* do you do?"

"Well, all sorts of things. I sometimes till the fields, or seed them. I've taken part in harvesting. I've repaired barns and tended the animals. Whatever Mr. Greczko orders me to do, I do. He hasn't complained about me, has he?"

"If he did, he'd have no cause to. My Janek is a hardworking and an honest man, unlike some I could name," said Anna. She looked directly at Kamila.

"Anna! Shh! You've no right to speak to Miss Kamila like that."

"What do you mean by that, Anna?" But Anna pursed her lips and refused to enlarge.

Kamila smiled at her, and turned to Lisinski, "Can you read and write?"

"Yes, ma'am. My father taught me. Mister Karol's father taught him, he always said."

Kamila took out from her bag a piece of paper and wrote *Do you know the month and the year it is now?* "Can you read this for me and write the answer?" He read it out perfectly and wrote *It is May 1850*. "Very good, Lisinski!"

Lisinski looked pleased with himself and his wife glowed with pride.

"Why I've come to see you is this. Mr Greczko is no longer working for us. My aunt has dismissed him. I've come to you because I think you may be suitable to take over his job. Obviously the pay will be increased accordingly. How do you feel about that?" Kamila looked from one flushed face to another and the relief therein.

"But I don't know anything about—."

"I do know that. But if you are honest and faithful we will get on well together. You must know that I too haven't had any experience, but I'm learning. Well?"

"I'm honoured you've chosen me, but—."

"He'll do the job, Miss. I guarantee that he will be honest and faithful. He's never anything else." Anna looked proudly at him.

"Right! Let's have a trial period of, shall we say, three months? If you don't like the job you can let me know. And if you don't like that work, you won't be turned out of the cottage. You can just go back to your present job. By the way, you have the option of moving into Greczko's cottage, if you want."

"No, Miss. We wouldn't want to move. Janek's father and grandfather lived here and Janek has done a lot of work here on the place. Would you like to see what's he done in the bedrooms?" said Anna.

"I'd love to." The two women left the table. Again Kamila was impressed at the cleanliness. Anna took her to the children's rooms. An amazing sight greeted her. In each of the bedrooms there were two large beds, but because there wouldn't have been enough room on the floor of the bedroom, one bed was suspended above the other, with a ladder leading to the top one.

"How very clever!" said Kamila. "And there is enough room even for an adult to sit up in each! I think I've made a right choice, don't you think, Anna?"

"Yes, I do, Miss."

Back in the living room she said, "You're very talented, Janek! Have you seen this somewhere else—putting the beds like that?"

"No, ma'am. I was thinking that the children will need more room when they become teenagers and it seemed the obvious thing to do."

Kamila nodded. "Now, about this job. Can you come to the house in the late afternoon, so that my aunt can meet you and she can discuss the job with you? I'd like to be there too because we'll be working together. I'll be home about four." She stretched her hand and shook hands with him and Anna, who also curtsied.

Outside, Jordan was sitting on a log, at the front of the cottage, sucking a straw. As he saw Kamila, he stood up. Seeing that she was going to the horses, he cupped his hand for her foot, so that it was easier for her to jump onto Bessie, although she was getting used to mounting her even without help.

They waved their goodbyes to the Lisinskis and proceeded down the hill towards the road. The more she analysed her opinion of Lisinski, the more she was sure that he was an excellent choice. She just hoped that he would live up to her expectations. She was impatient for her aunt's opinion.

When she told Elizabeth of her choice, her aunt put her hand to her mouth pensively and looked into the distance.

"Lisinski….of course! I do remember the family! They've been on the estate for four generations. I don't remember your uncle teaching any of them to read or write. It must have been before I had married or even met my husband. He sounds a good choice. I look forward to meeting him."

Lisinski came on time and was introduced to Elizabeth. After she shook hands with him, his hands went back to turning his cap nervously.

"I do remember your family now. When my husband was about five he fell into a large pond that used to be on the east side of the house and it was your grandfather who pulled him out. I remember hearing this story when I first met my husband."

"I don't remember the pond, ma'am."

"No. It caused such a panic that it was filled in within a week. Now, my daughter-in-law tells me that you're willing to take on Greczko's job."

"I did say that I have no experience—."

"Yes I know you haven't. But you will soon learn. There's just one thing that perhaps I ought to warn you about. And it's this. Greczko may try and cause some trouble for you both," she looked from Lisinski to Kamila and again Lisinski, "so do be on your guard."

" Don't worry ma'am. I'll look after Miss Kamila. I'm not scared of him or his whip. He won't bully any of us again." The two women exchanged glances.

CHAPTER 7

Lisinski knew all the workmen and women and Kamila saw that he was well liked. Despite professing that he knew nothing about running the estate, she saw that whatever problem occurred, he knew what was required to rectify it.

They didn't see Greczko but had heard that he was working at a nearby farm as a labourer. They both felt that, perhaps, whatever danger Elizabeth had anticipated from that man had passed.

Despite that she was now busy and preoccupied with running the estate, each morning she eagerly awaited the delivery of letters and became despondent that there were no replies to the numerous letters she had written. Whenever, rarely, one came, she tore it open, only to have her hopes trampled upon, yet again by the boots of bureaucracy. *We regret, we do not know the whereabouts of your parents. We are not permitted to ...*

Elizabeth came down the stairs. "Disappointment again?" She said.

"Yes."

"Have you written to St. Petersburg?"

Kamila looked up. "You knew…?"

"Yes. At first I thought you were expecting letters from your parents. Then I saw the postmarks…"

"I'm sorry—I didn't tell you—it's not that I wanted to keep it a secret—."

"It's alright, Kamila."

"I've written to *so* many. It's as if Mother and Father have dropped into an abyss. I've followed up every helpful suggestion, and yes, I have written to St. Petersburg."

"No answer?"

"No." Elizabeth nodded and put her hand onto Kamila's arm.

"Let's go to breakfast."

Although all the sitting room windows were open, the heat was still so oppressive, that Elizabeth's breathing was more laboured than before. She frequently wiped her face and neck and Kamila fanned her. A tray was brought in with fruit juice made from berries grown in the gardens.

"I wish we could have some rain," said Kamila. "I would help the soft fruits to swell as well as cooling us. I don't recall a July being this hot, do you?"

"No. Let's see if they predict any in the next few days. Not that these predictions are any good. I almost feel that the farmers are better at forecasting the weather than these so called experts." She picked up the newspaper and started to read it with interest. "Doesn't your friend Amelia live in Krakow?"

"Yes, why? Has something happened there?"

"Yes. *There have been extensive fires at the weekend, destroying three hundred houses, the Dominican and Franciscan convents, the churches of St. Barbara and St. Joseph, the Episcopal Palace, the polytechnic school and several other public buildings*. Dear me! Seven streets have been burned down. They don't mention which ones. It seems that it was the work of a band of incendiaries that started the fires in different quarters of the city at the same time."

"Did they catch them?"

"Some of them were caught in the act. Citizens of Krakow demanded martial law to be proclaimed so that any caught in the act, could be shot on sight."

"And did they get it?"

"No. It was refused, but they formed a court martial and the culprits were brought before it immediately."

"It sounds as if this was in the actual city, and Amelia lives on the outskirts. But what a terrible thing to do, especially to such a beautiful city!"

"At least it doesn't appear that they have damaged the more important buildings. And now they've called out the troops to patrol the streets."

"Was there any political motivation for this?"

"It doesn't say."

"Perhaps I ought to write to Amelia then."

"I think you should."

The three months of trial had passed smoothly and Lisinski was now employed permanently to the great satisfaction and relief of Elizabeth and Kamila, and overwhelming joy and pride of Anna and Janek Lisinski.

Lisinski was taking Kamila to see a newborn calf, which wasn't very well and not suckling, when someone brought them an urgent message that one of the barns, in the opposite direction was on fire.

"You go on to the fire and see what you can do, Janek. I'll have to go to this calf," said Kamila.

"But, Miss Kamila, your aunt said you were not to go anywhere without me."

"Don't waste time. You go to the fire. I'll be alright. Go on." She nudged his horse.

The barn where the newborn calf had been born was not too far away, but to reach it, the road went through a coppice, as on both sides there was bog land. Kamila looked at the full canopies of the trees and took delight in the fragrance of the coppice, the leaves and bark and the wild flowers and mushrooms. The ground was uneven with lots of rabbit holes and their progress had to be slower. It was only when Bessie snorted with apprehension that Kamila brought her attention back to earth.

Ahead, on the path stood a stocky man, with black hair and eyes, legs astride, and the whip in his right hand, smacking his leg.

Although she had never met him, she knew immediately who it was. Greczko. She froze. She could have turned and galloped off but that was not in her nature. She gripped her whip in readiness and clenched her teeth.

"Let the horse pass, please," she said coldly.

"I don't know that I will. You don't know me. But you will. Oh, you will!

Through you I lost my job." By then he had grabbed the reins.

"Let go of the reins!" She raised her whip but he caught hold of her and dragged her off her horse. She fought with a ferocity she did not know she possessed. He tore open her jacket and blouse and was about to hit her with his fist to stop her screaming when four women started to run towards them shouting, having dropped their baskets, full of mushrooms that they had been collecting.

"You're lucky this time. You won't be next time," he snarled, his face so near hers that she smelled the rancid smell of rotting teeth, and then he disappeared into the wood.

They picked her up off the ground, "Are you alright, Miss? He didn't harm you?"

Kamila couldn't answer, she was trembling so much, but shook her head. They pulled her blouse together to cover the scratched chest wall and the jacket and looked her over.

"If we had a pin or two we could pin the jacket and you wouldn't look too bad. It's only the buttons that have been torn off. Has any one got any pins?" The woman who was pinning the jacket together, said, "Where are you going, Miss? You really shouldn't ride alone, a lady like you."

"Yes, I know." Kamila said at last "I was with someone…. I haven't far to go."

"We'll come with you—."

"I'll be alright now, thank very much. I only have to go to the farm, just past the coppice."

"Then we'll walk with you to the end of the coppice, won't we, girls? Miss, mind you wait for us for a moment."

They helped Kamila onto Bessie and the went back to collect their baskets.

At the end of the coppice, "Goodbye, Miss. You'll be alright now?"

"Yes. Thank you so much. Thank you for all your help."

She had decided not to tell her aunt what had happened. But she would tell Janek

Lisinski. And she made a mental note to be on her guard from now on. She shuddered at what he had intended to do to her.

She found the calf lying on its side, motionless, in the straw. It was thin and smaller than normal.

"Tell me about this. Was the birth easy?"

"Yes, miss. But this here cow is an old one and it came 2 weeks early."

"Has the little one suckled at all?"

"No, miss. It ain't."

"Can you get me some milk from the mother, please?"

"Oi've just done that, and tried to feed the little `un."

"Did he take any?"

"No, miss." The man shook his head. He brought the bucket with the milk to Kamila. By now Kamila was sitting in the straw by the calf. She tried to feed, the still warm, milk through her thin fingers but there was no response. She rubbed the calf, but although breathing, there was no other response. She looked around the barn but saw nothing that would help. And then her eyes fell on her whip and the leather gloves lying on top of it. She wasn't sure if the idea would work, because the gloves were fairly new. She filled the glove with milk and put the fingers of the glove into the calf's mouth, squeezing the glove. At first there was no reaction and then she saw that the calf gulped.

"He swallowed!" she said, and started to rub his tummy. Again she squeezed the glove. Gradually the whole of the glove was emptied. And another. They tried to get him to stand up but he was still weak. She continued to feed him until he refused. They became aware of the sound of hoofs and commotion outside.

"Miss Kamila! I was so worried. It's quite late," said Lisinski, looking down at her amidst the straw, and then briefly at the herdsman, "Hello, Tom."

"Oh, Lisinski, I'm glad you've come. I suppose there's no way we can take this little one and the mother to one of the barns nearer the house?"

"Not tonight, Miss Kamila. Tom, do you think he'll survive until morning?"

"Oi didn't think so before, but now, yes. Oi can feed him in the night Miss, and even sleep in the barn."

"Do you know, Tom, that's exactly what I was thinking of doing myself." She laughed with relief at the expressions of horror on the two men's faces. "That would be fine then. Feed the little one about twice in the night, and make sure the milk is fresh and warm. I'll come early in the morning and bring with me some honey and herbs. Don't forget to rub his tummy. I think it will help with his digestion."

"Oi'll do that, miss."

"What about the Mum? She won't trample on the little one?"

"Oh, no, miss. She's always been a good mother. She'll lie down and oi'll make sure the calf is by her belly. Don't you worry, miss."

"Alright then, Tom. You stay with them overnight and I'll come about two hours after sunrise." She gently placed the calf on the straw, brushed her skirt. "You might as well keep the other glove. It may become useful too." With that, she and Lisinski left. She was surprised how late it was.

As they were returning through the coppice Kamila told Lisinski of her encounter there, just a few hours previously.

"It would have been better to take the road around the bogs. It's only slightly longer but there is nowhere for anyone to hide. Even if someone were lying on the ground, you'd see him from afar. But what am I saying? I won't let you go alone anywhere, ever, again," said Lisinski.

"No, that's not practical. It means that I'd be like a heavy weight that you have to drag around. Each one of us has something to do. Take yesterday—by the way, how was the fire? I forget to ask."

"By the time I arrived, the men had most of it under control. It was soon put out. And fortunately we had moved the dry bales of straw to another barn as this one's roof was leaking."

"In view of what happened to me, could it have been started deliberately?"

"You mean by Greczko? I don't think so. It started in the bales that had become wet and with the scorching days we've had in the recent weeks it's possible it started on its own. Haystacks in the fields can start to burn, as the temperature inside the haystack increases."

"I didn't know that. How interesting! Will it be possible to repair the barn or is the damage too far gone?" said Kamila.

"No, I think it will be possible to repair. I'll see to it tomorrow."

"By the way, please don't tell anyone about what happened to me today. I don't want my aunt to be worried."

"I won't tell."

On arrival home, Kamila went straight upstairs to wash and change her clothes and asked Mary to burn all the clothes she had worn that day.

"Miss Kamila, what happened? These are torn-."

"Nothing happened." It was quite obvious from the way Mary continued to look at her that she didn't believe her.

"Was it Lisinski?" she said quietly.

"Lisinski? Mary how could you even entertain such a thought? I would trust my life with him."

"Then?"

"Nothing happened."

"I really aught to show these tears to the mistress-." said Mary as if she was thinking aloud.

"That's blackmail! I didn't think you were capable of that. If I tell you, will you promise not to tell my aunt?" Mary nodded. "….so, you see, it's only my clothes that have been damaged."

"They are too good to burn. When they are washed and repaired they'll be as good as new."

"I never want to see them again. Surely you can understand why I want them burned? Only Lisinski and you know of this. Please don't let any one else know."

"I won't. You are right. It is best to burn them."

She yawned and stretched her arms. Goodness, how tired she was! She would gladly have gone to bed, but felt she should see her aunt. She hadn't seen her all day. When she saw her, she was glad, because Elizabeth didn't look too good. Kamila encircled her aunt in her arms and kissed her gently, as she was sitting in the armchair.

"Aren't you feeling too good, Auntie?"

"Don't worry, child. It'll pass. How was your day?"

"....so I'll have to go early in the morning to the calf. And Lisinski will start the repair of the barn tomorrow. I think I ought to go to bed early tonight."

"Yes. Certainly if you plan to be there at sunrise!" Elizabeth smiled. "I'll retire early today too, although I haven't been as busy as you. Oh! I nearly forgot! There's a letter for you." She moved a few books and handed the letter to Kamila.

"It's from Amelia." She opened the pages and read. At first she was overjoyed. She was being invited to go to Amelia's for a month. Kamila loved the ancient city of Krakow, where Amelia's family lived. She had been in Krakow before and fell in love with it at first sight. She looked up at her Aunt, her tiredness disappearing like magic. "She wants me to come over for a while."
"Then you must." The excitement in Kamila's face was not lost to her aunt.

"No. I can't at the moment. There's too much to do. And besides I've got to go to the calf. I would like the little chap to live. Besides, I wouldn't be able to go to any parties they are bound to invite me to. After all, I'm still in mourning. No, I shall write and apologise." Kamila folded the letter and put it on the table. As there was a little time till dinner was served, Kamila went to look up her mother's notes and prepare the herbs to take to the calf.

As she was searching through the notes, Amelia's words kept coming foremost in her head, so she couldn't concentrate on the notes. *Stop it. Stop this nonsense at once. I can't go and that's that.*

She made notes of what she required to bring with her and was delighted when she read her mother's writing *...to feed a young, poorly animal use a glove filled with milk or warm water, preferably sweetened with honey.*

When she had time to think of herself, and remembered Amelia's invitation, she suppressed her regret. Her feelings were strengthened whenever she looked at Elizabeth. Dr. Roger came quite frequently and at the last occasion took Kamila's hand and said,

"Kamila, I'm glad you are such a sensible girl. I'm talking about that invitation. Oh, yes, I do know about it. Your aunt told me."

"Well, at the time it was impossible for me to go away. Also, Auntie is looking so fragile. I'm so worried about her." Kamila looked appealingly at the doctor, willing him to tell her that Elizabeth would get better. But he shook his head.

"You must be prepared, my dear. She *is* fragile. I've seen deterioration in her since Karol died. Partly, I think she no longer wants to live."

"Oh, no! Please do something. Please say something to her. Tell her how much I love her and need her. She must try and live. I couldn't bear it. I really couldn't bear it." She buried her face in the doctor's jacket. He held her tightly and stroked her curly head as if she were a child.

"Kamila, it will be much more effective if *you* tell her how much you love her and want her to live than if I should say this. But though the circumstances of your coming here have been tragic, you presence here has helped her. Most especially when Karol was alive and at the time of his death."

"How can there be so much tragedy in one family? What have we done that God has punished us so?"

"You mustn't think of all that's happened in this way. God isn't to blame. Diseases do occur and because our knowledge in medicine is so limited, we can't cure them. That's not God's fault. It's ours, because we are so ignorant. Someday we will be able to treat heart disease and phthisis. But that day may be a long way away. The rest must be blamed on politics. Again the fault lies with people, you see, and not with God," said Dr Roger reprovingly.

When Dr Roger left, Kamila went to her aunt and sat at her feet. Thor, who was a constant companion to Elizabeth, moved over unwillingly. She put her arms around the thin frame (she hadn't realized how much thinner Elizabeth had become, until now) and poured her heart out, begging the older lady to try, to make the effort to live.

"Thor and I need you. We need you so much. We can't live without you." Elizabeth stroked her head just as Dr Roger had done.

"Don't say that. You have your whole life ahead of you, my child. Whatever is designed for us has to be so. I am a strong believer in destiny, aren't you?"

"I don't know. Can't you direct your life to how you want it?"

"I don't believe so. Perhaps, you can, but to some extent only. If something is to happen, it will happen, however much you try to avoid it. And I accept what is to be. I'm not afraid, nor have any regrets—except," her voice broke, "that of both of my sons dying before me."

Kamila put her head on her aunt's knees, not knowing how to comfort her.

"Don't be upset, Kamila. That's how life is. I'm lucky that I have you and having Thor with me every second of the day is as if Karol is near by. I know that you don't take him with you, when you go riding, for that reason. Thank you." She kissed Kamila's head.

Kamila arranged with Lisinski that she should stay more with her aunt. Now that the calf was gaining weight, she only visited him and his mother for short periods. She knew that she could trust Lisinski with every emergency and knew that each day he would report what was going on.

She didn't realise that up till that fateful Wednesday, she was living as if on top of a volcano. She would listen to Elizabeth's breathing. She would fuss over her, until Elizabeth lost her temper.

"Will you stop fussing like a hen. It doesn't become you and it's irritating me. Haven't you any work to do? Are you leaving everything for Lisinski to do? Hadn't you better see how the wheat and rye are? Have you forgotten the harvest?"

"I'm sorry Auntie. I didn't realize that I was fussing. Lisinski said yesterday that it'll probably be another two to three weeks to harvest, but I will go tomorrow to look myself."

Within two weeks Elizabeth passed away in her sleep. Thor howled non-stop, facing her bed. Kamila felt like joining him. She lost her appetite, lost weight. Staff frequently found despair written all over her and in her every move. Even Thor couldn't distract her. Mary went to see Dr Roger and it was he who arranged the funeral. Kamila seemed unable or unwilling to have her aunt buried. This was the last member of her family and she didn't want to part from her. Now she was truly alone in the world and the loneliness was unbearable.

Mary, who had been in service all her life, was forty, plump, soft and loving. It was she who held Kamila in her arms as the young girl cried. It was she who wiped her tears and forced her to eat a little and talked to her in soothing, motherly way although she had never given birth.

"It's time you was going out, Miss Kamila. You've been in the house for two weeks. Lisinski was asking when you was coming with him on his rounds. He'll be here in an hour, so I'm going to take out your riding habit and boots and things and I want you to be ready for him."

"I'll wear the breeches, then."

"No, you will not! Remember what your aunt said, *you are not the queen*."

"How do you know she said that? You were listening at the keyhole!"

"No, I wasn't. But there is not much that we don't know what's going on in here. Now get dressed."

Kamila found she was even more distressed on reading the letters of condolences that poured in, so she decided that she would open them later. They piled up on the tray in the drawing room. She would read them later, when she was not so upset…

THE CHILL FROM SIBERIA

As she was washing herself Mary knocked on the door and entered.

"Miss Kamila, you've got a visitor," she said, eyeing the pile of letters on the tray in her hand.

"Oh! Who?" She wasn't overly pleased. She didn't feel like visitors. She'd had some already and found these visits irritating. Once the sympathies and condolences were imparted, there were long silences in the conversations, as she disliked talking about nothing just to fill in the gaps.

"Your Aunt Zofia."

"Who?" Kamila stopped wiping her neck and shoulders. "I don't have any more relatives. I've never heard of a Zofia in the family."

"I've put her in the morning room. Hurry up and get dressed. I've left Lucy there with her—to fuss around the fire and that." She gave Kamila a strange look and went out. Kamila hurriedly dressed. So she does have another relative! She looked forward to meeting this aunt. She put dabs of perfume behind her ears and lightly ran down the stairs.

As she entered the room, she saw the back of a tall woman who was standing, looking out of the windows.

"Good morning! I am so sorry to have kept you waiting," said Kamila extending her hand to the woman. "If I had known you were coming, I would have been waiting for you."

"Hm. I wrote to you of my arrival. Didn't you receive it?" Kamila's mind flew to the pile of letters on the tray and was glad Mary had placed them in another room, where the woman couldn't see them, but her face flushed with embarrassment.

"I see that you have..." said the woman, seeing Kamila's embarrassment.

"There have been so many letters that I haven't yet read all of them. I can only apologise."

The other did not smile, as she took Kamila's hand. Her handshake was limp and half-hearted and Kamila released her hand with relief.

"Would you like some tea—or perhaps breakfast?" Kamila was puzzled. This woman had not smiled once and looked down her hooked nose at her. *Don't be silly. How else could she look, when she is so tall and you are so small*, she chided herself, refusing to believe her instinct that for some reason this was not going to be a pleasant visit.

"I've had breakfast, thank you."

"I'll ring for tea," and without waiting for an answer from the other, she went and pulled the cord. "Would you like to sit down?" and as the woman still didn't say anything, "I didn't know that we had—that Aunt Elizabeth had any relatives left. Her mother's sister, Anna, died at childbirth, if I remember correctly, and the baby was stillborn. "

"Yes, but the sister's husband remarried."

"Oh, I see. So you are from the second marriage..." There was a knock on the door and the tray was brought in and set on the table before Kamila. "How would you like your tea, Cousin Zofia?"

"Weak, please." *Weak and wet, just like her handshake,* thought Kamila.

"It's kind of you to come. I'm sorry I hadn't written to you. It was all so sudden. So sad. Did you see Aunt Elizabeth often?"

"No. We live in Chelmno."

"Oh! I see. That's in the Prussian Empire, isn't it?"

"Yes. Now it is." Cousin Zofia put her cup down, and looked around the room, the silver tea service and finally her eyes rested on Kamila. "I understand that you've been left all this—the estate?"

"Well yes. I'm—was Karol's wife."

"By rights, all this should be mine. I was Elizabeth's nearest relative since her son died before her."

Aha! So that's what brought you here, across so many hundreds of miles. Aloud she said lightly, "I think that you will find that everything is legally left to Aunt Elizabeth's son's widow. Besides, Cousin Zofia, you were born from *a second* marriage of Frank Turczyn and he was not a blood relative of Aunt Elizabeth."

In fact he was considered an undesirable choice for Anna, Kamila remembered. Many a time there were discussions on that subject when her father and her aunt were together. "So, you must have been born, during the Second Partition of Poland. How terrible! You poor thing!"

"I don't know—when was that? I'm not very good with dates."

"That was on the twenty-third of January, 1793." Kamila would have liked to say more but restrained herself, taking an intense dislike to the woman, her ignorance, her manner of speech and her obvious greed.

"No, no. I was born on a beautiful day in August, in 1792."

"Ah!" Kamila lowered her head to hide her delight. "Would you like another cup of tea?" and as the other nodded she poured it out for her. When she had replaced the teapot on the table she said, "Didn't Frank Turczyn marry your mother in 1794?" She was glad she happened to remember that that had occurred when her Aunt Elizabeth was four years of age.

The other woman realised she was caught in a trap. "Er, yes."

"Cousin Zofia—for the time being I shall continue calling you by that name, although you are not related to our family in any way *whatsoever*! I fear that your journey here has been in vain. No law in any country would consider that you had any claim on the estate. I am the legal wife of my Aunt Elizabeth's surviving son and of course my Father and Aunt Elizabeth were brother and sister, and Anna, of whom we spoke earlier was my grandmother's sister, as I'm sure you must know." The other woman began to rise haughtily, "No, please finish your tea and have more. You have such a long journey before you."

Kamila was elated she had won that unexpected battle, and suddenly felt full of energy and desire for hard work. When Mary came back to the room after

Benjamin had seen Cousin Zofia out of the house, Kamila burst out, "What an insufferable woman! You'll never guess why she came! And she's no relative of the family!" She told Mary what had happened.

"That's why I didn't want her left in the room alone when she came. I thought something would have stuck to her fingers. I know that kind. And common as muck."

"Oh Mary!" Kamila laughed. "She wouldn't have stolen anything. She came for much more than would stick to her fingers, as you put it."

"Hm! Have you finished with the tray?"

"Yes, thank you. But I tell you what? She's made me feel full of energy."

"That's a blessing then, 'cos Lisinski's waiting for you."

Lisinski told her that the gathering of the grain was nearly completed and that the crop had been good. She wanted to see and he willingly took her to the fields. She was glad to be under the glorious blue skies, and feel the warm west wind on her face. The smell of hay and the earth filled her nostrils and she was filled with love for this land. She jumped off her horse and picked a handful of soil and brought it to her nose.

"Do you think, we could have the grain wagons loaded and ready to travel to Gdansk by Monday? You'll come with me, of course. Trade should be good. I was reading in the paper that Russian crops have suffered greatly from heat and in the south, not only was the weather inclement but various insects decimated their yield. We may even have more trade with England. They too had dreadful weather."

"That sounds good. Yes, we'll be ready for Monday."

"Pity we haven't the rail system from here to Gdansk. It would have been so much quicker."

"What's that?" Lisinski looked puzzled.

"It's a new way of travelling. Apparently they lay down metal tracks and have engines, which pull wagons along these tracks by means of locomotives. These locomotives burn coal to produce steam, which drives them. I've read that they can travel at 50 miles per hour. There are a lot of them already in England. They started building these thirty years ago there, can you imagine? I wish we weren't so slow. I know that we definitely have a railway line from Krakow to Warsaw. I don't know of any more at present."

"It sounds very dangerous. I wouldn't like to travel in that. A horse is much more reliable."

Kamila laughed, "You've no imagination, Lisinski."

As Kamila anticipated staying in Gdansk a few days, Mary packed a small trunk. Just before it was to be locked Kamila sent Mary on some errand and quickly inserted a few items, before snapping the locks shut.

"Will you be wanting one of us to come with you? You'll need a personal maid." Mary had asked as she had packed. Kamila had not arranged that on coming to live here. She realised that this would have been frowned upon in her circles. But her life was so different from other ladies in her position that the turmoil of the last several months was only just beginning to settle. She felt as if she had just been through a huge tornado. So, she told Mary that she would be travelling with Lisinski and the men who would be driving the wagons.

"With men only! That wouldn't be fittin' for a lady not to have a maid. Your Aunt would not allow that. Daisy, too, says you should have a maid ."

"I know that. But there are reasons why I have to travel like that. I will tell you why when I return. So don't worry. I will be perfectly all right. Lisinski will look after me. He will make sure that no harm comes to me."

Mary's eyes narrowed but all she said was, "It *is* a blessing that he is reliable, but it's still not fittin'…It's not respectable for a lady like you…" But Kamila refused to change her mind.

CHAPTER 8

On Monday the whole household woke earlier than usual. As Kamila came to her carriage she saw Mary dressed for outdoors and holding a small bag.

"I thought I made it clear yesterday that I'm going with Lisinski and no one else."

"Yes, you did Miss Kamila, but I'm not letting you go all that way without one of the house staff going with you. Your aunt left me instructions that I should look after you." Mary waved a piece of paper, which was barely discernable in the dim light of the lamps. "Whatever you say, I'm going with you, even if I have to sit on top of the luggage." She set her lips in a grim line.

Kamila looked at her face and her stance of determination and laughed. "Oh, all right, then. We mustn't waste any more time. Get in."

"After you, miss."

The caravan of loaded wagons and Kamila's carriage set out long before the sun awoke and spread a glorious red and gold glow across the vast sky and warmed the land. They made short stops to change the horses and refresh themselves and arrived at Gdansk by midnight on the second day.

The hotels (which were a new idea) had already prospered in Gdansk as it was a large city and had an international clientele. The newly arrived travellers learned that premises were quickly filling up. Kamila was lucky to be able to have a set of rooms with a bathroom, on the first floor. Lisinski and the drivers of the wagons were accommodated in a nearby inn, after unloading the bags of grain in the corn hall and stabling the horses.

Next morning Kamila and Lisinski, followed by Mary, met outside the hotel to have a wander around the city and find out where they would have to go on the following morning when the actual sales would start.

The port was already busy. People hurried by with huge baskets or sacks laden with produce on their shoulders, heavy wooden wheelbarrows were pushed this way and that, so that it was almost dangerous to walk in the road. Tired horses threaded their way between the hoards of people, dropped cabbages and potatoes. Children, mainly boys, of six or seven flitted in between the wagons and horses picking up produce that had dropped off, putting their treasure in old sacks if they were lucky enough to possess them. Sometimes a trader would take something from his wheelbarrow and throw it in the children's direction. And each time the wind blew from the Baltic Sea, there was an overpowering smell of fish.

"Ooh! What a stink!" complained Mary every few minutes.

Apart from agricultural produce there were halls for materials, cottons from India, silks from China, buttons, shoes, hats, furniture and into these Kamila and her companions were able to wander freely and look with wonder at the splendid array of goods. But the halls where luxury goods such as coffee from Ceylon and Jamaica, white rice from Bengal, pink rice from Madras, sugar from India or Barbados or (less clean) from Mauritius was barred to women.

This made Kamila really angry. "How can they be so stupid, so limited in their outlook? Who cooks, looks after the kitchen and the whole house? Women do! And women should be the ones to decide what is good to buy and what is not!"

As they were turned away once more, Lisinski, in order to calm and appease his mistress suggested they stepped into the tea-rooms across the road.

"Ooh! What a lovely smell," Mary filled her lungs to capacity, "Coffee! And freshly baked bread!"

"In that case we will go there," said Kamila.

When they were settled at a table, waiting for the coffee to cool a little and eating hot bread dripping with butter, "So we now know for certain that they will not let me in into the corn hall, and I *must* get in there to do the sales and to buy things, so I propose that you," turning to Lisinski, " will wait for me outside the hotel and I will change into something more appropriate."

"Oh! No! You can't—," said Mary.

"Oh! Yes! I can." Mary had unpacked her trunk so had seen the items that she would never have packed into it.

Once in the hotel, Kamila took out from the wardrobe her "male clothes" as she called them. She had even had a hat made to fit her, as Karol's had been too big. Mary made disapproving noises in her throat.

"Look Mary! It's no use going on and on like that. I have to get into that corn hall and no way will they let me in as a woman. At the moment we are considered the wrong gender. But time will come, I'm sure when women will be considered on an equal standing. Anyway, tell me, how do I look as a young man?" She walked about the room, lifted the hat to Mary and bowed deeply, "Good morning madam."

Mary dissolved into a fit of giggles. With her eyes wet, she was able at last to catch her breath, "Ooh, sir I don't know any young man that wiggles his hips like you do. It is most fetching. All eyes will definitely be on you."
Kamila stopped and looked serious. "It must be because I walk as if I had a long skirt. Yes, that's it. Now watch." She took longer strides and barely moved her hips. "How was that?"

"Better. Swing your arms a little. That'll do. Now your voice. Can you lower it?" Mary turned away so that she wasn't looking. "I'm not sure, Miss Kamila. We'll have to try it out on Lisinski. He'll be better in advising you there."

"There's just one more thing, Mary. You can't be with me, so here's some money and I want you to go and buy yourself something. Wander about. Enjoy your day off and we'll meet later. And Mary, thank you for coming with me. For everything you've done for me since Aunt Elizabeth died. I couldn't have coped without you."

"Oh, Miss Kamila. I'm sorry I couldn't be of more use to you, with you going through such a lot and being just a young girl. Ooh! Such a lot of money!" Mary's eyes sparkled. "Thank you."

Outside Lisinski looked shocked when Kamila made herself known to him. She noticed with satisfaction that he had briefly looked at her disinterestedly when she came out of the hotel and then his eyes wandered back to the main door of the hotel.

"Miss Kamila!" he said.

"Shh! I'm 'sir' now! I thought that my name will be *Kazimierz* Wachowski, if I need to introduce myself and if anyone asks you. Is my walk all right and is my voice sufficiently low?" He nodded. "It's a good thing I have short hair, in case I have to remove my hat. Now, let's see how they will treat us today. Let's go to the corn hall."

This time no one stopped them. The hall was enormous. The entrances were wide, so that horse drawn wagons could be taken in, and the roof was high. Some of the produce was still being delivered and piled high with the aid of hoists and ramps.

Their produce was well displayed with notice "Wachowski Estate." There were bags piled high, of wheat, oats, barley and rye, and smaller bags on the floor as samples. Kamila was pleased and felt well equipped for the following day.

Just after seven in the morning the city became noisier with the increased activity. Kamila walked confidently into the corn hall with Lisinski beside her. His face appeared serious although she wasn't sure if his eyes were not laughing at her. But she had no time to dwell on such matters at present. She wasn't sure what prices various types of corn were being sold at. She only knew what the newspaper suggested—but that was several days ago, and the market may have changed. It was imperative that she should find out, and somehow be discrete about it. She was terrified someone would suspect her and expose her for what she was—a woman. Or else there may be someone who knew her aunt and her family.

But she mustn't think of that. Neither she nor Lisinski had been to one of these markets and these were so very different from the local ones she had seen in Luck or Kowel.

"Lisinski, I have to find out a bit more about the prices. I think you should stay here. These are the prices, as far as I know at present, should anyone inquire, but I'll be back as soon as I know something more."

Kamila started to walk between the rows of produce and eavesdrop if she saw a group of men discussing. Excitedly she made mental notes of the information she overheard.

"…I wouldn't do that again. Not after being cheated out of so much money. Cash is the best, in my opinion. Don't accept these cheques. Not here anyway."

"Oh, I never accept them anywhere. I believe in solid gold only."
Kamila felt she had to go back with that information to Lisinski. She almost ran and had to stop herself in time. "Have you sold anything yet?" she asked breathlessly and looked over the sacks.

"Mis—Master Kazimierz, you've just been gone one minute," said Lisinski. "You haven't found out the price already?"

"No. But I heard something that I wanted you to know, just in case I'm gone too long. That's about the payment by cheques. Don't accept them. Sales are only for cash." Briefly she told him what the men had discussed.

This time she went through different rows.

" ..and we've had a good year, thanks be to God, but those further east had terrible trouble. I have a cousin that lives there…"

"Those in the west didn't do too well either, with all that rain. The papers said that England had terrible downpours."

"And did you read that the crops around Sympheropol, in the south suffered severely from droughts."

"Yes, and on top of that to have had locusts devour your crop—I do feel sorry for them. Poor blighters! What a terrible tragedy."

"Yes, but that means our corn prices are higher than for some years…."

"Yes, and I'm happy to say that Russia is greatly alarmed at these rising prices." They discussed the prices.

The first speaker noticed Kamila, "Can I help you sir?"

Kamila cleared her throat, " No thank you. I was just interested in what you were saying."

Both men were now looking at her. The second man was a bit younger, perhaps around thirty, "We haven't seen you here before young man. Where do you come from?"

"Luck."

"Which estate is that?"

Reluctantly she told them. After all they could so easily find out by following her to her produce.

"Oh, I know the family. But I thought there was no one left of the family. Didn't Karol die in Siberia?" Kamila's heart was in her throat. She thought that any moment it would jump out of her mouth. *Don't be silly. Keep cool. Quiet now.*

"No, Karol escaped from there, but he did die—at home."

"I thought—I didn't know there were any more children."

"You wouldn't have seen me because I was away at school.*" God! I hope he doesn't ask which school...*

The younger man raised his head in acknowledgement. His curiosity was apparently satisfied. "So you haven't been here before?" Kamila shook her head. "Well, in that case we must take you under our wing, mustn't we Stanislaw?"

"Yes indeed."

"What's your produce? Grain mainly, isn't it?" Kamila nodded

They wrote down the prices on a piece of paper, advised on the method of sale by either waiting for customers or putting it into the hands of auctioneers. Because the yield had been so good they advised waiting for customers. " The Dutch will snap it up."

They told her that the grain market was here, in between the west and east branches of the river Motlawa. The latter she had crossed on coming to the city but had hardly noticed when they arrived at night, and that other markets were dispersed around the central wide road, The Long Market. The coal market was to the west of them, and the timber market was north of it, both by the canal, and directly north of them, the fish market.

"Ah! That accounts for the smell of fish whenever the wind blows!" said Kamila.

"If you think that's bad you should be here when it's really hot!" Both men laughed.

The noise in the hall was increasing with more traders, horses neighing impatiently whilst the produce was being unloaded. And the smell of saw dust spread thickly on the floor mixed with animal and human smells as well as different grains rose up to meet their nostrils.

"The hall will close at around four o'clock, you do know that, don't you?" said Stanislaw.

"No. I didn't. I knew it closed early but not the actual time. Thank you for telling me."

"Have you any plans for the rest of the day and night? By the way let me introduce myself. My name is Mateusz Kobulski and this is Stanislaw Skromny. They call me Mat."

"How do you do! How do you do!" They shook hands and Kamila introduced herself as Kazimierz Wachowski. Kamila searched her memory of those names and couldn't remember any such families although both were quite obviously gentlemen, from their bearing and the way they spoke and dressed. They couldn't be from the east because the huge estate of the Radziwil's covered a vast amount of Poland, being north-east. *Father's estate was adjoining Radziwil's, but much smaller and Karol's was further south, and I know most of the landowners between and around our two estates, albeit by name. So they must come from the west.*

"Mat comes from around Poznan and I am quite local, just beyond Starograd. We too live in the corn growing areas," said Stanislaw as if he had read her thoughts.

"So, have you any plans for later?" Mat was saying.

"We were thinking of looking around the city."

"Well, we can show you around, and in the evening we'll take you to a delicious place. Delicious, both in food and company. The girls are really out of this world," said Stanislaw, kissing his three fingers and blowing the kiss into the air. Kamila started to blush and was furious with herself for doing so, but still her colour was rising. Mat laughed heartily and slapped Kamila on the shoulder, so unexpectedly that she almost fell. She grabbed the nearby table but Mat had also caught her by the elbow.

"I-I don't think I can today. I already have a previous engagement for this afternoon and the evening. Thank you." She avoided looking at either of them.

"Well, if you go around the city, you must go and see our loveliest road—St. Mary's Road and St. Mary's church. Inside there is the most fantastic—and the largest in the world—astronomical clock. The man who built it had his eyes poked out, so that he would never build another one for anyone else."

"Oh, how horrible!"

"Don't distress yourself. It was way back in the thirteenth century," said Mat. "It really is quite wonderful, and has been working continuously since its completion, which is unbelievable."

"I will most certainly see these things. Thank you. Thank you for all your advice too. I think I ought to get back. So, will you excuse me gentlemen?" Kamila lifted her hat slightly and bowed.

"I hope we'll meet later?" Mat said and Stanislaw nodded.

"I hope so." She answered.

"Where are you staying?" She pretended she had not heard that as she hurried away.

When she arrived at their stand, she was breathless and hot. Lisinski looked at her enquiringly. "Are you alright Mis—ter Kazimierz?"

"Yes! But only just. I met two *very* friendly gentlemen." To her annoyance Kamila started to blush again. "But tell me, have we had any success?"

"Yes, we have. Two Dutch men came and these are their names—they want all the stock so they are coming back in an hour to see you."

"At the prices I had given you before?"

"No. I said that I wasn't sure of the price. That you would tell them but that our grain was of top quality. But they could see that as they looked at these bags." He indicated the smaller bags.

"I do hope they will buy all of it so that we can leave. I feel increasingly worried that someone will discover the subterfuge. These men I met—they knew the estate and my husband and his family."

"Then, how did you explain yourself to them?" Kamila told him. "Of course, you know what they will do to you if they find out, don't you?"

"No. What? Other than throw me out of here?"

"Oh no. I heard that they throw the impostors into the Baltic," said Lisinski.

"No!" Kamila was horrified and as she looked at him with terror, he started to laugh.

At the appointed time the two Dutchmen came. They were both tall and blond and spoke Polish beautifully. Kamila liked them instantly. They were friendly but businesslike too. They accepted the prices Kamila presented to them and within another hour their stand was cleared and the only trace that they had occupied a substantial amount of space in this huge corn hall were the clean flagstones where the jute bags had stood, surrounded by the saw dust that was spread all over the stone floor.

Kamila was elated. Not only with the price she had obtained but also that now they would be free to leave the hall and look at the city.

When they came out of the hall they looked around to see if Mary was anywhere to be seen. They had some lunch and waited.

"I'd like her to come with us. She may never be here again. But I don't know how long she'll be," said Kamila.

"You gave her the day off. She could return in the evening. Do you plan to stay tomorrow?"

"No. Our business is finished. I'm afraid in case I meet those two men I told you about. They promised to take me some place…" Again she started to blush. Lisinski glanced at her.

"In that case, I wouldn't wait for Mary—."

"Don't you think she'd be interested—?"

"Most likely she's already seen all these things. She can walk very fast. I once walked with her to the church and could barely keep up. And I've got longer legs than she has."

Kamila hired a britzschka and they climbed into it. They asked the driver to show them the city. They travelled along the Long Market and turned left to go to St. Mary's Road as this was the pride of the city with beautiful Buerger houses and stopped at St. Mary's Church to marvel at the huge, high astronomical clock that showed phases of the moon and positions of the sun as well as astrological phases accurately.

"That's strange. To have astrology inside a church."

"Why?" said Lisinski.

"Well, astrology is to do with fortune telling. You could say it's even heathen, and yet it's displayed in a most religious of places—this beautiful church. Poor fellow, whoever he was—to lose his sight for creating this remarkable clock. How barbaric! And all in the name of religion, presumably."

When they came to the mill—the largest in the world, the driver had told them—Kamila said, "Why not mill the grain and sell it as flour? It would take up less space, wouldn't it?"

"Mister Karol's father said that flour doesn't keep as long as the grain does. That's why we—the estate deals with grain and not flour."

"Oh! I didn't know that."

Kamila suddenly remembered that in her hurry to get away from Mathew Kobulski and Stanislaw Skromny, she had forgotten to do their own purchases. For a fleeting moment when Kobulski had caught her arm to prevent her falling, she thought that there was a glint of recognition in his eyes—that this was no young man but a soft female form under the male clothes. She had avoided the thought until she was out of the corn hall. Now the enormity of this hit her. They will have to go back to the other halls for their purchases and she might meet him again. Once more her heart was in her mouth, choking her with fear.

"We must stop. Ask the driver to take us back to the Long Market—preferably somewhere between the food hall and the stabling." Lisinski looked at her, puzzled. "I'll tell you why when we get off.."

The driver of the britzschka turned his horse in the direction of the Long Market and for a while the two occupants in the back enjoyed the fresh breeze on their faces and the sound of clip-clop of the horse's hoofs on the cobbled street. Their britzschka was dainty and most suitable for busy city streets, but they had passed others, which were bigger, sturdier, designed for long journeys and driven by 4-6 horses. Once in the Long Market the driver manoeuvred his horse with care between the milling people and other carriages. And the smell from the wide street rose up to their nostrils.

He stopped a little further than the corn hall, Kamila was happy to see. Lisinski helped Kamila down being careful, she noticed, not to betray that this was a lady getting off.

Kamila paid the driver and waited until he had turned the carriage around and was out of earshot.

"Now, we must go back, Lisinski. I forgot to do our own buying of necessities. And we must go home straight away. Also we can let the surplus wagons go back now, and keep the ones for our goods only."

"Didn't you want to stay on a day or so extra? Forgive me for being so bold, Miss Kamila but you've had a rough time this last year and haven't had any holiday or time to enjoy yourself."

"Thank you for considering that, but we have to go back—and soon. One of these men I told you about—I am sure that he knows I'm a woman—I almost fell and he caught my arm. Under normal circumstances it wouldn't have mattered, but here he will undoubtedly consider me of loose morals—and—and may take advantage of that knowledge."

"Oh! I see." He made a noise with his lips, which might have been a soft whistle.

"So will you go and tell the men to go back and I will go and look at the coffee and tea. You can join me there or perhaps you'd like to go and do a bit of shopping for your family?"

"No. I'm not leaving you alone. I'll go and see to the men. Miss Kamila, you wait for me by the coffee stands. Don't move from there. I'll be back as soon as I can." His voice had an edge to it.

"Alright, alright, I'll wait for you by the coffee. Would you like me to ask them to tie me to the stand there?" She laughed, touched that both Mary and he treated her with such tenderness. "Mary! I almost forgot her!"

"We can't go home without her. Mr Benjamin would murder us!" With that he started to run to the stabling blocks.

The food hall was smaller than the corn hall and not as lofty, and somehow seemed friendlier. Here it seemed the whole world had congregated. There were languages spoken between the traders that Kamila didn't understand. Only by looking at their faces and the names on the stands did she know who came from where. This hall was much cleaner and the smell pervading was of goods rather than what happened to fall on the floor, which too, was covered with sawdust.

There were great round red balls of Dutch cheeses, large yellow flat ones, and cured meats in net stockings There were hogsheads of white sugar from West Indies, Havana, Barbados and Bengal and brown sugar from Penang. Bags of rice were piled one on top of another. From Bengal it was middling white, and from Madras and Arracan, pink. Kamila looked with wonderment at safflower and gambodge from Bengal and Madder root from Bombay and wondered who would want to use these….

At last her nose picked up the scent of coffee and she made her way between the stands to it. There were not as many people around the coffee stands for coffee was very expensive. There were two stands. One was from Ceylon and the other Jamaica. She looked for bags that contained beans only. She remembered having read in the estate books that ground coffee sometimes had as much as 50% chicory added and Karol had always bought Jamaican coffee, which he considered the best, so she, too, chose this. And now she had to wait for Lisinski.

Meanwhile she considered which kind of sugar she ought to buy. Sugar was frequently adulterated with many substances. If there were additions of grape sugar, that wasn't so bad but sometimes fungi, starch granules or blood was added and even worse, lime or lead or particles of stone or grit. She decided that she would ask to taste, or at least look at it before choosing and let her instinct guide her.

She saw Lisinski running to her. His face creased with a smile of relief, as though he had expected someone to kidnap her, she thought.

"All settled with the men?"

"Yes, they're on their way."

"I've brought the coffee. Now let's go for tea and sugar and cheese. I suppose you didn't see Mary?" He shook his head.

They went to the sugar stalls and after looking at several samples she decided on the product from Barbados. They completed the rest of their purchases and made their way towards Kamila's hotel. And on the bench that they had sat on before was Mary, with one shoe off, rubbing her foot.

"Blisters?" Kamila asked.

Mary lifted her head, "Don't know. All I knows is that I'm knackered. Ooh! Sorry Mis—Mister Kazimierz."

"Poor Mary! But now that you're here, we are all going home. I'll look at your foot in the room. Let's go and pack."

Once settled in the carriage, Kamila breathed a sigh of relief and to take her mind of the last day she asked Mary what she had seen and done. Mary had indeed walked the whole of the city and saw most of the sights and now asked if she could take her shoes off.

"Oh! I never did look at your feet. Let me see them now."

"No! No! I can't let you do that. Them's bound to be dirty."

"Then at the next stop, wash them in cold and hot water and they will feel better. And of course take your shoes off now."

"Thank you Miss Kamila." Once that was done, Kamila asked if she had bought herself anything at Gdansk. Mary pulled the two boxes from the overhead shelves and took out two bonnets and a shawl.

"My! Two bonnets! You'll be the envy of the whole of Luck, let alone of the whole house. It won't cause you problems with the rest of the staff?"

"Ooh! This is not all for me. One bonnet," she pulled out a blue one, "is for Lucy." Kamila looked puzzled. "Maybe as you haven't met her. She's the scullery maid. Your aunt took her in just afore you came. She's only fourteen and church mice are millionaires compared to her."

"Where do her family live?"

"She has none. Her mom died, and dad, Gawd knows where the bast—, beg pardon Miss Kamila. He was a real good for nothing."

"And the shawl?" Kamila anticipated that this too was for Lucy.

"That's for her too. That kid's got nothing except her uniform."

"I'm proud of you. You are very kind Mary."

"No, I'm not. You see, I've been lucky, working for your aunt and the family. They was lovely people. Some of the gentry treat their servants something awful. Worse than animals. I was glad that Lucy came to us. She is a sweet girl. Never complains."

Kamila started to plan how she could help her staff more. There were all the clothes left following the death of Aunt Elizabeth, and then there were Karol's clothes. Of course they would need some alterations, to be suitable…..

They were now passing through a most beautiful part of the country, covered with large lakes, interspersed with trees, occasional houses on stilts. They all looked with fascination at the scenery, for when they had travelled northwards to Gdansk, it had been night, and there was no moon.

Finally they reached home. The clatter of unloading all the goods bought, excited voices of the servants, snorting of tired horses made Benjamin's greeting inaudible.

" Everything alright here? No problems?"

"No, no problems. But there was a—person that came." He indicated that he didn't want anyone to overhear. "Would madam like to go in first? "
Once inside, he took her bonnet and the light coat to hang up, and followed her to the drawing room.

"Well, who was it—that came?"

"He came to the front door, but as he looked a tramp I was about to send him off. It was dusk and he wore a hat pulled over his face. And he had a beard, so I couldn't see his face very well. He asked for Mr. Karol and he spoke like a gentleman. I told him that Mr. Karol was no longer of this world. He then asked for your Aunt, and on hearing that she had died too, he swore. He started to walk away and said angrily, 'Anyone else in the house, or are they all dead too?' I said that the mistress was away and will be back soon."

"What did he do then?"

"He walked away into the night, without a word."

"Who was he?"

"I don't know, madam. I called after him, 'Who shall I say called?' but he didn't answer. I told the cook and she said I should have asked him in. But you never know what could happen if you ask someone like that in, do you?" Kamila agreed.

It was three days later that just before the lamps were lit there was a ringing at the front door. When Benjamin opened the door, the visitor said

"Is the mistress home?"

"Er..shall I see?..sir…" Before Benjamin could say any more the man swiftly stepped into the hall and into the shadow. "Sir!" The butler pulled himself to his full height with indignation.

"Close the door," the man demanded and when the door was closed he added "Thank you. Now please go and tell your mistress."

"Who shall I say –sir?"

"I will tell her that myself."

"I'll just light the lamp before I go."

"No! Please go." And then with a wry smile, which was barely visible in the darkness added, "Don't worry. I won't steal anything. I won't move from the spot I'm standing on."

"Very well, sir." Benjamin eyed him suspiciously and then walked more briskly than usual to the sitting room where Kamila had just started to look at the correspondence that had arrived whilst she had been away in Gdansk. He knocked on the door and entered.

"Excuse me, madam."

"Yes, Benjamin? What is it? You look alarmed."

"You remember I told you of that person who came—."

"The one you thought was a tramp—."

"Yes. Well, he is here again. In the house! When I said 'I'll see if madam is in,' he just jumped in. He wants to see you."

"Alright. Send him in."

"Yes, madam, but I'll be just outside the door."

Kamila smiled at the man's concern and waited with interest for the visitor. When the man entered the room, he quickly looked at the windows where the heavy brocade curtains hadn't yet been drawn and stepped back into the hall, asking Benjamin to draw them. When this was done, he bounded across the room, an action which seemed somehow familiar to Kamila. But it was only whilst taking off his hat, and saying, "My name is Raphael Karbonski, your husband's friend –and yours I hope, Miss Kamila," that recognition dawned upon her.

Kamila looked into his face. It was considerably thinner than when she had last seen it. The same eyes but these eyes were no longer laughing at her. The same straight fair hair, but this time not very clean.

"Yes, I remember you, sir. Would you like to sit down?" The last sentence was said uncertainly and he had seen how she had looked him over.

"Don't worry. I haven't any fleas. I am very dusty, though. I've been on the road so long….I need your help. You are my last refuge. They are after me—."

"Who? What have you done?"

"Who? The secret police, the Russians….and what have I done? Not any more than Karol did when they sent him to Siberia, or your father—."

"Did you kill someone?"

"No, I'm no murderer, but if you will give me shelter, I would rather you didn't know any details. You know how they work. How dangerous …"

"For how long do you need this shelter?"

"Several weeks. Until the heat is off. Until they find something or someone else to occupy their minds. But the servants… can you trust them that none will gossip outside?….that's if you can put up with me for a while?"

"Yes, of course you can stay. I'm sure that neither Karol nor my aunt would have refused."

"What about the servants?"

"There are too many to be sure of that. I think it's best if I ask Benjamin. He knows them better than I. I think it would be best if only one was allocated to look after you, don't you?" She walked to the door, not wishing to summon any one else, and called Benjamin.

"Madam?"

"Benjamin please come in, and shut the door….Thank you. I wish to ask you something." When he was inside the room and the door was closed, "You've been with this family all your life, haven't you?"

"Yes madam. And my father before me, and his father before him."

"Yes, I thought so. This is why I need to entrust this confidence with you. You may have recognized this gentleman. He is a friend of the family and he needs to stay here for some time—in such a way that the other servants don't know or are suspicious." Kamila saw the look of recognition on Benjamin's face and was glad that she didn't need to say his name. "I thought that we could allocate someone whom you think is completely trustworthy, to look after him. Whom would you suggest?"

Without hesitation, Benjamin replied, "Theresa. She is quiet and it's impossible to get any information from her. She's also hard working. Will you also need a man servant, madam? Sir?" He turned to Raphael.

"No, I don't think so. The less people know the better." Raphael turned to Kamila for confirmation. She nodded her agreement.

"Ask Theresa to come, please. We had better prepare the suite in the east wing, and if anyone should ask, then the person there has some terribly contagious disease…."

"I'm not sure that I like that…" Raphael almost growled.

When Theresa came, Kamila repeated the instructions, stressing on secrecy.

"You need have no fear, madam. No one will learn anything from me."

"Thank you, Theresa. When you prepare the rooms could you make sure that when the curtains are drawn that not a chink of light shows through the windows? If there is any doubt about them, then change them for those brown ones with the green and yellow paisley pattern. Do you know which ones I mean?"

"Yes, I do. We took them down from the rooms in the west wing for the summer…"

"That's right…..Oh! I think Mr.Raphael will need to have a bath, so could you prepare that as well and I'll go and sort some of my husband's clothes …" She turned to Raphael and said, "I think you had better go with Theresa, in case any one comes in here."

"One moment, sir, I'll just go and check first." With that Theresa left the room and came back in a few minutes, "No one about, now sir."

When she was alone again she breathed a sigh of relief. She hadn't realised how fear and anxiety had enveloped her in that short period. Suddenly she remembered that she had not offered him anything to eat, "....Theresa will see to it. Anyway, he'll ask, surely...."

She left the room to go upstairs to Karol's room. She started to sort out Karol's clothes, putting on the bed only the clothes that Karol had not worn in the few months this year that she had lived in this house. She couldn't bear to part with the few that she has seen him in. When she came to his riding jacket and breeches, she clung to them as if in doing so it would bring him back ..... There was a knock on the door and Theresa entered.

"Yes, come in Theresa. Those things on the bed should fit Mr Raphael."

"What about some underclothes, madam?" Theresa said as she was gathering trousers, jackets and shirts.

"Oh, yes. I forgot about those. Perhaps you can sort those out for him. I'll leave you to do that then. I must go and deal with my correspondence...."

CHAPTER 9

Once she was settled on the sofa, she found that out of the bundle of letters, two evoked a verbal response from her. One was from her friend Amelia, *".....I have some news for you and am coming to stay for a few days. You did say that you didn't need me to arrange this ....that I would be welcome...so I should be with you by mid-day on Friday...."*

She laid the letter on her lap and looked worriedly towards the direction of the east wing where Raphael was having a bath. "Oh dear, oh, dear...."

The other letter was from that woman Zofia's solicitor, more or less repeating what that woman had said to Kamila—claiming the estate. And to this, Kamila's response was to throw the letter down. "Idiot! Imbecile!" she said to herself. "How can a solicitor take her word for granted, without first investigating it."

She went to the window and pulled the cord. Benjamin entered the room after first knocking on the door.

"Yes, madam?"

" Benjamin, could you ask the staff to prepare the rooms for a friend of mine, Miss Amelia. She's coming on Friday – goodness, that's tomorrow – I didn't realise."

"Which part of the house would you like her to be in, madam?"

"Oh, as far away from Mr. Raphael as possible. I think – perhaps, beside my rooms. Oh, you'd better warn Theresa so that she can tell him to be careful."

"Very well, madam."

Amelia arrived by mid morning, breathless, with pink cheeks as if she had been running instead of travelling in luxury in the family coach. The two young women hugged and kissed each other as if they had not seen each other for years, instead of just a few months. Amelia's luggage was taken up to her room. Kamila was amused that the amount of luggage she had brought was sufficient for two months instead of a few days. Amelia's delicate pink gown was complemented by Kamila's grey as they walked to the morning room, with their arms entwined about each other's waist, laughing and talking.

Kamila turned to her friend, "Well what's this exciting news?"

"I'm engaged to be married! Isn't that the most exciting thing you've ever heard?"

Kamila laughed. "I don't know about the most exciting thing… but I'm happy for you – since it makes you so happy! Who is the very lucky man?"

"His name is Noah Cynicki. He is a banker. Very rich—."

"Not that that's important to you—."

"—no, but I don't think my Father would have cared if he was poor."

"No, of course not. In such a case one would always wonder if he wasn't a fortune hunter, and I've heard of a lot of them. But tell me Amelia, with that name Noah, does it mean that he is Jewish?"

"No, thank goodness! But I did wonder that too, when I met him. No, he assures me that he is a Roman Catholic."

"I suppose it wouldn't have mattered if he had been Jewish, as we have this tolerance to all these various religions here, in Poland. We are lucky in this—."

"Ah! That's right! And of course it was the Jews that took over the banking and other businesses. They appear to be so good at finance. But I wouldn't have liked to have to convert to Judaism though. Their way of life is so different."

"You haven't said where you met him and what he looks like."

"Well, I met him at a ball in Krakow, shortly after I came here for your wedding. He dances divinely. After our first dance together, he wanted every dance with me thereafter but all of them were already booked, except the last three, so he put his name down on my card for those." She got up and started to dance in the room as if an orchestra was playing.

Kamila laughed, "You always were a romantic. Careful, Amelia, I think our tea is arriving." A dreamy Amelia stopped just as the door was opening. "Is he interesting? To talk to?"

"Wait a minute Kamila and I will tell you. You are so impatient! You wanted to know what he looks like first." She lifted the cup of tea to her soft lips, and said as if mesmerized, "He has brown eyes, large eyes and bushy eyebrows and curly brown hair—a bit like yours. He is quite tall—my height—but then I'm tall, aren't I? His voice is very deep and he is forty. He is interested in most things but his favourite subject is—."

"Money!" Kamila finished.

"As a matter of fact, I was going to say finance! So you didn't guess right!"

"It's the same thing!" And they fell about laughing as if they were ten year olds instead of young ladies. "Amelia, he sounds just the right sort of person for you. But you became engaged so soon after meeting him!"

"Hark, who's talking! You got married in less time that it took for that ball in Krakow to end."

"Ah, but that was different—."

"Yes, I know, my dear. I'm sorry—." She paused for a moment. "Noah visited us so often after that, that it was obvious what his intentions were and as I really liked him so much that, when he asked Father for my hand and as Father had already asked me in anticipation of the question, he agreed."

"And the wedding—."

"—will be in a year's time. Firstly propriety demands it—although Noah would have preferred it next week! Besides I want you to be out of mourning so that you can come to my wedding. Noah says you must be a very special person in that case."

"Thank you for that. I would love to come to your wedding."

"Oh! I do hope you can meet him soon. I'd like your approval—."

"And what if I didn't approve? Would you give him up?" Kamila couldn't help teasing her excitable friend.

"I'm sure you will love him."

Kamila took Amelia riding to show her the estate and the work that she did and described their trip to Gdansk and how exciting that city was, for Amelia had never been further north than Warsaw. She described the fascinating goods that were being sold from other countries, but she did not tell her that she had masqueraded as a man in order to get into the corn hall. She felt that, although Amelia was her best friend, she might inadvertently say this to her family, or Noah…..no, this was best kept a secret.

She took her friend to see the little calf and her mother that she had grown to love but saw that Amelia was truly a city girl and was not particularly interested in animals other than to ride or eat them. And as for the fields, her friend admired the beautiful landscape and the ultramarine skies as an artist might have done. *Yes, Noah sounds just right for her.*

She started to wonder about herself and discovered that, city life was not for her, that parties and balls all her life would not fulfil her, as she knew that they would Amelia. She realised that she hungered for the earth. And the beauty of the landscape and the vast skies had deeper meaning than just the superficial magnificent panorama. For her it somehow meant her mother and father. For her the land was as necessary as water for a thirsty animal. Yes, she needed to have her roots buried deeply in this fragrant soil.

One morning Amelia had gone up stairs to get herself ready because she was going to see her cousin who lived nearby. Kamila had quite a lot of paperwork to do and was glad she would have this time free to do it. She was in the study with the door ajar so that she would hear when Amelia came down the stairs, when Benjamin coughed to draw her attention.

"There is a gentleman, asking if he could see Mr. Kazimierz, madam."

"Mr.Kazimierz? There's no –oh!" Her eyes shot to Benjamin's face. She couldn't be sure if he knew that it was she. "Who is it? Did he give you his card?"

"Yes, madam. Here it is. A Mr. Kobulski."

"What did you say to him –when he asked for Mr. Kazimierz?"

"I said, 'I will see', sir.'"

"Oh! So you know." She saw that there was amusement on his face.

"If I may say so, madam, there was no other way of achieving what you did. Shall I ask him to wait in the library?" His eyes looked upwards and Kamila understood that he wanted to put the visitor as far as possible from the stairs.

"Thank you. Yes, do that. And when Miss Amelia comes down, you'll let me know?"

"Yes, of course, madam."

Kamila wiped her moist hands on a handkerchief. She looked at herself in the mirror. Her face was flushed and there was perspiration on her nose. She mopped this up and looked fiercely at herself. *Don't be foolish. He probably knew the truth when he caught your arm when you nearly fell and the fact that he is here – so what? Remember what Benjamin said – there was no other way....*

She adjusted her skirt and blouse and made her way to the library. She opened the door quietly. He was looking out through the windows. He turned round on hearing her enter and came up to her.

" Ah! Mr. Kazimierz." He took her extended hand gently and gravely bent down and kissed it. She still didn't say anything. And he was still holding her hand, "Don't be afraid. You see I had to find out the truth...." She pulled her hand out of his and at last found her voice.

"Would you like to sit down, Mr Kobulski?" She indicated the leather chairs by the highly polished big oak table, but first he drew out another chair for her.

"You knew?"

"Not at first. It was only after I caught your elbow, I began to think. And then I remembered quite definitely that Karol had had only one brother who had died in a riding accident. And now that Karol was dead, who was this charlatan masquerading as family? I had to know. I know I have no right...."

"No. I am not a charlatan. I *am* family. I am Karol's wife—widow. My name is Kamila. My father was Karol's mother's brother."

"Was?"

"Yes. My aunt also died, soon after Karol; and my parents were sent to Siberia—that is, my father was sent and my mother chose to go with him—."

"Ah! Yes, I remember reading about your parents in the papers. I am so sorry about them. Our history is riddled with so many tragedies…….But tell me—for I read every single item—there was no mention of Karol getting married in the papers—."

"No. It was a quiet and a sad occasion for all of us under the circumstances. The ceremony was held here in the house. Karol was dying, you see—." She suddenly felt that she could not continue. It was all so painful.

Suddenly there was a knock at the door and Benjamin came to say that Miss Amelia was ready to leave.

"Will you excuse me please? I have to see my friend off."

"Of course." He rose from the chair and pulled hers out again as she was rising from it. She thanked him, noticing what lovely grey eyes he had, and that thick brown hair, slightly speckled with grey.

As she walked with Benjamin at her side, she said, "Once Miss Amelia's coach has driven away, could you arrange some refreshments for us and I think it will be more comfortable in the sitting room, please. Oh, and take Mr. Kobulski to that room…"

"Yes madam. I'll just wait until Miss Amelia goes." *Yes, you had better do that, otherwise Amelia might prefer to stay, as he is so handsome*, Kamila smiled to herself.

"Have a lovely time, Amelia. Give my greetings to your family." They hugged. "When will you be back? Will you be back for dinner?"

"Oh, yes, I'm sure I will. I don't like to travel when it's dark. You never know if you could be attacked. One hears of these highway men…."

"Don't be foolish," Kamila laughed, "we don't have highway men in Poland. They would either freeze to death or starve to death if they waited for a coach with anyone who had anything worthwhile to steal. Especially in these parts."

Amelia climbed into the coach, the coachman lifted his reins and Kamila turned back to go to her visitor, still laughing at Amelia's faintheartedness.

Matthew Kobulski rose as she entered the room. "Your friend—is she leaving?"

"No, she's only going to see her cousin who lives nearby. She'll be back before dark." Kamila was anxious to discover what he was thinking. "The tray should be arriving any moment. So, please tell me—tell me what you would have done if you had discovered that I was a charlatan?" She smiled.

"I don't know, if I could have done anything legally, because Karol was the last in the line, wasn't he?" Kamila nodded. "But I would have tried something. At least I would have tried to make you very uncomfortable." At this Kamila laughed,

"There was no doubt that you did that anyway. I was terrified." At this, he took her hand, as they were sitting on the sofa.

"I am truly sorry."

"And you will report all of this to your friend Mr. Stanislaw Skromny?" She removed her hand from his hold and went to sit in the armchair.

"No. Why should I? I promise—no, I swear on oath—that I shall not tell a soul—on one condition though." She looked at him with surprise, unable to fathom out what he had in mind. "That I may see you again….perhaps under different circumstances….as a friend? I would like to get to know you…" Kamila was glad there was a knock on the door and Mary came in with the tray with tea and cakes and canapés and placed on the table beside Kamila.

"Would you like anything else, madam?" Kamila immediately translated these words and Mary's expression, *Shall I stay here? I am not happy with you being on your own with this man.* And she almost laughed aloud. And not for the first time she was touched by the protectiveness her staff were showing her. "Thor wants to come in. Is that alright, madam?"

"Oh, yes. Do let him in. I haven't been with him for some time." As Thor came running in, barking, Kamila caught him by the collar and reassured him by patting,

"Did you want anything else madam?"

"No, thank you, Mary. Everything is just right. But, just, a moment Mary—Mr Kobulski would you like to stay to dinner? You could then meet my friend. She'll be back then." She looked at Mary, knowing that that would be with Mary's approval.

"No, thank you. I mustn't. I have a prior engagement. But perhaps on another occasion?"

"All right Mary. Thank you."

"Thank you madam, sir."

"He obviously loves you. Why did you call him Thor?"

"It was Karol who named him so. He gave him to me as a wedding present. He wanted him to protect me."

"Which he is doing now."

"Yes." She released Thor and he went over to the visitor and sniffed his legs. Kobulski put down his hand so that he could sniff that too, and started to stroke him. Friendship was firmly established.

Once the door was closed he resumed the subject of seeing her again. She poured out the tea, and handed him the cup.

"Well, Miss Kamila—I may call you that?" She nodded. "Can I call on you again?"

"Mr Kobulski—."

"Please call me Mat—for Matthew."

"Very well. Mr Matthew—."

"*That* makes me feel like some Biblical figure. I feel that I should be dressed in a long, thick, white gown with a staff in my one hand and with the other stroking my very long beard." He stood up and assumed a position looking heavenwards. Kamila began to laugh. He joined her.

"You were saying?"

"I told you that I have only recently been widowed, and therefore I do not think it would be seemly to plan just yet. Maybe in a year's time? I did care for Karol very much you know."

"A year is such a long time. But you wouldn't turn me away if I came occasionally?"

"Of course not, how could I? I am, after all, in your hold."

"Oh, I wish that that were so! How I wish that that were so." She blushed. "I'm sorry. I'm always embarrassing you—."

"No. Not at all."

"Tell me, when did you get married and when did Karl die?"

"Our wedding was on the fourth of April, this year and Karl died five weeks later. I thought he was getting better—."

"It was Siberia that killed him I suppose, like so many—."

"No, it was consumption."

"Yes, but—."

"You are right of course. And now my parents are there and I don't know exactly where,"

"Have you tried to find out, Have you written—?"

"Oh, yes. I can't tell you how many places I've written to and talked to every possible person. There seems to be a wall of silence."

"I'll try and make some enquiries. I know a few contacts."

"Oh, thank you so much."

He took out his gold watch and said, "I regret very much that I have to leave you. It was most interesting meeting you under these circumstances and I hope we will be able to spend a lot of time together—soon."

"That may prove to be difficult since you live in the north and I live in the south and there is a great distance in between!" By now he was holding her hand again.

"Ah! But we may soon have a network of railways between us. Have you ever been on a train? No? Right! Then I will take you on one."

"I was thinking that it would be wonderful to have a rail from our south-east to Gdansk when we need to travel there. Transporting the produce would be so much easier."

"For you perhaps, but *I* wasn't just thinking of business facilities…." he said gently, as his eyes swept over her face as if he was stroking her it with his hand.

He kissed her hand and she was glad that he didn't omit patting Thor, and left.

The room felt somehow empty and she was glad of Thor's company. She reflected on the future—but shook her head. It was too soon to think so far ahead. One didn't know what would happen in a year's time. She mustn't think—of the ideas he had put in her head. She had work to do. She got up and with Thor following her, went back into the study.

She had not heard the knock at the door, being so engrossed with the paperwork concerning the running of the estate. But Thor had heard and with a bark and a leap over her legs, he was waiting at the door, wagging his tail. It was Benjamin to ask where she would like to have her lunch.

"I haven't quite finished here, so could I have a tray brought here please?"

Benjamin came again. "I'm sorry to disturb you once more, madam, but I have a note for you, from Mr. Raphael."

Kamila unfolded the note and read, *If I don't see you soon, I shall go mad in this ivory tower.* "It seems that our guest is bored, Benjamin. Perhaps he could come down for an hour. I don't know when Miss Amelia will be back, but I think one hour should be safe enough. And into the library. Do you think? He might like to choose a book to take his mind off..."

"Oh, he has already been having books from the library, madam." When he saw Kamila's alarmed expression, he reassured her, "Oh, Theresa was getting them for him. He would give her a list of authors.... Yes, I think the library would be the safest. I'll see to it myself, madam."

Kamila stayed a few more minutes in the study, replacing her ledgers, bills and receipts in their proper places and then made her way again to the library. When she opened the door she saw that he was already there. Thor growled and Kamila caught him by the collar and took him out of the room.

"Miss Kamila! Thank you for allowing me to come down, from releasing me from the incarceration in the golden tower—." He almost ran to her, grabbed her hand in both of his and kissed it, and continued to hold it.

"I thought it was an ivory tower—." She said dryly as she pulled her hand away.

"Whatever the colour or texture...I've missed your company."

"It's not as if you've had my company all that often—."

"No. But up there the mind can play tricks..."

Kamila laughed. "It'll be safe for you to be down here only for an hour. I have a friend staying with me and she'll be back shortly after that. I gather Theresa is looking after you well..." She looked him over. He had shaved, his hair had been trimmed and he looked younger. Karol's clothes that had been worn before he had been sent to Siberia, fitted Raphael well, except that the trousers were slightly short, but only slightly.

"I thought you might have visited me, to see if I was comfortable…"

"That would not have been possible. Anyway, you are supposed to have some terribly contagious disease."

"Ah! I had forgotten. But, tell me how is it that Theresa is allowed near me, if I am so contagious?"

"Oh! She's had this disease so she is immune to it."

"Oh! I see! Ah! But now that I've held your hand that means that you can come and see me." He seemed to be as pleased as a little boy to have caught her out.

" Most certainly not! Besides, I'm quite busy."

Benjamin came to collect Raphael. "I wanted to see what next to have—books, I mean, but I suppose I had better go before the clock strikes twelve.

It was Benjamin who said, "And before the princess sees the carriage turn into a pumpkin."

The carriage wheels on the dry cobble stones of the drive were heard long before they could see it arrive, with Amelia. She entered the house like the late autumn breeze, warm and fresh and bubbling with news from her cousin.

Amelia stayed another week.

"Promise me that you'll come and stay with me soon. Mother was saying, just before I left that we had known each other for so many years and you've never been to see us! That time when you were due to come some tragedy had occurred—."

"Yes. Both of my brothers had been—murdered, shot."

"There's always something dramatic occurring in your life! Perhaps now you'll be able to come? You said you now have a very reliable overseer. So please come. Will you?"

"Alright. But at present I can't. I have to prepare for the winter. Maybe in a month's time? As later—there may be an early winter. I promise—I'll write to you." They hugged each other.

Kamila watched the carriage ride away until she could see the light dust rising from the distant road, and only then did she turn back to go into the house, suddenly feeling very lonely. She called Thor and he appeared beside her as if he had been waiting just for such an invitation. She played with him for quite a while, not knowing that she was being watched through the windows—by Raphael, and from beyond some distant bushes— by someone else..

She and Lisinski inspected all the barns and cottages, made sure there was enough fodder for all the animals for the winter and checked that all the animals were healthy. And when all this was done she wrote to Amelia that she was coming for that promised visit.

She arrived at Amelia's home in the afternoon.

"Oh! I'm so happy that you are here at last." Amelia grabbed Kamila's hands and danced a circle. Her parents laughed as they watched with pride their beautiful daughter's excitement.

"Amelia! You'll both be dizzy—and you haven't introduced us yet!"

"Oh! I'm so sorry, Kamila. I forgot…"

Her hugs left Kamila breathless and bubbling with laughter. Her parents, Mr. and Mrs. Pasiak welcomed her with warmth, as she had imagined they would.

They lived in a large mansion just outside Krakow, surrounded by five acres of carefully designed gardens. It had been bought from a palatine who had emigrated to America. Amelia's father's wealth came from the salt mines nearby and the property reflected their wealth. Opulence was visible in every room. Kamila reflected on the difference between their property and her family's. This house and the gardens would not have been out of place in Paris but somehow in Poland it stood out.

Amelia took her upstairs to show her, her set of rooms. She was so excited at her friend's arrival that she barely stopped herself running, mimicking the voice of the Academy's mistress who taught them deportment, "….now, now ladies… walk slowly…imagine you are carrying a jug of water on your head. Imagine, Kamila who would want to carry that on one's head?"

"Well, the women *do* in India and Africa. Not on beautiful locks like yours though!" They laughingly reached the top of the wide red-carpeted staircase and turned left. Paintings by famous artists hung on all the walls. Kamila wanted to stop and look at them, but Amelia wouldn't let her and hung onto her friend until they reached Amelia's rooms.

She flung the door open and waited for Kamila to enter. "There!" she said as if she had made a discovery or was unveiling a works of art. "What do you think?"

"It's just you!" said Kamila, walking in slowly, for the whole of the room—this being the sitting room—was decorated in yellow. There were draperies and ribbons, silks, taffetas, organza and brocades and all in delicate lemon. There were ornate mirrors and furniture with inlaid rosewood and delicate cabriole legs. Her bedroom was equally richly furnished. It was quite obvious to Kamila that Amelia was very proud of these rooms so she didn't ask who had chosen this décor. Despite all the hues of yellow she didn't find the surroundings unbearable, but only amusing.

"Since meeting Noah, I've had a whole new wardrobe—well, almost. Do you want to see it?" She went to the wardrobes and flung all the doors open for Kamila to see.

"Yes of course I do! But tell me, is it he who insisted on it?"

"Oh no! It was because I wanted it and Mother had these sent from Paris. Aren't they divine? This one is pure silk – from China. And this one is for the ball in Krakow next week – in honour of some banking achievement—I can't remember what though…You'll come with us, won't you? I know just the person for a partner for you. He's—."

"Amelia, you know I can't come to any ball—have you forgotten? That I am still in mourning?"

"Oh, I did forget. I'm sorry. Oh, dear, I can't leave you here all alone—."

"Please don't let that worry you. It wouldn't bother me if I was left behind. I can always read. Let's see how the days go, shall we? Or I could leave earlier."

"Oh, no! Not after I've longed for you to come here. I'd rather not go to the ball."

"My! That is a sacrifice! I wouldn't want you to do that. Don't let's think about it now. Things always work out somehow. Now let's have a look at these beautiful gowns." Kamila laced her arm through Amelia's and led her into the huge wardrobes.

Eventually both girls collapsed into the armchairs. Amelia, proud to have shown of her possessions and Kamila, overwhelmed.

"Do you think Queen Elizabeth I of England had as many gowns as you?" Kamila said smiling.

"Oh! I don't know. In her position, I'd have had a great many more. How many did she have then?"

"I don't know. Probably thousands! She loved dressing up. Apparently she had a hundred wigs when she died."

"Ugh! I'm glad that they are no longer fashionable. Come on, let's go down. It must be time for tea and I am starving!"

Tea was held in an equally luxurious sitting room. Amelia's mother poured out the tea and chatted about the various gowns they had looked at. Suddenly the door burst open and two boys of about twelve or thirteen blew in and came to an abrupt stop just before the table.

"Ah! I thought that they would put in an appearance as soon as food was on the table. Please note where they are standing! By the food!" said Mrs. Pasiak. "Boys, come and meet Amelia's friend from the Academy. The blond one is my youngest, Andrew and this one," she pulled him forwards, "is his friend, Ian. He is spending a few days with Andrew. This is Mrs. Kamila Wachowska." The boys bowed. They did that with such solemnity that Kamila almost laughed.

"How do you do, Andrew? How do you do, Ian?"

"I don't understand," said Andrew, "Isn't the Academy for *unmarried* young ladies? Married people are *old.*"

"Andrew! How can you be so rude! Apologise instantly!" He apologised and hung his head. "Miss Kamila was unmarried then. But she has left the Academy—as indeed so has Amelia, as you well know." The lad blushed for having been so forward and looked at his feet.

"Alright! Go on and have your tea. Let me pour it out for you." Mrs. Pasiak arose from the armchair. Kamila's gaze followed her. She was a handsome woman, tall and slender, an older edition of Amelia. Her hair was still blonde, and what grey there was, was hardly visible. Kamila was amused that she tried so hard to speak in a manner that was suitable for their new found wealth – and sometimes it didn't quite work out – and, by comparison, her husband didn't bother. People had to accept him as he was, rough—an unfinished product—as God made him. And he had no intention of changing.

Almost as if Mrs.Pasiak had heard Kamila's thoughts, she said, "My husband won't be in until later. He frequently works quite late."

"Your gardens are beautifully designed. Were they like that when you came to live here?"

"Oh, no! Not at all! It was all rather plain. Left to nature, I'd say. One year we had been to France and saw the palace and the grounds at Fontainebleau and I must say we both fell in love with those gardens. So I found an Italian designer and that is the result! Would you like to see them?"

"I would love to."

There was still plenty of light left when they walked in the gardens. At first the boys stayed with the group but soon became bored and started to chase each other. Kamila wished she could have joined them and somehow this reminded her of her brothers and how they used to run and she, being the youngest, always the last. And it was always Adam who came back for her. *Oh! Adam! How I miss you both!*

Mrs. Pasiak touched her hand and brought Kamila to the present, showing her a particularly favourite design and special plants. They came to an ornate bench and sat down in the sunshine but it was only for a short time for the elongating shadows of the evening soon covered them as if with a blanket. But it was a chilly blanket. Amelia shivered and they decided to return to the house.

The view of the house was even more impressive from the garden side. It was a two storey, cream coloured building set on a hill. The windows were symmetrically placed and of the same size, nine at the top and eight at ground level, with a door in the centre and under the roof there was a beautiful ornamental frieze. Yes, this house went well with the geometrically designed gardens, thought Kamila.

On entering the house, Amelia showed Kamila her room. It was decorated in creams and light browns with a thread of gold here and there.

"Mother thought you might like this room."

"Oh! It's beautiful. So very elegant!"

"Your trunk has been unpacked." She waved her hand in the direction of the wardrobes. " Do you want to rest before dinner?"

"I would like to refresh myself first! You haven't given me any time to do that, in your enthusiasm!"

"Oh! Kamila! I'm so sorry. I was so excited at your coming I forgot. Please forgive me."

"I wasn't reproaching you, Amelia! I, too, was looking forward to coming here and meeting your family at last. But I think I will lie down for a while and digest all that I have seen. What time do you want me to come down?"

"In about an hour. Father should be home by then. I'll come and waken you."

"I shan't go to sleep." But when eventually Kamila lay on the bed her eyes closed and she fell into deep slumber, dreaming of her brothers running away from her…

CHAPTER 10

She was woken as promised and both of the girls went down the wide stairs side by side.

"You slept so heavily I had a job to waken you! But as I recall, you always slept well."

"Didn't you sleep?"

"No, I couldn't. I was thinking of all the places I could take you to. I don't want you to get bored. Would you like to go to Krakow? Perhaps you'd like to see the salt mines and the beautiful carvings the miners have done? They are really quite astounding."

Kamila laughed. "I never get bored. And I do know Krakow quite well, but if you wish to go, then of course I'll come with you. No, I haven't been down the mines. It does sound most interesting. But for my sake alone we don't have to go. "

As they entered the dining room they saw that only Mrs.Pasiak was there. Amelia looked around, "Hasn't Father come home yet?"

"Yes. He has. He'll be down presently. So we can sit down. Miss Kamila, you sit here and you here, my love. Andrew and Ian have already had their dinner and have gone to their room to play."

Mr. Pasiak came in, smiled at Kamila and sat down, "I hope that daughter of mine hasn't exhausted you with her enthusiasm, Miss Kamila."

"Oh! No! Not at all." They then told him in turn what they had been doing and Kamila said how beautiful the house was and how perfect the gardens were. This made him very pleased and made him puff out his chest with pride, almost like a bird.

"I owe all of that to my wife."

Since there were only four of them, the table had had the unnecessary leaves removed so that it became a large round table. It was covered with heavy linen tablecloth with lace around the borders and serviettes to match. The cutlery was polished and of good quality and the crystal sparkled and gleamed.

The butler hovered by the sideboard, pouring soup into the plates and when all the members were served, he brought a small silver dish with a serviette on top of it to Mr. Pasiak, but before he was able to place it on the table (Kamila presumed that that was where it was destined), Mrs. Pasiak said sharply, "No!" and the dish was withdrawn. Mrs. Pasiak's lips were pursed tight and her husband's face was suffused with red. Kamila couldn't guess what this was about and nobody explained. Amelia's eyes were fixed onto her plate as if there was something interesting in the soup.

After a short prayer (it was customary) they began on the soup. Unfortunately after the second spoonful, Mr Pasiak started to cough and with such an explosive force that his dentures flew out and landed in the soup tureen which had been placed in the centre of the table. It was Kamila's misfortune to be sitting opposite him and the displaced soup flew onto her clothes and a little onto her cheek. Fortunately it wasn't very hot by then. Chaos ensued. The butler flew to her side with a cloth, but she had already scraped back her chair and was on her feet.

Mrs. Pasiak was shouting something and Amelia was saying "Really Father! How could you?" whilst running to her friend. "I'm so sorry, Kamila. Are you alright?" Whilst wiping Kamila's cheek, "It hasn't burnt the skin."

"No, no. It wasn't hot."

"—well, you didn't let me take them out. If I'd had them out, it wouldn't have happened—it's your fault…"

"Will you excuse me? I'll go and clean up." With that Kamila left the dining room where the noise increased. She ran upstairs and stripped off her blouse and the skirt as this too had some wet patches, and went to wash her face. There was a knock on the door, and expecting it to be Amelia, she bade the knocker to enter. It was one of the maids.

"Excuse me, madam. The mistress asked me to take your clothes to launder. And can I help you in any way?"

"No, thank you. I've already washed. I don't think that it went through my underwear, do you?" The maid looked her over carefully.

"No, madam. That's all clean. I will look after your beautiful clothes personally. They should be ready tomorrow. Will that be alright?"

"Yes, thank you. What's your name?"

"Olga, madam. Will that be all madam?"

"Yes, thank you Olga." As the maid left, Kamila put out another, this time navy brocade, skirt and a white blouse with navy trimmings and white lace. Thank goodness that the stained blouse was pure cotton and the skirt wasn't such heavy weave as this skirt, she thought wryly. She dressed and went downstairs intending to ask for a piece of bread and maybe cheese since these were not on the table at the time of shower of soup. But when she entered the dining room, she noticed firstly that Mr. Pasiak was no longer in the room, and that the tablecloth, serviettes and cutlery had been replaced with fresh and the butler was placing the plates for the second course.

"I hope you'll have some of this pork. It really is delicious. The cook has some secret recipe which she won't divulge," said Mrs. Pasiak.

"I—." Kamila couldn't say that she couldn't eat anything now, and finished lamely, "Yes, thank you."

"I expect she feels quite sick as indeed I do—."

"Amelia!" Her mother said sharply. "Don't! I warned you before."

"Oh! Mother! Don't be such a hypocrite! As if it didn't happen! The worst possible thing did happen. Kamila is a very intelligent young lady. She's bound to come to some conclusions."

"Not the worst, Amelia." Both women looked at Kamila with apprehension on their faces. "The dentures could have landed in *my* soup or on me." They all laughed and the tension was dispersed.

"You may have noticed that a small plate was to be put beside Father, and that Mother forbade it. Quite rightly, in my opinion. But he finds he cannot eat with the dentures in his mouth, so he has this disgusting habit of taking them out, and placing them on that plate. We don't look at him at that time and they are covered with the serviette afterwards."

"The few people that I know that have dentures, have them secured with a loop of silver or gold wire to the adjacent teeth at the back somewhere and they can eat with them in. And I've never known them to fall out," said Kamila.

"They didn't fall out. They shot out. Like a bullet," said Amelia.

"Believe me, he's been to the best dentists and had the most expensive dentures you can buy. These are made of porcelain. And I was told that they can be secured by wire or strong thread only if you have some of your own teeth at the side. Well, he hasn't. Didn't your parents have any problems with them?"

"None of my family had any dentures. In fact I don't think that any of the family lost any teeth, except the milk teeth." She smiled impishly. "We've all had this tradition drummed into us, that we have to clean out teeth twice per day with crushed salt."

"And you really did that?"

"Oh! Yes! I remember when I was little, Grandmamma, on my Mother's side, used to stand us in a row and inspect our teeth as if we were horses."

After dinner they retired to the sitting room where shortly afterwards Mr. Pasiak joined them. For a moment he stood in front of Kamila, cleared his throat noisily, "I hope you'll forgive me for what happened there, Miss Kamila." He jerked his thumb in the direction of the dining room.

"Please, don't think about it. It could happen to anyone."

"Not to anyone! Only you, Father—."

"Amelia!" said her mother sternly.

"I usually eat in my room when we have company, so I can take the damn things out and only afterwards join the rest of the company, for a smoke. You don't mind if I smoke, do you?"

"No. Of course not," said Kamila as the question was directed at her, but he still looked in the direction of his wife, who inclined her head. He lit his cigar with an ember from the fire, puffed several times, and turned to his daughter.

"Well, young lady, is that Noah coming to see you tonight?"

"I don't know…"

"I'm sure he is. He comes and sees her every day, you know Miss. Kamila." said Mrs. Pasiak.

"I don't know why he doesn't just live here. He's always here," said her husband.

"He can't live here, you know very well. People would talk and I can't have Amelia's name tarnished."

"Good heavens woman!"

"I wish you wouldn't say that. It's so common. What will Miss Kamila think?"

"I *am* common. And I don't give a toss what *anybody* thinks—beg pardon Miss Kamila. As I was saying, Noah could come and live here instead of renting that house in Krakow, cramped with that uncomfortable furniture. As for propriety, this house," he waved his hand above his head, " is large enough for the two of them not to meet for three years or more."

"I think that Noah likes the journey here and anticipation of seeing you Father!"

"Me? You mean *you*! I do think I can hear the carriage!" They all listened but could hear nothing. Amelia ran out of the room to look out of the windows that looked onto the front drive but it was empty. With disappointment written on her face, she returned to the room.

"There's no one there."

"Oh! Didn't I tell you? The wheels that I heard were five miles away." He puffed on his cigar.

"Oh! You!" Amelia stretched her arms to him in a mock attack and he laughed. Kamila laughed too and thought that even though he was what was considered "rough" he really was a very kind man. He had piercing blue eyes, unlike Amelia's, and a large bristly moustache and wiry hair that stood on end, to match. Thank goodness that his daughter inherited her mother's looks, for what could she have done with such hair? On the other hand, he did have something about him that was pleasing and arresting.

Shortly afterwards Noah did arrive and was announced into the room. He greeted the parents of Amelia and then was hurried along by her, to her friend.

"This is Noah. And this is my best friend Kamila." He lifted Kamila's hand to his lips.

"I'm so glad to meet you at last, Miss Kamila. Amelia is constantly talking about you, I therefore feel as if I've know you a very long time."

Mr. Pasiak poured out vodka for Noah and himself and wine for the ladies.

Kamila leaned back in her armchair and observed the company. It was evident that Mr. Pasiak approved and liked Noah. But was this reciprocated? She couldn't tell as yet. But what did that matter? He wasn't marrying Mr. Pasiak. He was marrying his daughter, and it was obvious that Noah couldn't take his eyes off her. Equally obvious was that Amelia was aware of this and positively basked in the warmth of that affection.

He was elegant and the cloth of his clothes was of the very best. His eyes were indeed large and brown as Amelia had described him and he did not have any Jewish features.

It was almost as if Amelia had read her thoughts, because she said, "Kamila wondered about your name, Noah."

"You mean, about its being Jewish? This has always been a source of great embarrassment to my brother and me."

"No! Please—" said Kamila.

"I don't mind telling you this, so please don't be upset, Miss Kamila. My Mother has always loved Hebrew names—of the old testament— and named my elder brother Amos and me Noah. We were at least grateful that she didn't name us Israel or Hosea or, heaven forbid, Ishbosheth! Why she couldn't have chosen names such as Mark or Luke I don't know."

They all laughed.

"I'm surprised that the priest christened you with those names. They usually refuse to christen children, if the names chosen are not Roman Catholic," said Mrs. Pasiak.

"You don't know my Mother! She's very persuasive. I'm sure that she could even convince the Pope. She certainly convinced the priest that as Christ was a Jew, we had no right to refuse names that were so reverent in the Jewish history. And as an example, she said, that without Noah, none of us, including the priest, would be here now. In the end she had the priest thinking like her, just as she had wanted him to! You wouldn't believe that even the dog is called Zebulum!" This time the whole room reverberated with laughter.

"She sounds as if she would make a very good ruler of our country," said Mr. Pasiak. "We could do with someone like that. Couldn't you somehow get her into the Seym?"

"She'd have to masquerade as a man, though," said Kamila, and then regretted having mentioned this.

"She'd have to cut off her hair and whereas she'd love to rule the Seym and the country, I'm sure she'd refuse to cut off her hair," said Noah.

"Why is that?" said Mr. Pasiak.

"Her hair reaches to her ankles. I suppose you've never noticed this, with it being woven around her head."

"She could keep her hat on--," said Mrs Pasiak.

"Not all the time..," said Kamila.

On the fourth day of her visit, a man arrived with a message for Kamila. It was Jordan.

"Mr. Benjamin asked me to deliver you a message, madam. Lisinski's wife Anna is very ill with pneumonia and Lisinski is beside himself with anxiety and grief. They've tried everything and just before I left they were thinking of calling the priest to give her the last rites. Mr. Benjamin asks you—no, he said, begs you to come."

"Thank you, Jordan. Of course I'll come and you can tell me the details on the way." There was no point in chastising the man that she was not called earlier. Most of the people on the estate were very independent and accepted their fate but here it was different. They all knew how she appreciated her special relationship with Lisinski and his family and didn't consider that they overstepped their position.

Amelia and Mrs Pasiak had been listening, and murmured their sadness at Kamila's sudden departure but all understood the necessity for it. Mrs. Pasiak organised for the horses to be rubbed down and fed and given water and for Jordan to go to the kitchen for refreshment. Meanwhile Kamila and Amelia ran upstairs and quickly started to take her clothes out of the wardrobe and drawers as a maid packed them into the trunk.

"Take me directly to the Lisinski cottage, please Jordan." It was already dark and when they arrived there shortly afterwards, they saw a light through the window. Somehow it seemed a welcome sight and to Kamila perhaps a hopeful one. Lisinski came out, looking drawn and haggard.

"Miss. Kamila!" He was all choked up and couldn't say any more.

"Benjamin sent Jordan for me. How is she?"

"Very bad. The priest left two hours ago."

Kamila entered the cottage and came to Anna. Her eyes were closed and her breathing was shallow. Her skin was flushed, hot and dry but her lips were blue. Kamila suddenly became aware of all their children in the background of the room, and when she looked towards them she saw a host of huge frightened eyes.

"First of all, she can't stay here. We must take her to the house. But how will you manage to look after the children, Lisinski?"

"My eldest, Catherine, is thirteen and very capable. She'll manage. Catherine come here."

The girl came forward and curtsied. "It will be easier to look after your mummy in the big house and you can come and see her. I'll arrange for meals to be sent for all of you." She turned to Jordan. "We must go and arrange all this. I'll send a cart over and you can then put her down flat for the journey. She

must have the absolute minimum of disturbance."
The men looked puzzled, "We usually use a door for lifting the injured," said Lisinski, "I could take this one off."

"No. That'll take too long. Make a sort of a hammock. Have you got two long poles?" Lisinski nodded, "Then wrap a sheet around them, with a space for her body in between the poles. The sheet should go round about four times. Transport her thus."

As Kamila and Jordan set off, Lisinski and Catherine made preparations to make the hammock.

Once home, she called Mary and Benjamin to come and see her. "I'm bringing Lisinski's wife here. I can give her better care in the house. Get a room prepared for her."

"Which room do you want her to have, Miss Kamila?" said Mary.

"The one next to mine. It's large and airy."

"When is she coming?" said Benjamin.

"One of the men has just gone over with a cart."

The room was prepared. Lamps and a fire were lit. She wrote a note to Dr Roger, begging him to come and sent Jordan with it.

Once the cart returned with Lisinski and his wife, they found it quite easy to take her upstairs. Doctor Roger had not yet arrived and Kamila worked by instinct, as she had no knowledge to guide her. When she touched her night attire, she found it soaking with perspiration. Mary was there to help her.

"Mary, we must take this off. Can you bring some of my nightgowns, towels and a face cloth and warm water? We'll wash her down." She started to take her wet nightgown off and noticed how thin Anna had become. In no time at all, Mary was in the room and two other maids. They lifted her up to a sitting position, took the nightgown off and noticed eight circular red marks on her back and two on the upper part of the chest wall. The outer rims of the circles were very red, and deep. "My God! What's that?"

"She must have had dry-cupping done, madam, quite recently by the angriness of them," said Mary.

"What an idiotic thing to do! I'll deal with them later!" She pursed her lips. "Hold her like that for a moment, whilst I wash this area." Gently she wet the back and dried it, and when they placed her down repeated this to the front, making sure that the sheet underneath was not wet. "Bring me more pillows. I think it'll be better if she's in a more sitting position.
They put a clean nightgown onto her, and continued washing the rest of her body.

With her body in a sitting position, she already looked better, but still her eyes were closed.

"Will you call Lisinski in, please?" When he had entered, she questioned him about those marks. "Did you do these?"

"Good heavens, no! It was the local midwife. She deals with all of us. I didn't want it doing but she said it was the only way of relieving the congestion from within. There was nothing else that could be done, except bleeding—."

"Bleeding!" Kamila almost shouted. "It's the most barbaric thing ever considered."

"I knew your views on that and didn't allow it."

"Has she had any drinks, or any food?" Kamila's voice was now more gentle.

"No. It came out again."

"Mary, bring some very sweet warm tea." And when it was bought, Kamila tested the heat by dropping a spot on her own arm, and being satisfied, she opened Anna's mouth and put a teaspoonful onto her tongue and waited. After a long while, they noticed that she swallowed it. The process took a long time but by the time Dr. Roger had arrived she had managed to drink the whole cup.

He examined her, just as he had examined Karol so many months ago, and then straightened up. "She has double pneumonia, and really, my dear there's very little that can be done." Kamila told him what she had done so far and he nodded with approval. As to the dry-cupping, his opinion was that it was useless, "—just putting the patient through more pain, and the person who did this has burned the poor girl. But that's least of her troubles. It's important to give her lots of liquid, because she's burnt off such a lot with the fever. Keep wiping her body and face with a moist cloth. This should bring the temperature down somewhat. If she shivers, don't pile things on her. Shivering is a method that the body is trying to cool down."

"I understand. Are there no medicines she could have?" Asked Kamila.

"She can't have things like belladonna or laudanum as her breathing is already very suppressed. Have you got any oil of Eucalyptus?"

Kamila shook her head, "I don't think so. Have we?" She turned to Mary who shook her head. "What about herbs?"

"There, I think your Mother would know more. Have you looked at her notes and the collection of herbs?"

"No. I haven't had time—."

"Let me think, now." He stroked his chin for a while. "Common Horsetail is effective, as drinks, and Hearts Tongue Fern, again as drinks. Do you know how they look?"

"No. I don't know them at all. And I'm sure there are none of these in Mother's collection."

"What about thyme? Wild thyme? That probably is the best."

"Yes! I not only have this dried but we have lots in the kitchen garden. I don't know if it is *wild* thyme, though."

"If it's the garden thyme it's even better. It's more potent. Look at your Mother's notes. But it is perfectly safe to drink, inhale and even have it rubbed into the skin. Otherwise what you've started doing is wise. Keep her upright, propped up so she doesn't slide down or fall sideways. I have known patients who died in such falls. Make sure her head and neck are upright and not lolling to the side."

"We will. There will be someone with her all the time."

"I'll come again tomorrow, my dear, as obviously you value her well."

Kamila thanked him and walked with him down the stairs and to the front door. There he stopped, and touched her cheek, "Even so, be prepared that she may not live. She is very gravely ill."

"In that case, I'll add prayers to all the other things."

"You do that, my dear. See you tomorrow."

Kamila went straight away to the bags of dried herbs and found thyme. She rubbed it and sniffed at it and thought it would be better to get some of the fresh from the garden. She decided to get it herself. She took a lamp with her and, having found it, again pinched some with her fingers and sniffed it. Yes, this was stronger.

She went to the kitchen, and the cook took the herbs from her, seeing that Kamila was looking for something. "Let me do this, madam. What do you want doing with these?"

"I want to have them ground up. But first wash them. Then grind them as fine as possible. Then divide them into two portions. One will be to make a drink, just like tea, but firstly the thyme is to be soaked in boiled water for about half an hour. The other half I'll have in a jug of boiling water, upstairs so that we can rub it into Anna."

"We'll do that. I'll get the girl to bring it up to you. Can I make you something to eat and drink, madam? You haven't had anything since you arrived."

"So I haven't. I forgot. Perhaps, in a while. First, I'd like to give this thyme to Anna."

"Forgive me being so bold, madam, but while we are preparing this, and it will be a while, you could have something yourself. Mary's just been down and said that Anna is comfortable."

"Alright, I'll sit here."

"No, madam. A lady like you shouldn't be seen eating in the kitchen. You go to your room and we'll bring it to you as quick as lightening." Daisy had just come into the kitchen and the Cook looked at her pleadingly.

"Come now," Daisy spread her arms to guide her out of the kitchen.

"So I have two of you against me now! Alright, Cook, thank you."

She went to the sitting room, and sat in an armchair and almost immediately closed her eyes. She must have dropped off because she didn't hear the tray being brought in and only jerked herself into consciousness when Daisy touched her. Surprisingly she felt refreshed even after such a short sleep.

The light meal and tea also helped. She hadn't realised that she was hungry.

A knock on the door brought Benjamin, "A message from the Cook, madam. The jug has been taken upstairs."

"Oh! Good. Thank you."

She quickly made her way to Anna's room. Anna was sitting in the same position as she had placed her. She noticed a cup of steaming concoction on the table beside her. She tasted a spot from her hand—it was very hot—and wrinkled her nose. Despite having honey in it still tasted bitter. Mary was wiping Anna's face and neck with a moist facecloth.

"Let's use this thyme, instead of plain water, Mary."

They lifted her forward again and repeated what they had done before and when dry replaced the nightgown. The room was filled with the fragrance of thyme. This was reminiscent of when she was nursing Karol and using rosemary, and Kamila decided to try this on Anna a little later.

When the infusion had cooled a little and she was giving it to Anna, a teaspoonful at a time, they noticed a small grimace on Anna's face.

"She doesn't like it," said Mary.

"No. But it's good to see that. Where's Lisinski?"

"I've told him to go home. He was getting under my feet," said Mary.

"I'll go and get some rosemary and we can rub that into her chest as well." And again she chose the fresh rosemary.

On her return journey she suggested that they would have to take turns in staying with the patient, but Mary said, "I've already arranged that, madam. There will be two of us at any one time. You look all in, why don't you go to bed? I'll call you if we need you or if anything happens. Go on, madam."

As if realising only now, how tired she was, she stifled a yawn. "Alright, thank you Mary. I think I will. But call me."

"Yes I will. Goodnight madam."

"Goodnight, Mary."

CHAPTER 11

She quickly jumped out of bed and throwing a shawl over her shoulders ran to Anna's room. Mary was still there and with another maid they were giving her another drink.

"How is she?" and then "Good morning." She nodded to the two women.

"Good morning, madam. She's no worse. This is the fourth drink she's having since you last saw her. Oh! Lisinski came just as you had gone to bed, and stayed with her about an hour. He would have stayed longer but I sent him packing."

"How many times have you wiped her over?"

"Three times, and we did it with the thyme. Oh! And we had to change the sheets. She had a little accident."

Kamila touched Anna's neck and then the chest wall, a little lower. "I'm not sure, but she doesn't seem as hot as yesterday."

"Yes, we thought that too, didn't we, Basia?" She turned to the other maid, who nodded.

"I'll get dressed and then you can go and have a rest yourselves. You must be tired."

"Don't worry about us. You go and get dressed and have your breakfast, madam. Two other girls will come to take over. I'll show them what to do. They'll be here at eight."

"Alright. But I won't be long."

"I'm sorry to interrupt your breakfast, madam, but I have a message from Mr. Raphael," Benjamin said.

"Goodness, I had completely forgotten him! Is there a problem?"

"I don't know. He just wondered if he could see you for a while?"

"Do you think it's safe for him to come down?"

"Yes, I think so. All the staff are in different parts of the house, and I'll send them there if they are not, during the time he's here, if you wish to see him, madam."

"I suppose I had better see what he wants."

He went away and shortly afterwards, Raphael was ushered into the room.

"Good morning Miss Kamila."

"Good morning. Have you had breakfast? Or would you like some?"

"Thank you. I have my breakfast very early, although I wish I didn't today, so that I could have been in your company."

"Are you bored then?"

"Not really, but lonesome—for you!"

Kamila flushed with some annoyance. She wasn't used to such familiarity. "I have told you before, Mr. Raphael, that you do not know me, and therefore you cannot feel such—" She was going to say "emotion" but decided that it would be interpreted differently, so said coolly, "a feeling."

"Maybe we haven't known each other for a chronologically long time, but since you were Karol's wife, and Karol and I were very close friends, I do feel an affinity—no, even a closeness, if I may be so bold as to say—between us."

"Then I'm sorry for you," she said aloofly. "You asked for shelter. You have been given it. But this is wasting time, and I have many things to do, what is it you really wanted?"

"I haven't seen you for over a week. Theresa said you were away. You didn't even tell me that you were going away and now you are so busy. What's happening?"

"Mr. Raphael, I wasn't aware that I had to report everything or anything to you! Yes, I was away in Krakow. And yes, I am busy. My overseer's wife is very ill and we are nursing her here in the house."

"Here? In the house?"

"Yes, what's wrong with that? You seem shocked."

"I am shocked. You mean to say you transferred her from her—from her—."

"Cottage. Yes!"

"Why couldn't she have stayed in her cottage?"

"Because it was overcrowded and she could get better care here."

"Miss Kamila! People with our breeding—a person with your breeding—doesn't have peasants living in and certainly not nursing them like—."

"Human beings?" Kamila finished angrily. "May be *you* wouldn't. But, if you say that my husband and you were such close friends, you certainly do not know our family. Because Karol would have done just that, so would have my aunt and most certainly my parents. I value my overseer and his family very much. But apart from all that, I don't think that any of this is any of your business." Kamila was standing by now and her cheeks were bright red with anger, her eyes flashing as she walked off, leaving him in the room.

And she didn't hear his apology, "You're quite right. Forgive me."

She walked upstairs seething. The cheek of the man! He really was impossible. How presumptuous! How was it that Karol and her aunt thought so much about him? She couldn't see. She wished he would leave…but she couldn't turf him out…no, not for Karol's sake, she couldn't.

When she reached Anna's room, all her attention was on Anna. The maids said that they were about to rub her down again and Kamila said that she would like to do this, to see if she could detect any change. The maids positioned Anna, in a way that Kamila had instructed them. The nightgown was removed. Kamila massaged the back until the solution of thyme and rosemary sank into the skin, taking great care with burnt areas. Any moist areas were wiped off. The same procedure was applied to the front and a clean nightgown was put onto her.

By the time Dr Roger arrived she had had another drink and was reclining on the pillows. He examined her carefully, and turned to Kamila, "Her lungs are no different, but, although her temperature is still high, it is slightly lower than last night and her respiratory rate—her breathing—is better. But don't raise your hopes too high. How many drinks has she had?"

"About six cups, I think."

"Well, increase these to twelve."

Kamila nodded. "What about some food? Is there anything …"

"You have to be careful, because she's not fully conscious yet, and she may inhale anything solid. You could try fresh apple mashed into a pulp, and some rice, very well cooked. But do be careful how she's fed."

"We will be careful. In fact, I'll give her these more solid foods myself. When I put the tea on the tongue she did swallow it after a while," said Kamila. Dr. Roger nodded. .

Kamila sent a request to the kitchen for the mashed apple.

Meanwhile, Lisinski arrived to see Anna. Kamila greeted him, and when she told him what Dr Roger had said, the tension left his face and he buried Anna's hand in his face.

The apple mash arrived. Kamila placed a teaspoonful onto Anna's tongue and waited. Nothing happened for a while, so Kamila stroked her neck as if she were feeding an ill bird, and whispered encouraging words, and eventually that spoonful was swallowed.

A sigh of relief was heard from all in the room. Kamila continued feeding Anna until the whole cup was emptied and with relief she thanked God for helping her.

"I'll leave you with her now, Lisinski. Talk to her. I think it'll be good if you talked about the children and things that she's interested in." She turned to the maids, "I'm just going into the garden for a bit of fresh air, if you should want me."

Thor ran to greet her and she bent down to hug him. It was so good to feel the warmth of his body and his obvious affection for her. When she let him go he barked and ran around her with delight so that at last she laughed with him. She walked in the gardens for quite some time, playing with Thor, until her self-composure was regained, after the clash with Raphael.

In the afternoon she went to the study with the letters that had arrived during her absence. On looking through them she found a letter with just "Miss Kamila" written on the envelope in an unfamiliar hand. She slid open the envelope and unfolded the paper.

"Dear Miss Kamila,

How can I ask you to forgive me? How right you were to be so angry with me! How I deserved it!

I've been highhanded and pompous and arrogant. I have been so out of touch with real, kind, gentle people for so long, that I had forgotten that they existed.

I really feel so close to you and your family that I can only offer this as possible justification for my inexcusable behaviour. I therefore beg your forgiveness—and I do so, on my knees. And I ask you humbly if you could find it in your heart, to let me be in your company for some part of your day, whenever you can spare the time.

Yours very truly,

Raphael."

Kamila's first instinct and desire was to squash the letter and throw it into the fire. Instead she folded it and put it in the envelope and placed it on the shelf in her writing desk, and started to deal with her other correspondence.

On the morning of the third day Anna opened her eyes and looked into the brown eyes rimmed with dark eyelashes and a halo of gold hair, of a young girl bending over her and thought she was looking at an angel.

"Am I in heaven?" she asked weakly.

The girl laughed lightly, "Not quite! But near enough! You're in the big house." She then called to Mary to come, who came running from the corridor.

"Oh! You've come to! Miss Kamila will be pleased. I'm Mary and this is Basia. I'll just go and tell Miss Kamila."

Kamila almost ran to the room. "Hello, Anna. I'm glad you're with us at last. How do you feel?"

"Very well, thank you Miss Kamila," she said slowly.

Kamila laughed gently, "I doubt if it's as well as that."

"What am I doing here?"

"It was easier to nurse you here, so we brought you here. Your husband and the children have been to see you every day. Now, would like something to eat? Do you fancy anything?"

Anna shook her head. "I'm not hungry."

"Mm, but we've got to feed you up. Do you think you could eat some scrambled egg?"

"Yes, thank you."

"Mary, could you arrange that with the Cook please?"

Kamila offered to feed her but she said she'd manage on her own and Basia held the plate for her. When it came to the tea, Kamila held the cup as Anna's hand trembled a little with the exertion.

The day after Anna left a request came once again from Raphael to see Kamila. Could he have tea with her? Kamila sighed in desperation, but agreed. She had asked for two cups "just in case someone came" and once it was brought in she settled down to it. Benjamin negotiated Raphael's journey to the sitting room.

"I'm so glad to be in your company again. Thank you for letting me come down." He kissed her hand.

"That sounds as if, indeed, I'm keeping you a prisoner in a tower," said Kamila coolly, "Whereas the choice is yours, if you want everyone to see you. Or has the danger passed?"

"No, the danger will remain for as long as I am alive. Are you afraid for me?"

"It's difficult for me to answer that. I don't know the circumstances," she raised her hand when he was about to explain, "nor do I want to. I think it is better that way. You said so yourself when you first came. But I do wonder—shouldn't you let your wife and family know that you are alive, and safe? They must be very worried about you."

"My family consist of my parents and one younger brother. As to a wife, alas, I have none."

"I'm sorry. When did you lose her? Forgive me, I should not ask this. I should know that it may still be painful."

He laughed. "It isn't painful, for I've never had one!"

"Haven't you ever wanted to get married then?"

"Oh, I have. I've even been engaged." It was obvious from the expression in Kamila's eyes that she would have wanted to enquire much more, but forced herself to remain silent. She had frequently been told that she was too inquisitive. So he continued, "We were engaged for two years. Her name was Eleonora. She kept asking me to fix a date for the wedding but it was always inconvenient for me. I always had something more important to do months ahead, some interesting meeting to go to or to arrange. Eventually, after two years she became angry and gave me an ultimatum."

"Oh, dear!" Kamila suppressed a smile, imagining the scene.

"You may laugh! But she called me some terrible names. I was really quite hurt. You see she was twenty by then, and felt that she should have been married by that age, with at least two children."

"What did she call you then?"

"The worst was that I never was and never will be ready for marriage as I was always postponing the date. She called me Raphael the Unready. You know, how they named mediaeval kings, Ethelred the Unready."

"I'm surprised you've even heard of Ethelred the Unready. I bet you don't know another thing about him."

"Well, you are quite wrong. Did you know that he spent his wedding night in bed with his wife *and his mother-in-law*?"

Kamila burst out laughing. "I don't believe you for a second."

"You see—you wound me, too. What Eleonora said really pierced me to the core and still hurts even after twenty years." His expression suggested that he had swallowed something indigestible.

Kamila was still laughing. "She must have had a great sense of humour."

"I don't agree. She didn't mean to be funny. She was being extremely sarcastic and intended to wound me and succeed she did."

"Wouldn't you think that she was right to break it off? Otherwise you'd be engaged to each other when she was all wrinkled and grey, and you had hair sprouting from your ears and nose, but none on your head apart from a long flowing beard."

"I can see that you are on her side."

"What about the last twenty years? No long engagements?"

"You are laughing at me so I won't tell you." He picked up his plate and loaded it with canapés and started to eat.

There was a knock on the door. Raphael sprang up and looked wildly around, but as the door was opening they heard Benjamin say, "It's only me, madam." And when in the room he closed the door, and turned to Raphael, "I think we had better go to the tower, sir." He looked sideways towards the door.

Raphael thanked Kamila again and left, escorted by Benjamin almost like a prisoner, thought Kamila, and felt sorry for him.

Now that Anna was so much better Lisinski and Kamila went back to their routine and were more busy, preparing for winter, which was predicted to be hard.

Anna's illness forged a closer bond between the staff and Kamila. It became obvious that the house staff were more faithful to their mistress than before and Raphael judged that they would not divulge his presence in the house to anyone outside for fear of harming their mistress in any way. But outside, he would not venture.

It was at one of these evenings that quite naturally the conversation turned to his favourite topic, his love of Poland, and how this had affected all their lives. The table had been cleared.

"You see Miss Kamila the problem that really arose in our country, was when they introduced the *liberum veto* into the Seym. That was the worst thing, because the magnates, the most powerful and the most wealthy were virtually spitting in the face of whoever ruled the country, simply by sending their minor staff to the sitting of the Seym, and simply vetoing whatever was proposed."

"I thought the problem was that they allowed the king or queen to be chosen from anywhere, even from other countries, rather than from our own aristocracy."

"Well, that too had problems because, the magnates would or could vote for whoever would pay them more, or who would give them something else in exchange, like huge acres of land."

"That, together with the veto meant, in that case that the king was only a puppet," said Kamila.

"Exactly! But we have had some excellent sovereigns as well. So the system of election was a good way, in a way, and this would have worked magnificently, had it not been for human greed. In fact the system of election was even better than the hereditary monarchs who believed that they ruled by divine right like the kings of England and France." He fell silent for a moment. "We were once such a huge country, so powerful and now look at us! Just a tiny Kingdom under the Russian boot! Such a pretentious name for such a small piece of land! Just a strip barely 250 miles wide from River Bug to just past the River Warta! Is it any wonder that there are always people willing to plot some uprising or other? I've always thought that we were like a volcano, ready to erupt. That's why so many of our people, good people, who loved our precious country have died for it. You only have to look at your family—Karol, and your parents banished to the wastes of Siberia."

"Not only they. Perhaps you don't know this, but my brothers died for that cause too. Adam, he was only eighteen, my age—he was hung from the citadel. Michael was even younger, seventeen, and he was shot. The crowd caused a commotion so as to give him a chance to run away but the soldiers foresaw this. A man jumped out in front of him to protect him. They shot him too."

"I didn't know of this. So your parents had only you left?"

"Yes. It was a terrible time for us all. Probably worse for my parents, for I was away at school…."

"When did this happen?"

"Two years ago. 1848, although, now, it seems such a long time ago."

"Ah! I remember…."

"As to Karol, you wouldn't believe it, he said just before he died that he wouldn't have changed anything that had happened, meaning his being sent to Siberia. He tried to make me understand that that love for the country was so great, that it was worth dying for it." She looked at him with huge, accusing eyes, as if he had said the same words. "And now my parents have gone the same way and I shall never see them again. I've tried so hard to find where they are so that I can write to them, send them parcels, have letters from them. I've lost count how many people and organisations I've written to. Nobody seems to know. Or maybe they do know and just don't want to tell me. I don't understand why it's not possible to get any information."

"Ah! Those who know are not allowed to say. You see, political prisoners are not allowed any privileges of contact with the outside world."

"I didn't know that. No one told me that. I think that it's a form of cruelty—mental torture—for them and for their families."

"Of course it is. Kamila, my dear—you don't mind my calling you that? You are so very young, it's difficult for you to understand. But it's in our blood, this binding love for our country. It's in you too. Perhaps you don't even know it yet." Seeing the unhappiness in her eyes, he took her hands in his and held them tenderly. "That's why Eleonora was so wild with me. Do you know, I had a globe atlas standing on my desk, the one that you could swivel around, and she picked it up and hurled it at me? And screamed, 'You love the world so much, you marry it!' I didn't know that the woman had such strength! Imagine what she would have used when she was mad at me, once we were married? I think I escaped with my life there."

Kamila started to laugh. He kissed her hands, "That's better. I don't like my Kamila to be upset." He continued to hold her hands, now in one hand, and with the other he stroked her cheeks.

Kamila gazed at him in wonder. Why! He was so kind! She surveyed his face as if she was seeing it for the first time. Why hadn't she noticed those clear blue eyes that had previously laughed at her and now were looking at her with such tenderness, and a beautiful straight nose? And he could be so funny. Why had she disliked him so much? He was really quite charming. No wonder that Karol and her aunt liked him so much.

His face was very close to hers and she smelt the tobacco on his moustache. He brushed his lips over her forehead, and then her nose. The sensation of his touch left her skin tingling with pleasure. She quickly withdrew. She was aware that her face was flushed and her heart beating fast.

"You mustn't!"

"Why not? Why can't I show you—."

"It's not right!"

"Who says so?"

"The society!" she said.

He looked around the room, and she could see that he was laughing at her again." I can't see anyone else here but you and me. Oh! I forgot to look here!" He lifted the heavy tablecloth and looked under the table, "Society! Are you there? No answer. You see, no one here either."

"In that case, I say so! Goodness! Look at the time! I'm going to say good night Mr. Raphael."

"In that case, good night to you too, Miss Kamila. Sleep well. Please dream of me." He gave an exaggerated bow and laughed lightly.

But it was a long time before Kamila could get off to sleep. For one, her heart would not quieten. For another, her thoughts disturbed peace and tranquillity that she liked.

She woke early, dressed and long before breakfast set out with Thor for a long walk. The sun hadn't risen yet but already there was a glow in the east. There was low mist on the ground giving an eerie feel to the land. Although the slight breeze was chilly, the day promised to be warm and at the pace that she was walking she felt only the exhilaration. Thor ran forward and whenever he was out of sight, Kamila called him and he returned and always touched her leg or her hand to reassure her that he was protecting her.

She bent down and cupped her hands around his face, "That's a good boy. Stay with me. Don't go too far." And he didn't.

She watched the sun awaken and stretch its arms across the eastern sky, sending rays of orange and pink and red across the ultramarine background. Then the dark blue became a cool pale blue and the warm colours suffused the entire vault of the sky. They walked for another hour before returning home for breakfast.

She changed her clothes as the lower part of her skirt was damp and she had almost finished her breakfast, when Benjamin came to say that Lisinski would like a word with her.

"Ask him to come here, and could I have another cup please?"
Lisinski came in and stood by the table, "Good morning, Miss. Kamila. I'm sorry to interrupt your breakfast, but we've had another fire."

"Sit down, Lisinski. Benjamin is bringing another cup. Ah, here it is. Have a cup of coffee."

"Oh, I couldn't Miss. Kamila—."

"Don't be silly. Look, I'll ask Benjamin to sit down. Will that make it alright? Benjamin—."

"I'm sorry, madam. Thank you all the same. But my breakfast is waiting for me," said Benjamin.

Kamila poured out the coffee for Lisinski, and once Benjamin had left, Kamila indicated the chair but he still shook his head, "My clothes may have some mud on them and the maids will curse me for that." He smiled and then his expression became serious. "I think, and the men who put the fire out, think the same, that this time it was started deliberately. No one saw him distinctly, because it was very misty, but from the outline of the body, we think it's Greczko again. He was seen running away."

"Oh, that horrid man! Was there much damage done?"

"Fortunately very little, because one of the men had a toothache which kept him awake so he decided he might as well start work early. Part of the roof and a portion of the wall were damaged. So he and another man put the fire out quite quickly."

"Will it be possible to repair it fairly promptly?"

"Yes, of course. The men have already started to do so. It should be finished by this evening or at the very latest, tomorrow."

"And how is that man's toothache?"

"It seems that putting the fire out, cured it!" Lisinski grinned widely. "But seriously, Miss Kamila, what are we to do with this Greczko? He's obviously got it in for you. He is a danger to you."

"Yes, he is. But unless he is caught red handed, we can't do anything. And we can't take the law unto our own hands."

"Hm, pity! I'll find out where he's working."

"You still won't be able to do anything about it. I'd better go and see this barn then."

"There's no need really, Miss Kamila. The hay hadn't caught fire and the repair is under way. Why I was so concerned is that on no account are you to go out on you own. Not even walking in the night like you did this morning!"

"Ah! I've been spied on, have I? I thought the whole house was asleep."

"They all care for you. You are their precious egg, if I may say so?"

"You want me to ask Benjamin to accompany me for my walks?" She smiled mischievously.

"Or Fred." This time he laughed. Fred was the groom who only talked to the horses.

"Heaven forbid! I'll stay in the house."

Kamila did go with Lisinski to inspect the barn. It was a fair distance and riding side saddle wasn't the easiest. By now most of the staff knew that she had

had some breeches made, but each time she wanted to wear them, Mary appeared and folded her arms across her ample chest and her lips became a straight line of disapproval.

The roof of the barn was damaged where the fire had travelled upwards from the wall, and it was obvious that the arsonist tried to set the door on fire, but for some reason, the door didn't catch fire but the doorpost did, and the adjacent wall. Ever since the previous barn fire, Lisinski had requested that all the barns were securely locked. He also, now, suspected that the other fire had been started deliberately.

The men were doing a good job, Kamila saw. She asked to see the man who saved the barn. Lisinski called him over, and said that his name was Jacek.

"Mr. Lisinski told me that it was you who saved the barn. I wanted to thank you, Jacek"

"'T was nothing. Oi couldn't sleep."

"Because of your toothache?"

"Yes, ma'am."

"And how is it now?"

"It's gone, ma'am." He gave a grin exposing a front gap of three missing teeth. "It's the smoke, you see ma'am."

"You mean it removes the pain?"

"Oh, aye, it does do that." This time it was Kamila who laughed, and said, "Well, if you have a problem again, you tell Mr. Lisinski."

"Yes, thank you, ma'am."

CHAPTER 12

Lisinski took her to other parts of estate that needed her attention and eventually they returned when it was already twilight, with Lisinski bringing her right to the stables, and only then leaving her.

She washed and changed her clothes and went down to dinner. Almost instantly, Raphael joined her.

"You came in late today!" he said.

"If you had wanted to eat early, you could have asked Theresa or Benjamin," she said.

"And miss seeing you? Not for anything in the world! I'd rather be hungry for a week!"

"That's foolish talk."

"Foolish or not, it's true. So where were you all the day?" So she told him but omitted telling him about Greczko.

"And did you sleep well?"

"Yes, thank you," she said and hoped that he would not see that this was not the truth.

"And did you dream of me?"

"No. Now, would you like some more of these potatoes and perhaps some more of the meat?" She was glad that she could distract him with the food.

He asked if he could smoke, she nodded.

"I'm a great burden for you. I wish I could be of some help. I wish I could accompany you on your travels around the estate, but I dare not," he said seriously for a change.

"No, I don't think you had better venture out. There is a man called Greczko, who worked for my aunt whilst Karol was in Siberia and later when he was home." She told him what brought on his dismissal and how he had stopped her once and that he seems to bear a grudge towards her……" He's just the sort to inform the officials."

"He certainly does. But now it worries me your going about on your own. And those fires, you think that they were started deliberately?"

"Lisinski and the men do. With this last one, he was seen running away."

"Oh, how I wish I could get my hands on him!"

"Well you can't." She offered him a plateful of tiny cakes that the cook made especially for Kamila, "Do have some of these, they are really mouth watering." He stretched his hand to take one and suddenly dropped the cake and clutched his chest with both hands, his face white and contorted with pain.

Kamila jumped up, " What's the matter? What's happened?" She led him to the armchair and knelt before him. He groaned quietly. "Shall I call the doctor?"

He shook his head. He was so still for such a long time that she thought that he had died and touched his face and neck. Eventually he lifted his head and she saw that colour was returning to his face.

"I'll just ask for some more hot tea. Just rest. Put your head back and close your eyes." Once the tea was drunk, she said quietly, "Are you feeling better?" He nodded. "What happened, Raphael?"

"Don't worry my dear Kamila. I'm not going to die just yet. I've had this pain intermittently over the last twenty years. It happens when I do a certain movement with my arm. I goes just as suddenly. In the aftermath there is only the memory of it."

"Have you seen a doctor about it?"

"Yes."

"And?"

"There's nothing that can be done. It's because—there is a bullet lodged in my chest."

"A bullet! Whose bullet? Who shot you?"

"One of the Grand Duke Constantine's guards. I didn't ask his name."

"Now you are being flippant."

"What do you want me to be? Serious?"

"Yes. I'd like to know how you happened to get it."

"Then I'll be serious, but first can I have some more tea?" Raphael now looked his normal self.

"Can't the bullet be removed?" said Kamila.

"I was told that it cannot. It's somewhere near some vital part. It was either going to kill me if it moved nearer that part or work itself out of the body. It has done neither. Tell me, didn't Karol ever talk of the insurrection of 1830?"

"Is that when it happened?" He nodded. "No, never. Not to me. I wasn't even born then!"

"I'm sorry, Kamila. I keep forgetting how very young you are."

"Was Karol involved in it too?"

"Oh, yes. He certainly was."

"All I know of it, is what we learned at the Academy."

"Would you like me to tell you about it? It was the most exciting time for us."

"Us? Who is that?"

"All of us, who took part in the insurrection."

"I should very much like to hear about it."

"Let me bring you that atmosphere leading up to it. In the latter part of 1830 the patriots of Poland were determined to free our country from the oppressor. You see the July French Revolution had fired their enthusiasm and they passionately wanted to follow that example. The circle of conspirators grew like ripples in an ever widening circle. It had been brewing for a long time—five years at the very least. There was increasing discontent at the universities, I mean, due to constant interference from Russia, sacking of important heads of departments, and closure of these departments. Two of my friends, both sub-lieutenants, Wysocki and Zaliwski were the leaders of this conspiracy. And the outbreak was planned to take place at the end of February 1831." He chewed on his cigar.

"So what happened to bring it forward?"

"Tsar Nicholas, that despot, sent an edict commanding the Polish Army to be placed on a war-footing in readiness to march against France. This tipped the scales. It filled the men with such anger that it precipitated the insurrection. On the 29th of November at 6pm eighteen young men rushed out of the School of Ensigns with bayonets and forced themselves into the Belvedere Palace of the Grand Duke Constantine."

"To murder him?"

"No. To assassinate him."

"That's the same thing."

"No, Kamila it's not. Since 1815 The Congress of Vienna set up a constitutional Kingdom of Poland and Tsar Alexander I, appointed his degenerate brother, Constantine as commander in chief of Poland's armed forces, and with the powers of a viceroy."

"Wait a minute! Don't you mean Tsar Nicholas?"

"No. Can't you remember your history? Alexander, Constantine and Nicholas were brothers, born in that order. Alexander died in 1825, and then Nicholas became Tsar."

"I'm sorry to interrupt again, but shouldn't Constantine have been the next Tsar?"

"Yes, he should have, but in 1820 he made a morganatic marriage to a Polish countess, Joanna Grudzinska and two years later renounced all of his claims to the Russian throne. He consoled himself by most barbaric brutality to the Poles."

"Oh! I see. I really didn't know that."

"Under his direction there was espionage and slander carried out in secret amongst private families. People were thrown into dungeons and forgotten, or transported to St. Petersburg into the forts and never heard of again. There was great discontent and secret societies were formed…….Now where were we before you interrupted? Ah! Yes! We stormed the palace."

"Were you and Karol among these?"

"No. We were in the section which was to storm the Arsenal. You see it was all very well organised. I forgot to say that there was another group of us that attacked the Russian cavalry barracks in the Lazienki Park. Now where was I? Ah, yes. Anyway the Grand Duke was in bed—."

"At six o'clock in the evening?"

"Yes. Will you stop questioning every detail? And he had only time to throw a cloak over his shoulders to escape the vengeance of the conspirators, and was bundled unceremoniously into the coach and driven out of Warsaw."

"Without a struggle?"

"Oh, no! He was an experienced captain and had a considerable force of Russian bayonets in the place but so determined were the conspirators that after a sanguinary and obstinate fight, they won."

"That's unbelievable!"

"Nevertheless it's true. After we broke into the Arsenal, the Russian troops gave way in every direction, abandoning it. We distributed more than 50,000 muskets amongst people, as the insurrection became general. There were cries of `To arms! To arms!` and songs of victory. The black plumes of grenadiers were discarded, and workmen, armed with hoes, scythes, hayforks and even sticks filled the streets. The white eagle of Russia was thrown off of facades of monuments and buildings. The mood was of exhilaration and mad delirium and belief that there was no doubt but that we would attain victory."

Kamila watched his face with fascination. His face was in the shade and the lamp behind his head made his blond hair shine like a halo. His eyes were afire with excitement and passion and she was captivated by this. She knew that he was in the past and hundreds of miles away, seeing the hoards of crowds roaming the streets of Warsaw, drunk on the victory and glory they had achieved. He suddenly grabbed her hands with such ferocity that it almost hurt.

"How is your pain, now?" said Kamila.

"Gone. Completely gone. Oh! Kamila, my love, if you could have seen that sight! You would have been moved to tears with pride." Still holding her hands, the far away look returned to his eyes and he continued. "The Minister of Finance and other important personnel formed a National Council and chose General Chlopicki and proclaimed him as `Dictator.` He was a poor choice, totally unsuitable to the situation."

"Why?"

"He was cautious and wanted to negotiate, not to fight. He wanted reconciliation with Russia and the whole of Warsaw wanted to be free of it. After all that's why we fought, why so many were lost. But he was fearful of the Emperor's wrath. Can you imagine? It's a wonder nobody throttled him."

"Why, what did he do?"

"Firstly, how he dealt with Constantine! The Grand Duke had encamped some miles outside Warsaw, with some eight thousand troops, bewildered and terrified at the suddenness of the revolt. Chlopicki allowed Constantine to depart unharmed."

"You mean, you would have murdered him?"

"He should have been assassinated or imprisoned, at least. But it wasn't only that. Can you believe it? He was escorted with his whole court, his army and his political prisoners all the way, as if they had been welcome guests? Next, he refused to allow the revolt to spread throughout other Polish provinces despite that the people wanted to march onto the enemy. Such heroism had not been known in the history of man. The generosity of people, both rich and poor, was unbelievable, outstanding. The rich raised enormous armies at their own cost. Women donated their jewellery to the cause. The monks gave half of their rations."

"Couldn't the people have overturned his decisions?"

"It seems that as a Dictator he had the power to check the spread of the revolt. Perhaps he thought that the wrath of Tsar Nicholas would be so great that he would have destroyed the whole of the country. Who knows? His next move was to send two ministers to St. Petersburg to negotiate with Nicholas. But the Tsar was so enraged he refused to see them. The manifesto for negotiation was sent back to Warsaw and arrived mid January with Nicholas' reply, neatly written by his hand.

"`I am the King of Poland. I will rule her. With the first cannon fired by the Poles, I shall annihilate her.` This was read to the Diet by one of those ministers mentioned. There were other derogatory and insulting remarks written by Nicholas."

"How frightening this must have been! And how chilling!" She shivered.

"Yes, but instead of making the Assembly tremble, it gave them further impetus to fight. One member of the tribune struck the hilt of his sword and asked them all if they were going to tolerate these insults. At first there was a silence and then another shouted in a deep voice, `There is no Nicholas!` I think it was your father and Karol's father who tried to calm the Assembly, to plan a sensible strategy. But the uproar spread to the whole city. Chlopicki resigned in a rage because the Diet refused to accept his timid solutions. But regretfully his replacement was equally spineless." Raphael stopped when he saw Kamila suppress a yawn. "Have I bored you?"

"Oh, no! On the contrary, it's fascinating. I just think it must be late. Goodness! It's past two! The Grand Duke would have slept eight hours by now." He laughed and kissed her hand for good night.

Kamila slept well and dreamt of the Grand Duke Costantine sitting forlornly barefoot on a an overturned log, outside Warsaw, in his nightshirt and a night cap. And throughout the day, going about her duties that image remained with her. I must tell Raphael about this dream she thought and laughed to herself.

In the evening, after dinner, she told him of her dream and they laughed, visualising the scene.

"Last night you said that my Father and uncle took part in the insurrection. I didn't know that. Father never mentioned that."

"No. I didn't say that they had taken part in the insurrection. It was Karol who told me that they had been at the Assembly. Otherwise we wouldn't have known what happened there, would we?"

"Wasn't it reported in the papers?"

"I don't think so. Not directly then. I think perhaps because it was a dangerous time."

"Who was the replacement you were telling me about last night, when Chlopicki resigned?"

"Oh, that was Prince Michael Radziwill. You see, someone was required to head the army. Why to God they chose him, I really don't know."

"Wasn't he a patriot then?"

"Oh, yes, he was, very much so. But a leader needs to be much more that just that. A poet can be a patriot, but you wouldn't choose him to lead an army, would you?" Kamila shook her head. "Well, he was timid and indecisive."

"I can't understand why they chose such unsuitable men."

"None of us knew, or can explain it even now. The Tsar sent a huge army under the command of Field Marshall Diebitch. Our army was only a third of that, or even less, but unbelievably it was a victory for us, with 5,000 of our men dead and twice as many of the Russian soldiers and the elite of their officers."

"When was that fought?"

"It was towards the end of February 1831. Had Prince Radziwill followed this up by attacking the Russians once it was nightfall, they could have wiped out the enemy completely. But what did he do? He retreated the army beyond the river, and Diebitch retreated into the forests." He stroked his upper lip as if he was considering the position now. "After five months, Radziwill was considered incompetent and was replaced by Skrzynecki."

"I hope he was better!" Kamila said.

"No. He was slow and his decisions were poor. But despite that, our army was still victorious in many battles, but with tremendous loses. After the Battle of Ostrolenka—this was where I received the bullet, but the exhilaration was so great, we continued to fight—you see, we were winning. I felt nothing till evening

"This was our victory again, by the way. Diebitch retired to his camp to drink and a few days later he was dead, seemingly from cholera. And Skrzynecki returned to Warsaw. As he stepped into the carriage he repeated the words of Kosciuszko, `Finis Polonia.`" Raphael's voice broke as he said these last words. They sat in silence, contemplating the gravity of these words.

"The Tsar certainly intended to annihilate Poland," Kamila said sadly.

"And certainly would have done, had you killed his brother

"Definitely. They were unquestionably planning to exterminate us. Despite that the whole world knew how bravely we had fought, what sacrifices had been made, and yet no one came to help us. No one wanted to be involved. Austria was too timid and completely abandoned us. England didn't even lift a finger. France was just an egoistical spectator."

"I thought that these countries were our friends!"

"So did we."

"And in the end Nicholas won."

"Yes. He won, because whomever the Diet chose it was always someone who wanted to resort to diplomacy, rather than to action, and however many of the enemy were killed there were endless columns of soldiers to replace them. Just like ants, they were. By the 8th of September after fierce fighting the commander-in-chief reluctantly signed the capitulation and surrendered Warsaw to Russia."

"Don't look so despondent. You look almost as if this was your fault!"

"I do because I feel it so very deeply! You see, despite the terrible conditions—there were tremendous rains and the men had to wade through mud—there were so many dead bodies about, and cholera—they still had the fervour and unlimited energy to fight off the oppressors for good. But what did commanders want? Diplomacy!"

"Perhaps they were trying to save lives."

"Pah!" he said savagely, "Diplomacy can only work if both sides are of equal mind. It wouldn't work with a savage who was drunk on his imperial power and had only one aim—to wipe us out to the last man. Oh, Kamila, if we only had had someone who was not only brave, for we have a lot of brave men, but who had the true spirit of our country. A good leader was needed, someone who would have overpowered the Russians, and once that was achieved, someone who could have led our country to be great again."

He talked passionately at great length of how the country should be run, and all the time he was holding her hands, playing with her fingers and looking far into the future.

"Had you any ambitions to be that someone?" She asked gently.

"I? Oh, no. You remember what Eleonora called me?"

"Raphael the Unready!" She laughed.

"Yes. Well, to some extent she was right, in that I've always been distracted by more exciting things and therefore, have never been one to complete things. To tell you the truth, my dear, I have never faced up to this fact until this very moment. Perhaps there is something in you Kamila that has made me tell you this. What is it?" He was looking at her earnestly.

"Being truthful? You know, *To thine own self be true*…My Father liked to quote that. Perhaps you are overwhelmed by a passion for an ideology?"

"With that you are quite right. My passion for our country is boundless, my love for this soil is limitless, for to me, Poland is my mistress, my mother, my wife and for Poland I'd willingly lay my life."

"Please, Raphael! Don't you say that as well! I couldn't bear it when Karol said the same words…" She couldn't finish that these were practically the last words that he spoke. Even so Kamila was fascinated by such eloquence for their country. So, when he brought his face close to hers and kissed her, she didn't resist. Although she was reluctant to part from him, she pushed him gently away.

"You didn't tell me about the bullet."

"So I didn't. By the evening I felt hot and ill. They took me to the hospital. The doctor couldn't get it out, and he was a very experienced army doctor. Whatever he gave me, helped, for not long afterwards I was able to go back into battle."

"So passionate you were about fighting—."

"You must understand that, Kamila. I couldn't abstain. So many of our men died."

"I think I should retire now. I plan to go to Luck tomorrow. Is there anything you would like me to get you?"

He was again laughing at her. "You could get me some of these cigars. I'll write the name down. Here." He handed her the piece of paper.

"Won't they think it strange that I'm buying cigars?"

"No. Why should they? They could be for your husband."

"Ah! But they know what happened to my husband. Could anyone work out from the brand that they would be for you? That's what I'm frightened of."

"I'm touched by your concern, my dear Kamila. Supposing that you said it was your friend—what was her name? Ah, yes. Amelia. That she asked you to get some for her father's birthday?"

"I'm not very good at telling lies, but that's a good idea. Well, good night, then."

"Good night, my dear." He laughed gently, seeing how she had distanced herself. "You are afraid of me, aren't you?" He held out his hands to her, but she didn't come near.

"No, I'm not. Should I be, Raphael the Unready?"

"Don't you dare call me that as well!" But she only laughed as she left the room.

Mary made it known that Kamila was not to go to the city on her own, so it was agreed that she should accompany her mistress, and Jordan drove them there. It had rained in the night but the day was dry and rather windy. Kamila loved the wind. She frequently talked to the wind when she was a child and she felt like doing that now but kept her peace. She didn't want Mary to know her thoughts….

Kamila looked out of the window of the carriage, "Look Mary how beautiful this countryside is! And soon we'll see the castle. There it is! Now we'll soon be in the centre, so here's some money and you go and have a look around, buy something for yourself and for Lucy if you like, and we'll meet outside the coffee house—or inside, if it's raining although I don't think it will. In about two hours."

"I'm not leaving you alone to walk in the strange town. It isn't right—."

"Now, Mary, we won't have any of that again. Anyway, this isn't a town, it's a city and it isn't strange to me. I've been here many times and I love it. There is a lovely cathedral of the Holy Trinity and St. Peter and St. Paul. You should go and see it."

"Cor! What a mouthful!"

"Yes, it is a bit. I shall go in there once I've purchased my things. So we'll meet in about two hours, alright?"

"I'm not sure—."

"Go on!" Kamila gave her a gentle push.

Kamila brought a few pieces of material so that the seamstress could make her some new blouses and items from the haberdashery and then she went to the tobacconist. As she was leaving, she almost collided with a young man who had just entered the shop.

"I do beg your pardon, Miss. Why! Isn't it Miss Kamila? Whatever are you doing here? Have you taken up smoking?" He laughed. "You don't remember me, do you?"

"Of course I do! Mr. Woitek. No, I haven't taken up smoking. I've been buying some cigars for my friend's father's birthday." She was amazed how easily that lie came, and was glad that Raphael thought of this excuse. And she was glad that the tobacconist would have heard this too. He had been too discrete to ask….

"But what are you doing in Luck? Wait a minute, Miss Kamila, I'll just collect my usual and we can go out and talk."

His purchase completed, they left the shop. He offered her his elbow, and when she hesitated he took her hand and threaded it through his arm. "I've got to hold on to you, you're so fragile, you might be blown away!" He laughed. "Pity it's so windy, otherwise we could have sat by the river."

"And paddled?"

"Yes. I think we'll go to this coffee house here." Once they were settled at a table and the coffee was ordered, he leaned on the table and looked earnestly into her face, "Now tell me what you are doing in Luck and how are your parents? I've been meaning to go and visit them—."

"You are too late…." She poured out all that happened to them in the last two years, since she had last seen him.

"I didn't know. You see I left the country. I had to. You see I belonged to the same group as Adam and—."

"Shh! Don't say any more."

"You are just like your father, Miss Kamila. That's exactly what he said to me when I last saw you. In fact it was he who told me to go away."

"Where did you go to?"

"France."

"What did you do there?"

"I taught languages."

"I didn't know. You taught them Polish? I wouldn't have thought it would have been much use to them." He threw his head back and laughed. His brown eyes sparkled and his untidy thatch of hair shook with mirth.

"No, I wasn't teaching them Polish. I'm what's known as a polyglot. I used to think that that word sounded as if one had swallowed a huge stone. I've always found languages moderately easy to learn and am fluent in six other languages. So I can teach in many countries. It's very convenient."

Last time when she saw him she had assumed that he was much older. He had treated her like a child, perhaps that was why he had appeared so much older, almost as old as her Father, and now she was surprised to see that he was probably about twenty seven or eight. Or was it that it was she who had grown up much beyond her eighteen years?

"Are you here all alone? No chaperone to protect you from being carried away—by me for instance?"

"No. I do have a maid with me, but I've sent her to have a look around and do her own shopping. She'd have a fit if she saw me now with a strange young man. And there's Jordan who drove us here. Goodness! I promised I'd meet Mary, and it's past the time. I really must go."

"Let me escort you. Mary must be very protective towards you then."

"Yes. She is. As indeed, all of the staff are."

"Can I come and visit you?"

"Yes, of course. It has been really lovely seeing you and I never did thank you for all you did for my family."

"O—oh! I see someone marching towards us with a grim expression. It must surely be Mary." It was.

When she was beside them, Kamila smiled and said, "It's alright, Mary. Don't look so disapprovingly at this gentleman. He was, and is, a very good friend of my family. He even held me in his arms when I was young." Although Mary frowned at this, she still curtsied to him. Kamila extended her hand to him, "Once again thank you for all your kindness to my family. I am so glad that we met again and I shall look forward to when you come to the house."

"I shall look forward to that time too. Good bye, Miss Kamila," he kissed her hand, "and goodbye Mary."

She turned to Mary as they were going to the coffee house, "Why do you disapprove of all the young men I meet, Mary? Do you think that they will swallow me up?"

"No, Miss Kamila but I do think that they have, er, designs on you."

At this Kamila just laughed.

When Kamila gave the cigars to Raphael, it came out that she had to use the excuse he had made up when she met Woitek.

He immediately bristled and said, "So! You had a rendezvous with this Woitek! You want me to be even more jealous than I've been to date. Was your maid with you when you met him?"

"No. I had sent her away—."

"Sent her away! How could you do that?" His voice was raised. "Ladies don't meet—respectable ladies don't meet men on their own, without a chaperone."

"Raphael, in the first place I had to send Mary away so that I could get you those cigars. In the second place, I met Woitek at the tobacconist's. In the third place, Woitek is a family friend and I don't see what all this is to do with you anyway. Whom I see or don't see is none of your business." At first she was inclined to feel flattered that he was being peevish at her seeing another man, and then she felt irritated and finally angry at such possessiveness. She picked up a book, resolved to ignore him.

He remained silent. She stole a glance at him and was amused to see a petulant look on his face. After a very long silence, he cleared his throat and when she eventually looked up he was looking at her.

"I suppose you are right to say all those nasty things. I have no right. But you see Kamila I fell in love with you when I first met you, even though you were so frosty and disapproving of me. I felt jealous of Karol—there he was dying, with nothing to offer you and you were getting married to him…"

"Please don't exaggerate so. You didn't even know me then."

"Don't you believe in love at first sight?"

"No, I do not," Kamila said emphatically.

"Why can't you be nice to me?"

Kamila was on the point of replying but instead pursed her lips and fetched her correspondence. He took up the newspaper and started to read.

CHAPTER 13

She searched for an official type of letter but there wasn't one that might give her news of her parents, but she did find one that gave her joy.

My dear Kamila

It is such a long time since I had any news of you. How have you coped with all the tragedies and responsibilities? I have recently been ill—nothing serious—but have been told to convalesce for a couple of weeks and I would very much like to come and see you if I may. I had in mind to come on this Thursday, 12th September.

Yours affectionately

Madelaine Prust.

Oh, my goodness! That's only a couple of days away. Thank goodness she had opened the letters that evening. She immediately wrote back an answer to go with the first post in the morning.

Oh, dear, Raphael will be none too pleased that there will be a visitor again, she thought and smiled to herself.

She told the staff that Madame Prust was arriving this coming Thursday and to prepare the rooms for her on Kamila's side of the house. She hadn't intended to go out that day, thinking that everything on the estate had been dealt with recently, but no sooner had she finished her breakfast, Lisinski arrived.

"Miss Kamila, something's happened to one of the fields that I think you should come and see."

"What's happened? What did that Greczko do this time?"

"Oh, no, it was nothing to do with him. Part of the field has disappeared."

"Disappeared? How can that be?"

"You'd best come and see."

Kamila ran upstairs and dressed in her riding habit and by the time she came down her horse was waiting for her. When they arrived at the field, there were some workmen with long poles, poking areas around what could be described as a hole. From the edge of the field for about the area of an acre, the field had dropped about thirty feet. Kamila walked towards the edge but the men spread their arms to prevent her progress and Lisinski took her by the elbow.

"Don't go nearer Miss. It be real dangerous. One of the men did. You see that `un covered in mud?" said the man with the longest pole. "We had a real job to drag `im out."

"How could this have happened? There aren't any caves under there. I'm sure of it." Kamila searched in her mind if there had been any mention of such a thing happening on the estate before. She felt sure that there hadn't been any subsidence before. She had read everything in the estate diaries that Karol and his father had kept.

"Could it have been the rains?" asked Lisinski of one of the men.

"But we haven't had that much rain," said Kamila.

"No, we didn't, but I heard that way upstream they 'ad torrential rain. It could 'ave swelled the river from there. And if you was to go a bit further upstream, Miss, you'd see that the banks have overflowed. And the river level is higher."

"By how much?" said Lisinski.

"By a foot."

"What's your name?" Kamila said. He was obviously a much more knowledgeable man than she had expected.

"Jakub Sroka, Miss."

"You're from this estate?"

"Yes, Miss."

"I'm sorry that I didn't know. I've only recently taken over."

"Yes, I know, Miss."

"I think I had better get a geologist to come and look at this. Do you know whether any more land will drop?"

"I've a brother that works on an estate up further north and he has often said that they have this happening, sometimes every few days or weeks."

"Then we must have an expert opinion. Only I don't know if there is someone like that in Luck. Meanwhile, I think we should mark off the boundary of the hole with fencing. This will show us if any more subsidence occurs and also, hopefully, prevent someone falling into the cavity."

As Kamila left with Lisinski, she said, "You obviously need to stay here, so I'll go home and get Jordan to drive me to Luck to see where I can find a geologist, because from tomorrow for about a fortnight I probably shan't be able to do that. I have my mistress from the Academy coming to stay."

"I'm not letting you ride back alone. As to the hole, I don't think it'll matter if it's not dealt with straight away. Anyway, it may even be good idea to see if any more land falls away, as Jakub said that it may do. So enjoy your company, Miss Kamila, and don't worry about the estate. I will look after it."

"Yes, I know you will. Thank you."

Mary again insisted on accompanying Kamila to Luck. It was difficult to know where to find the information about geologists but Kamila thought the town hall would be the most likely place. As Kamila marched up the steps with Mary, she shivered, for near here was where her brothers were killed and since that time she had avoided being anywhere near this place.

She drew her coat collar closer around her neck and stepped nearer to the maid. Once they were inside they had to adjust to the dimness of the entrance hall. They looked around but there was no one about. There were statues carved in a Romanesque style spaced around the hall. The floor was of marble. The ceiling was high and beautifully carved friezes all around, gave the building a feeling of having stepped into a bygone age.

At the far end of the hall there was a door, which looked promising, but when they knocked and opened the door the room was empty but there were books set untidily on the table, chairs and some on the floor, and papers strewn on the desk, as if someone had left the room in a hurry.

They stepped out into the hall again and stood uncertain as to what to do.

"How about calling?" Mary said.

"I've thought of that too. I think it's the only thing we can do." She called out several times "Hello" and eventually they heard a door bang and a voice said,

"Can I help you?" With the echo, they couldn't tell where the voice was coming from, and looked from side to side. "Look upwards. I'm here." He waved his hands and then they saw him. He was standing on a balcony which surrounded the whole of the entrance hall which they hadn't noticed. "Wait a minute, I'll come down." He clattered down some stairs that they couldn't see and suddenly appeared before them. "Now, what can I do for you, madam?"

Kamila introduced herself. "I wonder if you could tell me if there is a geologist in Luck. We've had some land subsidence and I need some advice and perhaps a survey."

"Let me see," he stroked his beard, "We did use to have one. At least the one I knew. Now, what was his name? Come into the office and I'll try and find it. Mind you, it may take a while. I'm not that tidy." He led them to the room they had looked into before.

Kamila laughed, "I know. We've seen the inside of your office." He stopped in his tracks and looked over the top of his glasses. "We were looking for someone—for you—we didn't touch anything."

"Ah! So you won't be shocked." Once inside the room, he found a chair, removed huge tomes from it and offered it to Kamila and to Mary he said, "I can't get at the other chair but you can sit on those books there if you wish."

Mary turned to where he waved his hand, and said, "That's alright, sir, I'll stand."

"I don't usually see ladies, so I'm not really prepared. It's usually the husbands that come here. And they don't mind the mess." He rummaged through drawers and by the sound of the noise he was creating, it was obvious that he was making them even more untidy.

"My husband is dead."

"Oh, I'm sorry. I didn't mean to sound inquisitive. Oh, I've found it! I didn't think I would!" He sounded as pleased as a boy. "His name is Stokowski.

Now, he's getting on a bit. He's possibly around sixty. I don't know if he's still working but he might know of someone else, if he's not able to help you. That's his address. Will you go and see him now?"

"Thank you so much for all your help. No, I'll write to Mr. Stokowski."

"When you see him, say that I was asking after him. He's a very pleasant man."

"I will. Thank you. Goodbye."

"Goodbye, madam."

Kamila wrote to Mr. Stokowski straight away, and started to read through the diaries to see whether there was anything about this field that she had missed. But she was soon interrupted by a knock on the door and Benjamin saying, "Excuse me madam, the cook wants to know when you will be dining tonight, and Mr. Raphael was asking for you." He smiled, "I think he is hungry."

"Is it that time already? I'll go and change straight away, so tell the cook, in half an hour please."

In the dining room, Raphael was pacing the length of the room, with his hands behind his back, and with his long strides he came to her, took both her hands, and was about to kiss her, but she withdrew, afraid that one of the staff would walk in.

"Are you still angry with me, that I haven't seen you all day?"

"What should I be angry about? I've been busy."

"Too busy to eat? Never mind that I may be dying of hunger!"

"Wasn't it only yesterday that you were willing to forgo eating for a week?"

"Oh! Oh! Perhaps that was a bit rash." He said sheepishly. "But what were you doing all day?"

Kamila described to him what she had seen in the field and asked him if he knew anything about subsidence, but he didn't. He said that his estate had nothing exciting like that happening there. Kamila looked at him thoughtfully and decided that if five acres of his land dropped in front of him he wouldn't notice. His head would be in a political cloud and even minor changes and nuances in *that* field, he would see and care about, but not an agricultural field. Oh, no, nothing as practical as that.

"After dinner, I'll have to go and look through the estate diaries and papers to see if I can find anything about it."

"I can come and help with that."

"No, thank you. I really must read through all of this myself."

"What about doing that tomorrow?"

"I won't have time. Oh! I forgot to tell you! Madame Prust is coming tomorrow. She taught me at the Academy. I'm really looking forward to seeing her."

"I'm not though. How long will she be here?"

"A fortnight or more."

"A fortnight! And what will I do with myself all this time?"

"Well, if you like, you can see if there is anything in the library on subsidence."

"How terribly, maddeningly interesting!"

"I thought you would find it so."

Although Kamila poured over the books, diaries and documents until two in the morning, there had been no reference to any subsidence in any of the fields. The only thing of relevance to that field she found was that that field had been scrubland and that the family started to till it about fifty years ago.

Kamila awaited patiently for the arrival of Madelaine. Not only because she liked the lady herself, but also, that she would have news of her other friends from the Academy and in some measure this would bring back her old life. So when her carriage arrived she didn't wait for Benjamin to come and tell her, but had ran out to greet her friend, as she stepped down from the carriage.

"Oh, I'm so glad to see you! It seems like a thousand years since I've seen you."

"I know, Kamila—."

"I'm so sorry, I didn't ask you how you are?"

"I'm recovered now. I had a chest infection, quite badly, it seems."

"Then I'm so glad you wanted to come here to convalesce. You couldn't be in a more beautiful place."

Madame Prust laughed. "Even more beautiful than Zakopane?"

They embraced each other and then Madame Prust held Kamila at arms length and surveyed her, "Hmm! You are very much thinner! And that carefree look is gone. Oh! My dear." And again she hugged Kamila.

"Come inside. It's cold today," and she threaded her arm through Madame Prust's arm. Kamila introduced Benjamin to the latter, as he took her coat and bonnet, and they went into the sitting room. "Now, would you like some refreshment now or would you prefer to go and have a rest first?"

"Not a rest, but I would like to have a wash. We've been travelling for many hours.."

"Yes, of course. How thoughtless of me! I was so excited at your coming— I'll take you to your room, and when you come down we'll have some tea."

When Madame Prust came down she had changed into a brown skirt and a cream blouse and somehow these colours made her look younger, and not as drawn as when Kamila greeted her on her arrival.

"Tell me all that's happened, because all I know is from that one letter you wrote me, shortly after arriving here." They talked at great length until lunch was announced, and through the lunch. It seemed that without the strict ruling of the Academy, they found that they had a great empathy towards each other. They laughed at the same things, had similar outlooks that by now Madame Prust asked Kamila to call her by her first name.

"You know Madelaine, I've never had a sister but if I did, I would have wished her to be like you."

"That would have been extremely difficult to achieve, since I'm so much older than you." Madelaine said with a smile. "It would have been more appropriate if I had been a second mother or an aunt!"

"Maybe, but you don't look that age and certainly don't behave like a stuffy aunt. That reminds me, there was a woman, called Zofia. I must tell you about her…"

Kamila showed her where the library was and various rooms downstairs and took her outside into the grounds, well wrapped up as it was still chilly. Although it was only the second week in September the first flurries of snow started to fall, great big fluffy snowflakes as they were walking through the gardens. They looked up at the slate grey sky and how the snowflakes circled round above their heads.

"Isn't it lovely? I adore it when the flakes are so chubby, don't you?" Kamila put out her hands to catch them. "Perhaps we should be getting back, otherwise Mary or Benjamin will come out for us. If you like we can go riding tomorrow. Do you like riding?"

"The only riding I like is in a carriage that has four wheels, but I don't suppose you mean that?"

"No." Kamila laughed. "Can you ride a horse?"

"Mmm. If you had said, have I ridden a horse, my answer would have been `yes`. I didn't fall off it, but I'm not very confident. I would rather sit on a chair than a horse."

"In that case, you have to gain that confidence. Besides, being in the country, you have to get accustomed to it. I have a lovely placid mare. She will be just wonderful for you. That's providing five feet of snow doesn't fall during the night."

The following morning when Kamila opened her eyes, her room was extraordinarily bright with the reflected brilliance of the snow on the ceiling through the windows. She always liked to open the curtains before she climbed into her bed. She ran to the window and marvelled at the beauty she saw. As far as she could see, the land and the trees were covered with snow. It had stopped snowing and the sun glistened on the white surface as if it was covered with a multitude of tiny diamonds. She quickly washed and dressed and run down the stairs with Thor close behind her.

She made her way to the stables and was glad that when she stepped out of the house, the path and the courtyard had been cleared off the snow. She walked to where Bessie was stabled and told her that she was to look after Madelaine…

"Morning, Miss." It was the other groom whose name she couldn't remember. "Can I do anything for you, Miss?"

"Good morning! I have a friend staying with me and I wanted to take her riding. She's not very experienced so I thought she could have Bessie…"

He clicked his tongue and surveyed the land briefly, "No, Miss. 'Tis not wise to go riding today, even for you. The snow is nearly two feet deep in places and underneath it could be icy and most definitely slippery. The horse could slip and break a leg. Wait a few days." He was stroking Bessie's neck, and the mare obviously liked his touch,

"Yes, of course you are quite right." She kissed Bessie and murmured a few words to her and then went to see Emblem,

"Be careful with him, Miss. He's not so even tempered as Bessie."

"I know you all say that, but Emblem and I are friends, aren't we Emblem?" She put her arms around his neck. He looked at her with his beautiful eyes. Was he asking her about Karol? "Karol is no longer here, my love. I will ride you from now on, and we will always be friends, won't we, my beauty?" She buried her face in his neck and he tried to nuzzle her.

"I can see that there is a bond between you, Miss. He's a strange horse. He only ever loved Mr. Karol."

"Yes, I know, that's why I think that he is so very special." Still petting him, she said, "Everything else here alright? The other horses?"

"Yes, Miss. The others are fine too." She kissed Emblem and thanked the groom and went back to the house.

When she entered the house, Benjamin was waiting for her, "Good morning, madam. I thought that you might like to know that your friend is down and I've shown her into the morning room."

"Thank you Benjamin. I've been to the stables to see if Madame Prust and I could go riding but the groom—I can never remember his name—do you know it?"

"I think it would have been Ignacy—a well spoken young man?"

"Yes. Anyway, he said we were not to go out."

"Quite right, madam." Kamila smiled at the way they all treated her as if she was a child.

She greeted Madelaine with the news from the stables.

"I must say, Kamila that I was greatly relieved to see all that snow this morning."

"Wouldn't you like to meet Bessie at least? You do like animals, don't you?"

"Yes, I do," said Madelaine uncertainly.

"I can see that Thor likes you the way he behaves when you are near. He doesn't even bark when you come into the room and the way he sweeps his tail lazily, means that he trusts you."

"I just haven't had much experience with dogs or other animals." By now they were walking to the dining room for breakfast. “When I was little we did have a dog, but once I was married—.”

“Married? I didn’t know you were married.”

“Yes. I’m not now. I’m a widow, like you.”

“Oh, Madelaine I’m so sorry. How insensitive of me!”

“Don’t be sorry. I couldn’t have continued living, had he lived. He was a terrible, cruel man. He was Prussian and so charming before marriage that my parents and I were completely taken in. It was only after the wedding, about a fortnight, he told me how he hated Poles and that the only reason he married me was so that he could lay his hands on my father’s business. My father had several distilleries. And when my father died about two years later, Kurt took over. He frequently beat me and held a gun at my temple.”

“How terrible! What an awful life you’ve had. When did he die?”

“In February of 1831. After the battle of Grochow.”

“So he died in battle? Was he fighting on our side then, seeing that he hated Poles?”

“No. Neither. Can you believe how humiliating it was? He joined the Russian army under the Field Marshall Diebitch to fight the Poles. But he didn’t die in battle. He died of dysentery. And do you know what I did when they informed me that he had died? I went to the church and I thanked the Lord that he had released me from that monster. To this day I thank God for that.”

“I can well believe that. What happened to the distilleries? Were you able to run them?”

“No. He had sold them and the money he either frittered away or sent it to his family in Germany. There was nothing left. Fortunately, father had put some away in my name, so I wasn’t quite destitute, but I still had to earn a living. I had had a good education, so I could teach.”

“And you never remarried?”

“No. I didn’t want to. Would you have wanted to marry after having that experience? Besides, women have to have financial backing to marry well—not that that helped in my case. Anyway, I loved my work and had no intention of making another mistake.”

“I would like to remarry some day. I can’t see myself running this estate for years and years.” Kamila said wistfully. “I did love Karol, but then I’ve known him all my life. But it wasn’t a proper marriage of course and we had such a little time together…”

Madelaine patted her hand, “Of course, you must marry again. It’s almost your duty. But choose carefully my dear. First of all make sure that you *like* him, never mind this so called love and—forgive me for saying this—lust. I’m sorry I’ve embarrassed you. But you see Kamila, I feel that I must indeed play the role of a second mother to you, because you have no one else to turn to now.”

“That’s true. Thank you. Would you like another cup of tea or anything else, or shall we go to the morning room and I'll tell you about my visit to Amelia?"

Two days later Kamila received a letter from the geologist, Mr. Stokowski, "*…as the snow has melted, it might be wise to have a look at this field as soon as possible, before the heavy frosts come. I will arrive at The Birch House at ten on Tuesday morning, the 17th of September, if that is convenient. Hopefully the weather will remain mild until then.*

I remain yours, Madam,

S. Stokowski."

Lisinski came every morning to see if she had any instructions and every evening to report on what's been happening, so she could tell him this news then. She felt she was going to like this man, and wrote back to say that she looked forward to meeting him on Tuesday.

Meanwhile she wanted to take Madelaine riding but a problem arose. Madelaine had no riding habit.

"Of course you could use mine—."

"And show the whole of my leg? Kamila, I'm much taller than you—."

"What about Karol's breeches and jacket. He was very tall—."

"Kamila! How can you even suggest that? It wouldn't be ladylike—."

"Queen Christiana of Sweden wore breeches for riding." Kamila was trying to suppress a laugh.

"That may be so, but Madelaine Prust of Warsaw is not going to."

"If you think logically, the clothes for women are really idiotic. Those huge voluminous skirts right to the ground, and that's just for walking in—or rather gliding about. How would she cope if she had to do any useful work? Even the shoes are stupid with no heel and heaven forbid if they peep out from underneath the skirt. That's almost like showing naked flesh! As for riding, how on earth is a woman supposed to ride and enjoy it when her skirt is larger than the horse?"

"That's because women are supposed to be ornamental, and we are not supposed to do any work. Don't you know that our qualities are supposed to be quietness and delicacy and preferably be deathly pale? A prosperous man desires his wife to have two virtues. One is to be a model of domesticity and the other that she should do absolutely nothing. In fact her consummate idleness is a mark of his social status."

"In that case we two are complete outcasts—."

"I don't belong to that category, Kamila. I *have* to work for my living. But you are!"

"Yes, I do. Because I am doing a man's job since my aunt discharged that dreadful man. But do you know what? I love it. I couldn't envisage a life of planning what gown to wear for the next ball and all that small talk. So you see

I do feel quite strongly about Queen Christiana. So, what about it?"

"Definitely no."

"Mm. I know! My aunt was about your height. Let's go and see if there is anything in her wardrobes." Kamila had given away many of her aunt's clothes to the maids after her return from Gdansk and had been pleased to see how they had altered them. They didn't find a riding habit in the wardrobe but Kamila was sure that her aunt would have had one, so they opened one trunk and found it full of beautiful evening gowns. In the second trunk they found what they were looking for.

Kamila took it out. "It's lovely, and the fashion hasn't changed in these. What do you think?"

Madelaine held it up, "You know, it even looks my size. Turn round Kamila, whilst I put it on." Instructions were obeyed, and when she was dressed she said, "Now look!"

"Why! It fits you perfectly. And you look very fetching in it—just like a country lady. Let's see the boots." They fitted but were a little tight. "You might as well stay dressed in these and I'll go and change. But first I'll ask Benjamin to tell the groom to saddle the two horses. I'll just run down to tell him that."

Once in the yard, Kamila and Ignacy, the groom, saw how inexperienced Madelaine was. She had to have several goes at jumping on Bessie, even with the groom's help and then she held onto Bessie's mane as if her life depended on it.

"Madelaine, let go of Bessie. You won't fall off. She is broader than an armchair—."

"I prefer an armchair—." The groom chuckled.

"I'm holding your foot, madam, so you won't fall. Now that other leg—bend it more at the knee. See! Now, you're sitting better. Now keep that position whilst you are riding. Don't hold the reins so tightly. Bessie isn't galloping away. There, that's better. Miss Kamila shall I come with you both?"

"I think he'd better, Kamila."

"I think my friend will be fine and Bessie is the safest horse you could wish for." She patted the mare and felt sure that Bessie was smiling.

"I'm not worried about Bessie. I'm worried if I should fall off. How will I be able to get up on to her again? I don't suppose she'll get down on her knees like the camels do?"

"Don't worry Madelaine. I'll give you a leg up. I won't let you walk back through the mud and if we're not back within an hour, Ignacy will come looking for us."

Ignacy took the reins and led Bessie out of the yard. "I should go on the south road, Miss Kamila. That one there is very muddy. Bye for now."

They rode side by side, Madelaine holding grimly onto the reins.

"Madelaine, hold the reins lightly. Bessie knows where she's going.

Imagine that you are in an armchair on top of—an elephant!" At this Madelaine laughed and relaxed and from then on began to enjoy the scenery. The skies were a glorious blue, without a single cloud, and the trees had turned all shades of orange and yellow. The picturesque countryside couldn't but help to delight the soul.

"If we go down here we'll come to the river Styr. During the summer I saw a kingfisher there." And it was a lovely spot, but she didn't suggest getting down as her friend looked relaxed. They rode beside the river until the bank became steep and then decided to return home.

They were greeted by a smiling groom. "No mishaps?"

"No. Bessie looked after me beautifully," He put his hands up to her waist, she automatically stretched her hands onto his shoulders, and he had her down. "Thank you, Ignacy."

He then went to Kamila because she had been riding Emblem. She patted and hugged each horse and thanked the groom.

"Will you be riding tomorrow Miss Kamila?" He looked from one to the other and they both nodded.

Kamila broached the subject of riding astride, being dressed in breeches but again this was frowned on so fiercely that she didn't mention it again.

That evening after dinner Madelaine asked if Kamila had a newspaper, and they looked for it but could not find it so Kamila summoned Benjamin and ask him where it was. He coughed and looked at Kamila, "I'll just get it for you, madam." Shortly afterwards he brought the paper.

"It looks as if the paper had been read. Do your staff read?"

"Yes. The majority do. Some are illiterate but my family have always encouraged those who wanted to learn and so did my aunt and her family." She didn't say who else there was who would have had the paper. She must remind Benjamin that the paper should be downstairs, during Madelaine's stay here.

" You started to train me in this horse riding too late, you know."

"Too late for what?"

"For the horse racing—in Siberia. It started on the 15th."

"I'm surprised that they have anything like that. Are you joking?"

"No. It says here that they race their breed of horse. Apparently they are quite small with curiously coloured coats, have huge heads with long shaggy ears, just as in the days of Zenglus Khan, and they can withstand being without food for forty-eight hours."

"That seems to be a requirement of any living thing there, but for much longer than that," said Kamila dryly and then fell silent. Then quietly, "You know, I wonder about my parents, so very often. Are they still alive? Exactly where are they? If only I knew where they were. I have had no letter or any news from them or about them. It's as if they've disappeared from this earth."

"I'm sorry, my dear. How thoughtless of me to mention that place. It's so vast and desolate that it's no wonder no one ever receives any letters unless they are brought by escapees."

"Don't distress yourself, Madelaine. I'd have seen it in the paper anyway, so don't blame yourself. And anyway, I think of them every day and wonder where they are. I do miss them both, but especially my mother." She fell silent again.

"Have you considered writing to Warsaw? Maybe they could tell you where your parents had been taken?"

"Oh! If you only knew! I've written so many… Even now, I'm waiting for three replies."

"I'll make some enquiries when I return."

"Thank you. ……Incidentally, I almost forgot, that on Tuesday I have to go with the surveyor to that field where we had that subsidence, I told you about, so I'll have to leave you. It's not a very safe area and I don't think you are a sufficiently experienced rider. You don't mind, do you? We have to take the opportunity whilst the weather is holding."

"No. I don't mind in the least."

Lisinski and Mr. Stokowski arrived almost at the same time and together with Kamila they rode to the field. Lisinski told him what had happened and that they had inserted fencing and that it was still in the same place, so no more subsidence had occurred. Stokowski didn't say much but jumped off his horse some distance from the edge and started to walk to the edge, looking carefully underfoot, occasionally measuring something. Kamila and Lisinski began to follow him on their horses, but he turned and held up his hand. "Go back to where my horse is, don't come any nearer." So they returned and waited for him.

At first they watched him, but as he just seemed to be looking, Kamila scrutinized her surroundings. She twisted her head this way and that as if she couldn't quite see something. Eventually she pointed to the field, "Do you think this field is slanting downwards, or am I imagining? There, can you see? Was it like that last time I was here?"

"No, I don't think so," he said slowly, "I think you are right, it is sloping."

Stokowski came back. "Tell me, has this area been forested before it was cleared?"

"I looked back at the records and no. There were no trees here. Just scrubland. And that was cleared around fifty years ago."

"And you've never had this happen here before?"

Kamila shook her head. "Not anywhere on the estate."

"There are two contributory factors, maybe even three. Firstly, we've had a very dry spell followed by a very wet one. Secondly, to the east of here, it is quite near the marshes. Excessive rain can cause what's known as bog-burst, where the underneath layers start to simply slide over each other. As indeed, this can happen, if the third factor is present. And that is if there is salt underneath—this gets washed away—and the clay becomes saturated."

"Do you mean that this has happened only this year or that it can take a long time to develop? That hole is very deep."

"Madam, this hole is only about thirty feet deep. It can be as much as *two hundred* feet deep. As to the time it has taken to build up this amount of water, it's difficult to say. I would think many years. Come, I want to show you something, but we have to go on foot. Now, Look!" He pointed.

"You mean the slope?"

"Yes."

"I noticed this too, whilst you were examining the area."

"This means that the whole of his field will probably drop—any moment in fact."

"I wasn't sure if it had been lopsided like that before. Lisinski didn't think so."

" I'm sure it wasn't. If it had been you would have had such soil erosion that after a year or two nothing would have grown here. Now come here. Do you see this crack in the earth and this one? And, please note that this is quite a distance from the hole. This is a sign that it's subsiding underneath the surface. This is where it'll break away from and it'll do so in a form of a crescent. Come, before it does so." He spread his arms to hurry them out of the danger zone.

"Is there anything we can do to prevent this? Perhaps we could plant some trees?"

"I can see your logic, madam, but actually this could worsen the situation. Pipes can be inserted to drain it, but this is going to be a very large area. Do you really need this field? Your acreage is quite large if I remember rightly."

"Yes." She mentioned the acreage. "You suggest leaving it?"

"It might be a good idea to wait and see how much subsides and when it settles—say, after the winter is over—and then we can decide what would be the best solution. Meanwhile, I'd suggest you fence it off from where the horses are and maybe put up notices of the danger."

"But they wouldn't be much use when such a lot of people are illiterate, would they?"

"I meant the pictorial kind of notices. Skull and crossbones in big, bold, black lines."

"You'll arrange the fencing then," she said to Lisinski, "and I'll ask Benjamin who could paint these notices. How many do you think we'll need?"

"How about eight or ten? If it isn't enough, more could be added later."

Kamila went in search of Benjamin. "There is Henry, who is quite artistic. He's a footman. He's always drawing. He could use the Cook as a model."

"Benjamin! How could you!" He smiled, for every one knew that he had a very soft spot for the Cook.

When Henry was brought to her and she explained what she wanted, he said that he could certainly do that but suggested that perhaps burning out the picture first and then painting it, would be more practical. He would have a word with the carpenter.

Kamila then went upstairs to wash and change and when she came down she was astonished that Madelaine was nowhere about. She ordered some tea and refreshments and asked where her friend was.

"Oh, she's gone riding, ma'am. That's all I knows ma'am," said the maid.

She called Benjamin. "I'm told that Madame Prust has gone riding. When did she go?"

"Shortly after you left, madam."

"Oh, dear! That's nearly four hours! What a foolish thing to do. She's not experienced enough to go on her own. Get Emblem ready, I'll have to go and look for her."

"She's not on her own. Ignacy wouldn't allow her to do that. He went with her. He'll look after her."

"That's a relief then. But they have been gone a long time."

"Shall I go and look if they are back?"

"No. Let her enjoy her freedom. I'm going into the office after I've had something to eat, if you need me."

"Very well madam."

When Madelaine returned, she was full of excitement. Ignacy had taught her a lot of things and she learned how to jump over hedges and ditches. "And I didn't fall off once!"

CHAPTER 14

One morning in the following week, when they came down, Madelaine said she had a book to return to the library and Kamila carried on to the morning room to wait for her. But before she reached the door, Benjamin hurried to her and in a subdued voice,

"He's here. He wants to see you, madam."

"Who?"

"Mr. Raphael."

"Bored again, is he? Where is he?"

"I've put him in the library."

"Library? Oh, my goodness, Madame Prust has just gone in there!" She was about to run to the library but stopped. After all, the deed was done. Madelaine and Raphael have now met. "In that case, Benjamin, I shall wait for them in here."

Before long both of them came to join her. She was glad that she didn't have to tell any lies on Raphael's behalf or explain anything to Madelaine.

"I apologize for encroaching on your time together, Miss Kamila." Raphael said.

"That sounds as if I had forbidden you to be with us."

He turned to Madelaine, "Miss Kamila can be very disapproving and frosty, you know."

"I have never known her to be so," said Madelaine, looking at Kamila.

"Shall we go and have some breakfast, otherwise it'll be lunchtime soon," said Kamila to them both. Kamila wondered what Raphael had told Madelaine and whether she knew why he was here….but she wasn't going to question either….nor was she going to tell Madelaine anything but the truth when the occasion arose.

At breakfast, Raphael was at his most flippant and it looked as if Madelaine liked him. She and Madelaine were now in the habit of riding and were going to go that morning, but when Raphael heard of this, he appeared downhearted.

"I've been longing for some company and now you're going!"

"Can you not come with us? Kamila?" Madelaine turned to her friend.

"That decision is not up to me. It's up to Mr. Raphael."

"I wish I could," he said.

"It wouldn't be safe, you are right," said Madelaine. Kamila breathed a sigh of relief, so he had told Madelaine the truth!

It made life easier. Kamila no longer felt guilty at leaving Madelaine alone anymore.

Towards the end of Madelaine's stay at the Birch House, whilst they were out riding, for the weather remained dry but frosty in the morning, Madelaine asked Kamila if she liked Raphael.

"Yes, I suppose so. I didn't when I first met him."

"He told me. But I think you like him a lot, don't you? I've watched how you look at him."

"I wasn't aware I looked at him any differently to, say, you."

"Kamila, please forgive me. I don't wish to be impertinent. I'm trying to fulfil my role as second mother. I can see how you could be attracted to him. You're lonely, hungry for love, very vulnerable in that respect. He is lonely for a woman. Again, forgive me—I mean *any* woman. Do you understand what I'm trying to tell you?"

"I think so," Kamila said slowly. "He told me that he loves me."

"And you? What did you say?"

"I didn't say anything. I didn't think that he was very serious."

"And do you love him?"

"I don't know."

"I've analysed him and I think that he is not for you. In fact I don't think he's the marriageable type."

"I think he more or less told me that."

"You've gone as far as that? Discussing marriage? Oh, Kamila!" Madelaine said with dismay.

"Oh no, no! I understood that in between the lines. He was telling me of his engagement to Eleonora. It was actually very comical….." Madelaine sighed with relief, and Kamila recounted that episode.

"See how you've altered my attitude to living in the country, Kamila! I'm beginning to think like a country lady and even regret having to return to Warsaw tomorrow. I've always thought that I never enjoyed anything as much as teaching. I shall miss Bessie—."

"I'm glad you've taken to riding—."

"I shall miss Ignacy—."

"Is that all?"

"You, of course."

"What about Raphael?"

"I'm not sure. I think of him only as if he's flown in, perched a while and will fly off again. He doesn't let down any roots, like you and I. Oh, I do enjoy it when he's fooling around in order to entertain us…."

The three of them supped together and each dressed for the special occasion. Aunt Elizabeth's trunk supplied a plain but beautiful lavender gown for Madelaine and Kamila took out from her own wardrobe, a pink blouse with grey lace and a skirt in brocade with these two colours in the weave. Even Raphael found something in Karol's wardrobe.

The Cook laid on a special dinner, Benjamin brought wine from the cellar and filled up their glasses again.

"Do you know, ladies, I don't remember when I was this happy before. How lucky I am to be in such enchanting and interesting company. Let's drink to that."

"And to your heath," said Madelaine.

"And may you find another Eleonora," said Kamila dryly.

"You see, Miss Madelaine. You see? Miss Kamila wishes me to be subjected to Eleonora's temper. My! It was fierce."

"No, no. You are mistaken—," said Madelaine.

"She sounds great fun—," said Kamila.

"Fun? Hmph! We were having fun until you brought her name up," said Raphael.

"… so what about Christmas, Madelaine? Will you come here?" said Kamila.

"Well, thank you my dear. Of course I would love to be with you. Will you be here, too Mr. Raphael?"

"If Miss. Kamila will still have me."

"It's not up to me, is it? It's your choice."

"You see Miss. Madelaine, what I mean? That frostiness?"

"I don't think that was frosty at all, was it Kamila? I think that maybe Mr. Raphael is more used to the Oriental attitude of women to men," said Madelaine with a smile.

"No, I cannot agree with you there. I have absolutely no experience of being in the company of such women. Whereas you two ladies have no experience of men, although one of you is a widow."

"You are wrong there, I'm afraid, because I too am a widow, like Kamila."

"I didn't know. Please forgive me. Recently widowed?"

"No. In 1831. After the Battle of Grochow."

"So many died in these battles in that year—," said Raphael.

"He didn't die in the battle. He died of dysentery—," said Madelaine.

"Like that Field Marshall Diebitch. Or was that cholera?" said Kamila.

"Oh, no, he didn't—," Madelaine and Raphael said together and laughed. Madelaine put out her hand to Raphael, to explain.

"At first it was reported that he had died of cholera, but the circumstances surrounding his death and that of the Grand Duke Constantine were singularly suspicious."

"Why?" said Kamila.

"After one battle, I forget which, he was visited by Prince Orloff, the favourite of Tsar Nicholas, and they supped together. Prince Orloff insisted on sitting next to the General," said Madelaine whilst Raphael was lighting a cigar, having previously asked their permission to do so.

"That night the General expired in great agony," said Raphael.

"Was Constantine there too?" Kamila asked.

"No." He puffed at his cigar. "Prince Orloff then left the camp at Pultusk, where the General died, and proceeded to Minsk, where the Grand Duke was staying."

"Wasn't he reported to have died of cholera too?" asked Madelaine.

"Yes. But the following day after arriving at Minsk, these two dined together, sitting next to each other, and that night, Constantine was dead too," said Raphael. "And the battle you couldn't remember Miss Madelaine, was the Battle of Ostrolenka."

"Were they poisoned or what?" Kamila asked.

"Poisoned," said Madelaine.

"But why?"

"On Nicholas' orders. Prince Orloff was the Emperor's envoy," said Madelaine.

"That ominous name Orloff sent a chill down the spine of whoever had to entertain anyone with that name." said Raphael.

"There were other murders in the family due to them," said Madelaine.

Kamila shivered. Raphael took the carafe and filled up her glass and then Madelaine's and his own. "You mustn't have a sleepless night! She'll have nightmares now. So let's change the subject. How about some music? Which one of you ladies will play? Or maybe both?"

"I'm not very good, but Madelaine, you play wonderfully."

"What would you like me to play?"

"Something romantic, or sentimental," said Raphael and his companions turned to look at him strangely, "I think that the occasion merits it."

Madelaine sat the piano and tested the keys, before playing tunes that were popular, followed by lullabies, nationalistic songs and classical pieces. Then she accompanied the piano with her singing. Kamila had never heard her sing before. Her melodious voice was soft and sweet and brought a feeling of longing and sadness. She leaned back in her armchair and closed her eyes. It made her think of her parents, for both of them played the piano well and her mother often sang.

At the end of the evening, Madelaine said her goodbyes to Raphael.

"Until Christmas, then," he said, and kissed her hand.

"Yes. Until Christmas. Goodbye." Madelaine said, but Kamila shivered and felt as if a chill wind had blown on her. And she didn't understand the feeling.

"Remember me to the girls and the mistresses, Madelaine. And have a good journey. I'm glad it has remained dry for today. Write to me, and I'll look forward to seeing you at Christmas."

"I shall look forward to that too. And thank you for such a lovely time—and for forcing me to conquer riding. Give Bessie a hug from me and thank Ignacy. I did go to say good bye to him but there was different lad there."

"That was Fred. Unless you are a horse, you won't understand each other." Kamila laughed. They hugged each other and Madelaine climbed into the coach.

That evening Kamila felt subdued, despite that Raphael tried to make her laugh and when they went to the sitting room, she still felt the haunting music from the previous evening as if the music notes were suspended in the air. Raphael sensed her mood and was gentle and tender.

"I'm not as good as Madelaine, but I can play for you if you like," he said lightly as he went to the piano. He started to play love songs, some that were known to Kamila, and some that were not . This time her eyes moistened but it was some time before he noticed that. And when he did, he jumped up and ran to her, "Oh, my love, my love." He gathered her in his arms and kissed her face as he cradled her in his arms, and this time she didn't push him away.

The following morning at breakfast, she stole a shy look at him and he caught her gaze. He blew her a kiss. She smiled. She felt that the world was beautiful, more beautiful than she had ever envisaged it and didn't know that beauty was shining from her.

Meanwhile, it started to snow again. She stood and watched through the window as great chunks of fluffy snow fell and gathered momentum.

"Isn't it beautiful? When it looks so enchanting, I wouldn't mind being snowbound for a year," Kamila said.

"I wouldn't mind it either, if I was snowbound with you."

Heavier snow fell and the house was now prepared for the winter.

It was the middle of October that a group of men rode up to the house and knocked on the heavy door loudly with ominous authority. Benjamin walked unhurriedly. He disliked such imperious demands to come to the door. When he opened the door, the leader had alighted off his horse, and barked a command for the men to spread around. Benjamin saw that all the men were in uniform and were armed.

"We would like to see your mistress." The leader said curtly.

"I will see if she's in."

As Benjamin was closing the door, he heard him say, "Oh she's in, alright."

Benjamin hurried to Kamila, "Madam, there are uniformed men who wish to speak with you. They had the cheek to say that they know you're in."

"Oh my God! How many are there?"

"A lot. About ten, I think. And they are armed."

"Quick! Run and warn Mr. Raphael. I'll go to them." Her hands were moist and her heart felt as if it wanted to jump out of her mouth. She wiped her hands on the handkerchief, and then her forehead and the nose, took several deep breaths and slowly and unwillingly went to the door and opened it.

"Good afternoon! I believe you wished to see me?" She forced a smile. She stepped down one step and pulled the door to but not closing it.

"Good afternoon, madam. We are searching for a man called Raphael Karbonski. We know that he was a friend of your husband's and wondered if he might be here. I believe you know how he looks as he'd been here earlier in the year."

How well informed they were! Kamila's mouth was dry and she looked from one man to another, looking terrified.

"Please do not be alarmed, madam. We will not harm you. We only want Mr. Karbonski. You see, he is a traitor and needs to be punished according to the law. I will accept your word as a lady if you say that this traitor is not in your house, and we will not search it."

"Whom has he betrayed? Surely not Poland?"

"He is a traitor to the Empire, to His Imperial Highness the Tsar!"

Unbeknown to Kamila, Raphael had not fled but had come down and was listening just behind the door, and at the words of the leader, he couldn't contain himself and flung open the door and came out to the men, spreading his arms as if to encompass them, his shirt sleeves billowing in the strong breeze.

"My countrymen! I am not a traitor. I am like you. We Poles have it in our blood, this love of our country! This is our heritage. Once our country extended from the Baltic to the Black Sea, but now we are just a narrow strip and even that is under the Russian boot. *You* know that I have not committed any crime, any betrayal of Poland. The Empire is Russia. We are not Russians. Come and join me, let us all fight together the Tsar and his Empire, and free our country from their tyranny. Let us have our country back again to be ours, as it used to be, so that we can be—." At that point there was a volley of gunfire and Raphael crumbled to the ground.

Kamila let out an unearthly scream, "No!" It seemed to echo off the walls and hang on the trees, heavily laden with snow, as if it was blood, dripping from the branches, and she fell on top of him sobbing. The blood spread across the back of his shirt and on to the snow.

Benjamin and all the house staff ran out to the scene. The soldiers had disappeared like cockroaches exposed to sudden light. The only evidence left that they had been, was the churned up snow where the horses had stamped with occasional clear imprint of a hoof, and broken twigs and dried plants that had poked through the snow, and the devastation of one person dead and a young girl who wanted to die with him. Kamila was now sitting in the snow, having turned Raphael's lifeless, pale body in her arms, holding him tightly and sobbing as if her heart would break.

The staff looked on with horror, temporally stunned into immobility.

It was Mary who made the first move to take her in her arms but Kamila was clinging so tightly onto Raphael that she couldn't lift her. Others came to her aid and with difficulty peeled her arms off the dead man and bodily lifted her and took her inside the house and all the time Kamila sobbed.

"Give me that tablecloth. Wrap it around her, and bring me a blanket. She's frozen. Get me some hot tea and put some brandy in it." They wrapped her up and laid her on the sofa. Mary sat beside her, rubbing her hands, talking gently to her. Benjamin came and whispered in her ear.

"We've put the body in the far side of the house. Shall I get the girls to lay him out, as you won't be able to leave Miss Kamila?"

"Yes and get them to clean him well and change his clothes." She too whispered. Kamila was crying quietly with long in-drawing of breath.

"Benjamin, I think we'll need to send for Dr. Roger and for Father Dominic."

"In that case I think I'll go for them both."

"That would be the best. Go for the doctor first."

Despite Mary's effort of warming up her mistress, Kamila shivered and her hands remained cold. Mary felt her feet and found that the shoes were completely wet so whilst taking her shoes off, she ordered the maids to hurry and prepare Kamila's bed and to be sure to warm it well and when it was ready the footman carried Kamila up the stairs. The fire in the room was banked up and the warmth was already spreading. Mary placed Kamila on the chaise longue and started to take her clothes off. She was pleased that someone had thoughtfully brought hot water, and she washed off every smudge and drop of blood off Kamila, rubbed her roughly with the towel and put on the warmest night gown she could find. There were two other girls in the room who helped and when they put her into the warm bed, Mary noticed that after a while the shivering lessened although not completely disappeared.

"Take all these things to launder. Oh! I've left her shoes in the sitting room. They are completely wet. I think I'll stay with her. I don't think she should be left alone." And all this time Kamila didn't speak. Every now and then tears rolled down her cheeks but they were silent tears and she seemed unaware of what was going on around her, what had been done to her by the motherly Mary.

Dr. Roger came and Kamila looked at him without recognition at first, but when he touched her and said, "Kamila, my dear—," she looked at him, her eyes widened so that he could see in them, the depths of her pain.

"Why?" she whispered and then started to cry. He gathered her in his arms and she clung to him fiercely.

"You did quite right to put her to bed, Mary. She's suffering from shock. Keep her warm, give her lots of liquids and don't leave her." Mary nodded and said that was what she had meant to do.

"But Doctor, what are we to do with the body?" She said it quietly so that Kamila wouldn't hear. "Have you seen him?" He shook his head. "He isn't from these parts."

"Yes," he said thoughtfully, " I see what you mean. The body should be transported to his home for burial. And someone from the house should go with it, but not—." He looked pointedly at Kamila.

"Well, that would have to be either Benjamin or me. We are the most senior of the staff, apart from the Cook, but I would like to stay with Miss Kamila, if you don't mind, sir."

"I would rather that you stayed with her too. I'll just give her some sedation and then we can go and see what information we can find out in his room."

Once Kamila was asleep they left her in the care of Lucy and went to Raphael's room and looking through his papers, they found a letter from his parents but that was dated a year ago! He also found poems written to a girl with dark blue eyes and curly hair and half finished letters. "Oh, dear," he said to himself, which didn't escape Mary's attention. He was in half a mind to destroy them.

"He wrote many more. He didn't even throw them into the fire, but left them in the waste paper bin. Theresa told me that she was terrified if they got into wrong hands, so she always burnt them first thing in the morning," she said.

"I was thinking of doing this too, but maybe his parents would want them as a keepsake. It's a blessing they don't mention a name."

"Some of the others did," she said.

"In that case, I'm glad that they were destroyed." He searched through the rest of the contents of the writing desk and found nothing else of importance. "I think I shall have to ask Miss Kamila for more information."

Dr. Roger went back to Kamila. "Kamila, wake up for a moment! Good girl! We have to let Mr. Raphael's family know. No, don't cry! Think! Do you know where he comes from? Do you know his address?"

"His parents and—and a younger—brother run the est—estate. The address is in Karol's address book—in Karol's room."

"Good girl! Now go back to sleep."

He went back to Raphael's room where Mary was still waiting. "Benjamin hasn't come back with Father Dominic yet?"

Mary shook her head. "I don't think so. The staff would have told me if they were here."

"Now, I must see the body first, and then I'll write and tell his parents what has happened——and I don't think that Benjamin will be able to set off with it till the day after tomorrow. I'll arrange a coffin and a hearse for that day then. You stay with Miss Kamila. We don't want her getting pneumonia on top of everything else."

"I will do that, sir and thank you for arranging all that. Will you come and see Miss Kamila tomorrow?"

"Yes, I will. Now let us go and see the body." When they arrived there, one of the maids who helped to lay Raphael out, was in the room.

"I'm glad you are here. Did you notice how many bullet wounds were on the body?"

"Yes, sir. We was saying the we counted three, two from the front and one from the side." She showed him the positions on the corpse.

"This room—keep it cold—no fires."

"It's a very cold room, sir, anyway, all the year round," said Mary.

"The sooner this is dealt with the better," said the doctor. "A sad business, this. I don't know him. You say, he's not from these parts?"

"I don't think so, sir. I'm sure not."

"Oh, dear! What an onerous task of writing to his parents. How does one tell the parents that their eldest son lies here, riddled with the Tsar's bullets?"

Early in the morning Kamila woke. Lucy bent over her, murmuring for her to go to go back to sleep, but Kamila grabbed her hand urgently and said,

"Where is Mr. Raphael?" Lucy didn't know how to answer. Was her mistress aware that he was dead? Did she remember yesterday, that terrible day? She knew that none of them would ever forget it, as long as they lived.

"Shh, now. I'll get you a hot cup of tea and then—."

"Where have they put Mr. Raphael? I want to go and see him." She became more agitated and started to get out of bed. "Lucy, if you don't tell me I'll go to every room until I find him."

"Alright, Miss Kamila, I will take you to him, but first have a hot drink." She pulled the cord and asked for the drink, found a dressing gown and slippers and put them in front of the fire. Once Kamila had drunk the tea and was gowned warmly, they went down the stairs to the chilliest room in the house.

Raphael was laid out on a long table, covered with white sheets and his body was covered up to his waist. He looked almost the same colour as the sheets and his pure white shirt but his face looked peaceful and younger than in life. Even his hair seemed fairer than when he was alive. There were candles lit in the room, around the table. Kamila laid her hand over his folded ones and whispered his name.

After what seemed like an age, Lucy touched her, "Come now Miss Kamila, it's terribly cold in here."

"You go, Lucy, I want to stay here a while." Lucy brought her a chair and went out. Twice more she came to ask Kamila to come back to her bed but she refused. Lucy was now very worried. The room was freezing and when she had touched Kamila she felt her hands were as cold as the corpse's. So she ran to the servants' quarters and into Mary's room.

"Mary! Wake up! I need your help. Miss Kamila insisted on going to see Mr. Raphael and she won't leave him. I've tried several times to drag her away. She's been there nearly two hours." Mary had jumped out of bed, washed her face and dressed quickly and they both ran down to Kamila.

Kamila was still holding his hands. Her eyes were swollen and the cheeks wet.

Mary put her arms around her. "Let go of him. You can't bring him back. You'll make yourself ill. Come away, back to bed. Later in the day, when you're dressed warmly you can come again. The coffin is arriving this afternoon. He will look more comfortable then." She took her hands off the body, and eventually Kamila allowed herself to be taken to her room. Lucy brought her another hot cup of tea into which they again put some brandy and Mary gave her the medicine prescribed by Dr Roger. Kamila slept until late morning and woke only when the doctor arrived.

He greeted her warmly and she clung to him for a while, and when he held her away from him to have a good look at her, he was pleased that she was a little more composed. He told her what he had arranged and that Benjamin would accompany the coffin on the following day. At that, Kamila became distressed and said that she would go instead of Benjamin…

"Kamila, on this occasion I have to take place of your Father, as I have known you all your life. Indeed, if you didn't have the responsibility of running this estate, I would have suggested that you come and live with us and in fact become my fifth daughter! Imagine, all these women in the house!" He raised his eyes to the ceiling, "So, I am sure that your Father would not have allowed you to go, and neither will I. If you prove to be difficult, I'll tell the staff to lock you in your room." But he smiled at the last threat.

"But I should go...... at least to let his family know."

"They already know—or will do so shortly. I've written to them in detail. If you feel up to it later, you can write too. But not yet. Let them get over this first shock. The life that he led must surely have made them aware that this could happen to him at any time. And indeed, quite obviously he knew that too. But you know, that by being here, hiding in your home, was a very selfish thing to do, for he put you and all the staff in a very precarious, dangerous position. They could so easily have shot you too and legally they would have been their right to do so, for harbouring a traitor. That's how the law stands, I'm afraid."

"He had no where else to go. And he was Karol's friend—."

"Yes and that's why they found him. As I said, it was a very selfish thing to do—."

"No! Don't say that!"

"My dear, maybe at present you can't see that, but you will in time. You're very much like your Father. He was very analytical and practical and so are you." He patted her hand. "Now, you can get up, but dress warmly and don't venture outside today. And before you go to bed I want you to have that sedative. I want you to sleep. I don't want to hear of your keeping your nightly vigil in that cold room. Promise?" After a while she nodded.

In the afternoon the coffin arrived and the body was placed into it. The staff made sure that Kamila was nowhere near. But she did go into the room later and stayed a long time.

It was felt that a carriage that could accommodate the coffin and Benjamin would be more practical. When the horses were changed, it would not have been possible to have black ones throughout the journey and the distance to be travelled was far too great to be ridden at a funereal pace, so a hearse was out of question. Kamila and most of the staff gathered in the front to see them off. When they were out of sight, Mary spread her arms like a mother hen and propelled Kamila and others back into the house.

Almost as if arranged, Lisinski came shortly afterwards to tell her the progress of the subsiding field and of other activities around the estate and he stayed a long time.

Kamila lost her appetite, cried, especially at night when no one would see her, slept poorly and even Thor couldn't raise her spirits. After four days Mary suggested that she wrote to Madame Prust to come and stay with her again, that she needed some company, but Kamila shook her head,

"I can't do that. She'll be working and won't be free until Christmas."

"What about Miss Amelia? She could come and be here with you. That's what friends are for, aren't they?" But again Kamila shook her head.

"I don't want any company just yet. I feel that I'd rather be alone. I think I'll go for a walk with Thor."

"Alright, but I don't want you catching a cold or pneumonia. The Doctor said I was to make sure you was looked after. "

"Don't worry Mary. If you want I'll come and show you that I've taken care to be warm."

Walking daily was heavy going through snow if there was no path. Thor raced about, barking with delight at being with her so often and, like all young animals he loved being in the snow. Certainly being out in the fresh air helped her emotionally, but it still wasn't quite enough. On her way back from such a walk she went into the stables and looked at the horses. She hugged Bessie and then went to Emblem and while she stroked him she told him what she planned to do.

Fred came out to her and asked if she wanted anything and she told him that she would like to have Emblem ready for riding on the following morning. No more snow had fallen and the air was dry, so she felt that riding would not prove difficult. Anyway she was quite an experienced horsewoman.

When she came downstairs to breakfast, she was dressed in breeches and jacket, and at first sight looked like a young boy. When Mary saw her, she opened her mouth and then closed it. After all what did it matter? There wouldn't be anybody about in this weather and even if there was, no one would recognise her.

"It's no good your disapproving my attire Mary. I'm going in this and that's final."

"I didn't say a word, Miss Kamila, did I?"

"No. But I know that look. I've seen it before—many times!"

Benjamin had been more diplomatic and had merely greeted her in the usual way as well as wishing her a pleasant time. He knew that she was only going riding for pleasure and not going on any estate business. Perhaps he would have said something on that score, had she been going with Lisinski. But perhaps he would not. Kamila was not sure. Ignacy was in the stables that morning to greet her and after a first glance of non-recognition, he grinned widely, showing perfect white teeth.

"Good morning Miss Kamila. I didn't recognise you at first. Emblem is all excited and ready." He brought the horse to her and gave her a leg up. Riding astride would be so much more comfortable and safer. "When can I expect you back?"

"Sometime before nightfall."

"Oh, no! Please don't be more than an hour, Miss Kamila otherwise we'll all be worried and I'll have go and fetch you."

"Two hours then."

"Alright, but not a moment longer—please."

"I promise."

"And which way are you going?"

"Towards the River Styr and then across the bridge and the road passed it, if it's passable." He nodded approval.

When they were well past the stables and on the road to the river she started to think of the last week and just as Dr. Roger had predicted to analyze the events. Had Raphael really loved her as she had loved him? And how she loved him still! Was he capable of loving for a whole lifetime as she had imagined? He certainly hadn't shown it during his lifetime, according to what he had told her. But what was the use of such questions? He was dead and what was left, were shreds of her love for him. *Oh Lord! I hope that that is all that is left of all this....*

They crossed the bridge and found the road which for some portion of it still had fresh dry snow and Emblem appeared to enjoy it. Kamila talked to him as if he was a friend who understood. She told him secrets she would not dream of sharing with anybody else. Eventually they came to the crossroads, signified by a carved, painted figure of Virgin Mary holding Baby Jesus. There was a peaked roof over the figures, covered with a clump of snow.

Kamila stopped at the figure and sent a silent prayer. She was not particularly religious but whenever she prayed, she did so fervently and perhaps that was why she felt some comfort at such times. She looked around. There were pinks and blues in the snow as it sparkled in the sun and she marvelled at such beauty. It was only when Emblem snorted with impatience that she looked down and patted him.

"Alright, my love, you want to go home. Come on then, take me there." Every day she went riding and all the time she thought of Raphael. Why had he come out to face these soldiers? Surely he must have known that they would at the very least arrest him and that one way or another he would forfeit his life? Did he value his life so little? No, otherwise he would not have been hiding at The Birch House, besides during their many talks he had said that he had such a lot to do, to help, with others, to set Poland free again, so that it could be great once more. No, he had valued his life and quite a lot and he was dedicated it to the cause, to patriotism.

Patriotism! That word again.

I could spit at the face of patriotism! How much more does it want of me and my family?

Two brothers, her parents, a husband and now someone whom she had loved so much and for such a short time! *If that was not enough, why did they not shoot me too? I was more than willing, and am willing now.*

She was not looking where she was going. Indeed, she allowed Emblem to go wherever he fancied. So she was unaware that there was someone else who was interested in the route she and Emblem took.

Therefore when Emblem reared and neighed with fright she was not prepared, and sitting relaxed and holding the reins only lightly, she was thrown high and fell. She lay crumpled in the snow. Emblem came to her and nuzzled her but she did not respond. He moved to the side and nudged her, but to no avail.

Kamila had not known that they had wandered on to another property. They had been travelling on a path at the edge of a wood and when Emblem neighed he was heard and seen as he reared, by Baltazy, who was standing on a ladder and repairing a window. He looked for some time to see if anyone climbed back on the horse, but no one did. But what he did see was a stocky man running away and he knew exactly who that was. That sight made him slide down the ladder with expertise and run in the direction of the horse.

It took him some time to battle through the snow, but no weather conditions ever deterred him from his purpose. When he reached the area, he approached Emblem without fear, patted him on the neck and looked down at the crumpled child. He turned the body over and thought that it was dead, so he lifted the lifeless body and placed it on the back of Emblem. As he took the reins, he looked at the ground. He saw footsteps that had come up to the body, and then ran away. He looked around to see why the horse had reared and saw on one tree a portion of a rope that had been cut off hurriedly. He cursed under his breath.

He patted the horse and took the reins, "C'mon boy. Let's take your poor little master to my master."

He carried the body into the living room where Thomas Orzel was reading a paper.

"This lad was thrown off his 'orse. Oi think he's dead. Oi'll just go and see to the 'orse. They must have been riding a long time…" Thomas nodded. Horses were important and needed to be looked after. He knew that Baltazy would rub him down and cover him with a blanket in the stable. He went to the body. It showed no life.

He lifted it under the arms and marvelled that such a young boy would be riding alone and so far from home. He had no idea who he was. He had never seen him before. There were no bones broken as far as he could see. He tentatively tried the neck. That seemed to be alright, and then he noticed a pulse in the neck. He started to loosen the kerchief and then the shirt but whether his eye fell on the delicate cheek or whether when his hand touched the softness of the skin, a memory was stirred from his distant past, he didn't know. He stopped what he was doing and called his housekeeper,

"Aniela! Can you come here, please."

Her buxom form appeared at the door in no time at all, "Yes, Mr. Orzel?"

"Baltazy has just brought this little chap. Thrown off his horse. He thought that he was dead. But I'm sure that I've just seen a pulse."

Aniela looked at Kamila, "I don't think it's a little chap at all. I think it's a girl even though she's wearing breeches." She took her large cap off to reveal short dark curly hair. "Look at the way the buttons are sewn…"

"I never noticed that."

Aniela did not bother to say that he never noticed anything. She had told him that many times. She took Kamila off his hands and laid her on the sofa and started to unbutton her jacket. He took a cushion and placed it gently under Kamila's head. As he looked at her he thought that he had never seen anything so beautiful. Just like a dark haired angel! He wondered who she was. Meanwhile, Aniela brought a bowl of cold water and a towel and was wiping Kamila's face and neck. Suddenly she stiffened and sniffed loudly.

"I can smell him!"

"Who?" said Thomas Orzel. But before she could answer, Baltazy appeared in the doorway.

"Out! Out! You smelly devil! Give me that poker, Mr. Orzel." But she had to get the poker herself and chased Baltazy out of the room. "I won't have him in the house, I've told you before Mr. Orzel. He can stay with the horses and the cattle. Even they smell sweeter than that, that…" She was lost for words to describe the malodorous Baltazy.

"But you made him have a bath a week or so ago."

"It was more like a month. I do hate that job but I suppose I'll have to do it again."

"He ought to have a wife—."

"A wife? A woman would have to be demented to have him!"

Whether it was the booming voice of Aniela, or her chasing Baltazy or the cold water being applied to her face, or the combination of these factors, but something made Kamila come back to consciousness. She opened her eyes and they were both amazed at the darkness of these blue eyes, surrounded with dark lashes. To Thomas Orzel the picture of an angel was complete.

"Hello, lass!" Aniela said, "How do you feel now?"

"Very well, thank you." She looked around the room and the two people standing by her. "Why am I here? Where am I?"

"You were thrown off your horse," said the man in a kind voice.

"Is my horse alright?" She tried to raise herself on the elbow and winced with pain.

"Yes, your horse is alright. My man has looked after him and he's in the stable at the moment. Where do you come from? What's your name?" Whilst Thomas was talking, Aniela took off Kamila's jacket to look at the elbow. She tested the movements gently and patted her hand.

"The elbow is fine lass, just bruised. I'll just go and make some tea for you both." She left but did not close the door.

"I come from the Wachowski estate. My name is Kamila Wachowska."

"Oh, I know it. I was there around springtime. I saw Mr. Karol. He wanted a puppy—."

"I remember—you brought me my Thor!"

"That's right."

"So your name must be Mr. Orzel."

"Yes. That's right. I am Thomas Orzel." Aniela came back with the tea, poured it out and put a piece of cake on a plate and handed it to Kamila. "And this is Aniela, my housekeeper. She runs the place really. It was probably her bellowing at Baltazy, that brought you back to us. Baltazy is the man, who found you and brought you here. He saw your horse rear."

"It could also have been the way that Baltazy smells, lass that brought you back to us. I'm sure that could waken the dead. Having him around, you wouldn't need smelling salts."

"Now, now Aniela, he's a good man to have around. Not lazy and he can do almost anything you want—."

"Except have a bath!" Kamila and Mr.Orzel laughed.

"I would like to thank him for bringing me here and looking after Emblem. I hope he didn't bite him. He's known to do that. He was my husband's horse, but we seem to get on well and I think he knows that I love him."

"You can thank him some other time, lass. I'm not having him here, and that's final!" Aniela folded her arms across her chest. "Mr. Orzel can thank him for you, won't you sir?"

"Yes, yes. I'll do that. Now, I think I had better get you home, young lady. Your people will be worried about you."

"Thank you so much. If you take me to the stables I'll get Emblem—."

"Oh, no, lass. You're not going alone. Mr. Orzel will take you."

"But Emblem—."

"He'll be alright here and I'll bring him over tomorrow. I think he must be tired too. But come and see him…" Aniela put on her jacket and buttoned it up and tied the kerchief around her neck, and touched Kamila under the chin gently.

"Thank you both very much. You are most kind." She was moved by their gentleness, and touched Aniela's arm to show this.

It was not far to the stables and when she saw Emblem she was loathed to leave him behind but instead she looked him over and being satisfied that he had no injuries, she put her arms around his neck. Emblem nuzzled her face and neck. She saw that he had been rubbed down and a warm blanket was on his back, his feet were deep in straw and he had been given oats.

Once again she thanked Mr. Orzel.

A one-pony trap was ready and waiting. Kamila was helped in and her legs were covered with a sheepskin rug. Mr. Orzel put on his warm coat and climbed in. The journey home took an hour. During that time Kamila told him that Karol had died and her aunt too, but that her staff were very caring, more like a family to her.

"—like your Aniela. She is such a kind motherly person. Has she worked for you a long time?"

"Yes, for over twenty years. My wife was a delicate thing. Aniela looked after her. And then when my wife died—following the birth of the second boy, she looked after the children. She brought them up. And yes, you are right. She is motherly."

"And your boys, do they work with you?"

"No. They are not even in Poland. Two years ago they left to explore the world. So they said. They never showed any interest in the farm. They were always restless, even when they were youngsters. They were eighteen and nineteen. They asked if they could go to Australia. So I let them. But when they arrived in Gdansk they met some people who had been to America. You can imagine my surprise when after many weeks I received a letter from New York."

"Are they happy there?"

"They were, but they are no longer there. They decided to travel west. They wanted to explore the country before settling down somewhere."

"Presumably they are not too lonely, having each other."

"That's right. And they were always close."

"I expect you worry a lot about them."

"Yes, of course. They wrote from various towns on the way. Whenever they could, they wrote. The towns were getting sparser and sparser. I followed their route on the map. But the last time I received a letter from them was five months ago. They said that they were going into really wild country. They were travelling north, possibly to Canada. If I didn't hear from them, I was not to not to worry." He grew quiet then.

"It's such an enormous country to explore and there is such wilderness. It must be very exciting for young men to see a new continent. I am glad you have such good people close to you like Aniela and Baltazy. They obviously care for you very much." The mention of Baltzy made him smile.

"Yes, I am lucky in that way. Aniela really runs the place. I don't know how I would cope without her. And Baltazy, he can put his hand to any kind of job. He's done repairs of every kind, looked after the animals. Many a time he's slept in the stable with an animal that's been sick. And it's true that he never washes—."

"Louis XIV had only three baths in his whole lifetime and he had to be coerced into these."

"I don't think that he was the only person who didn't wash—."

"No, I'm sure that you are right." Kamila looked around at the familiar land. "We are near The Birch House!" As they neared the house, Kamila saw in the distance Benjamin's figure standing in the drive.

Thomas Orzel jumped off and came to help Kamila down just as Benjamin reached her.

"Oh, Miss Kamila we were so worried about you. Ignacy and two other stable lads have been out searching for you. You've never been this long. And what's happened to Emblem?"

"Your mistress was thrown off her horse. She was brought to my place and the horse is alright too. I'll bring him over tomorrow."

"Benjamin, you've met Mr. Orzel before—when he brought over Thor."

"Oh, yes, I do remember you, sir."

"Will you come in Mr. Orzel?" said Kamila.

"No, thank you, it'll be dark in an hour. I think I had better get back. But I'll be back with Emblem tomorrow. Good day to you both."

"Thank you again, Mr. Orzel." He lifted his hat, turned the trap around and drove away.

CHAPTER 15

"Are you hurt, Miss Kamila?"

"No, I don't think so, but apparently I was unconscious and at first they thought I was dead. But I am *so* hungry."

"The Cook has something ready for you. Will you change first or eat?"

"I think I had better change. I've given enough shocks for the day. Will you inform the stable men that Emblem is alright, please?"

"Certainly, madam."

Mary came to see if she was alright and find out what had happened.

"Yes, I am alright but I don't know what happened. I might know a bit more tomorrow. Mr. Orzel will try and find out."

"It's that horse. He's dangerous."

"You are wrong, Mary. He is safe and intelligent and I would trust my life to him—."

"You nearly lost it today. And what would we do without you then?"

"What happened today was not his fault. If anything it was mine, in that my mind was miles away and I wasn't holding on as I should have. But I tell you what, Mary, riding astride was so comfortable….."

"Mm. But come the winter is over you won't be able to do that. People will talk. You can't have your name tarnished."

"We'll see," said Kamila with a smile.

She ate a very belated meal at first ravenously but after a while felt slight nausea and a headache, so she left the rest and started to read the letters that were brought to her. There was one form Madelaine, thanking her for the hospitality and saying that she actually missed riding Bessie, and how very enjoyable that last evening was and would Kamila pass on her best wishes to Raphael*.....Oh, dear, how am I going to tell her that he is dead? Shall I leave it until she comes for Christmas?* She laid down the letter. *I will leave that for another week or so. I must also write to his parents....*

There was also another letter with unfamiliar writing. When she opened it, she found that it was from Matthew Kobulski.

Dear Miss Kamila,

I hope that you have not forgotten me already. I certainly have not forgotten you. In fact I think of you constantly and remember our last meeting with pleasure. How could I ever forget that? It was so delightful!

By all reasoning we in the north of the country should have mild winters but I believe that we have had much heavier falls of snow than you. It is that Arctic wind that makes it so fierce. You remember my friend Stanislaw Skromny? He has written me that the Baltic is already frozen and they are skating on it.

It is a pity that the railway system has not connected Poznan and Luck, otherwise I would be there today.

I wonder what your plans are for Christmas and whether you would like to spend it with me and my family. My parents would love to meet you and I would love to feast my eyes on you again. I do realise that the weather may prove a bit of a problem, but I could arrange for a group of us men to dig a tunnel from here to your estate.

Your very faithful friend,

Mat.

She immediately sat to write him an answer, thanking him for his kind words and for the invitation but that her arrangements for Christmas had already been made. She would have liked to see Poznan, for she has never been there and of course to meet his parents. She hopes that they all have a very joyful time....

At mid morning, the next day, Mr. Orzel arrived not only with Emblem but with a driver. Kamila was told they were riding up the drive, so threw a shawl over her shoulders and ran out to greet them, but especially Emblem, who was trotting behind the carriage.

As Mr. Orzel kissed her hand in greeting, he said that the driver was Baltazy and he had something to say to her. Kamila, first of all, thanked him for rescuing her. He had alighted from the seat and taken his cap off. He looked delighted with himself and grinned broadly as she talked.

"Tell Miss. Kamila—do you mind if I call you that?" Kamila shook her head and he turned to Baltazy, "Tell her what you told me last night." So he started. Kamila listened very attentively, not taking her eyes off his lips, hoping that maybe by trying to read these she could understand him better, but she couldn't. The only thing that she was able to pick up was the word " 'orse" a few times. He talked at length and all she could see, looking at his lips was that he had one tooth in the upper jaw and three on the left side of the lower jaw, and his tongue was rolled into a pink round ball that kept bouncing in between them.

Kamila looked in desperation at Mr. Orzel. "I don't understand a single word. What dialect is he speaking? He's not from these parts, then?"

Thomas Orzel threw back his head and laughed. It was a deep spontaneous laugh, the laugh of a person at ease with his environment and himself. Baltazy also laughed, with equal mirth.

"He was born and bred on the farm. It's only since he lost his teeth that people don't understand him. We are so used to him now that I forgot that you might not have understood. So I will tell you."

"In that case, let us go in. Perhaps Baltazy could take Emblem to the stables—Benjamin will show you where—and to give Mr. Orzel's horses some shelter and oats. Would you like to go to the kitchen Baltazy? The Cook has just baked some delicious cakes."

Kamila asked for some tea to be brought to the morning room where she and Mr. Orzel now entered. She asked him to sit down and he waited until she was seated.

"What Baltazy told me quite horrified me. I think you should be made aware of these facts. Baltazy was standing on a ladder. He was repairing a window when he heard a horse neigh. He turned to the sound and saw it rear. You must have already fallen off, for he saw the horse standing on his hind legs. He waited to see if the rider got up onto the horse but he (you) didn't. He was about to get off the ladder to see to the rider, when he saw a stocky man run away from the scene—."

"Oh! I think I know who that might be—."

"You do?"

"Yes. Our previous overseer. He bore a grudge against my aunt and me."

"Ah! Well, Baltazy too, knew very well who it was. Their paths had crossed before. Greczko is his name. He threw a knife at Baltazy's brother and killed him. Is that the name?"

Kamila nodded. "Yes. That's the man. He waylaid me before. His favourite mode of cruelty here was the whip."

"He is a dangerous man. Anyway, when Baltazy reached you, you were unconscious. He—we all—thought that you were dead. He looked around to see why the horse had reared. He found that someone had tied a rope to a tree and must have pulled it taught for the horse to be so frightened. It must have been Greczko. He had cut it off in haste before making off. But Baltazy untied the rope and brought it home. He also marked which tree it was. He said that this time he won't let him get away with it, especially as he is such a danger to you. I will let him search him—hunt him down."

Kamila told him how it came about that Greczko bore this grudge against her.

"Miss. Kamila, it is quite obvious that this man intends to harm you. Please forgive me for being so bold, since we have only met yesterday. But please, I beg of you, do not go anywhere on your own. I will tell your butler and your staff to forbid it. If you need to go anywhere, let me know and I will accompany you."

"Thank you Mr. Orzel—."

"Won't you please call me Thomas?"

"Thank you Mr. Thomas. I promise not to go out on my own. As a matter of fact that time when he waylaid me he planned a fate much worse than death then……" Kamila shivered at the thought. How naïve she was to have thought that that episode was over! "How will Baltazy find him, because he obviously has travelled widely since he left here? And if and when he does find him what will he do with him? Will the law help at all?"

"Hopefully the law will take note. After all Baltazy was a witness to attempted murder. We'll see. He has his own methods."

"I hope he will not be in danger though—."

"He is very good at tracking animals. Even dangerous ones, you know. So he shouldn't have any difficulty with this monster."

"That's good. Incidentally I thought that Baltazy looked very smart," said Kamila.

Thomas laughed, "I'm glad you noticed. He'll be pleased. When Aniela learned that he was driving me here today, she made him have a bath. Normally there are loud protests from him. But this time he did it almost willingly! Years ago she used to make him strip outside whatever the weather, because she couldn't stand the smell. She used to fill a large barrel with hot soapy water. She had him soaking in it for up to an hour. If he tried to get out before she was satisfied, she would submerge him using a broom. You should have heard the screams. And all that he had taken off she would pick up with a long stick. Every item would be subjected to several hours of boiling." Kamila was laughing at the picture painted for her.

"I'm surprised he doesn't catch pneumonia bathing outside."

"Oh, nowadays he has it in the tack-room beside the kitchen. Anyway it probably made him all the hardier—you know, like the Russians. They make a hole in the ice and plunge into it. Very refreshing! You should try it, Miss Kamila."

"Oh, yes? What will people think of me then? Not only does she wear breeches when she goes riding but she swims with the icebergs. Anyway have you tried this kind of bathing? Are you talking from experience?"

"No. I like my baths in the normal way." He looked at his watch, "I think I had better go. I've taken up too much of your time as it is. But please take me seriously. Do not go out on your own. And if you want to go anywhere, let me know. I am willing to be beside you for your protection."

"Thank you so much for everything that you have done."

"I would like to come and see you again if I may. Say, the day after tomorrow?"

"Yes, certainly. I'll look forward to that." As she opened the door, Thor came running to her, but first sniffed Thomas's feet.

"Hello, Thor, my boy, how are you?" Thomas bent down and patted Thor with both his hands. Turning to Kamila, "He is a lovely dog. A right choice for you. I'm glad you have him."

"Yes, I am glad I have him. Thank you—for him too. He was also a great comfort to my aunt when Karol died. He seems to have this great understanding…."

On the following day Kamila did not feel too well. So after Lisinski's visit to report that there has been no apparent change in the subsidence of the field and that everything was fine except that Greczko has been seen in the vicinity, Kamila went to lie down in the sitting room, having first rubbed some oil of peppermint to her forehead.

Mary came to check how she was every so often, bringing her some tea and showing great concern.

"You must have fallen on your head when you were thrown. Don't you think you should call the doctor, Miss. Kamila? Perhaps you've broken something?"

"If I don't feel any better tomorrow, I will go and see Dr. Roger."

She did not feel any better. In fact she felt worse because she felt sick and could not eat her breakfast and the headache persisted. She prodded her neck and found painful areas which she had not noticed before.

As she was about to leave for Luck where Dr. Roger lived, Thomas arrived. She had forgotten that he said he would come. On learning that she was going to Luck, he insisted on accompanying her.

"I'll be perfectly safe. Jordan will be with me."

"I think you need another person with you. Supposing you fainted? He wouldn't be able to cope with the horses and an ill mistress."

"I've never fainted in my life…"

"You've never been thrown off a horse like that before."

"That's true. Well, alright, thank you."

On the journey to Luck, Kamila was almost sick twice and Thomas had to ask Jordan not to ride so fast.

"My dear Kamila! How lovely to see you! What brings you here?" said

Dr. Roger with pleasure.

"Dr Roger, I would like to introduce--."

"There is no need. We already know each other. How do you do, Mr Orzel? It's a long time since I've seen you."

"Yes it is. It's good to see you again, Doctor." They shook hands. "Miss Kamila was thrown off her horse three days ago." He looked to Kamila to continue.

"In that case come in here, my dear," said the doctor.

"Are you sure you have the time to see me, Doctor?"

"Yes of course my dear. I always would make time to see you. I told you that before. Anyway my appointments don't start until 2 pm today."

In his room Kamila told him of her symptoms and he examined her thoroughly. Yes, there were bruises on the back of the neck. She was lucky she didn't break it. But all her reflexes were normal. He didn't think she had broken anything. He then examined her further, asked more questions and when he finished and she was dressed, he looked at her with compassion.

"There's no other way to tell you this, but you are with child. Oh, my dear!" He watched her eyes fill with horror and for a moment thought she was going to faint. "Raphael's?" he said. She nodded.

"I was beginning to worry that—that—I might be. My God what have I done? *What have I done?"* He saw the horror in her face, her sudden understanding of the enormity of the situation. "I've soiled the family name. My parents would be so ashamed of me…"

"Kamila, my child, you will not have been the first or the last to be in this situation. I am sure that your parents would not be ashamed of you. They would stand by you. You were just unlucky and besides this, you were very vulnerable and lonely and Raphael may have calculated on that—."

"No. No. Don't blame him. He is not here now to defend himself. I must be equally held responsible. I fell in love with him. I tried to resist that. I really did try. He said he loved me, but I've thought a great deal about that since he died, and I don't know now. I must think what to do…"

"Is there no one whom you know who—?"

"—would marry me? You mean carry this off as if it was his child? No. I could never do such a thing. I wouldn't be able to live with such a lie."

"I don't necessarily mean hoodwink someone. You are such a beautiful girl and intelligent—there must be a dozen men who would marry you. I would offer a son if I had one or myself if you would have me, although I'm much too old for you—but I don't think my wife would agree to live in a harem." He was pleased to sec her smile. "There are other possibilities. You could go away, have the baby in some distant land or some other city. I have a friend in Switzerland you could go to. And have it adopted there—."

"No. I don't think I could ever live with myself, knowing I'd given away my child."

"Or you can brave it and still hold your head up high—."

"Yes, that is what I shall do. I can see no other solution."

"Remember Kamila I'm here whenever you want me. You are no less dear to me now than you were yesterday. If you would like to go to convalesce into the mountains, I have a house in Zakopane that you can go to. Any of my daughters will come with you."

"Thank you, Dr. Roger, but I think I'll stay at The Birch House. I have a friend coming to stay for Christmas. At least, I think I still have…a friend," she said slowly.

"I'm glad you've met Thomas Orzel. He is a good man. I think you will find he makes a very good friend. He is well known for the quality of his livestock, especially his horses."

He hugged her in parting and led her back to the room where Thomas was waiting.

As they left the building, Thomas looked into her face, and just said, "No broken bones then?" She shook her head. "Would you like to go and have a coffee?" She nodded. He held out his arm, "Take my arm Miss. Kamila. It's quite slippery underfoot."

He chose a corner table and ordered coffee, and asked her if she would like something to eat, but she just shook her head, and said quietly, "No thank you."

After looking at her a while, he said, "You are greatly troubled. Do you wish to talk about it? I'm willing to listen. I know that we haven't known each other long. However, I would like you to consider me as a friend." He wanted to touch her hand but felt that it would be considered inappropriate. He looked around the coffee room. The tables were placed quite far from each other and there were only a few people in the room, and no one whom he knew. No one had said anything to Kamila either when they came in, so he assumed that no one knew her either. He knew that she was not from these parts.

"You know Miss. Kamila, when I first laid eyes on you, I thought that—even in that ridiculous cap that nearly swallowed the whole of your head—that you looked like an angel. And then—when Aniela took the cap off and that dark curly hair—."

"Oh, Mr Thomas, believe me, I am no angel. If you but knew…" And suddenly, haltingly, she told him of Raphael, how she tried to resist falling in love with him…how now over the last several days when she tried to analyze this, she was not even sure if he really had been in love with her. Whether Madelaine had assessed him correctly that all he wanted was a woman, any woman. And the news that Dr. Roger had given her…and she did not even know whether Madelaine will abandon her when she knew how wicked she had been.

"Dear child, you are being too harsh. Too unforgiving to yourself. It's not a crime to love a man. Even one who does not appear to be worthy of your love. I am sure that this Miss Madelaine will remain your friend. Write to her, especially since she does not know of Raphael's death. It wasn't reported in the papers, you know. Ask her to come to you if it's at all possible. As for the pregnancy, that too is not the end of the world. You are a beautiful girl and some day you will meet someone who will love you for yourself."

"Who would want me—soiled as I am—now? And my parents—how hurt and disgusted they would be!"

"Firstly, you are not soiled. Do you think that loving a man physically is dirty? The whole world does not think that. Otherwise there would be no people on the earth. Do you think that the nuns in the convent are so pure and chaste? Not at all! How many times have they discovered bodies of babies buried in the cellars of nunneries? So stop that nonsense! Secondly, your parents would not be disgusted. They would continue to love you as before, if not more. If you were my daughter, you would still be as dear. I would never abandon you. And neither would they."

"No, I don't think that loving a man is dirty. It's just that I shouldn't have done it, since I was not married to him."

"That is only a question of a little piece of paper."

"Yes, but it makes a world of difference."

"If that matters to you so much, then I can offer myself to you. You can have me with your little piece of paper. The baby will then be registered as mine—."

"Mr. Orzel—Mr.Thomas! If you thought that I was asking you to offer me marriage, please forgive me. I wouldn't dream of cheating!"

"Please don't distress yourself. Just listen. I am a farmer and have dealt with animals all my life. My whole life has revolved around cattle, horses, pigs and sheep. I look at the position of an offspring from *that* point of view. Sheep are different, in that they are so stupid that you have to fool them. In case of cows, mares or sows, if the mother dies, her little one will be accepted by another mother, who has had one or more of her own. With sows there are so many in the litter that if one or more squeeze in for the milk they won't even be noticed. If a mother can offer *so* much—milk, love, warmth—to an orphan and can accept another baby—why should a mere male object to that? So *your* baby would be *mine* also, and I wouldn't treat that child any different to any other children that may come afterwards. So, there is no question of anyone cheating."

"But we are not animals. We reason and calculate and think—."

"Don't you think that dogs and wolves reason and calculate? If you observe their expressions you will see that they are calculating how to solve a problem. And they, too, would accept an orphan, probably even more so than domesticated animals. I love animals and have observed them all my life. I am considerably older than you. You are—what, seventeen?"

"Eighteen. I shall be nineteen in a fortnight."

"And I am forty. I am not from your social class, of course. But I do have a successful farm and am not penniless. I do have a very warm affection for you despite that we have only met a few days ago. I am more than convinced that this would grow into a deep love. Just think about that. If you want me, I am yours."

"Mr. Thomas, you are the kindest man I have ever met. Oh, dear! I think I'm going to cry. Oh, dear!" She blinked rapidly to prevent this.

"I wouldn't do that. That tablecloth is so lovely and it would be a pity to spoil it. How about another coffee? And perhaps a cake or something to eat?"

"I'd like another coffee but nothing to eat, thank you. But you have if you wish."

They made their way to where Jordan was waiting. Kamila felt substantially calmer than when she had left the doctor. She stole a glance at her companion. He was very tall, perhaps as tall as Karol, and thin. Whilst sitting in the coffee house she observed how kind his clean shaven face was. His fine hair was fair and slightly curly and when he looked at her she felt a friendship and warmth. She particularly looked at his hands and was pleased that the nails were clean, and observed how long his fingers were. Yes, he had beautiful hands, almost like a pianist. And yet they were strong hands. She had an abhorrence of seeing grime under the nails and remembered that her mother had been the same.

When they arrived at The Birch House, Thomas said he would not come in. He felt she needed some time to herself but advised her to write to Madelaine and he would come and see her in two days time, if she was agreeable to that.

"Yes of course, I would love to see you. And thank you for coming with me to the doctor and for all you've done."

He kissed her hand, and whilst still holding it, said quietly, "Do write to Miss Madelaine. Just say that Mr Raphael has died and maybe briefly how he died. And say that you need her. Goodbye Miss Kamila. Till the day after tomorrow?" He raised his hat and went to fetch his horse from the stables.

She sat a long time with a pen in her hand and a blank piece of paper in front of her, trying to formulate in her mind a letter to Madelaine. Eventually she started to write.

11th November, 1850

Dear Madelaine,

Firstly, thank you for your letter. I could not reply straight away because something so terrible happened that even now I am finding this letter very difficult to write.

During mid-October, armed men came to the house asking if Raphael was living here.

Instead of escaping, Raphael came out and asked them to join him to fight the Tsarist regime.

They shot him in front of me.

I wanted to die too and still do. I have now lost everyone that I have ever loved to patriotism.

I wish you could be near.....

Affectionately yours,

Kamila.

This time she folded the paper and put it in an envelope and put a seal with her crest over the join. Although she did not impart any more information, she did not wish for this letter to be read by anyone else.

She should really have written to Amelia as well but felt that at present her mood was so gloomy that it was bound to come out and decided to postpone that for some days.

I must think what to do! Her arm encircled Thor as he sat by her legs. She looked into his face and remembered what Thomas had said, that dogs did reason and think.

"What should I do Thor?" She sought the answer in his intelligent eyes but couldn't understand. All she could see in them was compassion. She laid her head back and the dog put his head on her lap as if to mesmerize her, and she fell into a deep sleep.

Over the next two days she thought constantly of all that Thomas had said including his unbelievable generosity of offering her marriage. Each time she came to that, she shook her head. It would not be moral for her to accept this. *I'd only be using him to get myself out of trouble.* After all this would basically be to save her face and it was her responsibility to face up to her actions, whatever anyone thought. And she came to think of Matthew Kobulski with regret. If it hadn't been for Raphael, she knew she would have fallen in love with Mathew. But that was all over now.

CHAPTER 16

Thomas too thought a lot of what had happened these past few days. For twenty years he had been alone. Oh, he had had fleeting thoughts of getting married again, but whichever woman he considered, he pushed the idea aside and often he did not even know why. His home comforts were more than adequately looked after by Aniela, his housekeeper, and his bodily needs by Margareta who lived in Luck. She made no demands on him and was always available when he wanted her. And now, having met a wisp of a girl, he suddenly felt younger and somewhere inside of him there was a large ball of an unfamiliar feeling. This ball seemed to be made of gossamer thread plaited with gentle tufts of happiness. He felt sure if he were to unwind this ball, it would encircle the world several times over. And he liked that feeling very much.

Several times he caught Aniela looking at him, but apart from raising an eyebrow she did not say anything. Sometimes he caught a smile on her face. Despite that they had known each other for such a long time, she still called him *Mr.* Orzel, but that did not stop her from bossing him about. She would tell him when his hair was too long, tell him off if he didn't shave, or inspect his socks that they were the same colour for he never noticed such trivial things. And if he were going to an important meeting or to the church, she would brush his coat, and swivel him around like a child to check that he was immaculate.

Yes, Kamila was right, he was lucky to have her to mother him, although she was only about ten years older than he. She had loved her husband since they had been in their teens, and married very early. All five of her pregnancies had ended in miscarriages and when her husband died she felt that part of her died with him, and she never wanted to remarry. It was then that she came to look after his wife….

Baltazy had not returned and there was no news regarding Greczko.
Thomas took a little more care with his dress the day he was going to see Kamila, and Aniela looked him over critically. He decided to take the trap rather than ride his horse.

Benjamin greeted him warmly, took his coat and hat and arranged for the trap to be taken to the yard, and led Thomas to the morning room. Kamila came forward to greet him.

"—And how do you feel today Miss Kamila?"

"A bit better thank you. Benjamin is arranging some refreshments in a moment." She felt a little awkward and he saw that.

"Aniela wished me to pass to you her good wishes. When I was due to leave she spun me round. She brushed bits off the coat. She scrutinized every part of my attire—inspected my socks to make sure they were matching. On occasions, I have been known to wear different colours."

Kamila laughed. "Are you colour blind then?"

"No. I just don't notice such things. It gets her really mad. Tell me, have you heard any news about Greczko? I haven't seen or heard from Baltazy as yet."

"No, except, four days ago—did I not tell you? My overseer, Lisinski said that Greczko had been seen in the vicinity. But that's all I know. To tell you the truth I wasn't paying that much attention to that news."

"So near? Please do be careful. Are there any barns near by that he could be hiding in? I wish I could see your overseer."

The tray with tea and coffee was brought in and placed on the table beside Kamila.

"Will there be anything else, madam?"

"No thank you Lucy."

"Thank you madam." As Lucy left the room, Kamila started to pour the coffee out.

"Lisinski may well come whilst you are here. Yes, there are various buildings nearby. I'll ask him to search thoroughly and then secure them. We had a problem recently, before the snow fell, where that horrid man set fire to a barn, but one of the men saw this and put the fire out with only minimal damage to one wall and a portion of the roof. All our barns are securely locked nowadays, since that episode."

"That makes me more worried for you than ever. Please keep Thor beside you where ever you are, day and night. I almost wish I could be here with Thor." He said with a smile.

"Mr. Thomas!" Kamila said with pretended shock.

"I meant, entirely to protect you. But, tell me, have you thought about the things we discussed two days ago?"

"Yes I have." She then fell silent. It was so difficult to put her feelings into words.

"Perhaps I should have said that despite my great age—as I'm sure it appears so to you—I'm really in excellent health and quite strong—you have to be, to pull out some of those calves. In fact I can still do some cartwheels. Would you like me to show you? And I do have all my own teeth. See!" He bared his teeth for her inspection.

Kamila burst out laughing. It was spontaneous and free and he loved to hear it.

"It seems that all the men—or rather most of them that have touched my life—have been very much older than I. Karol was thirty six." She was about to say that Raphael was around forty but decided against mentioning him—or Matthew. But she knew that Thomas had read these unspoken words in her silence.

"In that case I may have—at least some—hope?"

"I have considered your offer. It is a most generous and kind thing you have done but I feel that this would be just to save my face. I've landed myself in this trouble. I should face it on my own and not burden you or anyone else with this. Indeed I think it would be immoral of me to accept. And I feel it would be callous of me to agree to such a marriage. I'd be labelled as a cold calculating woman for the rest of my life." And then more softly, uncertainly she added, "I don't think I am that. That is, I hope I'm not."

"No. I'm sure you are not. But as to being labelled—I thought that you didn't care what people thought of you—."

"Well, to some extent I do—."

"Forgive me, Miss. Kamila but I don't agree with you on this question of morality. I know that it appears that this solution is only to—as you put it—to save your face. I see it somewhat differently. Firstly, this would be to give the child a name. You know what a stigma is attached to such a birth otherwise. And this lasts the whole life of the unfortunate individual, not just his or her childhood. Secondly, you do need security of marriage. I'm thinking of this man Greczko in respect of that. Thirdly—perhaps selfishly—I would love to have a wife. I've thought of this over the last fifteen years and I haven't found anyone that I would have liked to share my life with until now. Please forgive me for being so bold, since we've met only very recently. And just to reassure you, that even if you hadn't got all this," he waved his hand to encompass the estate, "I would still feel the same. And what *I* have, would keep you in comfort all *your* life."

"But you don't know me at all. I might nag or have irritating habits, which will drive you to distraction. I don't know you well enough. And I'm sorry but I do not love you. "

"I *know* that. I wouldn't expect it. But I feel that you are friendlily disposed towards me, aren't you?"

"Of course I am. How could I help being otherwise?"

"Then that would be enough for a start. As for the irritating habits—I'll just have to bring you back here during the times you displayed them." He said with a boyish smile. Then more seriously, "And the feeling I have for you—. Well, I just can't describe it. It's overwhelming. It's as if I've been waiting for you all these years. But perhaps there is someone else? Of course, I must also tell you that I don't have this overwhelming feeling of patriotism that has been woven throughout your life.

"Don't misunderstand me, I do love Poland. And if I had to fight for it, I suppose I would do so. But my love is far greater for the soil and the horses and the cattle and sheep. And I am more likely to lay down my life for my horse than for an idea—for patriotism."

"There is no one else. And as I've said before I would not pass off this baby as some one else's. As for patriotism—at present there is a war raging within me against it. I have lost so much through it. I understand your love of the soil. I, too, love it. I love the vast ultramarine skies and the golden cornfields……Regarding marriage I must tell you that I am afraid—afraid of the unknown—."

"You mean because you haven't known me for a long time—."

"Yes, that too. I'm afraid if it should be a loveless marriage—."

"It wouldn't be loveless on my part, Miss Kamila. As I've told you, and if you didn't grow to love me, I'd accept that. Many arranged marriages are like that. What is important is, so long as we are kind and friendly to each other. That would make a happy marriage. Forgive me for this question but how far is the pregnancy?"

"Between six and seven weeks."

"Then I think you ought to make a decision quite soon. I don't want you to think that I'm putting pressure on you for my sake, but there is some urgency in the matter. Consider that there are three weeks for the bans before the marriage…..If I may suggest, please think of this child and its future rather than anything else."

Kamila became silent. What he said made sense. The stigma of being born out of wedlock would be there forever, however strong she was to cope with the disgrace. Would she be able to face this hurt that the child would suffer? She hadn't known anyone like that, but had only heard and read of such cases.

"Have you absolutely no doubts at all, that you want to marry me?"

"No, no doubts at all. It would make me the happiest man on earth."

After a long pause, Kamila said slowly, "Perhaps you are right. I should think of the future…..I don't know if I'm doing the right thing—I hope I am…. In that case my answer is—yes."

Thomas jumped up and ran to her and took her hands and kissed them. "You won't regret it. I'll make you a good husband. You'll see. I feel so happy, I could jump for joy, I could do those cartwheels—."

"I wouldn't if I were you. You might break the china, or worst still, a bone," said Kamila laughingly.

They then discussed the arrangements that were to be made. The following day they would go and see Father Dominic, who was also known to Thomas. Kamila chose him simply that he was the only one with whom she had most dealings.

They sat in front of the portly figure of Father Dominic and put forward their request. He looked from one to the other, and turning to Kamila gently said, "You are still in mourning. Can you not wait until the year has passed?"

Before Kamila could answer, Thomas put his hand over hers, and said, "Father, there is a reason why we wish to marry so soon. Because Miss Kamila is so recently widowed, we wanted a very simple ceremony performed by you. You've known both our families for so long. We thought that with the winter weather it would be easier to have a quiet wedding. But there is another reason. When Mr. Karol's mother was alive she asked Miss Kamila to take over the running of the estate. Greczko, who was the overseer at the time, was enraged at this and was subsequently discharged."

"She did that because I was grieving so much for Karol, who had just died."

"This man, Greczko, has borne a grudge against her all this time. About two weeks ago he attempted to kill her—."

"Before that, he waylaid me and intended to—I dare not even contemplate what he would have done if it hadn't been for a group of women coming towards us. He grabbed the reins and dragged me to the ground, all the time beating his side with the whip which I understand he used often. And he set two of my barns on fire—."

"And since the last attempt—she was unconscious for quite a while—we thought she had died. Since then, he's been seen near the house."

"And you think that by marrying this will solve the problem? Isn't that a matter for the police?" said Father Dominic.

"Father, you must know how hard it is to prove all this. However, one of my men did see him at the scene and has collected some evidence. It is in fact he who has gone to search for, and to catch Greczko. We hope he'll then bring him in so that the law can deal with him. And I've thought this over greatly. And yes, I think that by marrying I can give Miss Kamila the protection that she needs. Otherwise her life will continue to be in danger," said Thomas.

Father Dominic looked from one to the other, "I will have a word with the Bishop, but I don't think he will object. After all it's been how long—five months since your husband died?"

"No, Father. We were married on the 4th of April and five weeks later Karol died. So, it's thirty-two weeks, nearly eight months," said Kamila.

"Ah, yes. I remember. There should be no problem. The first bans will be called this Sunday, 17th November, so you can arrange your wedding for the beginning of December. I will let you know if there should be any change when I've spoken to the Bishop."

They thanked him warmly and left his office.

"Before we leave the cathedral, I'd like to say a little prayer. Do you mind?" Kamila said.

"I would like to do that too." He squeezed her hand and led her to a pew.

Coming out of the cathedral, he said, "Do you know what I feel like doing? I feel like dancing." He smiled at her. " Shall we dance?"

"In the street?"

"Yes. Right here."

"You don't want to do cartwheels?"

"Would you approve, if I did?"

"Certainly not. Neither."

"But don't you feel like doing something like that?"

"No! But I could race you to the carriage."

Kamila wondered if her happiness was purely relief or even gratitude. She stole a glance at Thomas. He really was a very endearing man and there was not a single thing about him that gave her any uneasiness.

"And now I shall take you for a most sumptuous coffee in celebration." He took her by the elbow and guided her to the most elegant coffee house in Luck.

"I would like to see Dr. Roger and tell him the good news," said Kamila.

"That would be a splendid idea. We'll go there after we've had the coffee."

"He's known me all my life, you know. And since my parents are no longer here, he's been like a father to me."

"I hope that he approves of me then," said Thomas, "although he's known me for over twenty years. He delivered my boys…."

When the doctor heard the news his face creased with pleasure. "Oh I am so glad my dear, so very glad." He gathered her into his arms and kissed her. "And congratulations to you Mr. Orzel. As Kamila is like a daughter to me—I delivered her, you know, so I've known her from the moment she came into this world—so I can now call you Thomas!"

"Yes of course, doctor. So you approve of me for Kamila?"

"Yes I do."

"As you know we haven't known each other very long but I proposed to Kamila quite a few days ago, but she refused me. I was fortunate enough that she changed her mind."

"How did you manage that?" said the doctor smiling.

"He said that I was to think of the future of the baby—being born out of wedlock…"

"Quite right!" said the doctor.

"There is just one thing, Doctor. You don't mind—that I'm not of—her social class?" For the first time Kamila detected an uncertainty in Thomas' voice. She was surprised because he had seemed so sure of himself.

"I don't think that you should even think of that. I know you to be of excellent character. You are hard working. Your financial state is healthy. I think that the two of you are very suitable for each other. I think that Kamila needs someone older, someone to look after her, just like you. And you Thomas—it's time you were married again, but I'm very glad that you waited until now! I hope, and I know that you will both be very happy. I am sure of that. And I give you both my blessing. Let me know the finalised date, because after all, I have to give my adopted daughter away."

They promised to let him know the date of the wedding and all three agreed that they would be in the cathedral to hear the bans read, and then they took their leave.

Back at The Birches they discussed their plans.

"I'll have to tell the staff…."

"And I'll have to tell Aniela. Somehow, I don't think she will be surprised. I wouldn't put it past her not to have woven a spell so that we would be together."

"In that case ask her to do her wonders on the Bishop that he doesn't refuse."

"I somehow don't think that he will. Now, we must decide where you would prefer to live—here or at the farm? But of course, the farm house isn't as big or as elegant as this house. And you haven't seen my house. But that can be arranged easily. To look at the farm is more difficult, this being winter. Where would you like to live?"

"I couldn't leave here because it was my aunt's legacy. I'd be frightened that the government would step in and confiscate all of this."

"I don't think that they could do that legally—."

"Ah! But they don't necessarily do things legally," she said.

"So, you'd prefer to live here?"

She nodded. "This house is big enough to house your staff as well. How many staff do you have?"

"There's only Aniela and two maids and Baltazy."

"He sleeps in the house?"

"As a matter of fact, he sleeps more often in the barn."

"Ah! That accounts for the smell that Aniela complains of! What about the estate and the farm? Can we run both at the same time?"

"I don't see why not. We grow different things. So, both places are well looked after. We should really speak to your overseer. And I think you should call your staff. They should be told that you are getting married again."

"You mean now?"

"Why ever not?"

Kamila went to the cord and pulled it. After a knock, Benjamin entered.

"Please come in, Benjamin. I have some news for you. You know how difficult it has been to run the estate for me, being a woman?" He nodded his head. "And with this second attempt on my life by that dreadful man Greczko, I've decided to marry again. Mr. Orzel has asked me and I have accepted. You are the first in the house to know."

"Oh!" At first he was surprised, but it had been obvious that he had liked Thomas, so he immediately said, "I am very honoured and I am *so* glad, Miss Kamila. Please accept my most sincere congratulations—and to you sir, too."

They both thanked him.

"I would like to tell the staff this. Could you assemble them in the drawing room in half an hour, so that they can all learn of it at the same time, please? Meanwhile keep this to yourself. And when Lisinski comes Mr. Orzel and I would like to see him too."

"Yes, madam."

She felt a little nervous when she faced the whole of the staff of the house, but took a grip on herself, looked at Thomas who gave her an encouraging smile and a nod.

"I have asked you all to come here as I have some important news to tell you. Since my husband died I have tried to run this estate as efficiently as I could and without all your support, I don't think I could have managed. But the attitude to women at present is such that it makes it exceedingly difficult as some of you may know." She looked at Mary, who smiled. "And you may know that when Greczko was discharged by my aunt, on departing, he threatened to have his revenge. This revenge appears to have been directed at me—although he had never met me at that stage—simply because I was to take over the running of the estate. Since then he has set fire to two of the barns and has attempted to harm me on two occasions, this last time with nearly a fatal result. But you all know about that. Mr. Orzel here," she indicated with her arm, " has asked me to marry him and I have accepted. He feels that once married, he will be able to give me more protection."

There was some murmuring among the staff, but Mary stepped forward. "I say this on behalf of all of us, Miss. Kamila. We are all very happy for you and wish you and Mr. Orzel happiness in the future. Has a date been set for the wedding?"

"Thank you. We went to see Father Dominic at the cathedral today. He thinks we can have the wedding in three to four weeks' time. The bans will be read from this Sunday. He just wants to verify with the Bishop, but doesn't think there'll be a problem. We would like the wedding to be a simple, quiet affair."

"Have you decided where you will live, madam?" said the Cook.

"Yes, we have discussed that. We think it would be best to continue living here. There will be no change in your positions. You will all continue with your jobs. Mr.Orzel's staff can move in here too. This house is big enough to house all of us. And we'll continue running this estate and Mr. Orzel's farm."

"What about this Greczko? Shouldn't we try and get him before he does any more harm, madam?" said one of the footmen.

"My man Baltazy has gone tracking him down. When he finds him we will give him over to the authorities." At this there was a murmur of disbelief that they would do anything. Thomas continued, "Baltazy was a witness to what Greczko attempted to do to Miss Kamila and has collected the evidence. Besides this, he has his own score to settle."

"I will let you know when we have a definite date," said Kamila. "That's all then, unless you have any questions?"

As they all filed out of the room, Mary stayed behind and came up to Kamila, "I really am glad at this news. It's time you had some happiness, Miss Kamila."

"Thank you, Mary." Kamila touched her arm.

Shortly afterwards Lisinski arrived, and had obviously been told the news. Kamila and Thomas repeated what had been said before and reassured him of his position.

"We haven't discussed this yet, but it may be that you will have greater responsibility—," said Thomas.

"Lisinski already does have that, haven't you?" said Kamila.

"You know Miss Kamila, whatever and however much more you want me to do I will do it," said Lisinski with a smile and he too, congratulated them.

Thomas then enquired about the security of various outbuildings and barns and they discussed how best to ensure Kamila's safety.

"Lisinski had requested that I didn't go anywhere alone after that first episode with Greczko, so has always looked after me," said Kamila. "But I do agree with both of you that the various buildings should be secured so that he doesn't do any damage again or can hide in them. I can' believe that this man can harbour so much hate towards someone whom he doesn't know."

"With vindictive people, time is of no essence. They will continue until they succeed. I'd give anything to know what Baltazy has found out and where he is at this moment," said Thomas.

" All the men on the estate were asked to keep an eye open for the two men. As soon as I know anything I will let you know, Mr. Orzel and of course you, Miss Kamila."

Once Lisinski left, Thomas said, "I regret that I must take leave of you. It's been a busy day for us. I am glad I've met your staff and especially Lisinski. I like him. You've chosen well." He took both of her hands, "I hope you will feel that you've chosen well today as well. I promise I'll be a good husband." His eyes were smiling as he lifted her hands and kissed them gently. "Until tomorrow, then?"

"Yes. Thank you. Until tomorrow."

CHAPTER 17

Kamila was relieved that the interview with staff had gone so well. For some reason she feared that they might indicate that they didn't like Thomas but it seemed that he had managed to charm them with his direct manner. She was somewhat amused that Mary, to whom she had felt closest, appeared to approve of Thomas, whereas, although she had never voiced this, she had not liked Raphael and mistrusted Matthew.

There were a few urgent letters to write, to Amelia and to Madelaine but would have to wait until the date for the wedding was fixed. And what about Matthew? Should she write to him? She didn't know. She wished she had someone to ask. Madelaine had not yet replied to her last letter….

Next day at mid-day Benjamin announced with a smile that she had a visitor but wouldn't say who.

"Well, who is it?"

Instead of answering her straight away, he opened the door wide and as the visitor was entering, he said, "Madame Prust."

Instantly Kamila was on her feet and flew to her friend, who caught her in her arms.

"Oh, Madelaine! How I've missed you! How I've wanted to see you!"

Madelaine hugged her tightly and then held her at arms' length.

"Well, you called, so here I am but unfortunately I shall have to go back on Sunday."

"But that's only the day after tomorrow!"

"I know, my dear, but we are a bit short staffed. One of them went skating and broke her leg so she won't be able to return until the very earliest, in January. What an idiotic thing to do! At her age too!"

Benjamin cleared his throat to let them know he was still in the room. Holding out his arms he said, "Shall I take your coat and bonnet, madam?" and whilst Madelaine was taking these off, he turned to Kamila, "Shall I ask the staff to prepare the same room as Madame Prust had before?"

"Yes, please Benjamin, and also lay another place for lunch." Turning to Madelaine, "Would you like a hot drink before we go in to lunch?"

"Yes, please. I'm parched. We tried to get here as quickly as possible."

"Very well, madam," said Benjamin and withdrew.

Once the tea was brought, Madelaine drank the first cup almost as hot as if it had come off the boil and Kamila was astounded. "I can't believe you've drank that! Haven't you burnt the inside of your mouth? Don't you feel it?" Madelaine laughed, "I'm used to drinking things this hot. Now tell me what's been happening here? I was really shocked at what you said in the letter."

"That 15th of October is so deeply ingrained in my memory—all our memories…." She described what had happened that day and the days afterwards. How she wanted to die. "The staff and Dr. Roger were wonderful. They all took over the arrangements and transport of Raphael's body—. Dr. Roger insisted—that—that I—stayed in bed."

"There, there, my dear. And quite right too! Raphael must have known that there'd be a day such as that—that they would eventually catch him and shoot him or, worse still, hang him."

"But, you see this needn't have happened. Benjamin went to warn him, so that he could have escaped or hidden, but what does he do? He comes out and asks them to join him in the fight against the Tsar. He didn't even finish his speech. There were several shots. One would have sufficed. He stood just three feet from them."

There was a knock on the door and they were told that lunch was ready. Over lunch they talked of Madelaine's journey here and what had been happening at the Academy. But once they were on their own in the sitting room, Madelaine said, "Where did Raphael live? He never mentioned this."

"He came from north-east, just outside Bialystok. Although he was the elder brother, he was hardly ever there. He wasn't interested in running his estate, so his brother and their parents looked after it."

"I suppose you might call him a professional patriot, if there is such a thing," said Madelaine drily.

"It certainly sounds a suitable description, for that was his blinding passion. When he talked about the part he took in the insurrection of 1830, and his plans for Poland, he was so captivating, that I was completely mesmerised." Kamila became silent, remembering those days.

And Madelaine observed her and then said quietly, "And you fell in love with him."

Kamila looked at her but did not answer.

"Have you written to his parents?"

"No. Not yet. Dr. Roger wrote to them explaining all that had happened. I do have to write to them but am finding it difficult…Now that you are here perhaps you can help me?"

"Yes, of course. I think you *should* write to them. If I were his mother I would wonder why you hadn't written. I would think that perhaps you didn't care…."

"Oh, I cared. How I cared! No one will ever know how much."

"I think I do know, my dear." She came over to Kamila and put her arms around her. Kamila closed her eyes to blot out the bitterness. "I searched the papers after I received your letter and it wasn't reported anywhere, you know."

"Yes, Thomas said the same."

"Who is Thomas?"

"There is so much to tell you, Madelaine! Thomas Orzel is a local farmer—."

"Oh! I've heard of him! And only recently. He breeds horses! Most wonderful breeds apparently! Imagine my knowing anything about that? A couple of weeks ago, I was talking to someone who had bought two thoroughbreds from him. And he held him, this Mr.Orzel, in a very high regard. I'm sorry, I interrupted you."

Kamila described how she met him and about Greczko.

"Oh my dear! You could have broken your neck. I'd like to get my hands on this Greczko! What wouldn't I do to him then!"

"They did think that I was dead. And you are not the only one that would like to do things to him. The whole of my staff, Thomas and his man, Baltazy, who has gone looking for him. You see it wasn't the first attempt…."

"You call him Thomas?"

"Yes, he's been most kind. He's like you….he comes almost daily…I wasn't feeling well following the fall and had a bruise on my neck. I was going to see the Doctor in Luck and he insisted on coming with me…" again Kamila became silent. Could she tell her friend what the Doctor told her? Or should she keep it a secret? She never liked dishonesty. She turned to her friend and found her looking at her pensively. "Thomas has asked me to marry him and I've accepted."

"And how long have you known him?"

"Since the fall."

"Are you in love with him?"

"Not yet. But he loves me."

"That's not difficult. And how old is he?"

"He's forty and a widower. I know you'll say that there is big difference in age, but Karol was thirty-six…" She didn't mention that Raphael was around forty too….

"When do you plan to marry?

"Possibly 8th of December. It isn't quite fixed."

"Three weeks! Why? Forgive me for that. I really have no right to ask this. But do you want to tell me why?"

"Thomas thinks it will be of some protection to me against this man Greczko."

"Kamila, look at me! You never were any good at lying. Is this really the truth?"

"Yes."

"But there is more, isn't there? I told you before that I must be in position of a substitute mother to you. You need someone like that. I felt when I held your letter that there was something—I felt your despair, just holding that piece of paper."

"There is more." Kamila gulped and stared at Madelaine with eyes that were expecting to see shock and rebuff. " I'm with child."

But neither came. Instead the older woman gathered her in her arms like a child, "Oh my little one, to bear this all alone! Does Thomas know? It's not his, is it? It's Raphael's?"

"Yes, Raphael's," whispered Kamila.

"Does Thomas know?"

"Oh, yes. I told him that day I saw the Doctor. He is very easy to talk to—Thomas, I mean. I had decided that I'd have to bring it up on my own. Dr. Roger suggested lots ways to get round the problem…… Anyway, after I told Thomas, he proposed there and then but I refused. A few days passed and he said that I should think of the future of this child, what a stigma it would be all its life, not to think of myself….so yesterday we went to the cathedral and arranged the bans…"

"I'd like to meet this Thomas Orzel."

"You will. He's coming tomorrow. He might even come today."

"And how do you feel about that decision?"

"I've been trying to analyze that. I feel elated and I don't think it's purely the relief over this predicament. I feel somehow safe and warm, because of him. And I look forward to seeing him. I like everything about him. I didn't feel like that with Raphael. I still felt all alone in the world, although I was in love with him—at least I thought it was love. Even if Raphael had proposed marriage, I don't think I would have felt as I do now. It's strange, Madelaine, but when I first met Raphael when he came to see Karol, I disliked him really intensley and thought he was a gigolo. And for a long time, whilst he was living here, I didn't like him."

"And yet you gave him shelter."

"Oh, I had to. You see, he was, after all, Karol's best friend and both Karol and Aunt Elizabeth liked him very much and thought a great deal of him. I don't regret that at all…."

Madelaine stifled a yawn, "Forgive me, but you know I don't like getting up before the birds do and I had to, today."

"Oh, Madelaine! You must be exhausted. Come, I'll take you to your room and you must have a lie down—."

"What I desperately need is a nap."

When they were by Madelaine's door, Kamila put her arms around her friend, "Thank you for coming and being such a wonderful friend. Have a good sleep. I'll waken you for tea—unless Thomas comes today."

"You must! I want to look him over as to the suitability—I'm joking to some extent. But I do want to see him. I want my Kamila to be happy."

As she descended down the stairs, she was considering how fortunate she was to have such a good friend and the relief she felt at her knowing everything. She must ask her what she should write to Amelia…. And then there is Matthew. Should she tell Madelaine the circumstances under which she had met him? And how could she phrase a letter to someone to whom she gave hope of his getting to know her better….

Having decided that she ought to try and write these letters herself instead of burdening her friend with that, she made her way to the study when Benjamin came to her with a letter on the silver tray. She immediately recognised the writing as that of Amelia. She opened it and read it as she slowly walked towards the study.

"Dear Kamila,

I haven't heard from you for such a long time but haven't had a chance to write to you because such a lot has been happening here.

My Father has recently been seriously ill but is now fully recovered. He had a stroke, which the doctors said was brought on by hard work. He lost his speech and was paralyzed down the right side. But we had a nurse to look after him and she was like an angry bear. She bullied him, forced him to practise speech and made him walk the room every hour. She was absolutely relentless and he would get furious with her and shout. All she said was, 'If you don't stop misbehaving I shall put you in a cold bath.' And she could have done that! She was an enormous woman. Because of her efforts he recovered. He was so grateful, he asked her to stay on but she told him there were more people in this world other than himself!

However this episode has frightened him so much—and Mother and me too, so that he has asked me not to wait until June before getting married. We did think that he was going to pass away. It was very worrying. Of course Noah is delighted with that request and we plan to get married towards the end of December. We would have liked it in January but the weather might be so bad with heavy snows that no one will be able to come. I would very much like you to come, if you can.

I did so enjoy your company when you came to see us. And my parents loved you, as I knew that they would. And my brother said that if you weren't so old (imagine!) he would propose to you! And there is only six years difference in our ages and his, but I suppose when one is only 12, six years more is a half of a lifetime.

Tell me what's been happening to you. Since you haven't written for so long, I presume that you have been tremendously busy. Apart from the episode of Father's illness, we have had a very busy social life.

Affectionately,

Amelia.

Kamila reread the letter and immediately sat down to answer it.

Dear Amelia,

Thank you for your letter. I am so sorry about your Father's illness. How wonderful that he has recovered completely!

*You are quite right that life has been very busy here. Not only that but traumatic too, as a lot has happened.. I have been planning to write to you.....*She described all the things that had happened, mentioned Raphael but not what he had meant to her…..the attempt on her life….and Thomas…*So, you see I too am getting married, and hoping this to be on the 8th of December. It'll be a quiet wedding, since it's only eight months since Karol has died and we too were thinking of the weather.*

I would very much like you and Noah to come. I suppose it's too late to ask you to be my bridesmaid or maybe maid of honour. Anyway I don't want to wear white. It'll remind me of my previous sad wedding. If your parents would like to come, I would be very honoured. Madame Prust will be here too.

Affectionately, your friend,

Kamila.

She took another piece of paper and started a letter to Matthew and was about to abandon this difficult task when there was a knock on the door. It was Benjamin with a smile, "You have a visitor, Miss Kamila. I've put him in the sitting room." Intrigued she followed him there and on opening the door saw Thomas. The pleasure on her face was not lost on either Thomas or Benjamin.

She almost ran to him, "I thought you weren't coming today!" their hands met and he bent down and kissed her gently after Benjamin withdrew.

"I had difficulties in staying away! Besides I wanted you to know the good news. I've just come back from Luck. I've seen not only Father Dominic but the Bishop too and we have their blessing. In fact the Bishop said he could do the actual ceremony, as he knew your family, but Father Dominic's plump face looked so down hearted that I didn't know what to say. So looking at Father Dominic, I said that we had wanted a very quiet wedding, because of all the tragedies your family has had these last few months."

"I'm glad you said that. Thank you. And did they give us a date?"

"Yes. We can be wed on the Sunday, 8th of December at 11 am. Do you approve?"

"Oh, yes. As a matter of fact I've just written a letter to my friend Amelia and mentioned that date, so now I can confirm this."

"Good. There's just one more thing we must do and that is to choose an engagement ring for you. I wasn't sure if you would have preferred to see the jeweller here or go into Luck. There might be a better selection there."

"Yes, alright. When do you want us to go?"

"How about tomorrow?"

"Oh, Thomas, I don't think I can tomorrow. You see, Madelaine is here. She arrived today in response to my letter. She has to leave on Sunday. She's having a nap at the moment, but I'll waken her soon. She wants to meet you."

"To look me over?"

"Hm, sort of." She smiled at him and looked at the mantelpiece clock.

"It's nearly tea time, so I'll go and call her, if you'll excuse me?" She went to the door, and said softly, "Don't go away."

"I won't."

She almost ran upstairs, knocked on the door and not hearing anything went in. Her friend was fast asleep.

"Madelaine!" she whispered, "Wake up!" Madelaine stirred but didn't open her eyes. "Thomas Orzel is here and you wanted to meet him." Madelaine was immediately awake, so that Kamila laughed. "We'll be in the sitting room."

Just as Madelaine came down, the tray was brought in and Kamila made the introductions. Thomas lifted Madelaine's hand to his lips and said,

"I am so glad you were able to come. Kamila needed you desperately."

"I am glad too and of course to meet you, Mr. Orzel. I've heard quite a lot about you recently."

"Really? I hope it wasn't anything bad."

"No. Quite the opposite, in fact."

"And now I'm embarrassed."

"You needn't be. It was to do with your horses," said Kamila. Kamila and Thomas were sitting on the sofa and Madelaine in the armchair. Kamila poured out the tea and Thomas handed the cup to Madelaine. Turning to her friend, "Thomas came with some good news. He saw the Bishop as well as Father Dominic—he, Father Dominic, had a lot of dealings with us in this house. He also married Karol and me. Anyway, they arranged for the wedding to take place on the 8th December. He said that the Bishop wanted to take the wedding—," and turning to Thomas, "you didn't say who, after all, will be taking it?"

"I don't know. Does it really matter?"

"If the Bishop takes it, it'll be expected to be a big affair," said Kamila.

"On the other hand, you can't tell him not to," said Madelaine. "As Mr Orzel says, does it really matter?"

"More importantly, will *you* be able to come to our wedding?" Thomas asked.

"I'm sure I'll manage it somehow. I do wish we had this railway system in this part of the country. It would alter so many things. It'll alter our whole way of life. They now have it all over the country in England, I'm told."

"Apart from saving time in travelling, it must be a godsend to transporting goods and maybe even animals," said Thomas.

"Yes, and grain to Gdansk," said Kamila.

"And I could be here in just a few hours," said Madelaine.

"Perhaps they could use steam power to build better farming machinery. What do you say to that, Kamila?"

"I think that that progress would be too fast for my workers! It'll be a long time before they accept such innovations!" Kamila laughed. "It might even affect you, Thomas, don't you think?"

"You mean that horses may not be needed? No, I don't think so. Not thoroughbreds. Horses will always be here. The love affair between man and these lovely animals will never die."

"Now about this wedding. Have you both considered whom you'll invite?" said Madelaine.

"Yes. I have Thomas' list here and this is mine, and we've both written to these people."

"And what are you going to wear?" said Madelaine.

"I shan't be wearing white. It would remind me of so many sad things, on the other hand I don't want to wear black!"

"Good heavens! I wouldn't marry you if you arrived in black!" said Thomas.

"How about a cream colour? Or blue?" said Madelaine.

"Not blue. But I, too, considered cream. What do you think about that Thomas?"

"My dear, I must leave that decision to you two ladies. I just want this to be a happy occasion for you and think that any dark colour would somehow signify all those tragedies that have occurred in the last nine months. I want you to remember it with sunshine streaming through the windows of the cathedral, as if it were spring or summer……whether we'll have sunshine on that day or not."

"Why! Mr. Orzel, that is quite poetic!"

"If it is, it is only because Kamila brings out these qualities. I have no leanings in that direction at all. I am very much down to earth, as I am sure Kamila will have told you."

"Being a farmer one would have to be," said Madelaine. "And where will you live? You haven't told me that yet."

"We have discussed that and think it would be easiest here. Anyway I couldn't sell this place. My aunt wanted me to have this since my parents' estate was confiscated."

"I regret I have to leave you, ladies. I'll leave you to discuss these details.... I'll see you on Sunday, then?"

"I am thinking of going to see my Mother's seamstress. Mother was always so beautifully dressed. Perhaps she could give me some guidance. I wish you could have stayed a little longer. But I mustn't say that. It's pure selfishness."

"No, it's not. You mustn't be so hard on yourself. It's natural for you to want someone to discuss these preparations. I am sorry too that I can't be here with you. But what about asking Amelia to come and stay—?"

"No. I couldn't. She doesn't know about—you won't say anything, will you Madelaine?" Kamila looked alarmed and beads of sweat stood on her nose.

"Of course not. Have you so little faith in me, my dear?"

"No. It's not that. But you weren't as shocked as I had imagined you'd be when I told you—."

"That's because I had suspected something of the sort."

"Oh."

"Don't look so down hearted, Kamila. Ask Amelia to come. It'll be fun for you to plan and choose together."

"No. I don't think so. Firstly she leads a very busy social life—I must let you read her letter—and she wasn't enchanted with this part of the country. I mean the country life. She's definitely a town girl. Secondly, you don't know her tastes. I might end dressed up in yellow like a daffodil, or a very pink embarrassed rose! I'd sooner rely on the taste of the dressmaker."

"Perhaps you are wise."

"Tell me, do you approve of Thomas? I saw that you were scrutinising him very closely, and I think that he knew that. I know that he expected it."

"Yes I do. I think he will be good for you. I think that you need someone older—."

"That's what Dr. Roger said— ."

"—And it's quite obvious he adores you, even though you've known each other such a short time. Yes, I like him very much."

"Perhaps fate intended for me to have someone older. Karol was thirty six."

"And Raphael older."

"Yes...." Kamila was on the point of mentioning Matthew, but that would have meant explaining the circumstances under which they had met, and after all, what was there to say? It was but a dream, a wish and nothing more.....

"You know, Kamila," Madelaine broke into her thoughts, "If Raphael had lived and you and he had married, he wouldn't have made a good husband. Not for you, nor for anyone else, I think. He was an adventurer. There would always have been something much more captivating and enthralling beyond the home. He would never have been home when you were delivering each of your children...."

"I don't like to speak ill of someone who is no longer on this earth to defend himself—."

"I am not being derogatory about him. I just am sure he was like that."

"You may be right. He was hardly ever at his home despite that he was the first born and should have taken an interest in running the estate, but he left everything to his brother and his parents...."

On Sunday Thomas arrived early and collected them to go to the cathedral. Kamila asked if Mary would have liked to go with them. The day was sunny and crisp. When they arrived Kamila was surprised to see quite a moderate amount of people gathered inside and said so to her companions, as they settled themselves in her family pews.

"Perhaps if you were a bit more religious and attended regularly you would know whether this was the normal amount or not," said Madelaine with a twinkle in her eyes.

"She'll soon know, Miss Madelaine, as she'll have to come here for the next three Sundays and maybe by then it'll become a habit," said Thomas.

At the end of the service Kamila introduced her friend to Father Dominic and they all thanked him for a lovely service and left to go back to Birch House. Thomas came in for a coffee but left soon after that as he knew Madelaine would be leaving soon.

Madelaine's trunk was already packed and waiting on the polished floor in the hall. Kamila's fears were all dispelled and she felt a great relief that Madelaine was still her friend and valued that friendship as if it was a priceless jewel. And above all, she delighted in knowing that Madelaine liked and approved of Thomas and she had felt that warmth between her friend and Thomas in the same way as if she had put her hands to a fire.

It was arranged that her friend should arrive on the Thursday before the wedding if she could get that time off, and if not, definitely on Friday. They hugged each other and as Madelaine was helped into the coach, Kamila said, "Thank you so very much for coming. You'll never know how much this has meant to me."

"But I do know!" said Madelaine with a laugh. "I know very well. Good-bye my dear. I'm looking forward to seeing the sumptuous gown you'll have. Say my good-byes to Thomas for me."

Heavy snow fell overnight and none of the roads were passable and a bitterly cold easterly wind blew. It was evident that neither Thomas would be able to come nor would there be a trip to Luck to see the dressmaker. And as the snow would block the roads for many days, Kamila asked for the seamstress to come and see her.

There was a knock on the door and in response to Kamila's "Enter," a woman of about thirty, tall and thin came in.

"You wanted to see me, madam?"

"Yes. You name is Bronia, isn't it?"

"Yes, madam."

"You know that I shall be getting married again on the 8th of December, and I was planning to go to my Mother's dressmaker to have a new dress made but now," she looked through the window, "I won't be able to. Tell me, do you think you could make me one? Are you good at dressmaking?"

The young woman's grey eyes lit with excitement. "I think so, madam, to both those questions. I used to sew all the clothes for the late mistress for the last ten years."

"Did you? I didn't know. Tell me do you recall a dress…" She described the dress that they had found in her aunt's trunk, which Madelaine wore that last evening that they were with Raphael.

"Yes, very well. I made that dress for her."

"I am impressed. That is a beautiful dress."

"Thank you, madam."

"When I married Mr. Karol I wore a new dress that my Mother had had made for me…..so I don't want anything in white. It would bring too many sad memories….."

Bronia lowered her head, and after a while asked tentatively, "Has madam chosen a colour?"

"Not really, although I have thought of perhaps, a cream colour. But this may not be possible since we won't be able to go and choose. Have you any ideas? More importantly are there any materials here in the house?"

"Oh, yes. There are a few. I think I know of one piece that would suit madam well. It's quite heavy brocade in cream, not too light a colour. There are threads of pale pink and pale grey. It was originally bought for a skirt, but madam is so little that I think I'll get a gown out of it, providing it isn't too—complicated."

"I don't want anything fussy. I like plain clothes."

"Shall I draw for you some ideas?"

"Yes, please. We might as well start now." She produced a pencil and paper and Bronia started to draw.

"How about bouffant sleeves?"

"No. It'll cut my size down further. Besides I don't like these mutton leg sleeves."

"You are right." She altered the sleeves to plain narrow ones. "I think if the neck line is open to the bust, you could have a white lace blouse with a high neck. I see you are wearing a high neck now. Do you like them high?"

"Yes, I do. Yes, I like that."

"Pearl buttons down the front. Now what about a hat? How about a Turkish one?"

"Oh, no!"

"What about a Russian fur hat, in white fur?"

"No, no! Nothing to remind us of them! And I don't want a bonnet. Even though they are fashionable I don't really like them. And as for wearing a coal-scuttle on one's head, that's definitely not for me!"

"And a poke bonnet prevents everyone from seeing your face except from directly in front. What about a Cossack hat—."

"No! I don't want that either—."

"Wait a minute, madam. I think if I make the hat in the Cossack style but out of the same material as the gown, with a narrow white fur trim to surround your face, it'll set off the beauty of your face. And perhaps a simple flower made of the same fur or of lace as on your blouse, on the left side. I'll see which looks better at the time. The beauty of a Cossack style is that it'll give you more height. There! What do you think of that?"

"I do like that. Yes, that hat does look right. And can you make all that in time for the wedding?"

"Oh, quite easily. What will you carry? Flowers may be difficult to get."

"I don't want flowers. I'd prefer a prayer book."

"Shall I bring you the material to see?" Kamila nodded. "There are other fabrics but I think they will be too dark. And I have to take your measurements."

"Would you prefer me to come to your work room?"

"No. It's no problem for me to bring these to you and I could do the measurements here, couldn't I?"

"Yes, of course. I'll tell Benjamin that we are not to be disturbed."

It was not long before Bronia returned. She was armed with several materials, a tape measure and pins. When she draped the cream brocade around Kamila and pinned here and there, there was no doubt that it was the right choice. It enhanced Kamila's colouring and made her eyes glow as if enchanted.

"And this we'll use for the blouse, ornamented with lace. What do you think, madam?"

"Yes, I do like that."

"It'll be cold. So, I think you ought to have a coat or a cape to keep you from freezing."

"Not a cape. I'm too small for that. What about a fur wrap? I think I saw one in my aunt's trunk that might be suitable. It's sable I think, so should go with the gown. And I have some gloves that will go with this."

"I know which one—the wrap—you mean. Yes, it would go well but when the gown is ready for its first try, we'll try the wrap then and if it doesn't look good, I'll make you a coat. I found some fabric that will go well with this one. It's a bit darker though, so not suitable for a gown."

"But will you have time to do all that in that short time?"

"Yes, I'm sure I will."

"Well, thank you for all that. It's a relief that you can do this. I don't know what I would have done if you were not capable of sewing all this."

"Thank you, madam."

Kamila was irritated that she had no news from any source and no means of communicating with Thomas. After all it wasn't as if she was experiencing her first winter in this part of the world. She had known winters where they were snowbound for weeks. But she had never been so very alone at such a time as she was on this occasion. She went to the library and browsed for a long time, before immersing herself in a novel and at last the irritation passed.

At long last came a visitor—Katarzyna Ludomirska, wrapped in furs and bringing with her an aura of frosty air.

"Auntie! Oh, how lovely to see you! How wonderful that you've come! I didn't think that anyone would brave his weather." Then noting the older lady's serious face, "It must be something important that brings you out in this." She waved her hand at the frosty window.

"It is. But first, come, let me kiss you." The greetings over and Benjamin having relieved her of her furs, they sat down to await the tea. "Now then, I'll come to the point. You've known me long enough to know that I won't beat about the bush. So, what's this about your getting married to a farmer? You're not in any trouble, are you? He hasn't been improper with regards to you, has he?"

Kamila laughed, "No, he hasn't been improper in any respect. I only met him about two to three weeks ago—."

"Two weeks ago! Are you mad? Have you lost your senses, girl? Next you'll tell me that this was love at first sight. I don't believe such nonsense. And to a farmer! Can he at least read and write?"

At first Kamila was amused at the tirade but now she saw that her "auntie" was truly alarmed that Kamila *had* lost her senses. "I didn't check whether he can read or write, although I think I saw a newspaper beside him—."

"Dear God! This gets worse. Tell me about him, and don't be flippant with me. I have your best interests at heart, Kamila."

"His name is Thomas Orzel and he is forty. He is a widower. He has two sons but they are in America or Canada. He is very kind and considerate and I like him."

"Like him! Hmph! How did you meet him?"

"I was thrown off my horse and lost consciousness and his man came to my rescue and carried me to the farm of Mr. Orzel. They were all very kind."

"You could have given him some money for that service. You don't have to marry him. You must withdraw from this alliance at once. Say that you were concussed and didn't know what you were doing when you agreed to marry him. Offer him money. He's bound to accept that. Farmers are always struggling. He is probably after your estate."

"He is very wealthy in his own right. He said that people might say that and that he'd marry me even if I was poor."

"Of course, he'd say that! Look at whom he'd be marrying! Not only young and beautiful but the status! Ladies in your position don't marry yokels. The whole society would rebuff you. Anyway what's the hurry? You have years ahead of you and there will be hosts of men strewn at your feet."

Kamila told her the attempt on her life.

"That *is* serious of course, but again, you don't need to marry this man in order to get protection. All you need is to employ someone to be with you when you go out. I can't imagine what possessed you to agree to that. Why he isn't even a gentleman—."

At this Kamila bristled and almost gritted her teeth. How she hated that demarcation! And she remembered many discussions on that subject at home with her parents and brothers. They all agreed that it was hypocritical and an empty title for any man to carry.

"But what ingredients does a gentleman require? All that constitutes a gentleman is that his yearly income is over a certain amount and that he should dress well, isn't it? Well, Thomas has much more than that amount and certainly he dresses according to the fashion."

"He should also have been educated and belong to the prestigious clubs."

"Ah, that I can't answer. About the clubs, I mean, for I don't know. What if your `gentleman` with the required attributes is sent to be educated but is too stupid to learn anything? Would he be suitable for me, Auntie?"

"Now you are being silly—."

"No, Auntie—forgive me for disagreeing with you—but I'm not being silly. I just want to establish what sort of person would be suitable as a husband for me. Supposing he wasn't `a gentleman` but was the top brain in the world, in something like astronomy or physics? Or a top expert in some other field? Would he do?"

"Well at least he'd be educated. Anyway since our last king, abolished all the titles, this has all changed and of course these people would be suitable."

"But do you agree that none of us has the capacity to know *everything* about every subject?"

"Of course, I agree but I don't see where this is leading us to. We were discussing your marriage to this man Orzel—."

"But Auntie, this *has* led us back to him. You see, he is apparently well known not only in Poland but also in Belgium and Holland for his horses. I didn't know this. It was told to Madame Prust, my mistress from the Academy, by someone important whom she met at some prestigious dinner in Warsaw. So you see he is an expert, as well as having these other attributes that you require. As for the clubs—I'm sure the doors to these would be opened if he wanted that."

"Kamila, you're just like your Father." Katarzyna sighed with resignation. "You're so logical and obstinate—you should have been a boy and studied law. I see that you are determined to go through this marriage. What I worry about is, when you've exhausted all the topics with him, what will you talk about after that? There is even a limit what you can discuss about horses. The gap between your status and his is a very wide one and it *does* matter, however King Stanislaw Augustus tried to narrow that gap. In fact it's not just a gap but an abyss. You see, I'm concerned for your happiness."

"Happiness cannot be guaranteed in any marriage. I used to think that it was but I've met many of my parents' friends that even in company they could barely disguise their hatred for each other."

"That's true. I even know whom you mean." Katarzyna smiled, "I'm sorry I can't meet him today, this Thomas of yours, but you will invite us to the wedding, won't you?"

"We deliberately chose this time of the year because I wanted it to be a quiet wedding in view of all the tragedies that have occurred. I wasn't sure if you'd come. Of course you and uncle are invited. And I thank you for coming, both today and for the wedding."

The tray of refreshments was brought in and over tea Katarzyna asked what Kamila was going to wear for the occasion. Kamila showed her the drawings that Bronia had made and described the fabrics.

"I can see that you are going to cause a furore with that outfit! But I like it and shall look forward to seeing you in it. Well my dear, I must be going. I'm glad I came and we had this discussion. You've given me some means of combat with those who will criticise you! And I'm afraid they will. But don't worry I'll do my best to protect you."

"Oh, Auntie, please don't worry about me. I've experienced such terrible things these last six months—indeed two years—that nothing can be as bad as those tragedies. They have made me so much older than my eighteen years. Perhaps that's why I'm not astounded by the difference in our ages."

"Tell me one other thing. Have you had any news from or of your parents?"

"No, nothing at all. Oh, Auntie, you wouldn't believe the number of places I've written to, including the Seym. I've followed up every suggestion given. And I'm no further in knowing where they are. Even to St. Petersburg—that was a long time ago and I still haven't had a reply. But what I've learned more recently is that political prisoners—I presume that's what my Father would be called—aren't allowed any contact with the outside world and that's why they won't divulge his whereabouts."

"I am so sorry. I wish I could give you some advice. We, too, made some enquiries to no avail. Well, look after yourself, my dear, and be happy with this Thomas."

"I will. Thank you so much for coming, Auntie. I'm so glad that you are coming to the wedding." They embraced each other and Katarzyna left.

Bronia worked on the gown and Kamila had had two fittings and was well pleased but when the fur wrap was tried, Bronia shook her head.

"It's too narrow. You will be cold in that. If this had been the autumn, that would be a different matter. I'll make you a coat. You can take it off once you are in the cathedral. The fabric is a thick wool and dark fawn in colour. I have an idea how to make it appealing to you." She smiled, but didn't enlarge on the idea. But by now Kamila knew she could trust this girl. She saw how beautifully she had made the gown, as it was very nearly finished.

CHAPTER 18

Towards the end of the week, the long drive from the house had been cleared of snow as far as the road and no more snow fell but it was still bitterly cold. And at last Benjamin brought her newspapers of the last four days and there were several letters. The one from Madelaine confirmed that she should be able to arrive by the Thursday before the wedding as they both had hoped. Amelia was full of excitement at their weddings that they should be so close together and she, Noah and her parents would be coming.

There were a few other letters. One whose writing was unfamiliar she opened it first out of curiosity. It was from Woitek, whom she had met at the tobacconist's nearly three months ago. She lifted her head and looked at the distance, was it really just three months ago? It seemed like a life time ago. She went back to the letter.

Dear Miss Kamila,

I've just seen in the paper that the first bans for your wedding were read at the Luck Cathedral last Sunday. I didn't know that you were planning to wed……. I've heard of Thomas Orzel and I understand he is a very kind man….. I just wish that I had been around for you when you needed someone through this tragic year. I hope, my dear that you will be very, very happy. I shall be thinking of you on that day, and I hope that I shall still be able to come and see you. Be happy, Little One.

Your very good friend,
Woitek.

Some of the letters were from her parents' friends, congratulating her and wishing her happiness. She put these aside. They needed to be answered. Explanations must be made why they were not invited, that it was to be a very quiet wedding…..

She noticed that her hand shook as she held the last letter. She knew that writing well by now. It was from Matthew.

"My dear Miss Kamila,

I couldn't believe what I read today in the paper. You never indicated that there was anyone after your hand in marriage, although, of course there was no reason why you should have. And I have no right to have expected you to tell me this.

Despite that, I can't tell you how distraught I am. You gave me hope. My heart was bursting with happiness as I travelled back home. You said to wait. To my suggestion of seeing you frequently you said that it wasn't seemly…

I waited.

There was not a day that I didn't think of you. That beautiful Russian song, 'Ochy Chorne' ('Dark Eyes') has been circling in my head since I met you. It was like an obsession. And it will haunt me for a very long time yet. Am I destined to regret for the rest of my life obeying a young girl's desire for propriety?

I must tell you that my parents are as devastated as I am, although they have not met you. They were looking forward to that pleasure….

But I must not distress you, which I expect I am doing. Please forgive me.

Please believe me that from the bottom of my heart I do wish you great happiness. And I hope that we will always remain friends and perhaps meet sometime, maybe even in the Corn Hall in Gdansk?

I remain your very, very good friend,

Mat.

Kamila put the letter on the seat beside her. How true, that she now appeared dishonest! She would never be able to explain….

"Oh, Mat! You'll never know now that it could never have been as you had wished."

She wished that Thomas was with her and could hold her but it was Mary who knocked on the door and entered the room.

"I came to see what time you'd like your lunch Miss Kamila—what's the matter?" Seeing her forlorn face she came and sat by Kamila and put her arm around the girl's shoulder. She glanced at the last letter lying on top of the others and saw the signature.

"There! There! My love!" She turned Kamila's face towards her. "He wouldn't have been as good as Mr Orzel will be for you. He had a bit of Mr Raphael in him, you see. I know he was so charming and *so* handsome. But you have made the best choice with Mr. Orzel. I am sure you will be happy with him and I am glad you chose him. I know that in time you will love him very deeply." Kamila freed herself from Mary, took a long trembling breath. "Now, go and bathe your face in icy water, paying especial attention to your eyes. You'll feel better and refreshed. You want to look sparkly, not down in the dumps, don't you? If Mr. Orzel comes you wouldn't want him to think that you didn't want to marry him, do you?" Kamila shook her head.

"Thank you Mary—for being here—I think I'll lie down with a compress on my eyes, then," said Kamila.

"Yes. That should help. And I'll put your letters inside your desk in the study."

Kamila nodded and went upstairs, whilst Mary gathered the letters.
She bathed her face for a long time. Mary came to see her, and thinking that she was asleep, she covered her with a rug. Kamila murmured a sleepy thank you.

When she came down, she set about answering the letters that had arrived that day, including the one to Raphael's parents, which she found very difficult but felt she could no longer postpone in writing. She took a sheet of paper and looked out of the window at the snowy landscape. But she didn't see that. Instead she saw the blood stained snow and the hoof marks on the snow…

21st November, 1850.

Dear Mr. and Mrs. Karbonski,

I apologise most sincerely that I haven't written to you earlier. It was not for lack of regard or bad manners, but because that terrible day in October when your son was shot in front of my eyes was so fresh—and still is—that I couldn't bring myself to write about it. And it is still very painful to do so. None of us will ever forget it.

Mr. Raphael was a close friend of my husband Karol, and I met him for the first time in March when he came to see Karol, who died shortly afterwards.

When Mr. Raphael came in the late summer and asked for refuge, I naturally gave it him. He didn't tell me why they were after him, for my safety, he said. He was thinner than when we saw him in March and had been living rough.

When the soldiers came the butler warned me and then went to warn Mr. Raphael so that he could hide or escape. And he could have hidden so easily. But instead he chose to come downstairs and listened behind the door as the men were questioning me.

When they said that he was a traitor against the Tsar, he came out to them and tried to convince them to join him in the fight against the Russian regime….They didn't even give him a chance to finish what he was saying. Three shots were fired. Each one would have been fatal. Blood stained the snow…I held him in my arms, but he was no longer in this world.

Doctor Roger is a family friend, almost like a father to me. He said he would write a letter to you and he made all the arrangements. I wasn't in a fit state to travel...

Please forgive me for not having written, and please accept my very deepest sympathy on the loss of your son, Mr. Raphael.

Yours truly,

Kamila Wachowska.

She inserted the letter in an envelope and sealed it with her family crest stamp. And now she straightened her shoulders, told herself to pull herself together, and took out another piece of paper.

She dated it and wrote.

Dear Mr. Matthew,

You are quite right. Mr. Matthew does sound biblical but on the other hand Mr. Mat doesn't sound right, so we will have to accept the first.....

Thank you for your letter and the sentiments therein. Yes, it was a distressing letter because it makes me sad that you felt that I had somehow betrayed you, hadn't been truthful.

Yet how could that have been? We had met on two occasions only. And each time for such a brief time. You wouldn't have had the time to get to know me....

I thank you for your good wishes for my forthcoming marriage, and I too hope that we will remain friends—always.

If you should be in these parts of the world please do come and see us. We will continue to live at the Birch House because my aunt wanted me to have this estate so that it would remain within our family and I am the only one left, as you know.

Perhaps it is a little early, but I wish you and your family a very joyful Christmas and a very happy 1851.

Yours sincerely,

Kamila Wachowska.

She gave a deep sigh of relief and perhaps satisfaction, that at last this difficult letter was finished. She put this in an envelope and sealed it. She gathered all the letters and took them to the hall where Benjamin took them off her for posting.

She then made a rough list of the number of people likely to come to the house for the wedding reception and went to the kitchens to discuss the menu for that day, knowing full well that the Cook would want to make a very special occasion of the day. They would also need to prepare the rooms for all the guests.....

Whilst she was having lunch, Thomas arrived, with shining red cheeks like apples and globules of ice all over his hair, that glistened like diamonds. He was shown into the dining room. Kamila rose, eyes alight with pleasure and ran to him. He held his arms open and kissed her as his arms closed around her. She stayed for a moment like that and savoured how comforting it was to be in his arms. She pulled herself away, laughing, “You’re just like an icicle! Come and have some lunch and warm yourself up.”

“How have you been? I’ve missed seeing you and was worried about our delay in going to Luck. You said you had to go to your Mother’s dressmaker—.”

“Oh, that problem has been overcome! The seamstress here has come to the rescue. My gown is nearly finished and it’s beautiful. She really is a talented girl.”

“Can I see it?”

“Yes, on our wedding day!”

“Come on, let me see it, otherwise I won’t buy you an engagement ring!”

“I’ll think about it. Have some lunch first.” She smiled.

After lunch she asked for Bronia to come to the drawing room and to bring her creations for Thomas to see.

“You haven’t brought the coat…”

“No, madam. I would rather you saw it when it was finished.”

“How do you know if it’ll fit me if I don’t try it?”

“Oh, it’ll fit.”

Turning to Thomas, Kamila said, “She is being very secretive about this coat.” And the seamstress laughed gently but didn’t say anything.

“I think the gown is very beautiful, Bronia. You are a clever girl,” said Thomas.

“Thank you, sir.”

“Thank goodness we can now go and choose the engagement ring,” said Thomas.

Mr. Stern took them to a room at the back which was decorated and furnished in a most elegant fashion.

“How beautiful this room is! How very elegant!” said Kamila.

“Thank you, madam. My wife designed the décor. She’ll be pleased with your comments when I tell her.”

“Does she do this professionally? Has she been trained in this kind of work?”

“No, madam, she just has that knack and enjoys planning it all. Would you like to sit here madam, and you, sir here? I’ll bring a few trays.” When he came into the room again he carried a square leather box which he placed on the table and opened the side door to the box. The trays were one on top of another and placed on runners so that he could slide each one out. He spread the trays in front of them.

“Has madam any particular idea of what would appeal? Sir?” But both of them shook their heads.

Mr. Stern picked one or two rings for Kamila to try but after trying she put each one back into the velvet tray.

"The majority of couples choose diamonds, but you have such unusual colouring, that perhaps I could suggest a very dark sapphire? Try this one." Kamila slipped it on her finger, and looked at Thomas. He just spread his hands.

"I'm not sure. It's so dark, almost black. No I don't think so."

"What about rubies?" He took out yet another tray.

"I do like them," said Kamila, as she tried one and then another but seeing her indecision Mr. Stern brought out another tray, of emerald rings.

"Now these I like better still." Eventually she chose one with the emerald in the centre surrounded by small diamonds in an oblong design and both the men agreed that this was best suited to her. Even the size was perfect for her slim fingers. Thomas asked to look at it, and once in his hand he took her right hand and placed it on her fourth finger and smiled at her.

"We shall also need two wedding rings." Mr. Stern asked his assistant to bring him the wedding bands. These were not difficult to choose. They would both wear them on the right fourth finger as this was the custom. Kamila already had the wedding band which her aunt had supplied for Karol to give to his bride. This had been worn on the right hand for the few weeks that Karol had lived and after his death had been transferred to the left hand.

"Would you like the wedding bands engraved sir, madam?"

Thomas looked at Kamila. He didn't want to say that he would have liked that very much. He was sensitive to the fact that Kamila may feel that he was being possessive and as always, he tiptoed as if in presence of a wild animal, which he didn't want to frighten. So he was overjoyed when Kamila said,

"Yes, I would like that. What do you think Thomas? How about K and T holding hands? Can you do that?"

Mr Stern laughed. "I'm sure we can do that." He fetched a piece of paper and started to draw various designs until they were both pleased. "Do you want the wedding date inscribed there too?"

Kamila immediately said, "No. In this case, I'm superstitious." Both men laughed. "We can have it inscribed afterwards."

When they were outside the shop, Kamila threaded her arm through Thomas' arm. Thomas looked at the clear blue sky. "I do hope the weather holds for us and remains like this. If we have a heavy snowfall we may not have any of the guests that you have invited. You'd better be prepared, my love."

"When Mr. Stern suggested inscribing the date, I was thinking of an even more dreadful thing—that *we* may not be able to get to the cathedral if we are snowbound! And then what?"

"Don't even think such things," he squeezed her arm against his body. "Anyway, I've asked the One Above," he looked skywards, "to help us in that. And if we are snowbound and can't get to Luck that day, then we'll get wed as soon as the weather allows. Everyone knows how severe the weather can be in these parts—."

"Don't even say it Thomas! Just in case—."

"You really are superstitious! I wouldn't have believed it of you! My Kamila, who rides the countryside in breeches and is so practical and capable of running such a huge estate on her own!"

"I am not really superstitious. It's just that—I didn't want to be in the firing line—and hoped that everything would go smoothly—that this would to some extent predict our life together."

"Are you still afraid, then?"

"No. Not like before. I'm just apprehensive for that day."

Again he squeezed her arm in reassurance.

"Let's go and see if the Styr is frozen and if any of the ships are stranded in the ice," said Thomas. But when they reached the bend in the river, it had not yet completely frozen over. Ice had formed at the edges but it was still negotiable. They stood and admired the scenery, with the castle in the background.

"It's getting cold. Let's go home," said Kamila.

On the way to the carriage they had to pass the cathedral and Kamila wanted to go in for a little while so they entered. They knelt in one of the pews and Kamila closed her eyes to pray, to ask God to look after her Mother and Father, to help with the forthcoming wedding and to make their marriage happy like her parents' had been and to thank God for Thomas…"

Just then Thomas touched her arm, "We ought to be going, my love."

When they came out, there was a man, wrapped up in all the clothes he possessed, with a tray hanging from his neck, selling amulets of the Virgin Mary. He hadn't been there when they went in. Thomas asked him for one and pulled out a handful of coins and gave it to him. The man thanked him numerous times and threw blessings on them both.

"I am glad you did that. Thank you, Thomas," said Kamila as he gave her the amulet.

The days ahead were busy with the preparations for the wedding. Thomas came on Sunday and they went to hear their bans read again and after the mass they met Woitek. Kamila was particularly glad to see him. He represented a thread with her parents and her childhood. She introduced him to Thomas and was glad that the two men seemed to like each other. When they invited him to the wedding he said he would only be able to come to the ceremony.

A few days later a letter arrived from Raphael's mother. Kamila opened it with some impatience and anxiety.

22nd November, 1850.

Dear Mrs. Wachowska,

Thank you for your letter. I too feel that I should have written to you to thank you for helping my son during the last dark days of his life. Your friend, Doctor Roger wrote a very sympathetic long letter. I am glad that he also enclosed some of Raphael's writings and amongst them there were some poems. He also said how Raphael's death had affected you so I assume that you must have had some affection for him. I know that your husband Karol and your aunt loved him. And of course we have met them both although it was a great many years ago.

Despite that, all of us in the family knew that this might happen, it nevertheless is a terrible devastating loss. From the age of eighteen or even earlier, he had this passion and perhaps I could call it even a mission, to free Poland. Once he left the university, he was hardly ever at home. Sometimes we didn't see or hear from him for many months. Eventually when he was about twenty eight he asked if he could give his inheritance away to his brother as he had no interest in the estate, so long as he could have a regular income. So this was arranged and we saw even less of him than before.

So you see he chose to live in this dangerous way. And this is why I am grateful to you that he was with you, with someone who undoubtedly showed him some warmth, and that although he was no longer alive, you held him in your arms. I am sure that his soul or his spirit would have been happy at that moment. My husband and I therefore thank you from the bottom of our hearts.

I hope that we will meet one day.

Yours very sincerely,

Jadwiga Karbonska.

Kamila put the letter down, remembering the horror of that most dreadful day

She didn't hear the knock on the door or as Benjamin entered. He hesitated and came up to her and touched her arm, "Madam, would you like me to call Mary?"

Kamila raised her head and shook her head but Benjamin already had pulled the cord with the prearranged summons and Mary came into the room.

"Come on upstairs and freshen yourself. Benjamin says that Mr Orzel is on his way and I'm not having you look like that!" Kamila briefly looked through the window and didn't see anything. She allowed herself to be taken to her room with Mary following close behind.

Mary poured her a bowl of cold water and watched as her young mistress splashed her face with it. As she handed her the towel she looked at her blouse and pointed that there were a few wet splashes. She went to the chest of drawers and searched out the prettiest blouse.

"Are you going to wear this skirt or shall I get another one out?"

"There's nothing wrong with this skirt. In fact it's rather beautiful in these subdued colours and it's very warm. Why are you making all this fuss?"

"Don't you know? Because our Miss Kamila is nineteen today! Happy birthday!" She pulled out of her pocket a small package and gave it to Kamila, who opened it, and inside was a handkerchief embroidered with rosebuds all along the edge.

"It's beautiful! Thank you, Mary. Did you do all this embroidery?"

"No, it's a combined effort. Lucy did all the embroidery, but she did allow me to do the stalks under her strict direction. And that was only because I insisted that I wanted to embroider something. She said I didn't have an artistic bone in my body."

"You have other gifts, Mary and above all you have an enormous heart. I don't know how I would have coped without you. You seem to have an instinct that brings you to me whenever I feel low or upset. How do you know? You mother me and are my friend and you boss me!"

"I don't think any of the others would have the courage. Besides you are so young, you need it sometimes…"

"We had better go down if Mr. Thomas has come—."

As they went down Kamila asked Benjamin where Thomas was.

"He hasn't arrived yet madam."

"I thought you said that he was here?" Kamila said to Mary.

"No, madam, I didn't say that. I said he was on his way. He would be on his way if he was still at home putting his socks on, to come here, wouldn't he?"

"Oh, You!"

"But I do have this letter for you, madam—and a few more." He gave her the letters on the silver tray. It was from Madelaine wishing her a very happy birthday and saying that she wasn't able to get any time off to come for this week, especially as she wanted to come for the wedding.

"I do hear a carriage this time." Benjamin went to the window and then to the door for the carriage was not that of Thomas but bringing Amelia and Noah.

"How lovely to see you both!" Kamila said.

"We couldn't miss not seeing you today, could we?" Amelia glance at Noah. "how does it feel to be nineteen?"

"Very old!"

"You look it," said Amelia.

"Ooh! You wait! I'll get my revenge someday. Did you hear what she has just said, Mr Noah?"

"She's rude like that to me too, Miss Kamila. No manners at all."

Amelia hugged her and wished her a happy birthday and Noah kissed her hand and voiced the same. By now Benjamin had taken their coats and hat and bonnet and they were in the bright morning room where there was a welcoming fire crackling. Kamila ordered some coffee. Thor was weaving in between, wagging his tail furiously as if he too wanted to proclaim his good wishes.

"So where is this Thomas that has swept my darling friend off her feet?" said Amelia. Thor barked and jumped up and down with excitement.

Kamila laughed and patted him, "All right, boy. All right, love."

"Yes, Amelia was simply dying to see him before the wedding and of course to see you on your birthday—."

"Come and sit down—."

"So where is he?" Amelia said again. Kamila was about to say that she hadn't hidden him in her sleeve, when the door opened.

"Right here!" said Thomas with a smile. Kamila ran to him. Their hands met. She came forward with him and made the introductions. He then bent down and kissed her on the cheek, "Happy birthday my dear." Kamila was amused how her friend surveyed the elegant Thomas, for he always managed to look neat and tidy, but must have taken still greater care today. And Thor jumped up to him to greet him too.

"I'm just wondering whether you've all conspired to bring this day about. It seems that Benjamin was in on this and so were the staff…. Well did you? If so how could you? After all you Thomas and Amelia didn't know each other? Well?"

"Now you'll never know, will you?" said Amelia and Noah laughed.

"Thomas?" But Thomas just spread his hands and smiled.

When the coffee was brought in on two large trays Kamila noticed that the Cook had made a lot of special cakes and everything was presented so artistically, she made a mental note to go and thank her after the visitors had gone.

"How lovely the trays look—and the delicious cakes. Please thank the Cook and the staff. I shall see them later."

Kamila poured out the coffee for each one of them and handed out the plates.

Noah and Thomas seemed to be engrossed in a conversation, so Amelia took the opportunity to give Kamila her birthday present. She drew it out of her bag. "I really didn't know what to give you, so Mother suggested this. I hope you like them."

Kamila opened the package. It was a long string of pearls. Kamila put them on and they reached below her waist. "How very lovely! You are always up to date with fashion, so tell me, are they being worn this long?"

"Perhaps not quite yet, but they will. They were always in fashion. They look so beautiful long, but you can always double them up if you would feel more comfortable that way. Mind, you might have to wear the national costume then!"

"I think that is really more suitable for children and village girls. All those beads and ribbons and floral skirts and fussy frilly blouses! Definitely not for me! Thank you Amelia and please thank your mother for suggesting this. It's a very kind thought. I have a cream blouse that will make them shine even more ethereally." She gave her friend a kiss on the cheek and then they set to discussing their individual wedding plans.

"So now you've met Thomas, what do you think?"

"I like him very well. Of course I don't know him yet. But by first impressions—and I value these very seriously—I do like him. More important is that you should be happy with him. And somehow I'm not surprised that he is older. After all your Karol was quite old. Thirty eight?"

"No. He wasn't old!" Kamila laughed, "He was thirty six. But that was different—."

"Yes I know. You always were more serious than all the others in our class. I sometimes observed you and wondered why you were so different."

"Did you? I didn't know."

"I didn't want you to catch me doing that, but on one occasion, one of the mistresses caught me at it and took me aside and said how rude that was." Kamila laughed. "I often wondered whether it was because of all the tragedy that had befallen you and your family….Yes, I don't think an eighteen or nineteen year old young man would do for you. You'd be like a grandmother compared to him…"

"Amelia! What an awful thing to say!"

"Forgive me—."

"I don't think I will."

"—you know I'm not very good at expressing myself like you are. I didn't mean to offend you—."

"You didn't. I was only joking."

"—but you frequently had that faraway look which was so serious. And your opinions have always been so mature. Yes, I think you need someone older, but not just anyone. He would have to be someone very special. Is he—special?" Amelia looked at Thomas.

"Yes. He is special. I've never met anyone like him," said Kamila softly following her friend's gaze. And in her heart she knew she felt this to be true.

Kamila described how Bronia had made her a gown and wouldn't show her the coat….

"But why? Supposing it's awful or you don't like it? I would insist! After all you are the mistress and she is only a servant—."

"There is a different relationship between my staff and me than in your home. You see, they are all so protective to me as if—as if I was their daughter and strangely, I don't mind. They look after me with such tenderness that I am really touched. The other day I had a letter which was very upsetting." Amelia raised her brows in question. "It was from the mother about her son who had died. He was Karol's friend. Anyway, Mary came into the room, put her arms around me….. I can't envisage this happening to you and a maid."

"No, of course not! I would have gone to Mother."

"Yes…"said Kamila softly. "So having seen what Bronia did with the gown, I trust her implicitly. Besides she has this instinct that instantly knows what would be best for me. Wait and see! You of course will be all in white."

"Yes, but I haven't got my gown yet. It's due to arrive from Paris any day now. I'm dying to see it."

"I expect it'll be covered with pearls and jewels and will weigh a ton!"

said Kamila with a laugh.

"As a matter of fact, it *is* embroidered with pearls and semiprecious stones." Her eyes became dreamy, imagining how she will look in it. "It's out of this world."

"Tell your father that in Gdansk they have this fantastic hoist for these exceedingly heavy weights. I'm sure he would be able hire it and have a platform on wheels made. They'll be able to lift you and place you on the platform and wheel you into the church right up to the altar. Otherwise, if you have to carry this weight all the way up to the aisle, you'll be so tired by the time you arrive—if you arrive there—you'll just curl up with exhaustion at the feet of the priest…" Kamila threw back her head and laughed, whilst Amelia feigned readiness for a fight.

The men turned to look at the young girls, each delighting in what he saw. Thomas wanted to capture the sight in front of them and the sound of Kamila's laugh and keep it in his memory for ever. The men came over and wanted to know the reason for and to join in the merriment.

"Kamila was being so sarcastic about my wonderful wedding gown……"

"You know Amelia, Kamila may be right in that it may be very heavy—," said Noah.

"It's probably already been sent and the ship has sunk under its weight somewhere in the English Channel—."

"You see what I mean? I don't know why I call her my best friend."

"But Miss Amelia, it is only one very good friend who could say such things to another." Thomas said.

"Amelia, I'm sure you'll be the most beautiful bride in the whole country—no, in the world and I can't wait to see you getting wed in this dress," said Kamila. "But more practical matters now—shall I ask the staff to unload your luggage and put them in your rooms?"

"Oh, no thank you Miss Kamila. We are not staying overnight," said Noah.

"We are going on to my cousin to stay a couple of days. They haven't met Noah yet and because we don't know if they'll be able to travel to Krakow in depths of winter, I want them to get acquainted with him. In fact we'll have to be going soon."

"Oh, then thank you so much for spending some of your time with me—us," said Kamila. "I hope you'll be able to come on the 8th December, though."

"I'm sure we will. Both Noah and my Father said they'll battle through the snow even if it's very heavy—."

"O—oh! Don't even mention that, Miss Amelia. Kamila is most superstitious on that subject," said Thomas.

"Kamila—superstitious? Never!" There was a knock on the door and Benjamin announced that Dr. Roger had arrived. Kamila ran to greet him and he gathered her to his protruding front in a bear hug and wished her a happy birthday.

"You remembered! Thank you so much!"

"Kamila my dear, how could I forget? I remember how you looked when I delivered you nineteen years ago. You don't look much different now. Perhaps a shade longer…" There was laughter in the background.

"What a day! First Amelia says I'm like a grandmother and now you say I'm like a newborn. What am I to think?"

"What I meant was that you are as enchanting now as you were then. We all looked at this tiny mite with dark wet hair and beautiful eyes and each one of us was bewitched." He touched her under the chin and looked tenderly at her. And Thomas knew exactly how they had all felt nineteen years ago, for he was experiencing this same feeling now. "I almost forgot to give you this. My wife chose it. I hope you like it." He pulled out a small package from his pocket. Kamila brought the package to her nose and sniffed it. "Tobacco?"

"Now, now, Kamila you know very well that once something has been near me it's likely to smell of *my* favourite perfume," he smiled.

"Before I open it, I'll just ask for some more coffee. We'll all have some?" Everyone nodded.

When she opened the package, she took out a delicately decorated porcelain flagon of perfume and the fragrance reminded her of fields and blossoms which hadn't yet opened and fluffy clouds racing across the sky. She closed her eyes to savour the perfume.

"Oh, thank you. It really is beautiful, not only the flagon—that is exquisite—but the perfume, it reminds me of our landscape—." Amelia came to smell it on Kamila and look at the bottle.

"No wonder! It's called *Prairie*. Mm! It does smell good on you."

Kamila went over to Dr. Roger and kissed him. "Please thank your wife. She's a lady with great sensitivity. I think this perfume symbolises what I love about this land."

Noah looked at the clock. "I regret, we have to leave now. Do have a wonderful birthday—be happy, Miss Kamila."

"We'll see you in December," said Amelia.

Dr. Roger also had to go as he was seeing patients in the afternoon. After they all departed, Thomas took out his very tiny present, a black velvet purse-string bag.

"I didn't want to give you this until we were alone because it is of great sentiment." He waited until she opened the bag and took out a gold brooch. It was in the form of a hand loosely holding four stems each of which ended in a green peridot.

"Your wife's?" Kamila said gently.

"No. She didn't like jewellery and only ever wore the wedding ring and she was buried with it as she had wished. No, this brooch belonged to my maternal grandmother. So you see, my dear it is of great sentiment and I think it's fitting that you should have it."

"It really is so beautiful! So delicate! Thank you Thomas." She went to him to give him a kiss but his arms encircled around her and he lifted her off her feet. She laughed and when he lowered her he put his head against hers for a few moments, delighting in the moment of tenderness.

"You know Thomas, these four peridot branches? They will always signify to me that on the fourth day of knowing me you proposed?"

"Yes, I did think of that. I hoped that you would think that too. Are you counting the days as I am? Only thirteen more days to go! Are you looking forward to the day?"

"Yes I am. Yes, definitely." They then discussed which rooms they would occupy and which day Thomas and his staff would move in and it was decided that it should be gradually over the week before the wedding, as the staff would be busy preparing for the celebrations.

The rooms that Kamila and Thomas would occupy would be the ones that had been her aunt's. The rooms were at the front of the house, decorated in pastel colours with intercommunicating door with dressing rooms leading off them. Meantime until the wedding Thomas would be given at room in the different wing of the house.

Aniela and the maids from his place would be resident in the servant's quarters. As for Baltazy, they hadn't decided where to put him, as Thomas didn't know if he would want to move, and he could stay on at the farm as indeed would all the other men who looked after the animals.

CHAPTER 19

On the day before the wedding Bronia asked Kamila if she had time to try her trousseau. Kamila went to her bedroom to wait with excitement. Bronia and two other maids came shortly afterwards carrying armfuls for Kamila to try.

"Heavens, Bronia! What's all this? I thought that it was going to be just the gown and the coat."

"I thought that madam should have everything to make it a happy day," she said with a smile.

"I do hope you don't expect me to wear a dozen petticoats or corsets or bustles because however beautifully made, I don't wear them."

"Yes, I've noticed. Would you like to try the gown now?"

"Yes, I'd love to. I'm glad that you haven't made the skirt voluminous as is fashionable—."

"I couldn't have even if you had wanted to. There wasn't sufficient fabric and besides you did say you didn't want it like that. Now I'd like you to put on these two petticoats because the skirt needs to be spread out a little at the bottom and they are very simple and fine material," seeing that Kamila was going to object, "Besides you will need them for the extra warmth. I've made a third one if it looks as though these will not be sufficient." Kamila donned the blouse and the gown, and Bronia surveyed the effect.

"It does need that third petticoat. You see how it falls in at the bottom?" She showed her the areas that needed filling out to convince her mistress. Kamila put on the third petticoat and saw that it did make a difference. Bronia then produced the coat. It was a darker cream colour and although wool, very light in weight. It was simply cut with a white fur collar and delicate pink satin lining which was visible as Kamila walked. When the hat was in position, it gave Kamila a little extra height and the narrow white fur trim did indeed enhance Kamila's colouring. "I've put a detachable fur flower as it looked better. And there is a muff to go with it."

She stood away from Kamila, and then walked around her. "Well, do you like your creation, Bronia?"

"Yes, madam, I like it very much. You look fantastic. You really do! But more importantly, do *you* like it?"

Kamila looked at herself in the mirror, turning this way and that and walked about the room enjoying the whisper the satin made. "I like it very much. Your creation is very beautiful. I do like the hat too. You were right about the Cossack style. Imagine if we lived in the late twenties, I would have had to have a hat so large that it could shelter two other people from the rain. And the women had to wear these hats even indoors. I remember my father being furious when they went to the theatre and the woman in front of them was wearing one and they couldn't see anything. He asked her to remove it. My mother was so embarrassed. Yes, I do like this Cossack hat and I like the simplicity of the gown and the coat. But I have a feeling it'll shock those who see it in the cathedral. Some women may even faint at the sight!"

"Because it's not as fashion dictates," Bronia said with a smile.

"Yes."

"And will you mind? After all if you have the courage to go riding—."

"I know. You were going to say 'in breeches.' But they won't know that, will they? No, I won't mind. I'll just have to carry some smelling salts for those poor creatures."

Bronia had also made for her very delicate night attire and a camisole and asked if Thomas was having something new made.

"Do you know, Bronia, I never asked? Isn't that dreadful?" She thanked her for the beautiful trousseau and asked her if she would like to come to the cathedral to see the reaction to her creations.

"Oh, yes madam. I would love to."

"Very well, I'll tell Mary. She's arranging for some of the staff who can come."

When Thomas came, Kamila greeted him warmly and told him of Bronia's creation and how pleased she was with her work.

"I never asked you if you were having anything made for you. It was very remiss of me and I apologise for that."

"You have nothing to apologise for, my dear. Yes, I have had a new pair of trousers and a frock coat made and a new shirt and a cravat. But I won't be as pretty as you. I can guarantee that. I'm just glad that we no longer have those pinched-in waists. They were so uncomfortable. And do you remember—what am I saying? You weren't even born then! I was thinking of those collars which we, men, had to wear. They were so high and kept in place with a cravat or a stock, that it made it impossible to turn the head or to lower it. Thank God we haven't that now, otherwise I wouldn't be able to see my lovely Kamila. Now tell me, isn't Madelaine coming tomorrow?"

"Yes, I think so. She said it would be Thursday. The house is full of excitement. I can feel it in the air. I frequently hear the maids singing whilst they are going about their work. Can you feel the excitement when you come here?"

He laughed. "I think my sensitivities are tuned in at a different level. If my horses or cattle were full of excitement, I would definitely know. But there is something like that at the farm. Aniela seems very happy. Tell me, we have to go to confession on Saturday, don't we?"

"Yes."

"I was thinking that I'll bring some of my things tomorrow and Friday, to leave Saturday free for last minute things."

"That'll be fine. Your room is already ready and so are the rooms for Aniela and your house staff. So you're all arriving by Friday? I'll tell the staff."
Kamila asked to see Mary to discuss the domestic arrangements. Mary knew that Thomas' staff were coming but she didn't know that there was a special relationship and position that Aniela held in his household.

"So you see Mary, Aniela has a special closeness to him. She looked after his first wife, brought up his boys with tenderness, and has looked after him, almost like a mother to them all—."

"Or a wife in every way?" said Mary, raising her eyebrows and looking at Kamila pointedly.

"Mary!"

"Beg pardon, Miss Kamila, but it would be the most natural thing in the world to happen. A widowed man, lonely—don't misunderstand me, I do like him."

"No, I'm sure that she is just mothering him and not what you think. I've seen her with him. She was like that with me. She had never loved anyone but her husband and still does after all these years. I don't know how to fit her into our household. At the farm she looked after Mr. Thomas, cooked for them and looked after the farm workers to some extent. Here she won't be cooking. But she could continue to look after Mr. Thomas—."

"Won't he be having a valet?"

"I don't think he has one and to tell the truth I haven't broached the subject. They have lived so differently from us. I think it'll be better if they get settled in gradually and then we can see what is needed. But as for Aniela, I want you to treat her gently and be welcoming. Maybe discuss with her once she has settled in, what she would like to do. I would like her to be happy here too. It must be difficult to be uprooted after twenty five years in one place."

"All right Miss Kamila. I will do my best. Would you like her to come to the cathedral for your wedding?"

"That would be a nice gesture, but why don't you ask her yourself? I did tell you that Bronia wants to come?" Mary nodded. "Are there many of the staff coming?"

"Quite a few. Cook wanted to come but feels that her legs wouldn't last the day, so she's decided to stay at home. And Benjamin would have loved to come but feels that his responsibility is to be here to welcome every one on arrival, but I've promised to describe to them as is not coming every single detail." She smiled. "We're all looking forward to that day. We almost all feel as if we was the ones that are getting wed!"

"Yes, I can feel the excitement in the house." Kamila smiled.

"We're so happy for you."

"Yes, I know. Thank you."

The next day, amidst the hectic activity with the delivery of bits of furniture and trunks arriving from the farm, Madelaine arrived.

"Goodness! Is there a war on? Where are the cannons and the muskets?" she greeted her friend.

"I hope not! It's been like this since morning. But Thomas said I wasn't to let it worry me. He has organised everything with the staff and now that you are here we can go to the quieter part of the house. I see that your trunk has been taken up. Or do you want to go and have a rest.? You must be tired—."

"Not so tired as I was able to sleep most of the journey in between the changes of the horses. Pity we haven't that railway system in this part of the country. But I would like to freshen up a bit and then perhaps something to drink?"

When Madelaine came down and the tray was brought to the sitting room, Thomas came to greet Madelaine.

"I won't stay too long as there is still a lot to do but I had to come and see you. I'm so glad—I mean to say, we are so glad that you are here and were able to brave the weather—."

"The roads weren't so bad, the snow was impacted and snowfall is holding off until after the wedding."

"Oh I hope so, I hope so. Do I smell coffee?"

"Ah! So that's the reason you came to see us—," said Kamila.

"No, it certainly is not! I was looking forward to seeing you, and I hope my, friend?" He raised his eyebrows at Madelaine.

"Of course I am your friend too. Are you bringing all of the furniture from your home?"

"Madelaine thought that there was a war on."

"It does look like that." He said.

"Have your staff arrived yet?" Kamila said.

"No. I thought it would be best that they stayed there until after the wedding—I'm sorry my dear. I didn't tell you. It completely went out of my head."

"That's alright. The beds and rooms can remain prepared."

Madelaine immediately saw that diplomacy was necessary and asked whether he had brought all his furniture from the farm.

"Not everything, but there are a few things that I would like to have. I'm very attached to my bureau and the chair. My father bought them for me when I took over the running of the farm. My brother wasn't interested—."

"Your brother? I never knew you had a brother! You never said1"

"You never asked," he said with a smile.

"That's true. I'm sorry. There are so many things about you that I don't know," said Kamila.

"Imagine, Kamila! You'll have a whole lifetime ahead of you to find out all these and other things," said Madelaine.

"Mm," said Kamila uncertainly. "When will I meet him?"

"Quite soon. In a day or so. He's coming to the wedding."

"Well, tell us more about him? How old is he? What does he do if he's not interested in farming?"

"What a lot of questions! Have a bit of patience and ask him all this yourself when you meet him."

"I can hardly say `How do you do Mr. Orzel?` and then start interrogating him. Well, am I allowed to at least ask if the staff have to prepare a room for him and his wife?" said Kamila. "Won't you at least say how old he is? Does he look like you? What he does for a living? And what's his name?"

"Alright. He's 8 years older than I am. As to the likeness, I really don't know. As to what he does, that's also difficult. You see, he's a sort of a vagabond." He stared into his cup as if the coffee was of great interest.

"A vagrant—a tramp! Good God, Thomas! And you weren't going to tell me! Benjamin will have a fit if a tramp comes to the front entrance demanding admittance. And where shall we put him? I hope he doesn't have fleas."

"No, I don't think he'll have fleas. He didn't this last time I saw him. And don't worry, he'll stay at the farm—I'll tell him that he can borrow my clothes. That is, after he's had a bath," he said with a laugh. He finished his coffee hurriedly and excused himself from their company.

Kamila looked so shocked that Madelaine laughed, knowing her friend wanted to say many things on the subject but felt that it would be some form of betrayal of Thomas, if she did.

"I can read everything that's passing through your head, you know. Don't you think that Thomas may have been teasing you?"

"I dare not voice my thoughts. *I* didn't think he was joking. Didn't you hear him say that the brother didn't have fleas *this last time.* That meant that he had had them the time before that!"

"No, no! It doesn't mean that." But Madelaine couldn't convince her. In order to distract her, she asked if Kamila wanted to see the gown that she had had made for the great occasion.

They went upstairs, with Madelaine asking questions about Kamila's trousseau in order to channel the young girl's attention away from her future brother-in-law. Once in her room she took out her gown. It was dusky blue with a delicate pink stripe and had the wide skirt that was so fashionable. When Madelaine held it to her body, Kamilla thought what a beautiful woman she was. Being tall, the billowing skirts looked good on her and the colour of the gown made her eyes darker and aglow.

"The gown is lovely and you will look so beautiful in it! I can see that all the men will fall in love with my enchanting friend—."

"Oh, you know I'm not interested in that. I like my life uncomplicated and on an even keel and after that one marriage, who would want to marry again? I just didn't want you to be ashamed of me—."

"Oh, Madelaine how could you say that? No one could ever be ashamed of you. You are intelligent and kind and if you look into that mirror, you'll see how beautiful you are."

When Madelaine showed her the bonnet, which matched her coat, Kamila said that *her* hat will shock the congregation.

"You call it a hat? Not a bonnet?"

"That's right. Come and see!"

By Friday evening an exhausted Thomas came to the sitting room where the girls were enjoying each other's company.

"Can I, at last, join you ladies?"

"Of course. You've been so busy that we've hardly seen you these two days," said Kamila as he sat in an armchair and stretched his long legs. "You've finished then?"

"I do hope so. If I've forgotten anything, so be it. I've asked one of the men to sleep at the farmhouse until Baltazy returns. I'm worried that there has been no word from him. I suppose Lisinski hasn't any news in that sphere?"

"No. He came earlier today and said that there have been no sightings of either of the men. I hope that dreadful Greczko hasn't harmed him."

"I hope not but I have great faith that Baltazy can hold his own even against that man."

"It's quite late. We should be going to bed too if we are to go to early mass tomorrow," said Kamila, getting up. Madelaine had just left them.

"Stay a little. I haven't seen you much, and besides, there is something I'd like to discuss with just the two of us in the room."

Kamila laughed, "After Sunday we'll have a whole life ahead of us—."

"Yes, but this needs to be said before then." He stood up and started to pace the room. "I don't know how to begin….well, it's this, regarding the baby—."

Kamila's heart sank, *Oh, my God, he's going to ask me to get rid of the baby after all….* and with a voice just barely audible said, "Yes?"

"—well …what I want to say is that once we are married and you don't want me to touch you until after the birth, then I will abide by your wishes—."

Kamila breathed a sigh of relief and told him what she had thought that he was going to ask her.

"How could you have thought that, my love? I told you that the baby will be *ours."*

"Thank you. I couldn't have done that—got rid of it—you know."

"I know. Nor I. But about—."

"Thomas, I couldn't ever have wished for a kinder, more considerate husband and I intend to be a proper dutiful wife to you in every sense from the beginning. Surely you wouldn't think that I'd be as ungrateful as that?"

Instead of being reassured as she had imagined, he looked as his feet and looked wounded. He was standing near her and didn't move and there was such silence in the room that she became aware of the ticking of the clock. So she took his hand in hers, and looking up into his face said, "Thomas? What's the matter?"

"I had hoped that it might happen—not out of duty or gratitude—but that because you loved me. Or at least, liked me—a little—perhaps. I know that I originally said that my love for you would be enough. That's if you found you could not love me. And I suppose that it would have to be if—."

This time she stood up and put her arms around his waist. "Oh! My dear Thomas! How clumsy of me to have put it that way! How hurtful! I see that now. Please forgive me. Of course I love you! I didn't think it was possible to fall in love so quickly. But it happened. How could I help but not love you? You are the kindest and most wonderful man I've ever known—."

"But you haven't known many!"

"That's true. But I must tell you this. Amelia said that it would have to be someone very special for me, and asked me if you fitted that description. Do you know what I said? That yes, you did. And you do."

At last the Sunday arrived. Bronia and Mary surveyed the dressed Kamila and were delighted at the sight.

It was Mary who said, "Have you got anything old on?"

"Yes. My shoes."

"And something blue? You must have something blue."

"I don't think so…"

"Yes, Miss Kamila you have. I've threaded a very narrow blue ribbon into your petticoats," said Bronia.

"Good girl Bronia, but what about borrowed?" said Mary.

"That's done too. The buttons on your blouse are borrowed."

"Really?" said Kamila looking at them more closely, "From whom did you borrow them?"

"I borrowed them from your aunt's blouse. But I sewed different ones onto it though." Kamila and Mary laughed.

"You know girls I didn't have any of these superstitious things when I married Mr. Karol. But I did have something that I would like to wear today. This! The Black Madonna—it was given me by my friend Miss Amelia. Can you fix it for me Bronia inside my bodice so that I don't lose it?" The seamstress immediately set to work with the needle and thread and the job was soon done. Kamila patted the area, "Thank you. To me this is more important than the old and the blue!"

When Madelaine saw Kamila's outfit she asked her to turn around. Kamila obliged and then put the coat and hat on and again kept turning to let them hear the swish of the satin lining.

"Stop! Stop! You'll get dizzy! You are making me feel quite giddy!" said Madelaine.

"Well, what do you think?"

"It certainly is different! The whole ensemble is beautiful. But which century are you from?" said Madelaine with a laugh. "My, but you'll cause a stir in the cathedral, when they see you. I do hope all the pews will be full."

It had been decided that Kamila would travel with Dr. Roger, who would give her away and Madelaine would travel with them. Thomas would travel in a different coach and the staff coaches would precede them about fifteen minutes earlier so that they would see Kamila arrive at the cathedral.

As they arrived into the outskirts of Luck they were greeted with bells pealing from various churches, calling the various denominations to prayer.

"It's as if the bells are ringing to announce your arrival Kamila," said Madelaine.

"It's rather fitting that they should do that, and look how brilliant is the sunshine. All a good omen, don't you think?" Dr Roger looked from one to the other of his companions.

"Surely you are not superstitious Dr. Roger?" said Kamila, but all he did was just smile. "And the bells are not for me. They always do that on Sundays. At Christmas they peal even longer."

When they arrived several minutes before the start of the mass, Thomas was already there looking tall and smart. The pews in the cathedral were nearly full. Kamila would have liked to see who was there that she would have known, but instead walked upright and looked ahead, with her arm on Dr. Roger's arm. She was amused that as they passed she heard whispering on both sides.

When they reached the first pew, designated for her family, each one knelt briefly in the isle, made the sign of the cross towards the altar, and then entered the pew.

Thomas leaned to Kamila and whispered, "You look absolutely fantastic, enchanting—altogether wonderful!"

"So do you!" she laughed, "but did you hear all the whispering after we passed? I'm expecting some of the women to faint." He chuckled. "By the way, is your brother here?"

"I haven't seen him yet. Perhaps he can't get rid of the fleas. I told him to be sure to do that, otherwise you'd never forgive me, would you?" She looked at him in horror but when she looked away he grinned.

After the sermon, given by the bishop, Dr. Roger and the pair came out of the pew, for the wedding ceremony.

As they came out of the cathedral they thanked the bishop and Father Dominic, who had helped in the mass. People stood politely aside until Kamila and Thomas were free, and then came forward to congratulate them and wish them happiness. There were many who said that they knew her parents and had seen her as a child. Some of them she recognised and to every one she apologised for not contacting them or inviting them to the reception but they had intended this to be a very quiet ceremony in view of all the things that had happened to her family in the last year.

And amongst the people who came up to them there was no Thomas' brother.

"He hasn't come then?" Kamila turned to Thomas.

"Who?"

"Your brother!"

"There were so many people here around you that he probably went on to the house. I think we've lost Madelaine now." He looked around above the heads. "Oh I see her! She's talking to the Pasiak family. I think we should be making our way home, don't you?"

When they arrived, they saw that quite a lot of coaches had already arrived. As she entered the house, Benjamin offered to take her coat, but she said, "Not yet Benjamin. There is something that I must do before that." She hurried along the corridor towards the kitchen and opened the door. Most of the staff that hadn't been able to come to the wedding were there and all stopped to look to where she stood.

"I wanted you to see how I looked since you were not there at the wedding." She turned round several times to demonstrate the swish of the satin.

"Isn't the coat lovely? And once we were in the cathedral, I took it off so that every one could see my gown that Bronia made. There was a lot of whispering as soon as I passed the pews. I wish I knew what they were saying." She smiled impishly at them and then thanked them for all the work they put in. "And now I must return to our guests." She left the kitchen amongst the murmurs of appreciation.

She hurried back to the main part of the house, gave her coat and hat to a maid and joined Thomas.

"Where were you? We were all looking for you? I swore on oath that I did bring back the beautiful bride." She told him where she had been. Champagne had been distributed and he now held the glass for her.

As Amelia and her parents came over to Kamila someone proposed a toast to the happy couple.

"I have to tell you what we overheard in the cathedral. After you passed us, there was some whispering and one woman said, `Fancy being dressed like that! Look how narrow that skirt is? If I can afford the most fashionable clothes I'm sure she can. And why not in white?` Another said, `It isn't her first wedding, that's why.` The first one again, `And that hat! Where on earth did she get that?` A man cleared his throat. He was sitting beside the first woman, so she must have turned to him, because she said, `Sir, you look as though you follow the fashion. Don't you think the bride's attire is entirely shocking and inappropriate?`"

"You didn't say that your curiosity was so overwhelming that you turned to look at them—," said Noah, smiling at Amelia.

"I was coming to that."

"So what did that man say?" asked Kamila.

"He almost growled, 'Madam, that bride is a widow and her wedding attire has great beauty in its simplicity in my opinion. The hat is charming and very fitting. If this wedding had been in Paris, she would have been all the rage of that city. She hasn't your proportions. If she wore such a voluminous skirt, she'd be entirely swamped in it and look like a mushroom.' There was a sharp intake of breath, and she said acidly, `Sir! Are you suggesting that I am not dainty enough?` He said, 'No, madam. I didn't say that, but merely that you are at least a head taller than the bride and the large skirts would be most becoming to you but not to the bride.' This seemed to please her for she started to ask him when he had been to Paris."

"What Amelia didn't tell you, is that she was completely dazzled by his cravat," said Mr. Pasiak.

"I must say that I was too. You should have seen it!" said his wife.

"Seen what?"

"Oh, Kamila! The size of the diamond in his cravat-pin! I've never seen anything so beautiful.

"What did he look like? Was he a foreigner?" said Kamila.

"He looked a foreigner, didn't he, Mother?" Her mother nodded, "But he had a good command of the Polish language. He was very tanned—or dark skinned."

"But who was he? Can you see him amongst the guests?" They all looked around but he was not there.

"Incidentally, my dear, what I overheard from a different group was how different you looked and how beautiful and sensible was the design. One woman said, 'I wish we had that kind of fashion rather than have to cart around tons of fabric around our waists,' " said Mrs Pasiak.

Benjamin came and announced for them to take their seats for the reception. The table was ornamented with beautiful dried flowers and fruits and nuts of the season and the guests started to go round the huge table searching for their place, marked by neatly written labels. Kamila wondered who had done them.

Once all of the guests had found their places, Kamila was glad that Amelia and Noah were near her but very disappointed that Madelaine was placed nearly half way down. But seeing her listening intently to the man sitting next to her, quietened her qualms that she would be isolated, especially when she heard her laugh. There were so many faces that she didn't know. Thomas had introduced her and she tried to remember their names and who they were, but had he questioned her now, she knew she'd not be able to recall them and put it down to the champagne. After all she wasn't very used to drinking….
She had asked Benjamin to discreetly give Mr. Pasiak a container with a lid and noticed that when it was brought to him he looked at her and winked. She didn't want him to abstain from having any of the delicious dishes that the Cook prepared, nor a repetition of what happened when she last sat at his table.

"Who is that man that Madelaine is talking to, Thomas? He must be one of your guests for I don't know him."

"Oh! His name is Marcus Morello. He plays the violin rather well and I thought that he might entertain us after the reception, if you like."

"That would be lovely! How considerate of you to think of that! Madelaine is very musical you know, so isn't it lucky that her seat should be next to his?"

He bent his head to hers and whispered, "Luck had nothing to do with it. I switched the place names with that lady with the orange feathers in her hair, but don't tell either of them that."

Kamila laughed. "You mean Mr. Morello and Madelaine? I certainly will tell Madelaine!"

"I really didn't want Orange Feathers to know. Her husband is probably wondering why he's been parted from his wife for the first time in twenty or so years."

"No, I don't think so. Both look as if they are enjoying themselves. And I am glad. They are very dear friends of my parents. The one you call Orange Feathers is Aunt Katarzyna and and that is Uncle Wladyslaw Ludomirski. I did introduce you to them before we sat down for the meal. Oh, look how Dr. Roger and his wife are laughing."

"Yes, I think it looks a happy gathering. Dr. Roger gave a very touching speech. And yes, I do remember Orange Feathers. Her husband didn't say much but she looked at my feet to see if I had brought the soil and horse manure from my farm on my shoes and asked me a lot of questions. In parting she said that if I didn't make you happy, she'll have my innards to feed to the dogs. Only she didn't use that word. She called them entrails, of course."

"Oh, dear. She has always been very forthright. But she—they—are both very kind people. I'm sure she'll warm to you."

But all he said was "Hmph!"

Amelia hurried over and took Kamila by the arm and led her away from the others.

"I've seen him!"

"Whom?"

"That man in the cathedral. The one with that—."

"—huge diamond?" Kamila finished with a laugh.

"Yes! And guess whom he was talking to? Madame Prust!"

"Really? I wonder who he is. Unless it was the musician—no, it couldn't have been him."

"Kamila, don't you know your guests?"

"No. Not Thomas' guests. "

When they returned they were shown into a large room adjacent to the dining hall. So at her request Thomas took Kamila to Marcus Morello, the man with a dazzling stone in his cravat-pin.

"This, my dear, is my brother—the vagabond." Kamila looked quickly from one to the other.

Kamila extended her hand slowly and said, "I thought that you said the gentleman's name was Marcus Morello?"

"Yes, I did—."

"Thomas didn't lie, Miss Kamila—my sister-in-law. You see, I've lived in South America and they couldn't pronounce the `rz` in our surname, so they dropped the `z` and I became `Orel`. Then they added my initial and there you have it!"

"Kamila was worried that you might have fleas—."

"Shh! Thomas! How could you!"

"Ah! The vagabond. Yes, I think that that is a very good description of my life."

"You've travelled extensively?"

"Yes."

Kamila wanted to know more about this man but he obviously didn't intend to expand. She couldn't question him further, so graciously said, "I'm glad that you were able to come to our wedding. Thank you for that." And immediately another question hung in the air. How could he have been informed so quickly and how could he have arrived here from so far away in time for the wedding? She gave him a long look.

"Marcus, put her out of her misery—."

"I could read your questions, you know. You have a very expressive face. I was due to arrive in Holland and Thomas sent me a letter. So the news of your wedding was waiting for me."

"It was fortunate that you were due to be in Europe at that time then," said Kamila.

"Yes, it was."

What an infuriating man! Isn't he going to say what he was doing in Holland?

Madelaine came to join them. "I see that you've met your brother-in-law, Kamila?"

"It seems that I was the last to know this. Was this deliberate?" She looked from Thomas to Marcus.

"No, definitely no, my lovely sister-in-law. I'm afraid I came to the cathedral very slightly late, so Thomas couldn't introduce us. The two of you were already in your pew." Because someone was calling her, he touched her hand, "We'll have plenty of time to talk later."

The guests had left and only Amelia, Noah, Amelia's parents and the family remained. There had been no opportunity for Marcus to play the violin.

"Thomas says you're staying at the farm, Marcus. You have no one to cook for you—oh, no! I'd forgotten that Thomas has left Aniela and the servants there. Or would you prefer to stay here? Shall I arrange for a room to be prepared for you here? There's plenty of room and you would be most welcome."

"You needn't worry about the help. Don't forget that I have lived in all sorts of places and under most primitive conditions in my life so I can cook and clean and wash. But it'll be very agreeable to have Aniela and the rest of the staff there. But thank you for the kind offer."

"You assume that I know all about you. I didn't know of your existence until a few days ago." Kamila looked reproachfully at Thomas.

"You mean my brother never mentioned me?"

"Not a word."

"You weren't ashamed of me, Thomas, were you?"

"Of course not. The events leading up to the wedding progressed so quickly and when I did mention you, the look on Kamila's face gave me the idea of teasing her—."

"And it was great fun," said Madelaine.

"You said you lived under most primitive conditions. Where was that?" Kamila said,

"South America has always held a fascination for me, ever since I read about it as a school boy. So when I left Poland I worked my passage there. Father had given me some money but as I didn't know what to expect, I decided to be as frugal as possible in my spending. When I landed I took any job I could. One of them was to join on an exhibition up the Amazon, as a cook and general dog's body. Believe me, after that experience I could really look after myself!"

"How fascinating and dangerous! Did your parents know what you were doing?"

"To some extent. But I was young and I was learning valuable lessons in life. I did write to them but it was many months before they would receive them and even longer before I heard from home. And it was usually Thomas who wrote to me."

"And then?" said Kamila.

"Oh, I worked in anything and everything. On ranches. In the forests. And then I worked in a mine. The mine collapsed. I was fortunate that I was so strong. I was able to pull some of the men to safety. One of them was the son of the owner, who was learning about mining from the bottom. The owner was so grateful that had I asked for a fifty percent share in the mine, he'd have given it me."

"I'm not surprised. What could be more precious than the life of a son?" said Madelaine. Kamila agreed.

"What did he mine? Gems?" said Kamila.

"Yes, that's right. Anyway, he promoted me, offered me a house to live in, but I refused. I had a small place of my own. Knowing that I liked travelling, when he developed some painful condition of his leg, he asked me to do the travelling for him, whilst his son looked after the mine. He wanted me to carry the gems to various jewellers. That's what I was doing in Holland. So I hope that now your curiosity has been satisfied, Kamila?"

Kamila smiled and nodded, "Yes, thank you. And when are you going back?"

"Quite soon."

"Don't you miss Poland? Not at all?" said Mrs. Pasiak.

"Well, I've lived away from this country for thirty years. So much has changed here. But at the cathedral this morning I did feel quite nostalgic….that perhaps I ought to…"

"I don't suppose that your wife and children would like our cold climate?" But he was still lost in his thoughts and didn't hear Amelia.

It was almost as if Madelaine could feel Marcus' preoccupation and deliberately diverted attention from him. "Kamila, have you made any plans for your honeymoon?"

"No, we haven't even discussed it. What do you think Thomas?"

"We haven't had time! But do you want to go at this time of the year?"

"That's true. Travelling would be a problem as the Baltic will be frozen. Perhaps we could go to England in the spring?"

"But Kamila how will we communicate with them in that country?" said Thomas with such alarm that they all laughed.

"Haven't you been in any other country then?" asked Mr. Pasiak with a grin.

"Come on Thomas, you've been to Belgium and Holland and Prussia when you were showing or selling your horses. And you had no problems there, did you?" said Marcus.

"Well, no, but all the people I had dealings with, spoke Polish, perhaps not perfect but it was easy enough to understand them."

"But you know, if you went to England, your wife speaks excellent English, don't you Kamila?" said Madelaine.

"I don't know about excellent—but certainly we'll get by. I could just manage to book a room in a hotel, I think."

"Don't you believe that. She has an excellent command of that language and a few others," said Madelaine.

"Thomas says you play the violin very well. Could you play for us? Please." said Kamila.

"How can I refuse such an endearing request? What would you like me to play?"

"Anything you like. I love the sound of the violin. I like Niccolo Paganini very much." Marcus picked up his violin.

At first there were well known classical pieces, then some popular Polish melodies. For these Madelaine accompanied him at the piano. As the atmosphere became mellow with the music and the alcohol, Mr Pasiak gave a very wide and somewhat audible yawn.

Mrs. Pasiak gave him an annoyed look, "Really! I wish you wouldn't do that—."

"I know—it's so common." He finished for her. The others laughed. "Sorry! I think I'm going to retire, if you don't mind."

"In that case—," said Marcus and picked up his violin and murmuring to Madelaine, they played a lullaby to finish the evening.

CHAPTER 20

Baltazy eventually came face to face with Greczko on the banks of the river Styr, north of Luck. He realised that Greczko was planning to cross the frozen river and escape into the village of Kolki. For days he had followed this man's tracks. At first he rode his horse but sometimes Greczko disappeared through narrow places where a horse could not go, so he had the horse stabled with a local farmer and followed him on foot, and each time Greczko managed to get away. He obviously knew the terrain like a fox and was as cunning.

On one occasion Baltazy followed his footprints—he came to know them so well—and these led to a tree and then disappeared. No new snow had fallen and there were no retracing footprints. He looked up into the tree and viewed each branch meticulously. There was no one hiding there. He looked at his surroundings. No footsteps to be seen within sight, just a coppice and vast fields of snow.

He examined the tree and the bark more closely. Yes, someone had climbed this tree, and very recently. Pieces of bark were torn here and there and there were scuff marks. Then he noticed a few small broken branches on one side of this tree and another tree facing it. Could it be possible? It must be! It was unbelievable that this man who was a little older than Baltazy and rather thick set could perform such acrobatics, for Greczko must have used his extraordinary long whip to swing from one tree onto another. He looked at the trees where the broken twigs and branches lay and followed these until he found his adversary's footsteps again.

And now he was a few feet away from him. Greczko faced him and snarled like a rabid animal. He cracked his whip with enthusiasm, in preparation to use it and to induce fear into the man opposite. Baltazy's only weapon was a knife but if he threw it and didn't kill him or worse still if he missed him, he'd have nothing with which to protect himself. He decided not to use it—yet. Greczko leaned back and swung the whip. Baltazy saw that he had aimed at his neck and instantly he ducked and at the same time put out his left hand in order to catch it. The whip did catch his cheek but he managed to grab the whip and pulled. But the other man was much stronger and as he savagely pulled, Baltazy couldn't bear the excruciating pain where the whip had cut his palm and had to let go.

Greczko had pulled so fiercely, hoping to drag the other man to him that his feet slipped on the high bank and he fell backwards. Under normal circumstances the ice covering the river would not have broken but because he had pulled with such brutality and speed, the ice did break as his bottom hit it and he fell into the dark abyss of the river Styr. Baltazy ran to the edge and was just in time to witness the end of the whip snaking after its owner. He hesitated, for by now he grudgingly had to admit to himself that he bore some admiration for this dreadful man. There were no branches he could have used to poke through the hole, and the ice was cracked for a couple of feet around the hole so that he couldn't slide onto it. He waited for quite some time, but there was no sign of the man coming up.

He turned away to make his journey home.

He was so tired and hungry, but doggedly he walked until he came to some dwellings. There he was given a hot soup. Someone was found who could drive him in his wagon to the next village where he spent the night. Eventually he arrived to where his horse was stabled and then to Thomas Orzel's farm. He stabled the horse, rubbed him down and covered him with a blanket, gave him oats and went to his room by the kitchen. As he entered the cold room his exhaustion hit him as if a boulder had fallen on him and he collapsed to the floor.

It was dusk and Marcus was in the process of lighting the lamps when he heard a noise. He went to investigate and found what looked like a pile of rags. And then he saw the foot. He kicked it. No movement. He turned the body over. It was very cold but still alive. He guessed who this was although he didn't recognise him.

When he said, "Baltazy?" there was no response of any kind. He quickly whipped off one blanket from the bed and threw it over the bundle on the floor. He then ran to the main house, calling, "Aniela! Aniela!"

She came running. "What's the matter?"

"Baltazy's back. Quick! Bring a bowl of hot water and towels. He's frozen." He collected an old thick night shirt that Thomas had left behind, more blankets and the warming pan. He put the warming pan into Baltazy's bed and knelt down to light the fire in the grate. Aniela brought the bowl of hot water and they quickly undressed Baltazy, noting that his clothes were soaking wet. He quickly washed him all over with the hot water and she rubbed him dry fiercely with the rough towel and put the night gown on him. They wrapped him in two blankets and Marcus carried him to the bed. Aniela then went to the kitchen and poured thick, hot broth into a bowl and together with large chunks of bread smeared thickly with butter brought them back to Baltazy. Marcus touched his cheeks, they were cool but not as cold as before. But his feet still seemed as cold.

"Baltazy! Wake up!" He shook him but the man just moaned. He shook him again. "Wake up! I want you to have something to eat." Eventually as if unwillingly, Baltazy opened his eyes.

"Mr. Marcus?"

"Yes. Now have this while it's hot."

"I did catch him you know, but—."

"Yes, yes! You can tell us later. First have this broth." Baltazy tried to scoop the broth with the spoon but it tipped out and he couldn't hold the bowl with his left hand, although Marcus had bandaged it. "Your hands are still frozen. Put them under the bed-clothes and Aniela will feed you. She's better at this than I." When the bowl was empty, he said, "Would you like some more?"

He shook his head. "But I would like to finish that bread." And this time he withdrew his hand from under the blankets, and ate the bread ravenously.

"Now go to sleep. You can tell me all about it tomorrow. Goodnight."

"Goodnight, sir and thank you."

Whilst Aniela prepared a hot breakfast, Marcus went to see Baltazy.

"Ah! Good! You are awake! The breakfast is ready. Do you think you can walk?"

"Good morning, sir. Of course I can walk. I'll get dressed and come."

"You don't need to get dressed. There's only the two of us here, and I think you should stay in bed today. Aniela won't mind."

"Oh, she will. I'm sure she'll chase me out. I must go and see Mr. Thomas—."

"You've done enough travelling for a while. I'm going to see him a little later and I think he'd want to come and see you. He was very worried about you. Here—put this wrap around and come and have breakfast."

Baltazy went back to bed after breakfast and Marcus saddled a horse and went to Birch House to see his brother.

"Oh, I am so glad he's back and not hurt. I know that Thomas was very worried that we hadn't any news of him, but so was I.," said Kamila.

"Well, he does have a very badly cut left palm. I only hope that it doesn't fester—," said Marcus.

"But you don't know how he came about having that, do you?"

Marcus shook his head. "I thought that he could tell us all that later. He was exhausted and frozen. All his clothes were sodden. I really thought I might have a corpse on my hands."

Thomas asked for a horse to be saddled.

"I really would like to come with you, Thomas—," but she looked at Madelaine, who instantly said,

"Don't worry about me, Kamila. You go if you wish."

"No—." Both men said at the same time.

Thomas said gently, "We don't know what he's been through. It may have been something terrible. I would really prefer that you stayed here, apart from the fact that you won't have Madelaine's company for that long. Besides, you don't understand him!"

"That's true."

When the two men arrived at the farm they were pleased that one of the workers had arrived and was working with the horses stabled near the house.

"Morning, Mr Orzel. Morning, sir. 'E's back then." It was neither a question nor a statement.

"You've seen him then?" Marcus.

"Aye. Oi seen 'is 'orse."

"Good man," said Thomas. "Can you stay at the house these next few nights, until Baltazy is fully recovered? Just in case Aniela needs you? "

"Yes, sir Oi will." They gave him the horses and went inside the farmhouse.

They needed to go through the kitchen in order to reach Baltazy's room. Aniela greeted them and said she'd bring some tea.

"How's the hand?" Marcus asked.

"A bit painful, but it'll be alright. I heal well."

"All the same, keep it clean and dry."

"I will." He then told them all that had befallen him in the trailing of his adversary. "—so I couldn't give him any help. The ice was cracked all around the hole—."

"But surely you wouldn't have wanted to save him?" Marcus said. "Didn't you say that he had murdered your brother?"

"Yes sir, he did. But, you have to have some admiration for his cunning—."

"Just as well it finished this way." Thomas said. "Now, let's look at that hand." When Aniela brought a bowl of warm water at their request and removed the bandage from the hand, they were dismayed to see the hand reddened and swollen and a lot of suppuration in the wound. "I think we must get the doctor to see this. Aniela, get one of the men to go for him. Tell him to ask the doctor to come straight away—that it's an injured hand."

"It'll be alright Mr. Thomas. I heal very well and quick. I'm lucky like this."

"That may be so, but this looks very serious and we can't afford to wait for luck to step in."

"In the meantime put your hand in this water. Let's wash off the pus and see what's underneath," said Marcus, noticing the wince on Baltazy's face as the hand went into the water. "Let it soak. I'll bring more water."

After several changes of water the hand remained red and the edges of the wound were swollen and white. The rest of the hand was swollen and an unhealthy colour. Marcus bandaged it with fresh bandages and asked Aniela to wash the dirty ones and boil them.

The local doctor arrived within half an hour. He didn't live very far and usually dealt with Thomas' farm men and women. When he saw the extent of the injury and inflammation, he shook his head, "'Tis bad. It ought to come off."

"Cut my hand off? Never. NEVER!" shouted Baltazy, becoming more and more hysterical.

"You'll get blood poisoning. Then you'll die," he said flatly as he looked at Baltazy from under great bushy eyebrows.

"I'd rather die than have no hand." Baltazy sobbed.

Aniela came to him and put her arm around his shoulder, "Shh! Wait and see what else the doctor suggests." Pleadingly she said, "Is there nothing else?"

"Yes. Poultices. Leeches. But he may still die. From blood poisoning."

"Ugh! I hate those cursed things, but I suppose I'll have to have them—."

"Anything else?" This time Thomas looked terrified.

"No." He gave them a bottle with the leeches and brief instructions. When he left the four of them exchanged glances. Each face reflected terror and distaste.

It was Marcus who chose to administer them, seeing that neither Aniela nor Thomas could even touch them. "In Brazil the natives used the leaves from a tree with great effect, but these don't grow on this side of the equator." He picked up one leech between his finger and thumb applied its mouth to the edge of the wound. "These are small compared to the ones they have in the Amazon. There, they are greenish brown and eighteen inches long." Aniela covered her mouth with her hand and turned away.

Back at the Birch House, Thomas related to Kamila all that had happened and how he was worried about Baltazy's hand. Kamila asked him to describe in detail how the hand looked so she had a picture of it in her mind as if she had seen it personally. She went to her mother's notes on wounds and was amazed that she mentioned leeches but she too must have had an abhorrence to the creatures. She mentioned plants that were for drawing out pus but of course they would have to be used freshly picked and this was winter. And then she read that honey was excellent for cleaning the wound……

"Thomas, I must go to Dr. Roger, to ask him about these. Will you take me to him, please?"

"Now?"

"Yes."

At Dr. Roger's house, they had to wait a little as he was still out but his wife brought them some tea and freshly baked cakes. When he arrived, once again Thomas described in detail how the hand looked and how old the wound was. And Kamila wanted to know about leeches. Was that the right treatment? "It somehow seems so barbaric, so antiquated."

"Well, yes, antiquated it is. They certainly have been used by the Greeks and by Indian physicians before that. Nevertheless people do use them now. In fact during the Napoleonic wars, not so very long ago, their use was frenzied to say the least and for every conceivable affliction. But as for barbaric? It may seem so to you, but treatment using leeches has saved many a patient from dying or losing a part of their body."

"But how do they help? Don't they just suck the blood?"

"They do, Kamila, but if placed at the edges of the wound, they will reduce the swelling—and quite dramatically too. But they do have other beneficial properties."

"My stomach turns at the thought. What about these notes of my Mother's about honey?"

"First of all, it's important to keep the wound clean, and the best way is to use salt."

"Won't it be painful to put salt into the wound, after all there is a saying—." Thomas said.

"No, no. You must put the salt into the warm water and soak all the pus away. You use about his amount of salt into this amount of water." He showed them with his hands. "Once you've cleaned the wound, smear honey into the wound. It's wonderful stuff and has amazing properties. Then cover the whole with a dressing. But if maggots were used they would eat all the pus and necrotic—dead—tissue most efficiently."

"Maggots! I do feel quite sick at the very thought of even seeing them, let alone handling them!"

"How often should the dressing be changed?" said Thomas.

"At first probably daily. Once it's started to heal, then every two to three days."

"Will you come and see him please, Dr. Roger?" said Thomas.

"But you say that your own doctor has seen him, didn't you?" Thomas nodded. "So it wouldn't be right for me to see him unless he, the doctor asked, and he isn't likely to do that."

"But why not? Why can't you see him?" Kamila said.

"Because of medical etiquette."

"But supposing that doctor doesn't know anything about your visit? *I* am asking you and I didn't know that he had been seen by anyone else….. Please, Dr. Roger, see him for me. I can understand his not wanting to live without a hand. Please—come and see him for me."

"Very well."

"Thank you." Kamila and Thomas said together. Turning to Thomas, Kamila said, "Have you enough bandages and honey at the farm or shall we bring some from the house?"

"I don't really know—especially bandages. Aniela would know—. We do have some honey."

"In that case we'll collect them from home first—."

"I'll bring the bandages, Kamila, so don't worry about them and if Thomas has the honey we can set off straight away."

Dr. Roger confirmed the previous doctor's diagnosis—that it was an exceedingly serious wound. Once again Aniela brought lots of warm water and the hand was soaked in the salty solution, until all the pus was removed. He applied four fresh leeches to the edges of the wound, "Now we have to wait until they swell up." Seeing that Kamila was going to ask him more questions, he continued, "That will take about twenty minutes. Incidentally, you must make sure that they bite the flesh where you want them to, otherwise they will crawl away. When they are full, they will drop off quite easily, so you catch them in this bottle. The hand will be less swollen and pinker but the wounds that the leeches produce will bleed so don't be alarmed at that."

"So do you used them again? And when?" said Kamila, now quite fascinated by the creatures.

"No. That teaspoonfull of blood that each one has sucked will be food for them for a year. If you pour some spirit or alcohol over them, they will die. Apply four more fresh ones in two days' time." He waited until the leeches were engorged and they dropped off into the bottle. "Note how much less swelling there is and the improved colour of the hand." And then he showed them how to apply the honey and the bandage.

"Now he needs to have this hand in a sling so that the hand is nearly as high as the shoulder—."

"Why?" asked Kamila.

"—so that the swelling drains away. And this is how you put the sling on." His fingers worked deftly. "You probably will need a lot more bandages because they will need to be washed very thoroughly. Now, you remember how you dealt with Karol's handkerchiefs?"

Kamila nodded her head. "You mean the disinfectant in the water?"

"Yes. But first they need to be washed well, then boiled for about forty minutes and then soaked in the disinfectant and then rinsed and dried."

"Will you remember that Aniela?" Kamila said.

"Yes. I will."

"Repeat what I've done today with the cleansing and dressing tomorrow. I'll come and see him in two days, unless I hear from you to the contrary. And you must not use this hand." He wagged his finger at Baltazy.

"I'll make sure he doesn't, Doctor," said Aniela.

"I won't. I promise. Anyway I can't like this—." Baltazy waved his hand in the air.

Kamila travelled daily to see Baltazy, sometimes with Thomas, sometimes with Madelaine and always there were willing hands of Marcus or Aniela to help her. Gradually her despair was replaced with optimism when she saw that the wound was cleaner and the hand much less swollen.

Preparations for Christmas and the New Year were overshadowed by their anxieties over Baltazy's hand and when Kamila and Thomas suggested that the staff of the farm come over to Birch House for the Christmas and New Year, they were surprised that Aniela and Baltazy said that they preferred to stay at the farm.

"—at least this year, thank you. You never know what mischief he'll get up to at the house, whereas here I can keep a close eye on him. Besides, we can have some of the men and their families here as we always used to, sir. He'll—we'll feel more at ease here," said Aniela.

Kamila arranged for some of the delicacies to be sent over with Mary and one of the footmen, and Aniela took the opportunity to show Mary around the farmhouse.

Meanwhile Kamila noticed that there was a blossoming friendship between Madelaine and Marcus but kept her peace and didn't even tell Thomas. She noticed that there was a difference in Thomas when he was at Birch House to when they were at the farm house but could not work out why there was this difference and what exactly it was. She was not even sure that Thomas was aware of this. Certainly she was not going to ask. After all there was nothing tangible, but on one occasion, after the three of them had been to the farm, she asked Madelaine tentatively if she had noticed anything.

Madelaine thought for a while, looking at her hands. "What exactly do you mean?"

"I can't quite put my finger on anything. He is always very kind and loving. Is it my imagination, or does he look happier—does he laugh more when he is at the farm? Have you noticed anything like that?"

"I can't say that I've noticed, but he did laugh more today. Perhaps he's just relieved that Baltazy is progressing so well?"

"I didn't think so. Perhaps it's the pregnancy that's making me so touchy? Anyway I don't like this feeling. Perhaps he's regretting having married me?"

"How can you say that! Of that I'm certain that you are wrong. How could he regret? You have everything in your favour in being a most desirable young lady, so put that out of your head once and for all. And besides it's quite obvious that he loves you very much." Madelaine made a mental note to be more observant and if an opportunity arose, to ask Marcus.

One evening Thomas took Kamila's hand and looked at her gently, "You know when you mentioned going on our belated honeymoon in the spring? I was wandering if we could go somewhere a little earlier, say January or February?"

"But the Baltic will be frozen then. Or were you thinking of travelling overland? Or have something else in mind?"

"Marcus says that it'll take a month to reach London from Gdansk, depending on the wind. So if we stayed there two weeks, we would be away nearly three months from home. I'd rather not travel so very far and be away during the spring as that is the busiest and perhaps the most important season of the year for the animals—."

"Oh, I see. Of course it is. I was being selfish—."

"No, my dear, you were not—."

"Where were you thinking of going, then?"

"I was wandering of somewhere in our country. Perhaps we could go to Zakopane? It should be quite magical there with the snow on the mountains. And it isn't so far to travel."

"My parents spent their honeymoon in the Tatras Mountains, you know. Yes, it is an enchanting place. But we can't plan yet, until we know how Baltazy's hand will progress."

"No. And of course, whilst Madelaine is here either," said Thomas.

"Or Marcus, for that matter. After all, you don't see him often."

"No, we can't take him into consideration. I don't know what his plans are. I don't think he's made up his mind yet—."

"He hasn't confided in you?"

"Confided about what?" He looked surprised.

She smiled but shook her head and refused to say more. "And of course, Amelia and Noah are getting married in January and we promised to go to the wedding. I had almost forgotten that."

"Will Madelaine come to her wedding too?" said Thomas.

"I don't think so. She'll have to be back at the Academy by then."

"So it looks as though we won't be able to go even to Zakopane. Not until the end of January."

"No," said Kamila .

It was true that they had to consider their animals, although there was plenty men to carry out the work. Her father always used to say that the eye of the master does more work than both his hands. Even she, who was so fortunate in having Lisinski to help, and she knew she could rely on him totally, she felt strongly that it would be better if she were around, and besides this she owed it to the memory of her aunt….yes, her father was right. Otherwise why did she go to Gdansk, instead of just sending Lisinski? After all, was a honeymoon absolutely necessary? And this last question she put to Thomas.

But to her surprise Thomas said, "Yes, I think we ought to go away, so that we could be alone. Just the two of us, don't you?"

Preparations for Christmas took their mind off going away. Kamila wanted to give presents to all the workmen and their families but both Madelaine and Thomas advised her against this.

"Wouldn't that involve a colossal amount of work? Besides do you know what they want? Why don't you give them money and then they can buy what they want for themselves?" said Madelaine. "Isn't that what is usually done?"

"That's what I do with my workmen," said Thomas.

"Which they will squander in the taverns, on vodka and wenches," said Marcus with a smile.

"The single men probably will, but it's up to them what they do with it, isn't it?"

"What about giving the money to the wife and not the husband?"

"I still would have liked to give some presents to the children. I remember how excited I was at this time of the year when I was little. You are right, of course, my parents too, gave them money. What about Lisinski and his family? And then some of the girls here in the house?"

"No, Kamila, you can't make exceptions. Jealousies will arise and you'll only create for yourself a problem for ever," said Madelaine. "Why don't you ask, say Mary or Benjamin, or even Lisinski for their opinion from their point of view?"

"That is the best suggestion I've heard. I'll do that. Thank you Madelaine. I'll do that right away but not in front of you all." With that she left the room and asked Benjamin to call Mary and for the two of them to see her in the library.

When she came back she confirmed to them all that they had been right and both Mary and Benjamin said that money would be best and maybe some extra meat for the workmen who lived in the cottages. "So that's what we'll do."

The fire was crackling in the large grate in the sitting room and coffee was being poured out by Kamila, Marcus took out a pipe from his pocket and inspected it. Seeing it, Kamila said, "You can smoke in here if you wish, Marcus. You don't mind Madelaine, do you?"

"No, not at all," said her friend.

"I don't think I've seen you smoke before, Marcus," said Thomas.

"No, I don't smoke. I was inspecting it, because this pipe is very special. When I slipped on ice this morning I thought I might have damaged it. But it looks alright."

They all looked at him but it was Madelaine who said, "Mr. Marcus has set us a puzzle. He owns a pipe but doesn't smoke. He leads us to believe that it's precious, but it looks rough and battered. Well? Are you going to tell us, Mr Marcus?"

"On one condition. If you call me just Marcus and I can call you Madelaine."

"Yes of course," she said. Kamila noticed a slight flush on her friend's cheeks.

"Thank you. Well this pipe unscrews like this and it has this false bottom—."

"Of course! For that diamond that everyone admired—," said Madelaine.

"How clever! I wondered how you travelled with it," said Kamila.

"You wouldn't believe the cut throats that travel the seas. If they knew about this pipe, I'd have been murdered many times over by now."

"But how do you hide the other stones that you have to transport?" said Madelaine.

"Ah! I have an equally battered crooked walking stick, which is crudely painted so that the junctions are neatly camouflaged. And of course I wear my vagabond's clothes—without the fleas, Kamila!"

"Those, he picks up on the boat from the company he keeps." Thomas chuckled.

"I can see you'll never forgive me for saying that…" said Kamila.

"Anyway, that stone obtained for me an invitation to your friend's wedding—."

"Amelia's?"

"The very same. And confirmed again by her mother."

"Well, I never!" said Madelaine.

"We can travel together then," said Thomas, "That's if you are going? Are you?"

"I told them that I probably won't be in the country by then."

"So you've made up your mind, at last?" said Thomas.

Marcus shook his head. "Not quite."

The Christmas and New Year festivities passed and Madelaine had returned to Warsaw but Marcus remained at the farmhouse. Aniela, by now was looking after Baltazy's hand to the relief of Kamila and Thomas, as they were preparing for Amelia's wedding.

A week before their departure Kamila complained that she had some pain in her stomach. Thomas was so concerned that Dr.Roger was called. After examining her, he straightened up, "Well at least the bleeding is not that heavy, I'm happy to say. But it means bed rest for a fortnight, I'm afraid—."

"But we were due to go to Amelia's wedding in a week's time. I promised her—."

"I'm sorry, Kamila. The answer is that you can't. The journey could make the bleeding heavy and it would not only endanger your child, but you could die in the process. I will not allow it."

"But what will I say to her? She doesn't know of this," she waved her hand over her abdomen. "And what shall I say to the staff?"

"Tell them all that you have a severe chill! As for the staff—." He raised his bushy eyebrows. "You'll be surprised how much they know of what happens in the house—in any house that they work in." Kamila flushed and lowered her eyes. "There, there, child, there's no need to feel like that. It's just life. Now, you write a letter to Amelia and say that I've banished you to bed for a fortnight."

Dr. Roger repeated to Thomas all that he had said to Kamila and reassured him that both Kamila and the baby would be alright provided she obeyed his instructions and had complete rest. As they walked to the carriage Thomas was very quiet. Dr. Roger stopped in his tracks and looked at him, "She will be alright. Many pregnancies have such problems, so you needn't be so worried."

At first Thomas didn't say anything, and then, "It isn't that—."

"What is it Thomas? You seem to be troubled."

"I was looking forward to going away with Kamila. No, please, Dr. Roger," he said as the doctor was about to interrupt, "I know it sounds selfish. But it wasn't that. I thought that if we were away from this house and everything," he waved his hand to encompass the house and the land, "we could be on the same footing, sort of....I feel that it somehow isn't right, for me to come and live here. This is Kamila's house. It makes me feel as if as if I were a pauper. As if I was after her wealth, with me being so much older and not of the same class—."

"Oh, I see. In that case, let's go back into the house. It's too cold to talk about this outside"

Once inside the sitting room, and the tray of tea in front of them, they sipped the hot beverage until the maid had left the room.

"May I ask, what brought this on, Thomas?"

"On two occasions when I was in Luck, I overheard snippets of conversation to that effect. Then I met someone whom I considered to be a friend. He greeted me with a hearty slap and, 'You've caught yourself a pretty large fish. Lucky you! All that wealth! Phew!' Do you know, it took all my willpower not to hit him. But since then I've had no peace. Each day I'm more aware of this. I now feel that perhaps every one thinks that."

"Have you told his to Kamila?"

"Goodness, no! I couldn't."

"I know it's no good giving you platitudes. People were bound to talk. You yourself had some misgivings, if you remember. What have you thought of doing, then?"

"The only possibility would be to sell both our properties. I would prefer to buy land somewhere else and build her such a house as she wanted. I'm not as sentimental about my farmhouse but Kamila's roots are here…"

"Yes….Although not quite, because her father's property was confiscated, but I understand."

"She loves this place, although she's lived here less than a year. But she's known it since childhood. And she has lived through so much in this short time—more than I in my whole life."

"I think you must somehow broach the subject with Kamila. I too don't see any other option other than moving to a different place. But, for the time being, I'd not say anything. You have time on your hands, this being winter. Wait until spring. Meanwhile I'll think on the matter and also keep my ears open for any outlets." With that they parted and Thomas was partly relieved, at least, that he had confided in the doctor…..

CHAPTER 21

Kamila lay in bed, irritated by her inactivity. She wrote letters to Amelia and Madelaine and filled her long empty hours by reading. Thomas felt this too and spent much time with her, telling her anecdotes from his life. It was on such an occasion when they were both laughing so much that they didn't hear Marcus enter the room.

"What's all the hilarity, then?" he said.

"Hello, Marcus! Thomas was telling me something—tell Marcus what you've just told me—about the antics of your animals."

Marcus drew a chair to the bed and looked at Thomas.

"Well—a man brought a four year old pony for his young son—no, no, not from me. This animal had had no training in its life and was very naughty. He wouldn't be caught, and when eventually he was, he threw the boy off. The lad had a broken arm so the father decided that the animal had to go and asked me to take him. I'm glad he didn't shoot the pony for he was really beautiful and it wasn't his fault that he behaved so badly. I spent many months trying to gain the pony's confidence in order to harness him without being bitten or kicked. His favourite trick was to kick in the crutch when you least expected it. You should have heard how my men cursed him for that. It was autumn and that day I had spent quite a few hours trying to coax him to come to my hand, to have confidence in me. All to no avail. So I sat on a bench by the fence to rest. After a short while, he started to back towards me. I thought, 'O—oh, here we go again.' But I was wrong. He continued to back and then put his rump on my lap—he *sat* on my lap."

Marcus and Kamila burst out laughing.

"Do you remember the time when a bull chased me—." Marcus started.

"And you wet your pants—."

"You would have done the same if you'd had him blowing fire at your heels and intended to have you for breakfast—."

"Bulls are not meat eaters—."

"This one was."

"Anyway, you deserved it." Thomas turned to Kamila, "He thought that he as a toreador and waved Mother's red blouse in front of the bull until it responded."

Once the laughter died down Kamila turned to Marcus. He had been away a few days and she wanted to know where he had been.

"Oh here and there," was all he'd say.

"You won't tell us where you went then?"

"Why do you want to know? You really are a very nosey young lady…"

"Yes, I know. I've been told that before. I apologise. I should have known not to ask." Then she turned to Thomas, "How is Baltazy's hand?" It seemed that Aniela was looking after him just as Kamila had wanted and the hand was healing well.

"Kamila, you sound as if you hadn't seen him for six months when in fact it's just three days. So there wouldn't be any dramatic change as yet," laughed Thomas.

"I know, but it does seem a long time. I wish… I wish…"

"Yes?"

"I wish it was spring and I could ride Emblem again."

"Is that whom you miss? Shall I ask the groom to bring Emblem to your room here?" But she just shook her head, fearing that if she said anything she would burst into tears. Thomas took her hand and held it between his until he and Marcus left.

Once downstairs he asked Benjamin to call Mary to him. When she came, he simply said, "Mary, could you go and cheer up your mistress a little. And it might be a good idea to take Thor with you. I think she needs a bit of company."

The two weeks yawned with tedium, and although she was happy that the pain and the bleeding had stopped, she was even happier at being allowed to come downstairs. Suddenly there were more people about and she went to the stables and talked to the horses. She had had a letter from Amelia saying how sorry she and Noah were not to have them at the wedding and that they too planned to go on their honeymoon in the spring. And she had a letter from Madelaine and was amazed to read, "…..and you'll never guess who paid me a visit! It was Marcus! We went to a concert and had two very pleasant evenings together. You can imagine what interest it provoked amongst the girls and the staff….."

"Well! Would you believe it?" She said to herself, "Oh, I hope…I hope."

Once the house was back to normal she again noticed that there was something troubling Thomas. Whilst she was in bed she hadn't noticed anything, presumably because he made every effort to keep her amused and interested. So now she decided to ask him if he was worried over something.

After dinner, they were in the sitting room, with Kamila pouring out coffee. She gave him the cup and looked at him searchingly.

"Thomas, is something the matter? I feel that there is something that is troubling you." He looked into his cup, stirring the contents. "I have felt that there was something for quite a few weeks, so please don't shake your head like that."

After a moment of silence, he sat by her and poured out his feeling, as he had done a couple of weeks ago to Dr. Roger.

"I see," Kamila said slowly. "I hadn't realised that would be a problem. Do you wish us to move to the farmhouse?"

"No. That wouldn't be suitable for you. You are used to living in much grander style. Furthermore, the farmhouse isn't big enough to accommodate all the staff."

"What have you in mind?"

"Perhaps we could sell both places and buy—or maybe we could build another place? Somewhere else, so that we are on neutral ground, so to speak."

"I couldn't sell this place, Thomas. Although this did not belong to my Father, my Aunt Elizabeth wanted it to remain in the family. My Father was her brother, but my uncle, her husband, was my Mother's cousin, so you see—."

"I know. Your roots are here. That's what I said to Dr. Roger—."

"You told this to Dr. Roger?"

"Yes."

"When?"

"When you fell—ill."

"And what did he advise?"

"Firstly, he said not to tell you at that time, whilst you were ill. He said he'd think on the matter."

"And has he made any more reference to it?"

"No, not really. Kamila, I just want you to know, that I'm not sentimental about the farmhouse. I could afford to build you a house such as you'd want. Your family have lived here for generations, so I do understand how you feel. "

"Let me think on the matter. We must consider the various options and discuss this more. We still have time…"

That night she had a sleepless night.

The snow started to melt. The daylight hours were longer and filled with hope as the awakening spring stretched its young arms. And still no decision had been made for their future.

Lisinski came to report on what happened and where, during the winter and what needed to be repaired and that he had met the surveyor, Mr. Stokowski as he was returning from the field that had subsided and could Kamila meet him there in two days' time?

This time Thomas came with the two of them and met the surveyor. Kamila introduced the two men, who shook hands and Mr. Stokowski congratulated them on their marriage.

"I want you to come to that area where we saw some subsidence last year. On foot again. Leave your horses well away, here……here we are." He looked at Kamila and Lisinski, "Can you remember the size of this crack when you last saw it?"

"It looks approximately the same to me. What do you think?" Kamila turned to Lisinski.

"To me too."

"Well it isn't. I measured it last year and today. It's wider by this much." He showed them the width of three fingers.

"So you think it's a significant amount?"

"Oh, yes, madam, it's very significant. You must remember that the thaw is only superficial at present. If I were to put a spade in here, I doubt if I could even get to the depth of one foot. The rest of the ground below is still frozen solid. If we have a hot May or June all this will fall away."

"So, how far back can we use the land?" said Lisinski.

"Certainly as far as where we have left the horses, but for safety, I'd advise a bit more. The lands and the rivers in this region and east of here are very treacherous with those extensive marshes. Why, I only heard from my sister that a body of a man was found in the river Styr, all tangled up in his whip and which he was still holding in his hand. His one foot was tangled in the weeds she said. Quite bizarre." He scratched his nose. Kamila shivered and Thomas put his arm around her and drew her nearer to him.

"Where did this happen?" Thomas asked.

"My sister lives in Kolki. It's about twenty five miles from here. So, somewhere near there."

"Do they know who he is?"

"No. They haven't identified him yet."

Kamila thanked Mr. Stokowski, who said he'd check the land again in a month's time, and they parted company.

"Baltazy will be pleased that Greczko has been found—." Kamila said

"Yes. I think he'll be relieved that Providence gave a hand and wrapped him up in his own whip," said Thomas.

"That's justice. I'm glad he's had his deserts," said Lisinski. "He was a sadistic so-and-so to all of us when he worked for your aunt, Miss Kamila. Everyone hated him. And feared him."

Two days later Benjamin came to Kamila and said, "You have a visitor, madam. He asked not to tell you his name." He smiled and said very quietly, "I think you will be pleased to see him."

"I hope so. I hope so, for the last time we had someone who wouldn't give his name—you know what happened. Where is he?"

"He's in the hall, madam. Shall I ask him to come here?"

"Yes please." She was sitting on the sofa in the drawing room and when the door opened she turned to see who it was. On seeing the familiar face, she jumped up and ran to him with outstretched hands. "Mat! How lovely to see you!"

He took both her hands and held them, looking closely into her face.

"How are you, Kamila? It seems such a long time since I saw you. How's married life?"

"Fine, fine, Mat. But why didn't you let me know you were coming?"

"And miss such a lovely greeting? I'm glad I didn't. I wanted to know how you'd welcome me. How are you really? Are you truly happy?"

"Yes, truly I am. I wouldn't have married otherwise."

He looked down at their hands, kissed each one but still held onto them.

"You know my thoughts on that. My parents are still lamenting at my having missed the opportunity."

She withdrew her hands and went to sit down. "Mat, you must have painted for them an unrealistic picture of me. They might have loathed me on sight."

"Never, never, never!" He was now sitting beside her.

"Were you on your way somewhere that you were able to drop in to see me?"

"No. My destination was you. I had a burning desire to see you. I couldn't stop thinking of you—."

"You mustn't say things like that now—"

"I know, I know, you're a married lady. Where is your husband? Will I be able to meet him?"

"Yes, of course but he's at the farm at present. He'll be back a little later today. You will stay to dinner, won't you?"

"I was hoping that you would ask me to stay longer than that."

"Oh, Mat, of course. I'll ask Benjamin to get the staff to arrange a room and how did you come? By carriage?" She noticed how elegantly dressed he was, and that he wasn't wearing riding boots and certainly was not splattered with mud. When Benjamin came she gave her instructions.

"Your luggage is in the carriage, sir? May I take it to your room?"

"Yes, thank you Benjamin."

"Can we have some tea, as well please?"

"I think that that's just arrived, madam." He went to open the door for the maid.

Kamila and Mat seemed to have such a lot to say to each other, as if they had known each other all their lives. He made her laugh. She felt her spirits rise. As they were laughing they didn't hear Thomas enter until he said "Good evening."

Kamila immediately jumped up and ran to him. He put an arm around her shoulders and kissed her on the forehead.

"Thomas, I want you to meet a friend, Mat Kobulski, and this is my husband, Thomas Orzel." By now they were all standing and the men shook hands, each eyeing the other.

"I must congratulate you on your marriage," Mat said and Thomas thanked him inclining his head. Kamila wondered at Thomas looking so elegant, considering that he had gone to the farm riding his favourite horse. He must have changed his clothes when he arrived…Benjamin, yes Benjamin must have suggested it.

As they talked Kamila couldn't help but notice the difference in the two men. Their manners were different and most of all the speech. She told herself off for this and to concentrate on the content of conversation—she didn't want to see the difference. She loved Thomas and she didn't want that social divide to spoil her marriage. She at last understood what it was that had made Thomas unhappy.

She asked Thomas if he would bring Marcus to dinner on the following day.

That night she came to Thomas and lay beside him. She was about to ask him to hold her tight but he seemed to understand instinctively for he spread his arms and as she cuddled up to him he wrapped his arms around her, like a blanket.

Once Thomas had departed for the farm, she asked Mat if he wanted to go riding or to see the estate.

"Not really. I haven't brought any of my riding clothes—."

"Mm. I don't think any of Thomas' or Karol's clothes would fit you—."

"I am not sure that I would like to wear either of your husbands' clothes. As you would put it, `It wouldn't be seemly`. Can't we just talk, or go for a walk, if you like?"

Kamila laughed, "I don't see why not. And you make it sound as if I have two husbands at present! "

"Well, if the situation were reversed, would you wear any clothes belonging to my two wives?" Kamila just laughed but didn't answer.

But they didn't have time to go for a walk, because Marcus arrived in the early afternoon. Mat found Marcus most interesting and asked numerous questions about conditions in other countries and especially America.

Eventually, Kamila asked, "Are you planning to travel around the world, Mat? Or just emigrate?"

"No, neither really. A very dear friend of mine is thinking of emigrating but I think he believes he'll become fabulously wealthy there. No, I have no wish to go there. I love this country too much."

"Have you no interest in travelling then? Have you not been to any other country?" said Marcus.

"Oh, I've been to Paris and Vienna and to Belgium, but it takes so long to travel that I can't say that it gives me that much pleasure. Besides, I lead quite a busy life on my estate. My parents don't do as much now, and I do feel guilty if I am away too long—."

"What about your wife, your family? Don't they want to travel? Especially since you live quite near the Baltic, your facilities are so much easier than, say, from here."

"As yet I have no wife—."

"Really? I am surprised that no one has caught you yet." Kamila didn't take part in this conversation.

Mat laughed. "Why the surprise? I gather you're not married either."

"Ah, but you see, I've been a rolling stone that gathers no moss for some thirty years and no woman would have wanted to go to the places that I've been to, or indeed live under the conditions that I've lived. But, you—you are different. You must have met some delectable creatures in your time and no one has captured your heart?"

Mat laughed, "Someone did—."

Just then there was a knock on the door, much to Kamila's relief, and

Benjamin entered the room.

"Excuse me, madam. Something's happened in the kitchen and Mary asks you to come straight away, please?"

Kamila jumped up, both men stood up as she excused herself and walked quickly with Benjamin. "What's happened?"

"It's the Cook. She doesn't appear to be well. I don't know anymore than that, madam."

When they reached the kitchen, the Cook was sitting on the chair and one maid was taking off her stocking, another giving her hot tea, holding the cup for her. Mary had just taken off her cap.

"What's happened?"

"She dropped a pan of hot water on her foot," said Mary. "But it isn't that so much, it's her speech—it's weird. Ask her something—."

Kamila bent to the Cook, "What's the problem Cook? Are you in much pain?"

The Cook shook her head and said something. Kamila didn't understand and asked her to repeat it and still she didn't understand. The Cook waved her right hand and said something.

They understood only by her movements, that the pan fell out of her hand.

Kamila examined her foot. Fortunately her long skirt had caught the majority of the hot water and her foot was only slightly scalded. Whilst the foot was being smeared with fresh cream and bandaged, Kamila took the empty cup and asked the Cook to hold it, and when she did, the cup swivelled and had there been anything in it, the contents would have spilled out.

"All right, Cook. Don't worry. I'll get Dr. Roger to come and see you and meanwhile, we'll put you to bed." The Cook became agitated and waved her left hand around the kitchen and at the table, but this time Kamila understood her movements even better. "No, don't worry about the cooking. Someone else will do it. If you like, I might even try." The Cook squeezed Kamila's hand.

Kamila wrote a note to Dr. Roger of all that she had been told and what she had observed and asked Benjamin to send Jordan with the message and a request for the doctor to come.

Kamila had decided not to ask her any more questions, fearing that she would just get more agitated and anyway Dr Roger would have to ask them again. By the time that the doctor came, the Cook was in her bed and dozing. When the two of them entered her room accompanied by Mary, the Cook opened her eyes.

"Hello! Dr Roger has come to see you."

"Hello." He said and shook her hand. "What's your name?"

"Her name is Dorota, Doctor." Mary said, knowing that Kamila probably didn't know it and thinking that the Cook wouldn't be able to say it.

"Tell me Dorota, what happened?"

"I had boiled some water. As I lifted the pan, it slipped out of my hand."

Mary and Kamila exchanged glances. She was able to speak!

The doctor examined her, asked to squeeze his fingers, push him away, pull him towards her….. asked her more questions.

When they left the room, Kamila said, "I don't understand. She definitely couldn't speak before—at least not to understand. It was all jumbled up. None of us could understand."

"I believe you," he patted her hand for reassurance. "What has happened is that she has had a minor stroke, or it may have been just a spasm of a blood vessel in the brain. I'm afraid that it means she'll have to be on complete rest for at least a month. Maybe even longer."

"And afterwards?"

"Most certainly she'll have to work much less. This has been a warning to her and to you. She's recovered now, but the next time—and there is a likelihood of another occurring—and then it could prove fatal."

"What you are saying is that I really ought to get some one else to be the cook and retire her, aren't you?"

"Yes, my dear, I am. It'll be more upsetting for you if she died, wouldn't it?"

"Yes, of course it would. Should she stay in bed this next month?"

"No. In fact I would like her to do some walking and when she is tired to go to bed but otherwise have a peaceful, less stressful life. Can she read?"

"I don't know. She does get an occasional letter from up north but that could be read by Mary or Benjamin….."

He nodded. "Pity. Well, I must be off. Bye-bye my dear."

"Thank you very much, Dr Roger."

Kamila returned to the patient and told her and Mary what the doctor had said. The Cook became distressed again and had to be calmed down. "…and when you have had your month's rest you can come and supervise and teach whoever is doing the cooking. Do you have anyone in mind for that?"

"Theresa. She can cook."

Kamila looked at Mary, and she nodded in agreement. "But she isn't as good as Dorota."

"I doubt if there is anyone as good."

Kamila wasn't the only one to have excitement that day.

Thomas noticed that his favourite eight year old cow, Clara, was in labour and when she gave birth to a healthy bull calf, he thought that she hadn't finished and examined her. To his amazement he felt more hoofs and pulled that one out too.

"Another bull! He is lovely," said Baltazy as he rubbed the calf down. They waited a while and saw that Clara was still straining.

Thomas again put his arm into her. "Good Lord! There's another one!"

By now he was sweating and his face was pink with excitement and exertion. Slowly he pulled this one out.

"This one's a heifer. She's a real beauty," said Baltazy.

"Three calves! My wonderful Clara!" Thomas gave her a hug. "You clever girl!"

"I ain't ever seen triplets, and they are a good size, ain't they Mr Thomas? A bit smaller than normal. What do you think?" The men lifted each calf in turn and agreed that they were around fifty five pounds, which was proved on weighing—about two thirds of the weight of a singleton. One of the other men cleaned Clara. She was given food and drink. Thomas went to the pump and washed himself.

He returned to the barn and patted Clara and when she looked at him with her gorgeous eyes, he felt sure she smiled at him.

He laughed, "Clara, old girl, I think my brain's addled, or did you really smile?"

When he returned home, he washed, and changed his clothes before entering the sitting room. It was Marcus who said, "We've had had some excitement here this afternoon whilst you were away. Ah, here's Kamila. She'll tell you—."

Kamila greeted him warmly, "I wouldn't call it excitement. I'd say it was drama. But all is calm at the sea now……"

"Poor Cook. It must have been frightening for her.... but *I too have* had excitement today with my Clara…."

"Thank goodness everything went smoothly and that you were there at the time, but I've never heard of a cow giving birth to triplets. Have you had them before?" said Kamila.

"No. It's very unusual. I have never had any."

"If *you* had had even a singleton, Thomas, you would have had fame as no other," said Marcus dryly, "But I do remember when I was a youngster we did have triplets but they were so premature they died soon afterwards. Poor Thomas wept so much that his eyes looked like boiled onions."

"I don't remember that."

Kamila turned to Mat, "What about you Mat?"

He shook his head. "No, I've never heard of any."

That evening at dinner Marcus announced that he'd be leaving early in the morning.

"I'm sorry to hear that. How long will you be gone?"

"I don't know Kamila. I'll see you when I come back."

"So you are coming back? I'm glad." He just nodded.

"I, too, have to leave tomorrow," said Mat.

At first a silence fell onto the company and then Thomas said how pleasant it was to have the company of the two men. They raised their glasses to toast them.

"It seems so quiet without Marcus and Mat," said Kamila. "You probably haven't noticed it much, because you've been so busy."

"I certainly miss Marcus. He's never stayed so long before." Kamila was sitting cross-legged on the bed, in the lovely white nightgown made by Bronia.

"I've had a letter from Madelaine today. I'm very excited about it and it answers many things about your brother."

"How so?"

"He's asked her to marry him."

"Really? The dark horse! He never even gave any inkling that he had thoughts of marriage. But I'm glad it's to be Madelaine."

"She doesn't say that she has agreed but all the same, I'm so very happy about that… She had said to me before that she would never marry after the unhappiness she had experienced with that first husband. Apparently Marcus has been up to Warsaw to see her many times and you'll never guess at this—he's left the diamond with her as a pledge."

"Well, I never! He's definitely serious. That solves another puzzle. Before he left he said to me that if I considered selling the farm with the stock, to let him buy it. I never for one second thought that he was serious and told him that by rights it should be his anyway, as he was the first born."

"What did he say to that?"

"Oh, that I had worked it for all those years to make it the success that it is—."

"Well, that's true."

"—that he had no right to it otherwise. This would release me to run your estate."

"Were these his thoughts or yours?"

"Yes. His."

"So you discussed our problem with him?"

"No, Kamila, I didn't. He must have guessed."

"He is a very clever man. But that still would not make you happy, would it?"

"I think it would make the situation even worse. People would point a finger and say, `I told you so. He was after her for the brass, after all.` I can just see them."

"Thomas, while Mat was here, he and Marcus discussed travel and emigrating. I didn't realise but an idea was born. Would you like to go and live in America, for instance? According to Marcus the land is fertile, depending where you buy it, labour is cheap and everyone there needs horses and cattle."

"But you wouldn't be happy. You love this land and this part of the country."

"I do, but we've both got to be happy. If you are happy, then I shall be too."

"I think we should sleep on it. It's a big decision. We must take some time to think on the subject. It would be such an enormous upheaval."

"But not too long. I am nearly five months pregnant. It would be safer to travel with the baby still inside me—and then we have to consider the weather, for travelling and when we arrive there."

"Whoa Kamila, whoa! Not so fast!"

Two days later Thomas returned home earlier than usual. Kamila was just about to go to her little office when he called to her.

"Are you busy?" She turned to look at him with surprise.

"Is something the matter?"

"No. I just wanted to see you."

She laughed. "It's only about three hours since we last parted. You've something on your mind. What is it?"

"No, nothing. I just thought we might go riding for a little while before lunch."

"Alright," she said slowly, not taking her eyes off his face. "As you see I'm all ready for that and Emblem is probably waiting." Once they had left the yard she looked at him enquiringly.

"We'll go this way towards that field that subsided—."

"But, Thomas, we had been there two days ago and there's no change—."

"We're not going to the field. Just be patient, my love."

After a while the path went uphill and when they turned off the main track, it became steeper. When they reached the summit, Thomas jumped down and lifted Kamila off her horse.

"Now, look! All this, as far as you see is yours—."

"Ours."

"No. Yours. Don't interrupt! Can you truly say that you'd leave all of that? You'd be willing to sell all this?"

She looked at the beautiful landscape. The house was hidden from the view by the trees. After surveying all the land around them her eyes came to rest on his kind, gentle face. "Yes, to the first question, if it would make you happy to live in another country. And no, to the second question because I couldn't sell it, but possibly rent it out….," she said quietly.

They looked at each other and after a while Thomas pulled out of his pocket a small package and gave it her.

"For you."

She unwrapped it. It was a small silver box with an inlaid ultramarine enamel lid.

"It's beautiful, Thomas, but why?"

"Open it."

She opened it. Inside there were four compartments. The larger one contained earth and the others, wheat, barley and rye seeds.

"The blue is for the sky. I couldn't capture the vastness of it. The rest is from your fields." She looked puzzled. "Don't you remember, my dear? You once told me that what you loved about this place. That was the vast blue skies and the golden cornfields. Well, if you get homesick when we are in America, you can open this box and look at this."

In answer, Kamila closed the box and put her arms around his waist and leaned her face against him. His arms encircled her.

"And remember, if after some time, you long for this place, if the contents of the box are not enough, we can always come back here…." he said.

Lightning Source UK Ltd.
Milton Keynes UK
UKOW041036130412

190660UK00001B/37/P

9 781906 791773